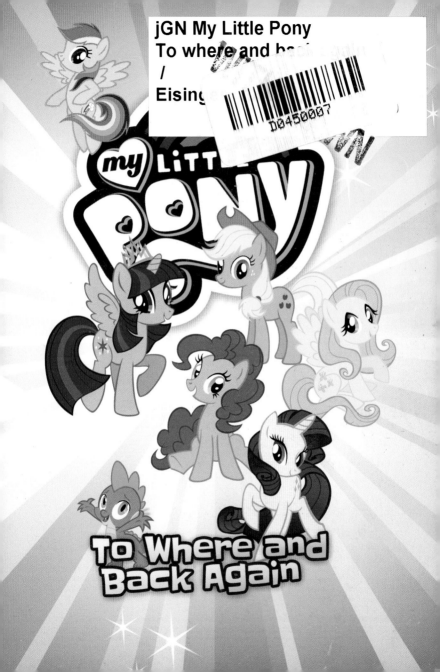

my LiTTLE PONY

To Where and Back Again

Special thanks to Meghan McCarthy, Eliza Hart,
Ed Lane, Beth Artale, and Michael Kelly.

ISBN: 978-1-68405-419-0
22 21 20 19   1 2 3 4

Chris Ryall, President & Publisher/CCO
John Barber, Editor-in-Chief
Robbie Robbins, EVP/Sr. Art Director
Cara Morrison, Chief Financial Officer
Matthew Ruzicka, Chief Accounting Officer
David Hedgecock, Associate Publisher
Jerry Bennington, VP of New Product Development
Lorelei Bunjes, VP of Digital Services
Justin Eisinger, Editorial Director, Graphic Novels & Collections
Eric Moss, Sr. Director, Licensing & Business Development

Ted Adams, IDW Founder

Licensed By: Hasbro

IDW®

www.IDWPUBLISHING.com

My Little Pony
To Where and Back Again

Story by
Josh Haber

Adaptation by
Justin Eisinger

Edits by
Alonzo Simon

Lettering and Design by
Gilberto Lazcano

Production Assistance by
Amauri Osorio

MEET THE PONIES

Twilight Sparkle

TWILIGHT SPARKLE TRIES TO FIND THE ANSWER TO EVERY QUESTION! WHETHER STUDYING A BOOK OR SPENDING TIME WITH PONY FRIENDS, SHE ALWAYS LEARNS SOMETHING NEW!

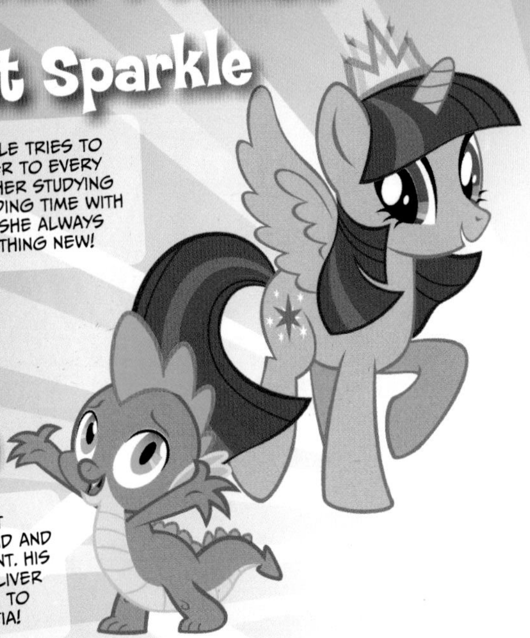

Spike

SPIKE IS TWILIGHT SPARKLE'S BEST FRIEND AND NUMBER ONE ASSISTANT. HIS FIRE BREATH CAN DELIVER SCROLLS DIRECTLY TO PRINCESS CELESTIA!

Applejack

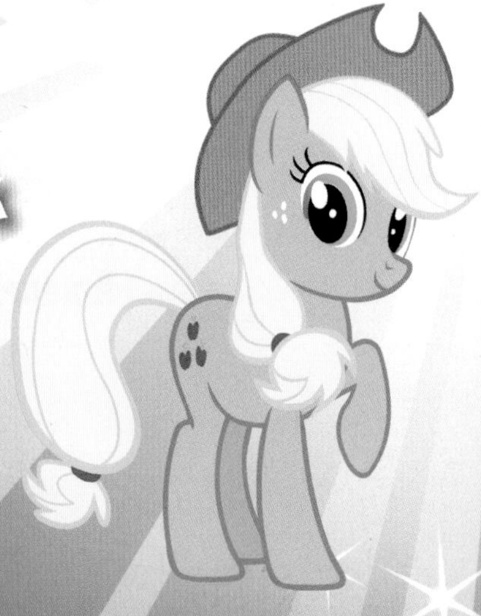

APPLEJACK IS HONEST, FRIENDLY AND SWEET TO THE CORE! SHE LOVES TO BE OUTSIDE, AND HER PONY FRIENDS KNOW THEY CAN ALWAYS COUNT ON HER.

Fluttershy

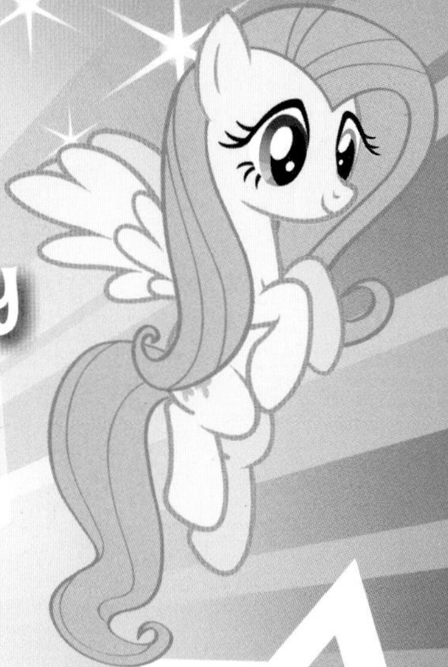

FLUTTERSHY IS A KIND AND GENTLE PONY WITH A BIG HEART. SHE LIKES TO TAKE CARE OF OTHERS, ESPECIALLY HER LITTLE ANIMAL FRIENDS.

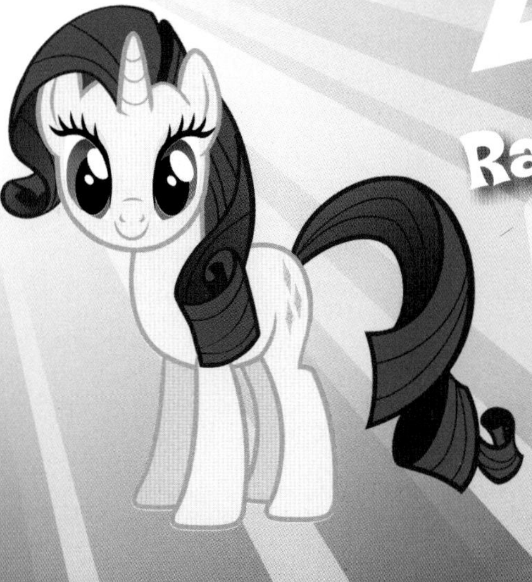

Rarity

RARITY KNOWS HOW TO ADD SPARKLE TO ANY OUTFIT! SHE LOVES TO GIVE HER PONY FRIENDS ADVICE ON THE LATEST FASHIONS AND HAIRSTYLES.

Rainbow Dash

RAINBOW DASH LOVES TO FLY AS FAST AS SHE CAN! SHE IS ALWAYS READY TO PLAY A GAME, GO ON AN ADVENTURE, OR HELP OUT ONE OF HER PONY FRIENDS.

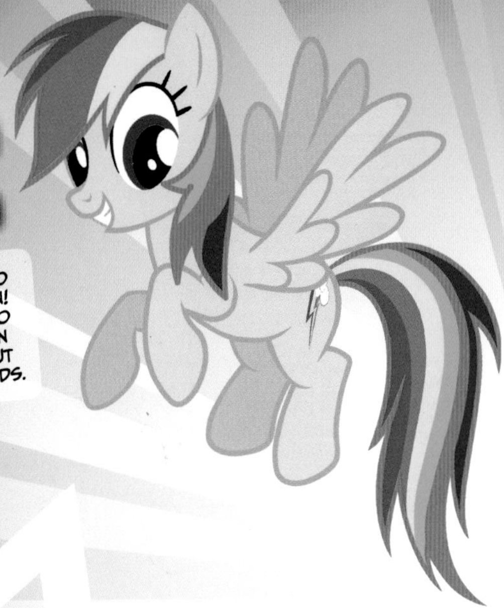

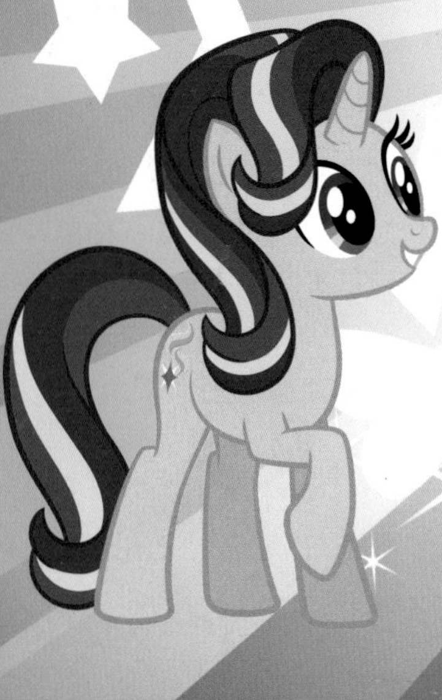

Starlight Glimmer

STARLIGHT GLIMMER IS A POWERFUL UNICORN, AND TWILIGHT SPARKLE'S PUPIL. ONCE CONVINCED THAT PONIES SHOULD SURRENDER THEIR CUTIE MARKS TO IMPROVE FRIENDSHIP, HER ADVENTURES WITH TWILIGHT HAVE TAUGHT HER OTHERWISE.

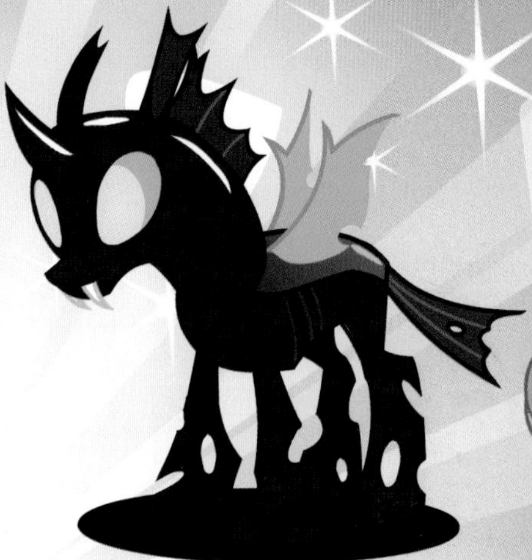

Thorax

THORAX IS A CHANGELING, BUT HE'S BEEN MORE INTERESTED IN MAKING FRIENDS AFTER WATCHING THE MANE SIX FIGHT OFF QUEEN CHRYSALIS DURING THE ROYAL WEDDING IN CANTERLOT.

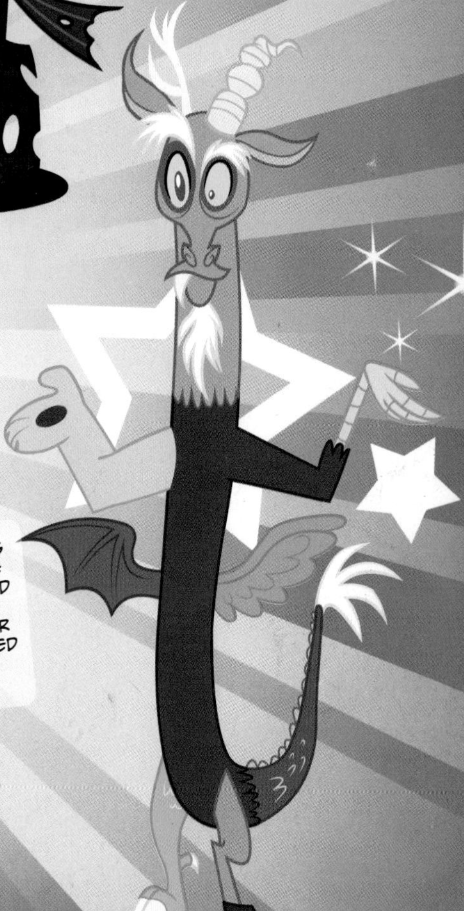

Discord

DISCORD IS A DRACONEQUUS ONCE IMPRISONED IN STONE BY PRINCESSES CELESTIA AND LUNA, USING THE ELEMENTS OF HARMONY. AFTER A LATER REFORMATION, HE DEVELOPED A DEEP FRIENDSHIP WITH FLUTTERSHY.

To Where
and
Back
Again

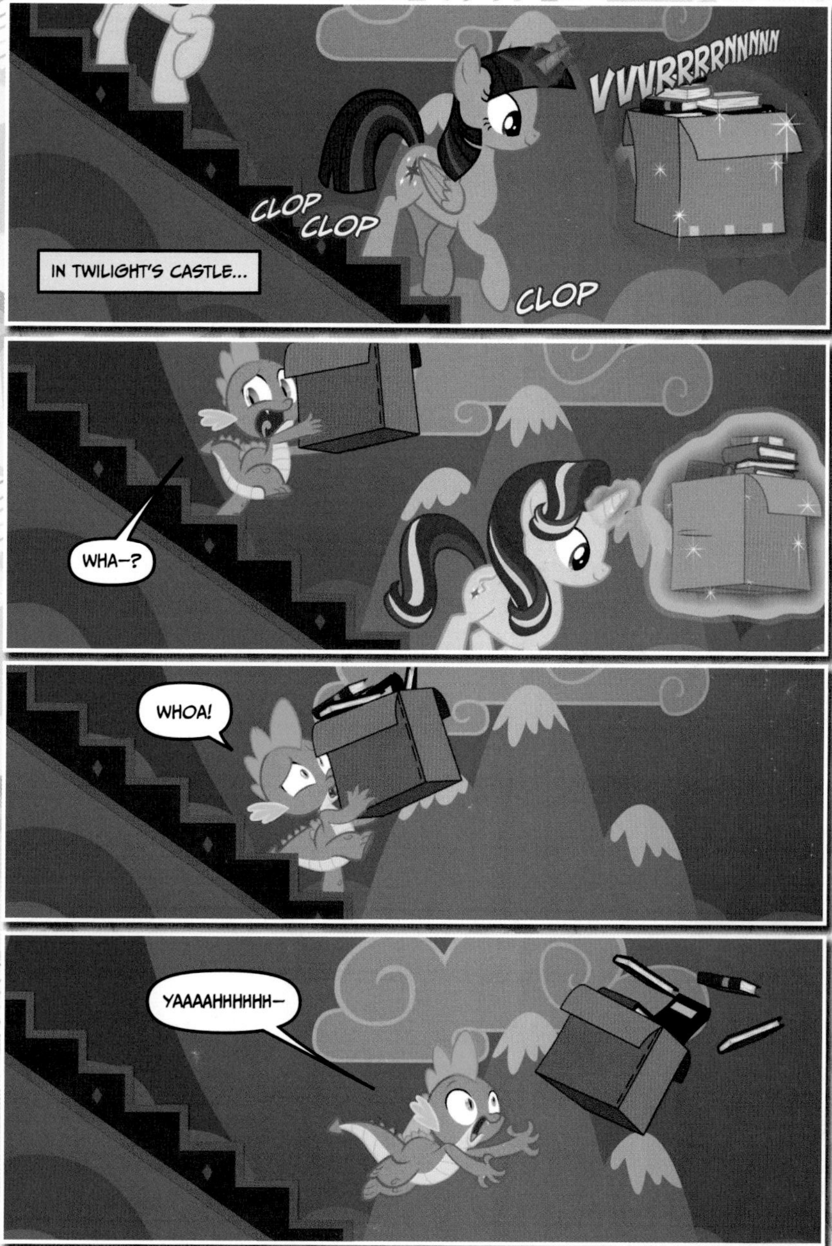
IN TWILIGHT'S CASTLE...
CLOP
CLOP
CLOP
VVVRRRRNNNNN
WHA—?
WHOA!
YAAAAHHHHHH—

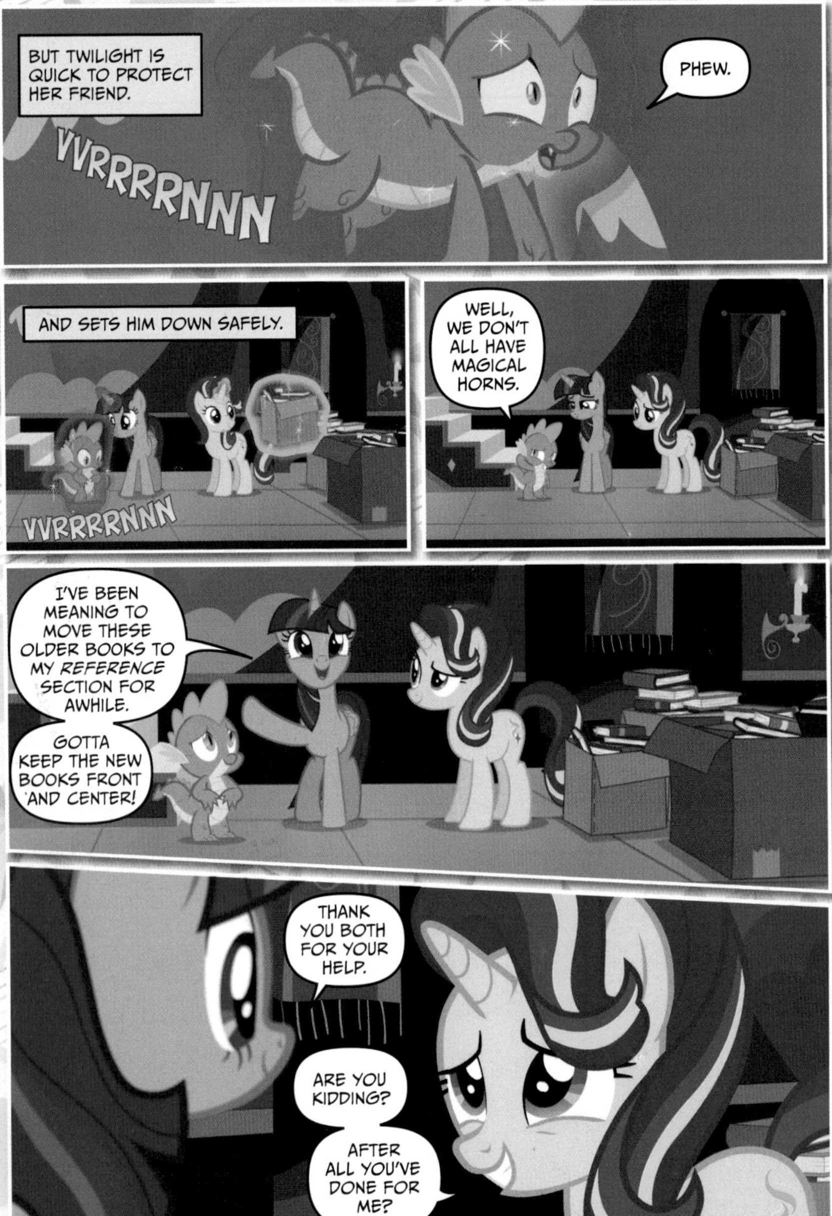
BUT TWILIGHT IS QUICK TO PROTECT HER FRIEND.
PHEW.
VVRRRRNNN
AND SETS HIM DOWN SAFELY.
VVRRRRNNN
WELL, WE DON'T ALL HAVE MAGICAL HORNS.
I'VE BEEN MEANING TO MOVE THESE OLDER BOOKS TO MY *REFERENCE* SECTION FOR AWHILE.
GOTTA KEEP THE NEW BOOKS FRONT 'AND CENTER!
THANK YOU BOTH FOR YOUR HELP.
ARE YOU KIDDING?
AFTER ALL YOU'VE DONE FOR ME?

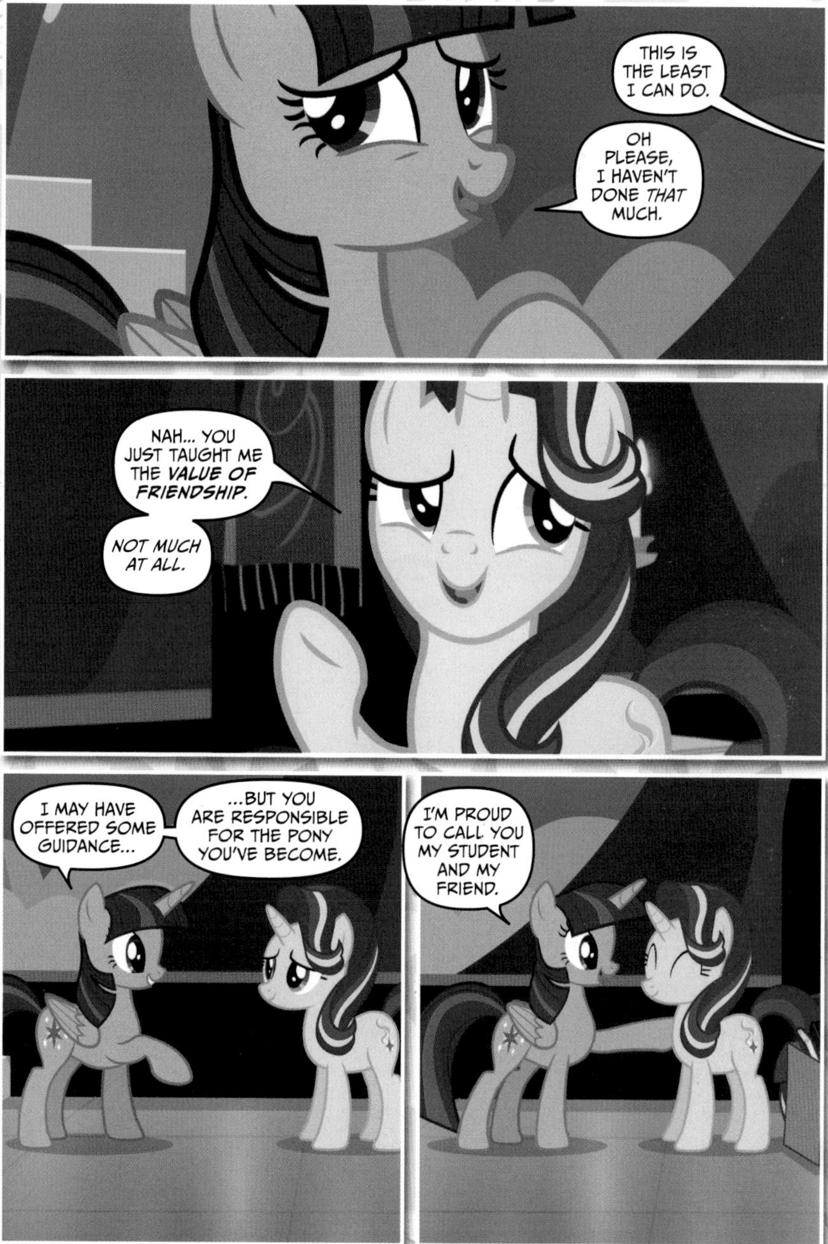
THIS IS THE LEAST I CAN DO.
OH PLEASE, I HAVEN'T DONE *THAT* MUCH.
NAH... YOU JUST TAUGHT ME THE ***VALUE OF FRIENDSHIP.***
NOT MUCH AT ALL.
I MAY HAVE OFFERED SOME GUIDANCE...
...BUT YOU ARE RESPONSIBLE FOR THE PONY YOU'VE BECOME.
I'M PROUD TO CALL YOU MY STUDENT AND MY FRIEND.

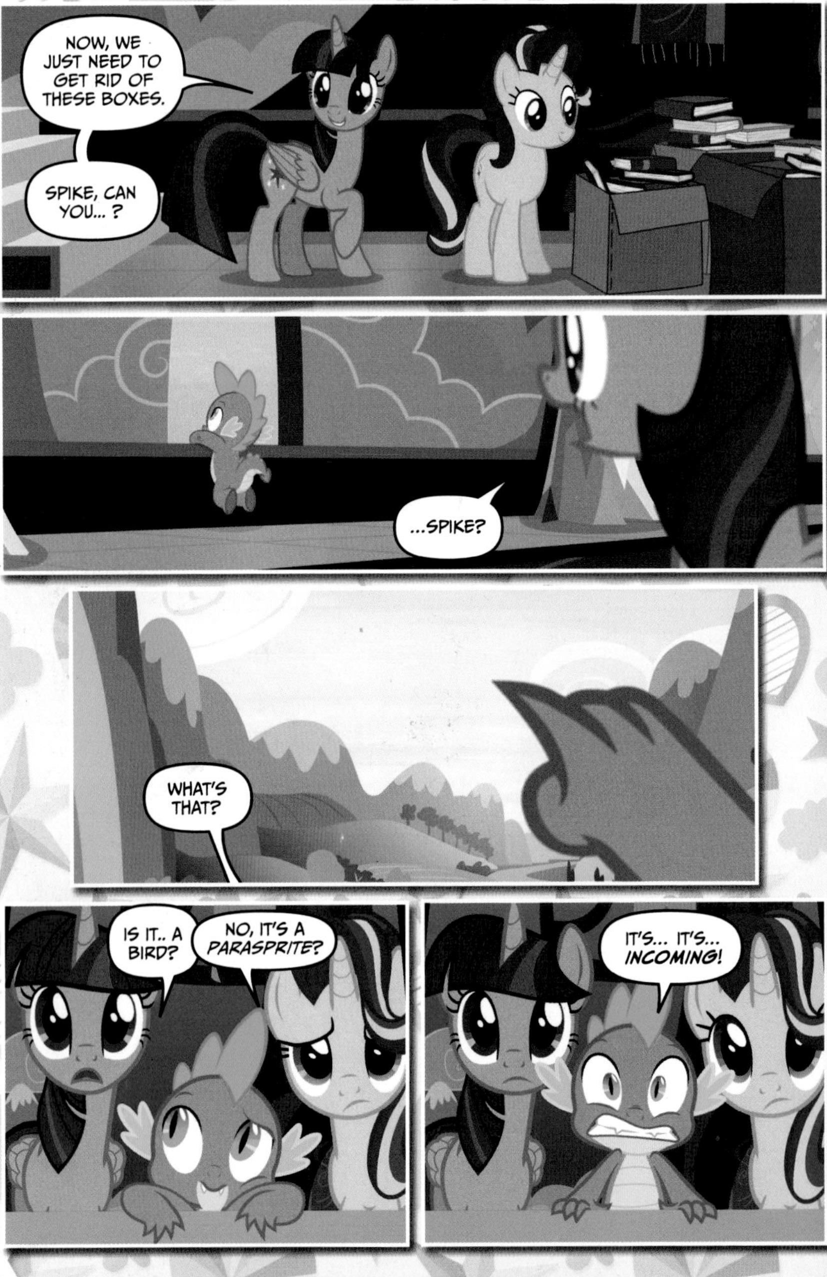
NOW, WE JUST NEED TO GET RID OF THESE BOXES.
SPIKE, CAN YOU... ?
...SPIKE?
WHAT'S THAT?
IS IT.. A BIRD?
NO, IT'S A *PARASPRITE*?
IT'S... IT'S... *INCOMING!*

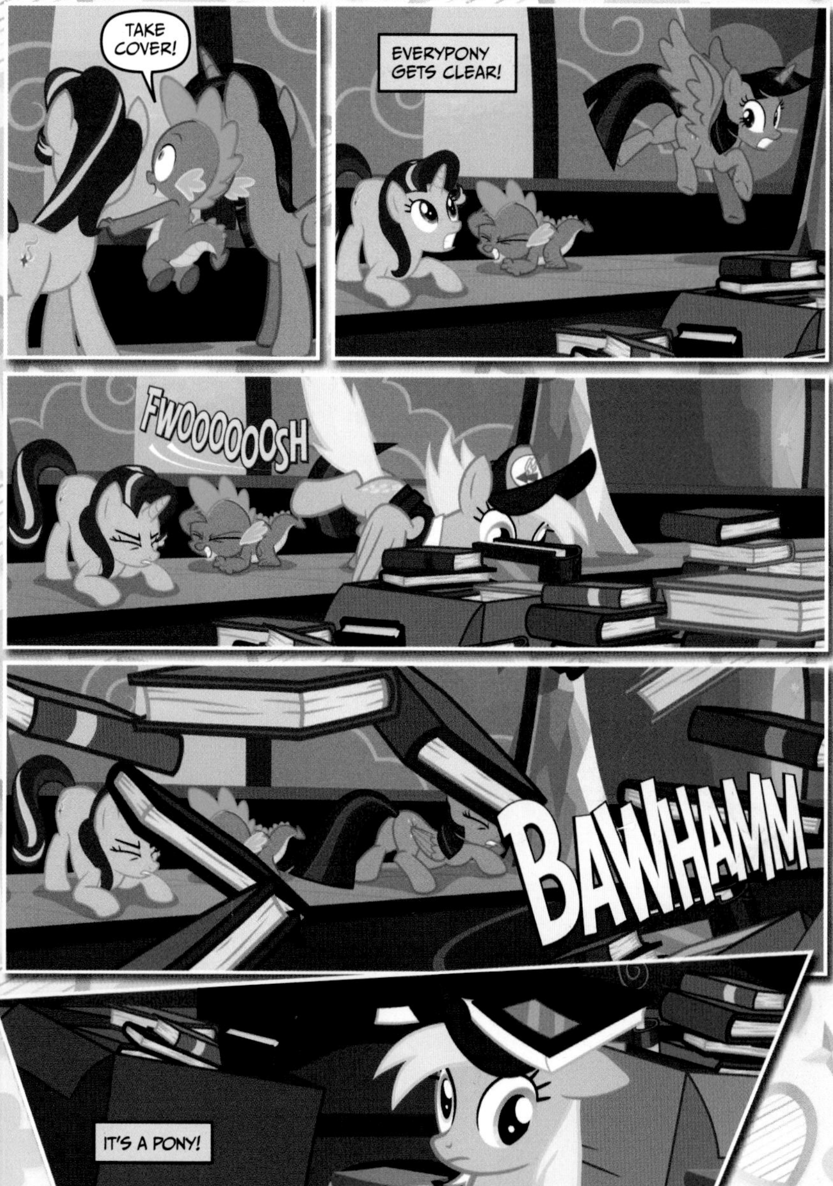
TAKE COVER!
EVERYPONY GETS CLEAR!
FWOOOOOOOSH
BAWHAMM
IT'S A PONY!

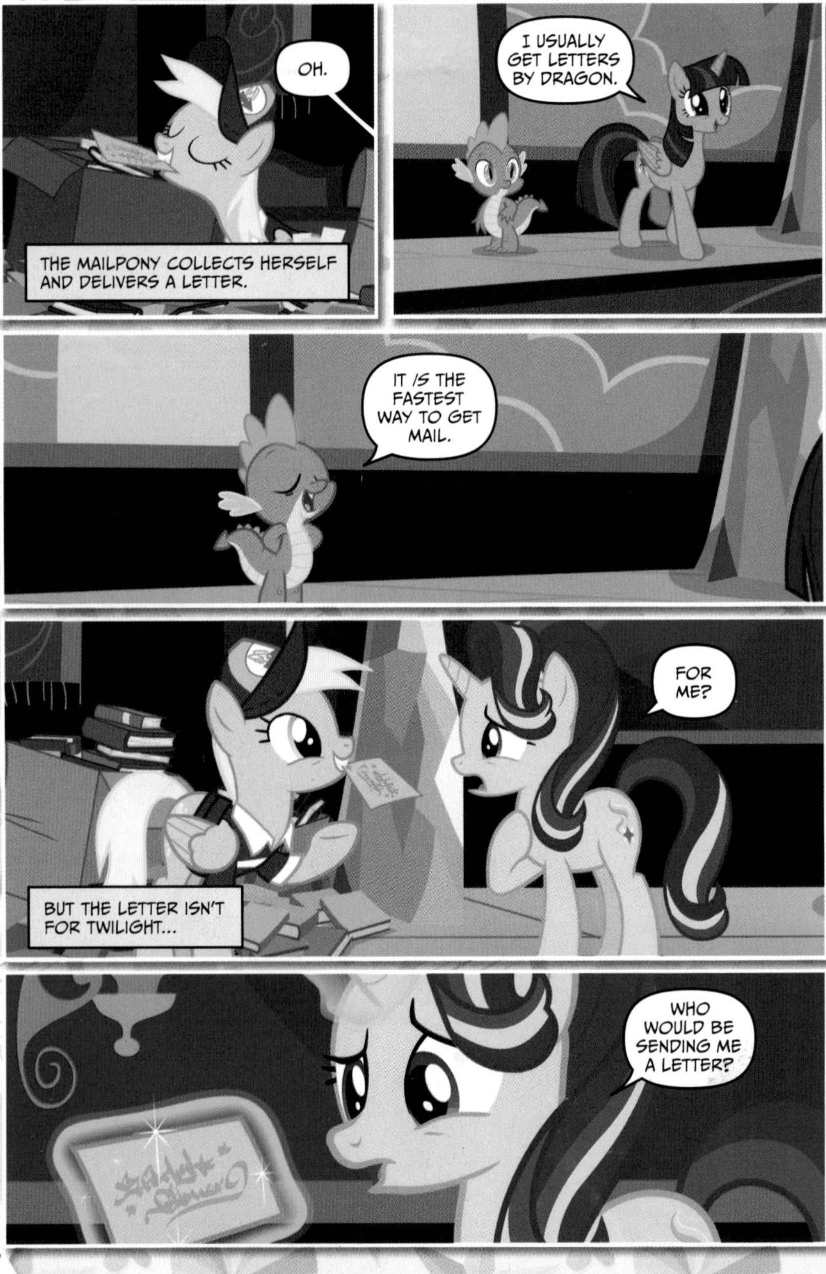
OH.
THE MAILPONY COLLECTS HERSELF AND DELIVERS A LETTER.
I USUALLY GET LETTERS BY DRAGON.
IT IS THE FASTEST WAY TO GET MAIL.
FOR ME?
BUT THE LETTER ISN'T FOR TWILIGHT...
WHO WOULD BE SENDING ME A LETTER?

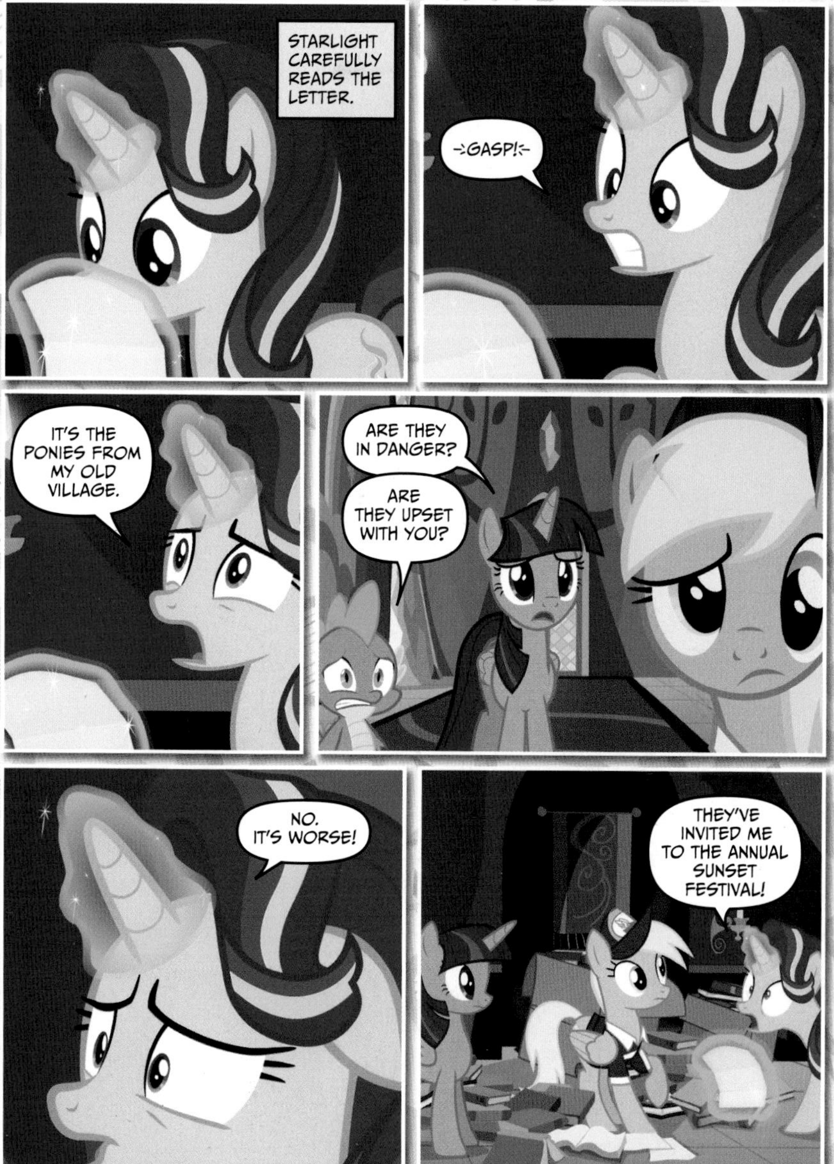
STARLIGHT CAREFULLY READS THE LETTER.
-:-GASP!-:-
IT'S THE PONIES FROM MY OLD VILLAGE.
ARE THEY IN DANGER?
ARE THEY UPSET WITH YOU?
NO. IT'S WORSE!
THEY'VE INVITED ME TO THE ANNUAL SUNSET FESTIVAL!

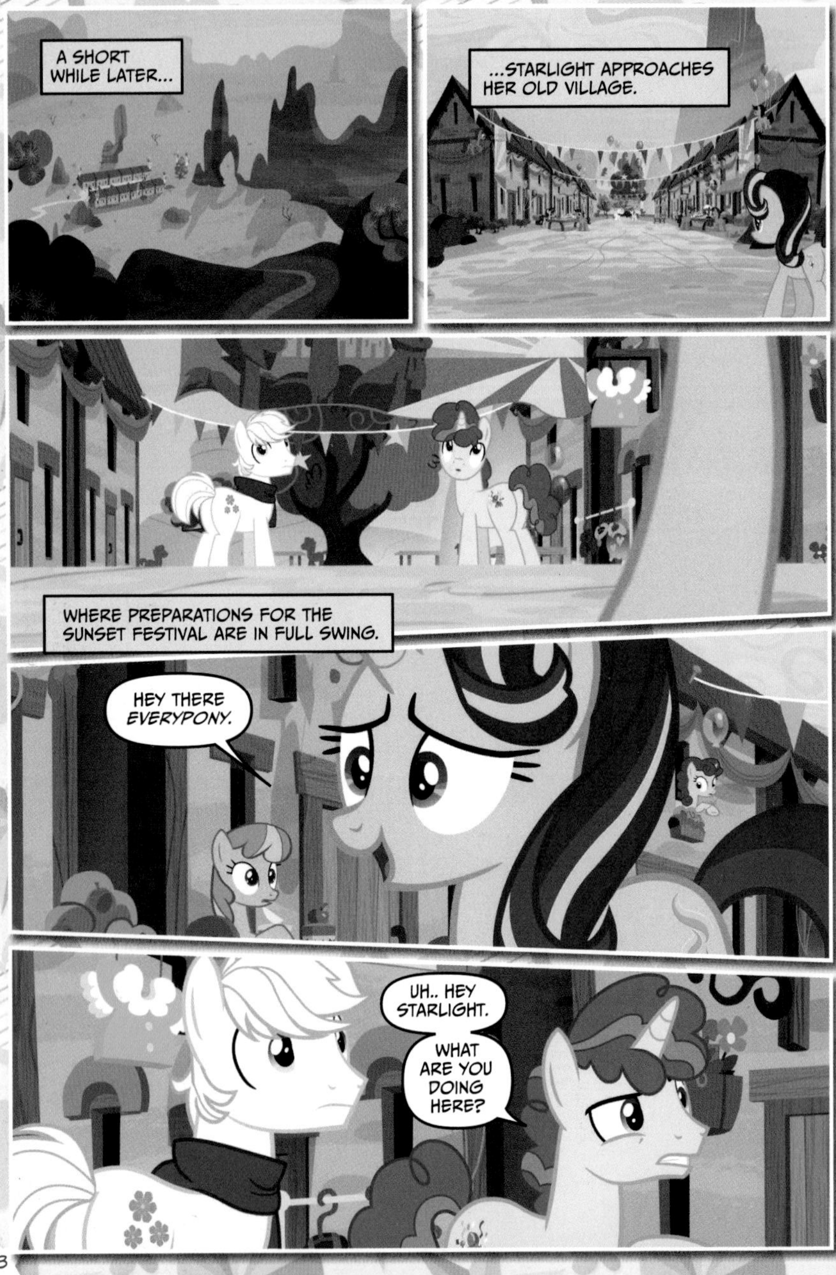
A SHORT WHILE LATER...
...STARLIGHT APPROACHES HER OLD VILLAGE.
WHERE PREPARATIONS FOR THE SUNSET FESTIVAL ARE IN FULL SWING.
HEY THERE *EVERYPONY.*
UH.. HEY STARLIGHT.
WHAT ARE YOU DOING HERE?

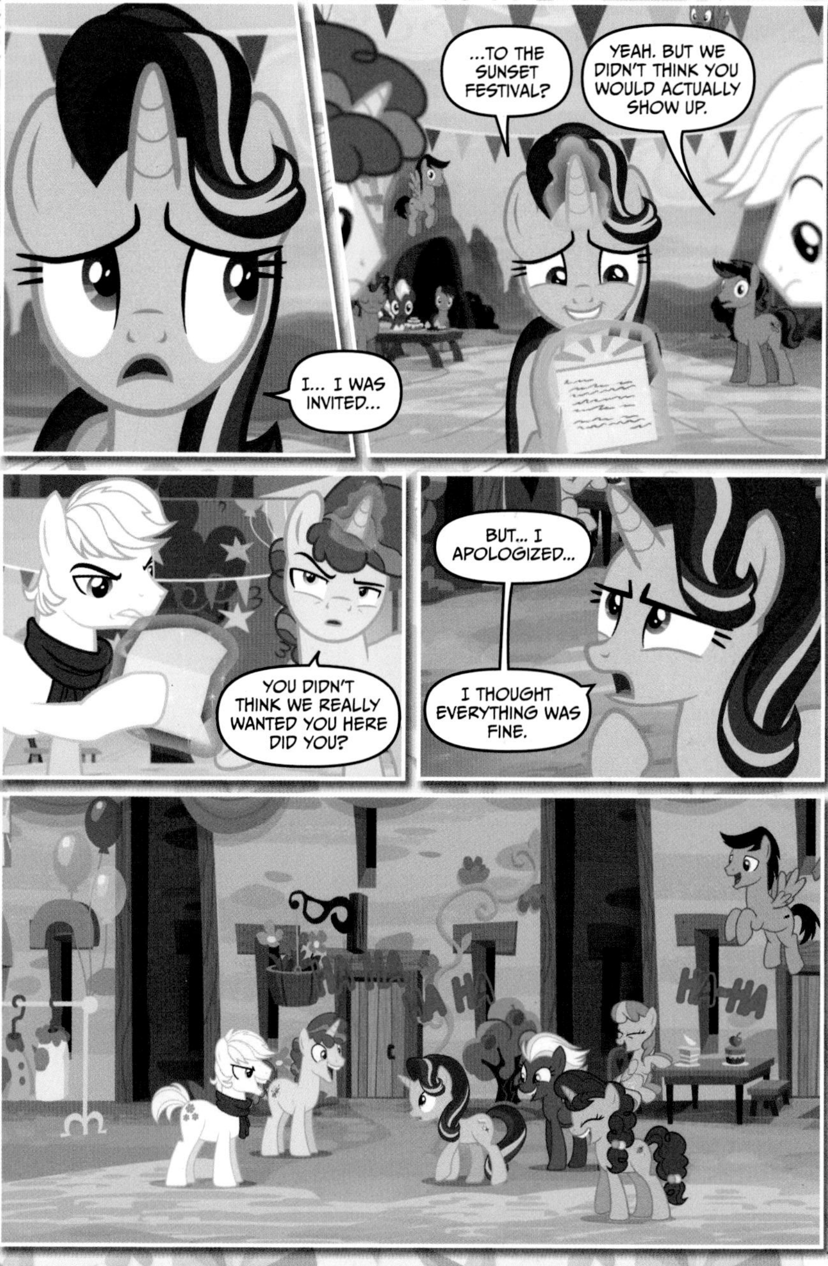
I... I WAS INVITED...
...TO THE SUNSET FESTIVAL?
YEAH. BUT WE DIDN'T THINK YOU WOULD ACTUALLY SHOW UP.
YOU DIDN'T THINK WE REALLY WANTED YOU HERE DID YOU?
BUT... I APOLOGIZED...
I THOUGHT EVERYTHING WAS FINE.
HA-HA

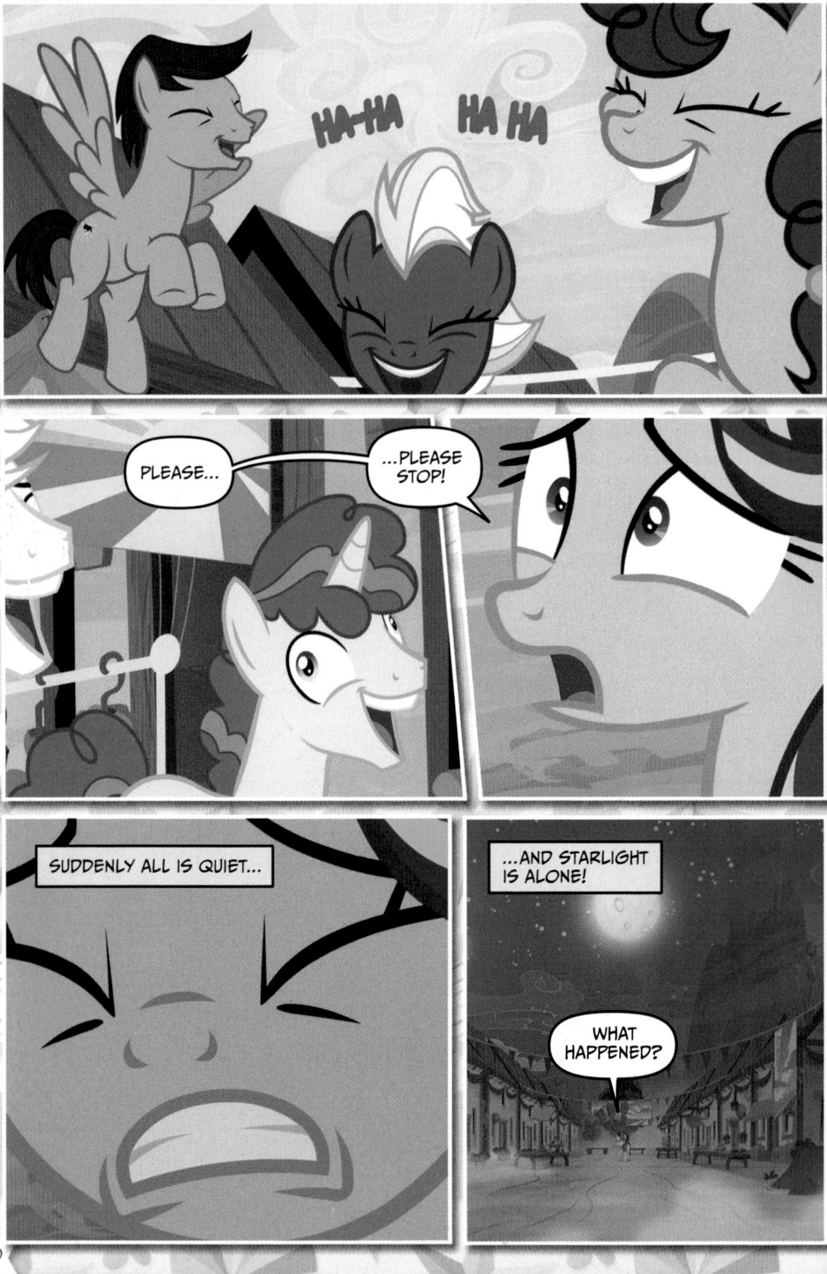
HA-HA
HA HA
PLEASE...
...PLEASE STOP!
SUDDENLY ALL IS QUIET...
...AND STARLIGHT IS ALONE!
WHAT HAPPENED?

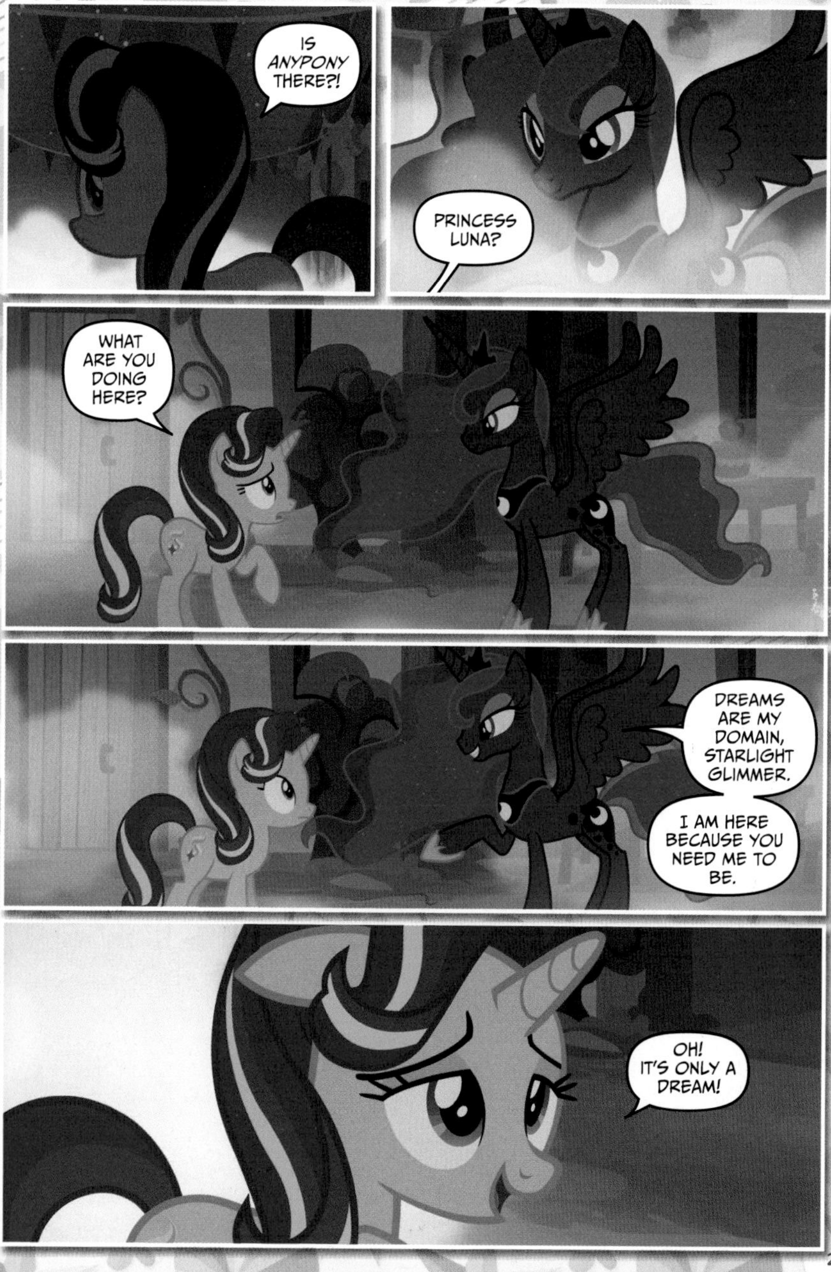
IS ANYPONY THERE?!
PRINCESS LUNA?
WHAT ARE YOU DOING HERE?
DREAMS ARE MY DOMAIN, STARLIGHT GLIMMER.
I AM HERE BECAUSE YOU NEED ME TO BE.
OH! IT'S ONLY A DREAM!

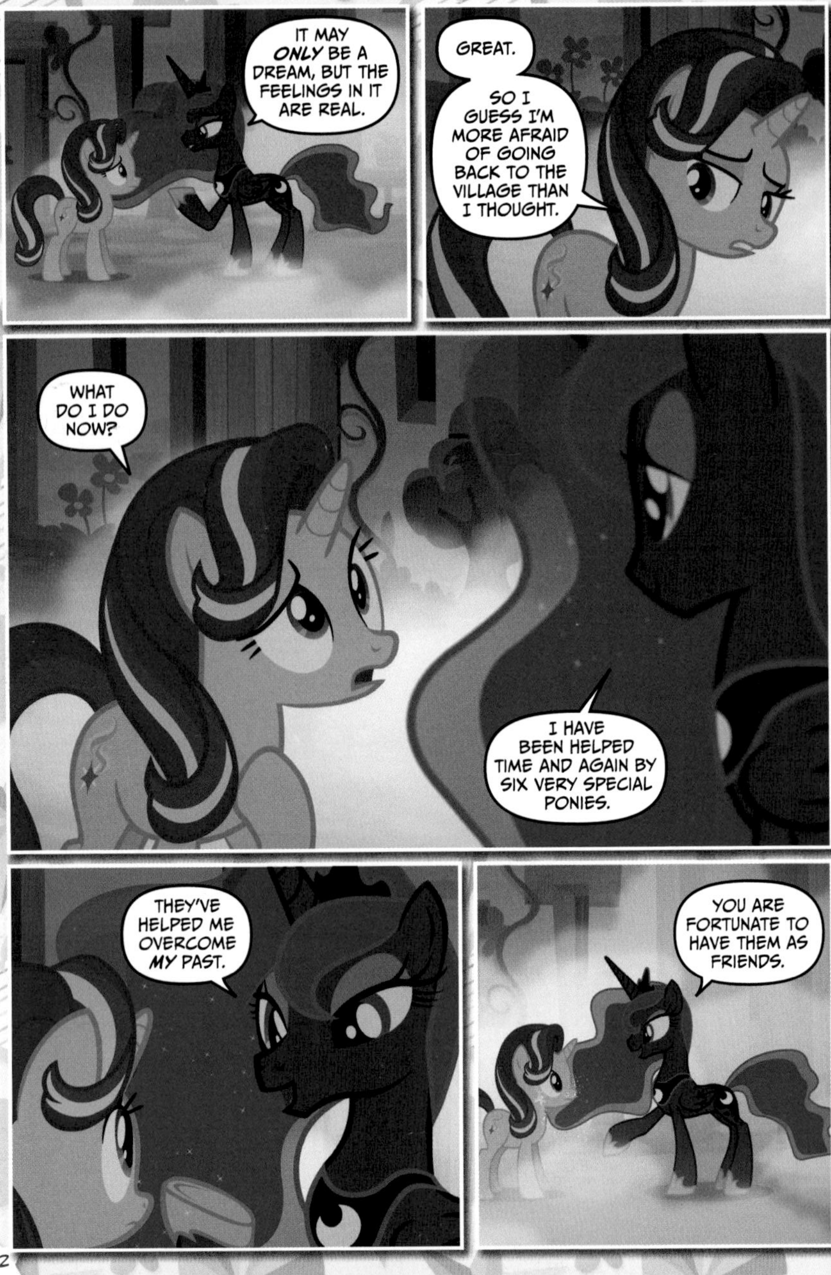
IT MAY ONLY BE A DREAM, BUT THE FEELINGS IN IT ARE REAL.
GREAT.
SO I GUESS I'M MORE AFRAID OF GOING BACK TO THE VILLAGE THAN I THOUGHT.
WHAT DO I DO NOW?
I HAVE BEEN HELPED TIME AND AGAIN BY SIX VERY SPECIAL PONIES.
THEY'VE HELPED ME OVERCOME MY PAST.
YOU ARE FORTUNATE TO HAVE THEM AS FRIENDS.

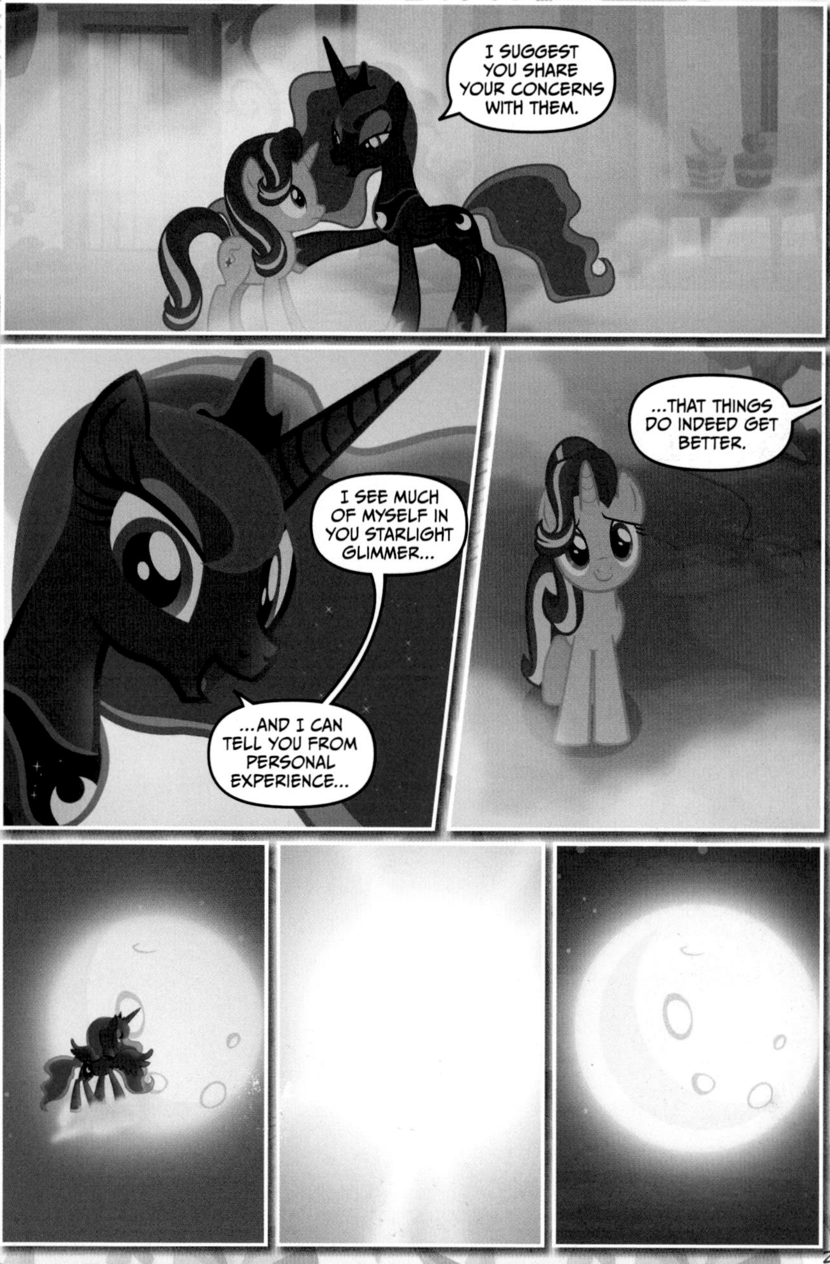
I SUGGEST YOU SHARE YOUR CONCERNS WITH THEM.
I SEE MUCH OF MYSELF IN YOU STARLIGHT GLIMMER...
...AND I CAN TELL YOU FROM PERSONAL EXPERIENCE...
...THAT THINGS DO INDEED GET BETTER.

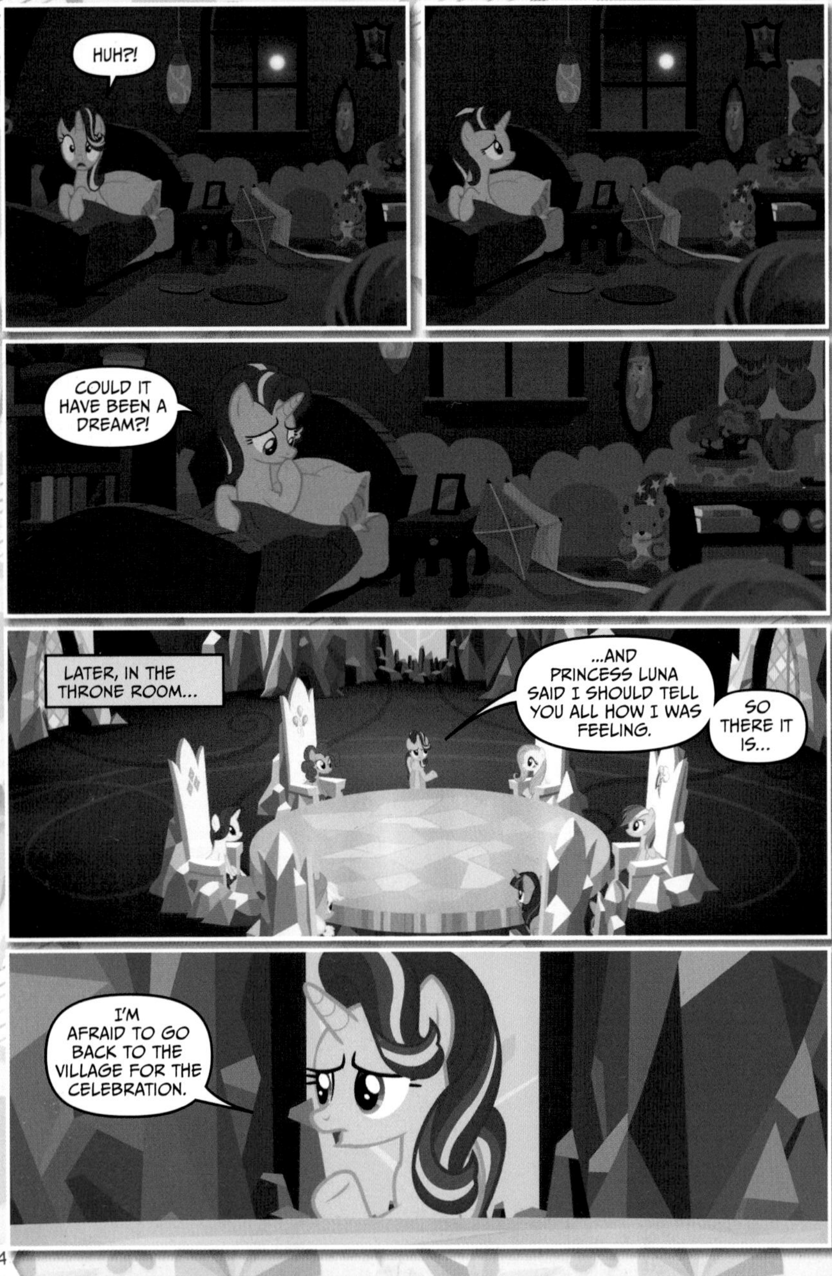
HUH?!
COULD IT HAVE BEEN A DREAM?!
LATER, IN THE THRONE ROOM...
...AND PRINCESS LUNA SAID I SHOULD TELL YOU ALL HOW I WAS FEELING.
SO THERE IT IS...
I'M AFRAID TO GO BACK TO THE VILLAGE FOR THE CELEBRATION.

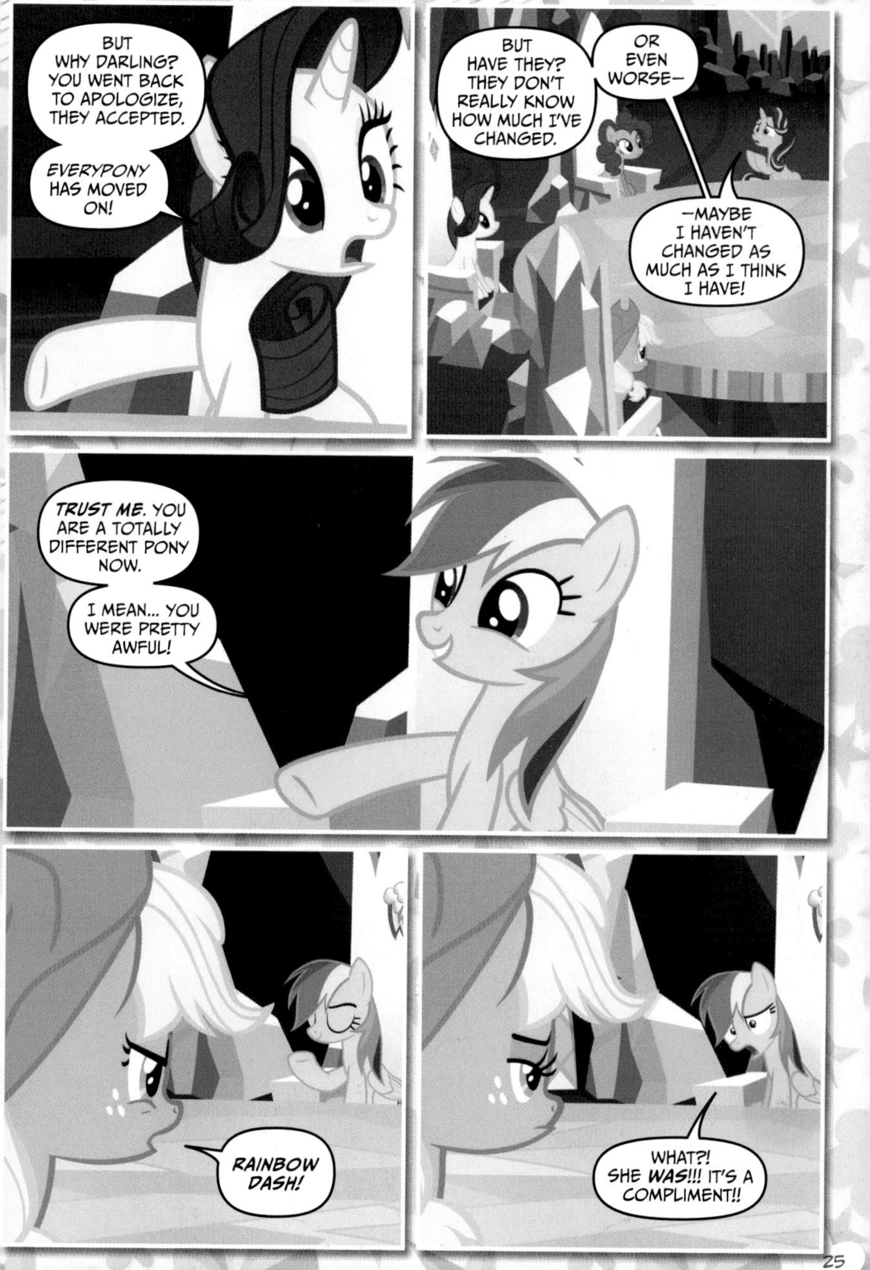

BUT WHY DARLING? YOU WENT BACK TO APOLOGIZE, THEY ACCEPTED.
EVERYPONY HAS MOVED ON!
BUT HAVE THEY? THEY DON'T REALLY KNOW HOW MUCH I'VE CHANGED.
OR EVEN WORSE—
—MAYBE I HAVEN'T CHANGED AS MUCH AS I THINK I HAVE!
TRUST ME. YOU ARE A TOTALLY DIFFERENT PONY NOW.
I MEAN... YOU WERE PRETTY AWFUL!
RAINBOW DASH!
WHAT?! SHE ***WAS!!!*** IT'S A COMPLIMENT!!

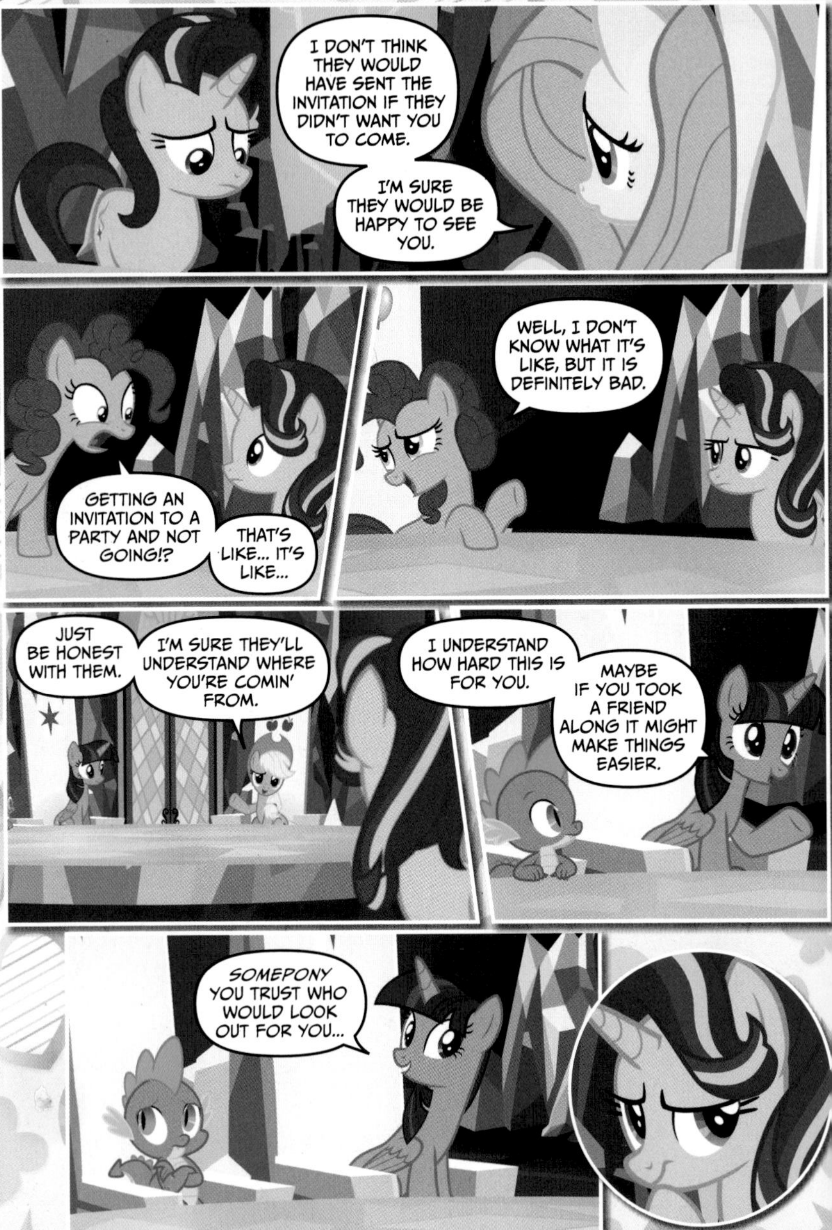

I DON'T THINK THEY WOULD HAVE SENT THE INVITATION IF THEY DIDN'T WANT YOU TO COME.
I'M SURE THEY WOULD BE HAPPY TO SEE YOU.
GETTING AN INVITATION TO A PARTY AND NOT GOING!?
THAT'S LIKE... IT'S LIKE...
WELL, I DON'T KNOW WHAT IT'S LIKE, BUT IT IS DEFINITELY BAD.
JUST BE HONEST WITH THEM.
I'M SURE THEY'LL UNDERSTAND WHERE YOU'RE COMIN' FROM.
I UNDERSTAND HOW HARD THIS IS FOR YOU.
MAYBE IF YOU TOOK A FRIEND ALONG IT MIGHT MAKE THINGS EASIER.
SOMEPONY YOU TRUST WHO WOULD LOOK OUT FOR YOU...

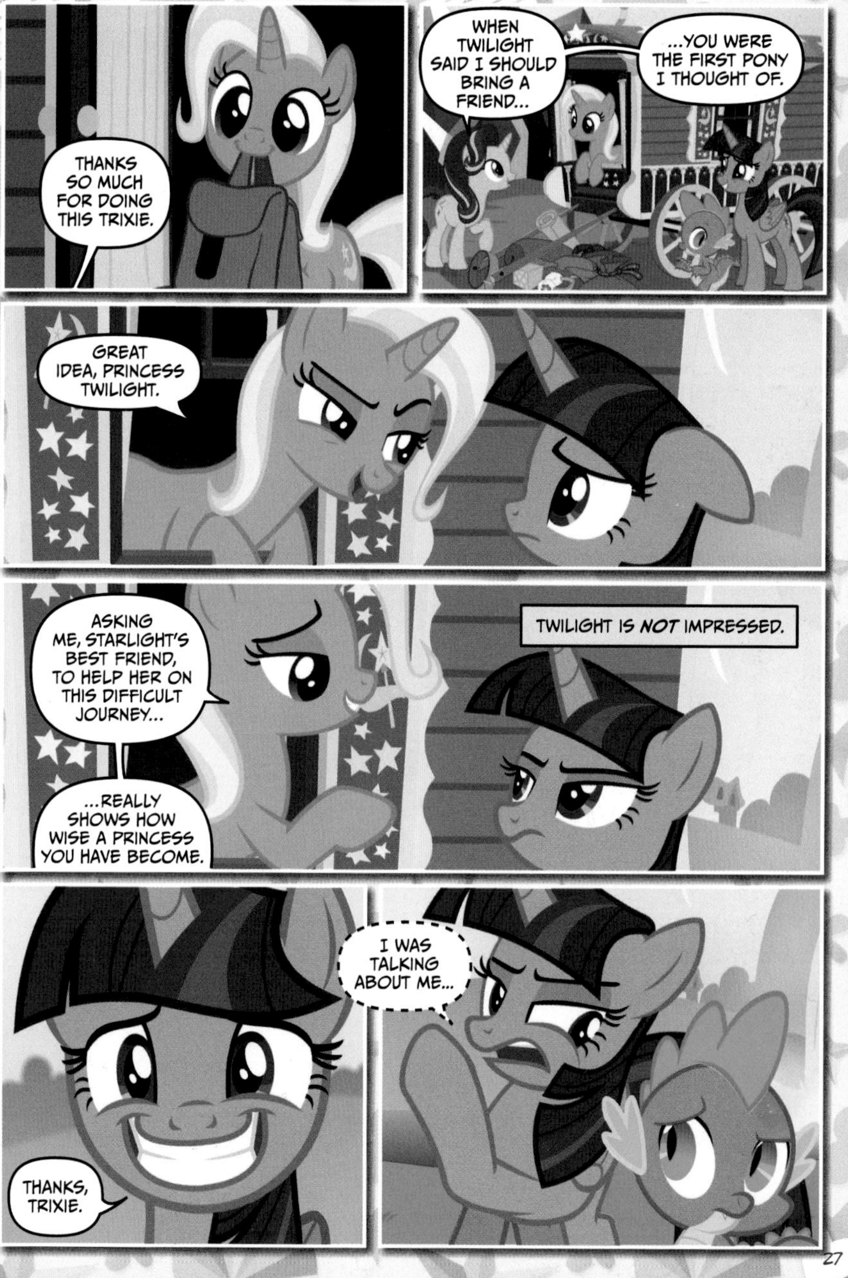
THANKS SO MUCH FOR DOING THIS TRIXIE.
WHEN TWILIGHT SAID I SHOULD BRING A FRIEND...
...YOU WERE THE FIRST PONY I THOUGHT OF.
GREAT IDEA, PRINCESS TWILIGHT.
ASKING ME, STARLIGHT'S BEST FRIEND, TO HELP HER ON THIS DIFFICULT JOURNEY...
...REALLY SHOWS HOW WISE A PRINCESS YOU HAVE BECOME.
TWILIGHT IS *NOT* IMPRESSED.
THANKS, TRIXIE.
I WAS TALKING ABOUT ME...

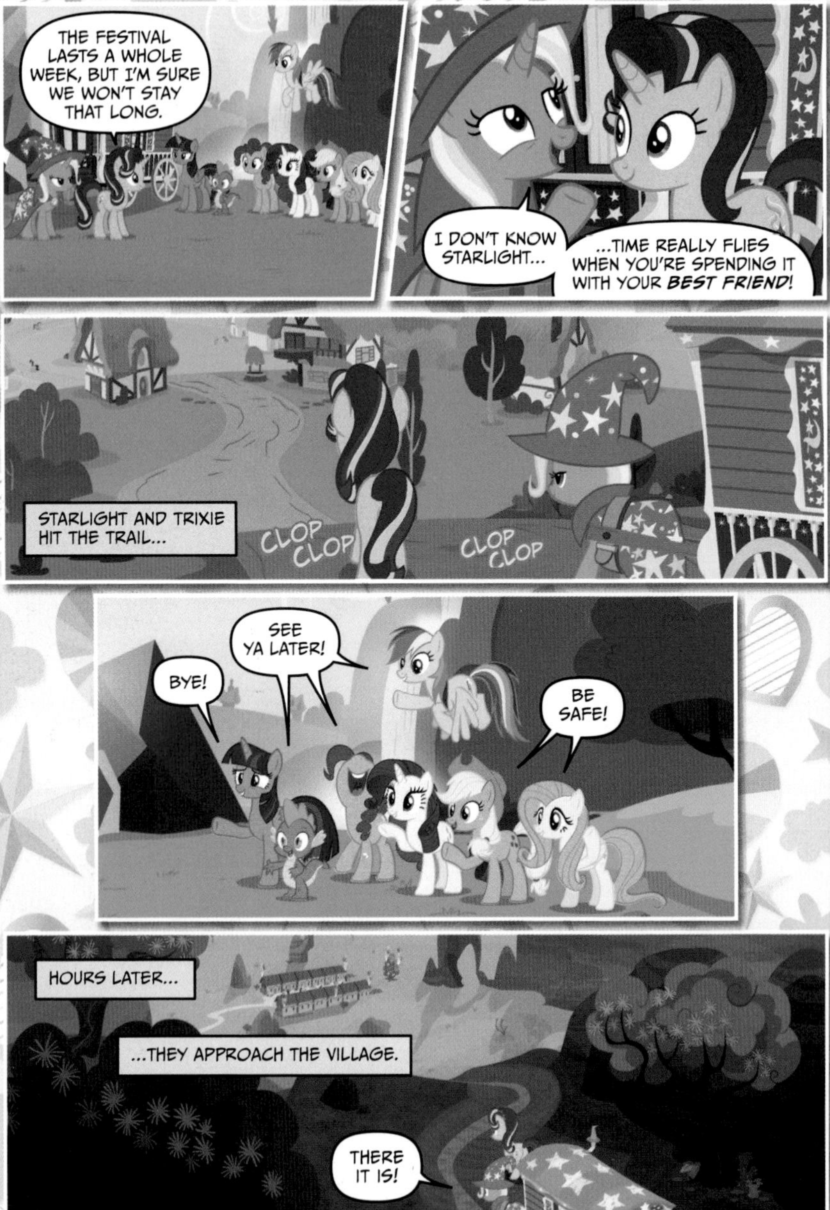
THE FESTIVAL LASTS A WHOLE WEEK, BUT I'M SURE WE WON'T STAY THAT LONG.
I DON'T KNOW STARLIGHT...
...TIME REALLY FLIES WHEN YOU'RE SPENDING IT WITH YOUR BEST FRIEND!
STARLIGHT AND TRIXIE HIT THE TRAIL...
CLOP CLOP
CLOP CLOP
BYE!
SEE YA LATER!
BE SAFE!
HOURS LATER...
...THEY APPROACH THE VILLAGE.
THERE IT IS!

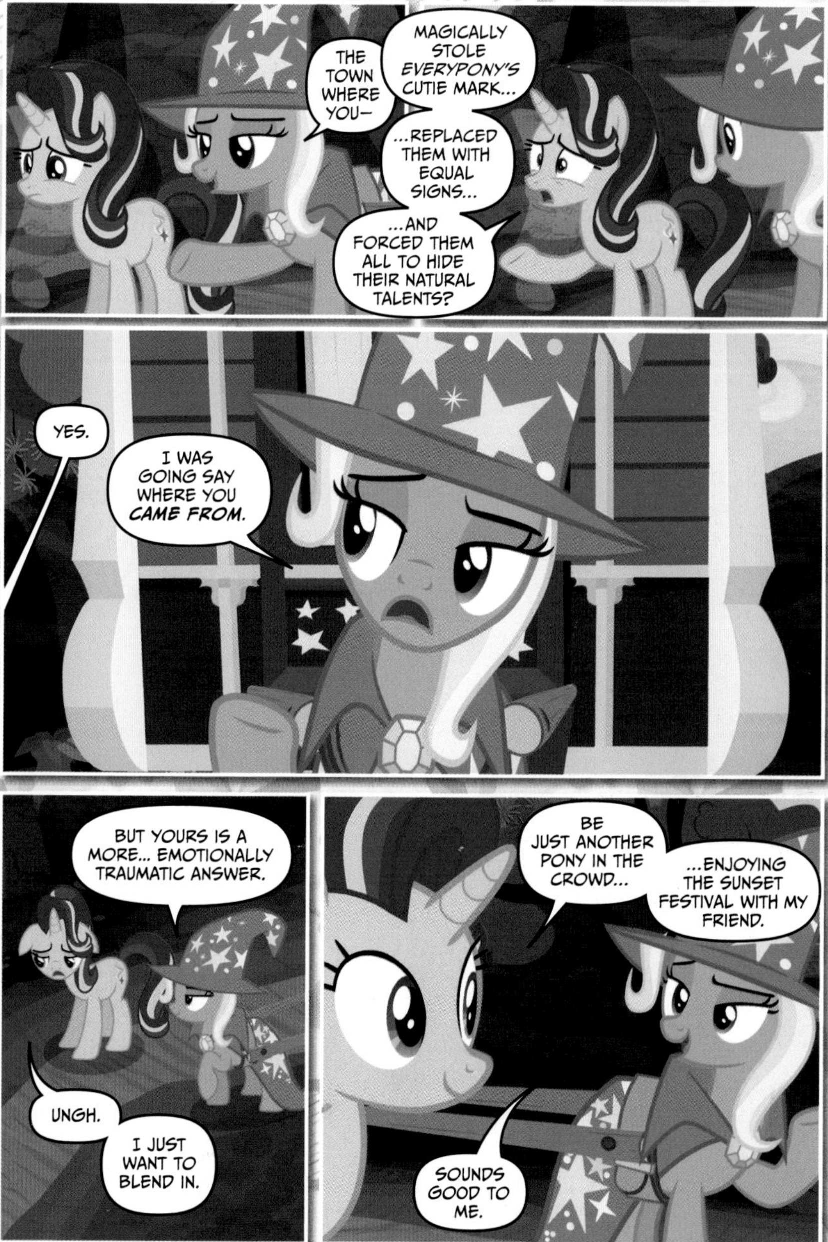

THE TOWN WHERE YOU—
MAGICALLY STOLE *EVERYPONY'S* CUTIE MARK...
...REPLACED THEM WITH EQUAL SIGNS...
...AND FORCED THEM ALL TO HIDE THEIR NATURAL TALENTS?
YES.
I WAS GOING SAY WHERE YOU ***CAME FROM.***
BUT YOURS IS A MORE... EMOTIONALLY TRAUMATIC ANSWER.
UNGH.
I JUST WANT TO BLEND IN.
BE JUST ANOTHER PONY IN THE CROWD...
...ENJOYING THE SUNSET FESTIVAL WITH MY FRIEND.
SOUNDS GOOD TO ME.

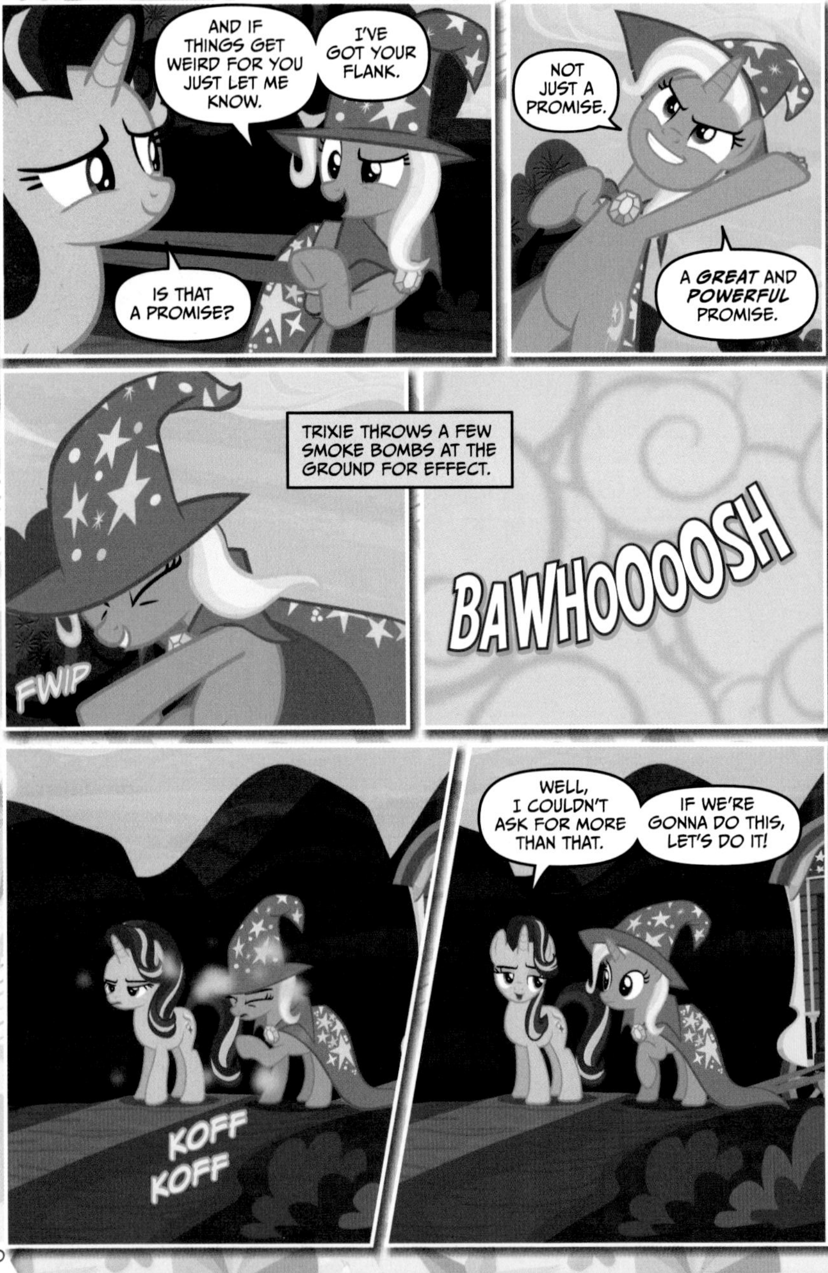
AND IF THINGS GET WEIRD FOR YOU JUST LET ME KNOW.
I'VE GOT YOUR FLANK.
IS THAT A PROMISE?
NOT JUST A PROMISE.
A GREAT AND POWERFUL PROMISE.
TRIXIE THROWS A FEW SMOKE BOMBS AT THE GROUND FOR EFFECT.
FWIP
BAWHOOOOSH
KOFF KOFF
WELL, I COULDN'T ASK FOR MORE THAN THAT.
IF WE'RE GONNA DO THIS, LET'S DO IT!

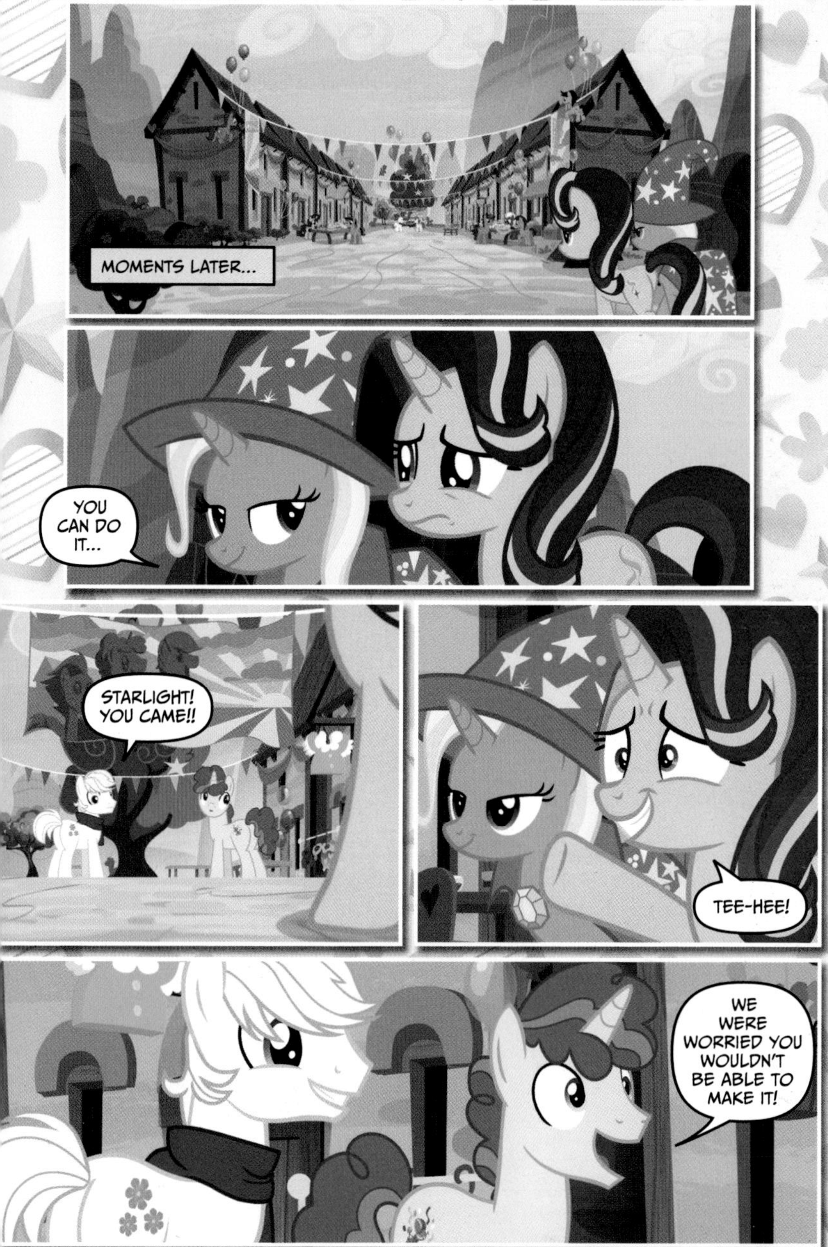
MOMENTS LATER...
YOU CAN DO IT...
STARLIGHT! YOU CAME!!
TEE-HEE!
WE WERE WORRIED YOU WOULDN'T BE ABLE TO MAKE IT!

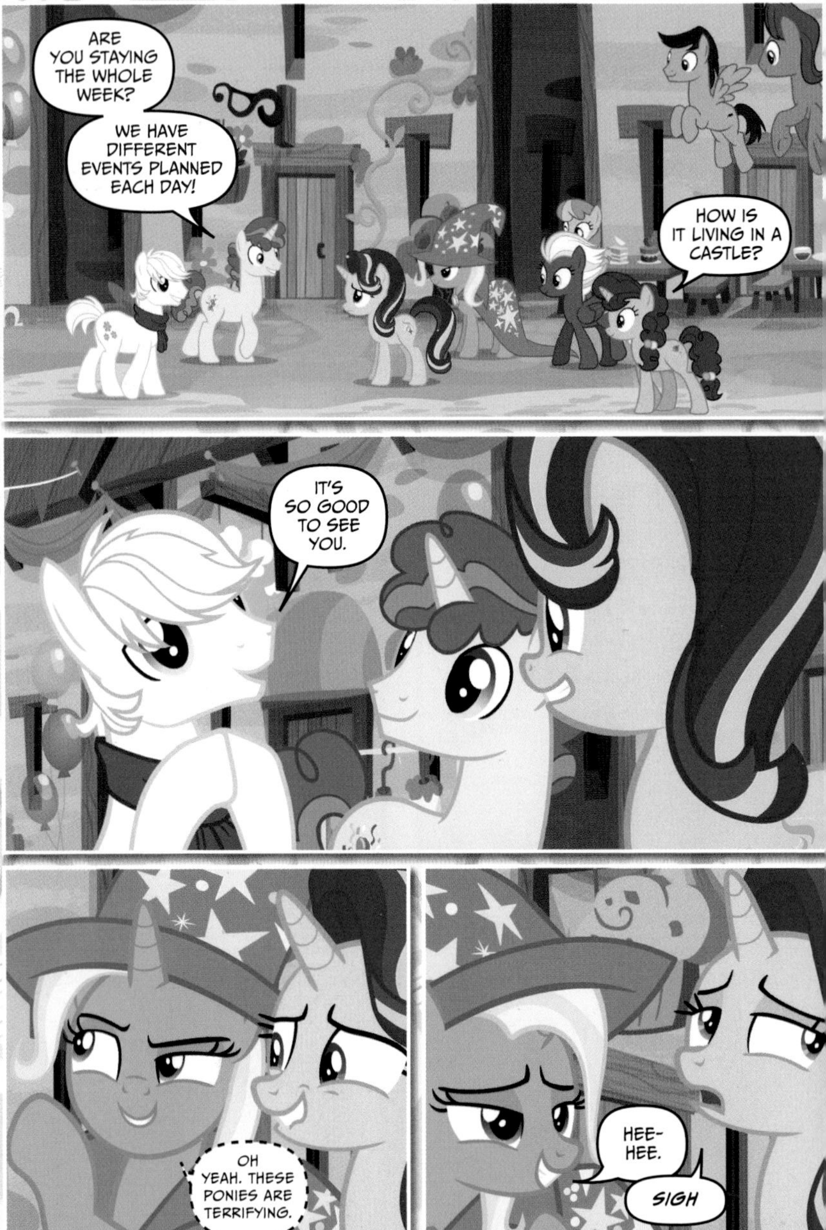
ARE YOU STAYING THE WHOLE WEEK?
WE HAVE DIFFERENT EVENTS PLANNED EACH DAY!
HOW IS IT LIVING IN A CASTLE?
IT'S SO GOOD TO SEE YOU.
OH YEAH. THESE PONIES ARE TERRIFYING.
HEE-HEE.
SIGH

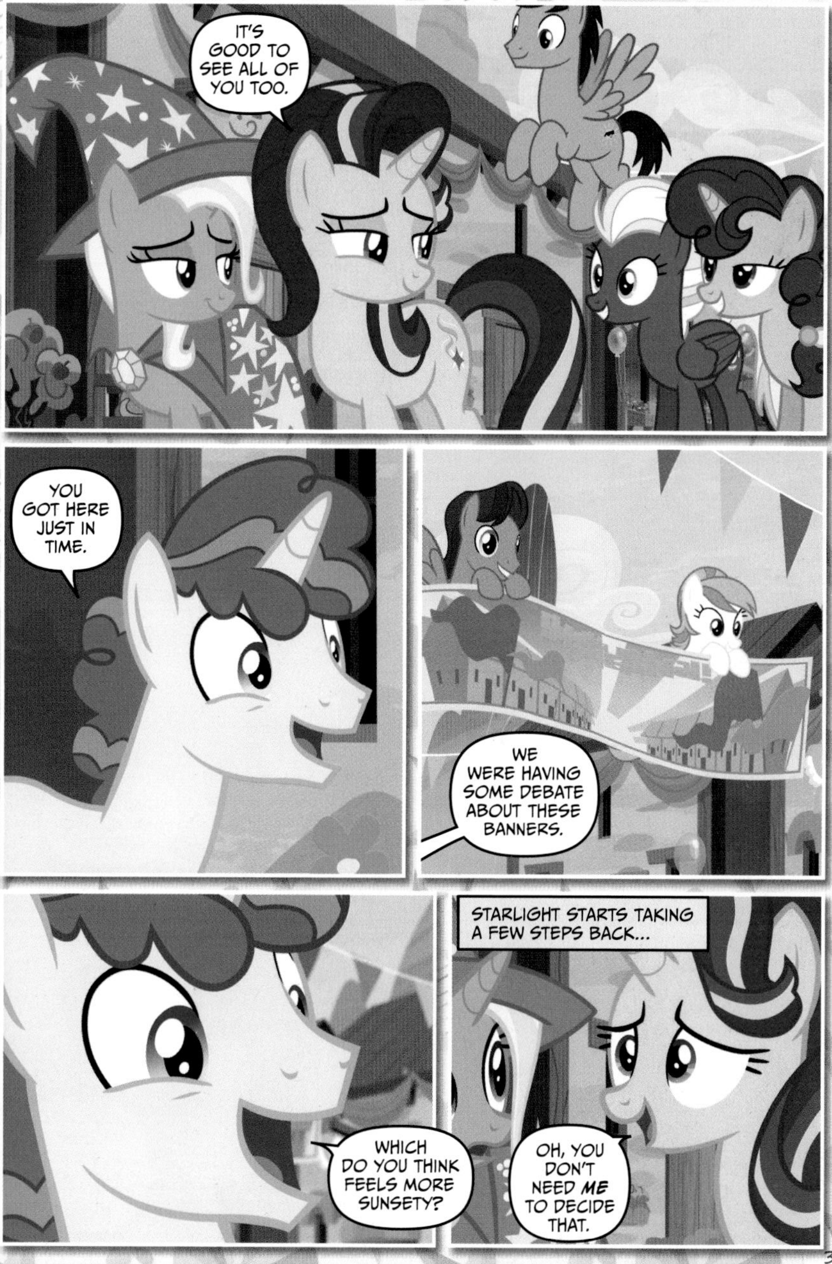
IT'S GOOD TO SEE ALL OF YOU TOO.
YOU GOT HERE JUST IN TIME.
WE WERE HAVING SOME DEBATE ABOUT THESE BANNERS.
STARLIGHT STARTS TAKING A FEW STEPS BACK...
WHICH DO YOU THINK FEELS MORE SUNSETY?
OH, YOU DON'T NEED *ME* TO DECIDE THAT.

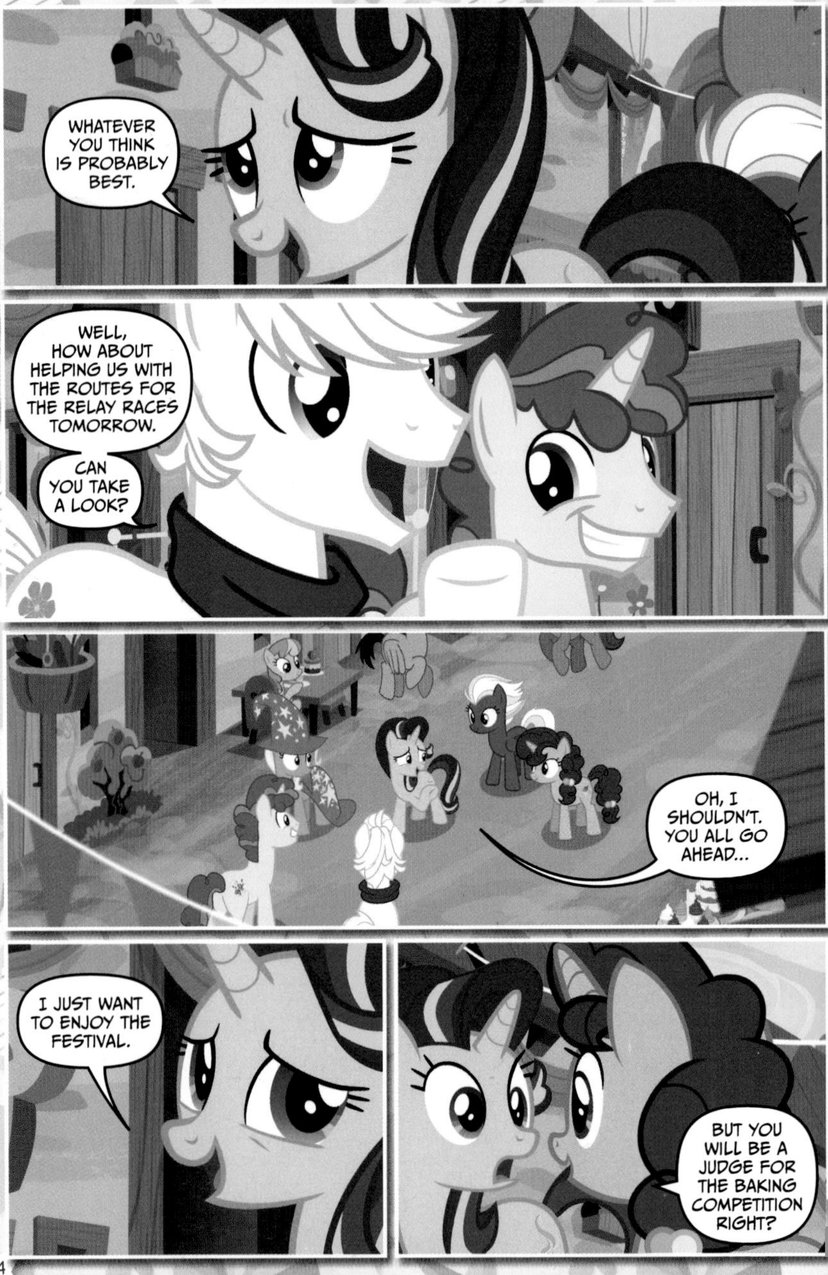

WHATEVER YOU THINK IS PROBABLY BEST.
WELL, HOW ABOUT HELPING US WITH THE ROUTES FOR THE RELAY RACES TOMORROW.
CAN YOU TAKE A LOOK?
OH, I SHOULDN'T. YOU ALL GO AHEAD...
I JUST WANT TO ENJOY THE FESTIVAL.
BUT YOU WILL BE A JUDGE FOR THE BAKING COMPETITION RIGHT?

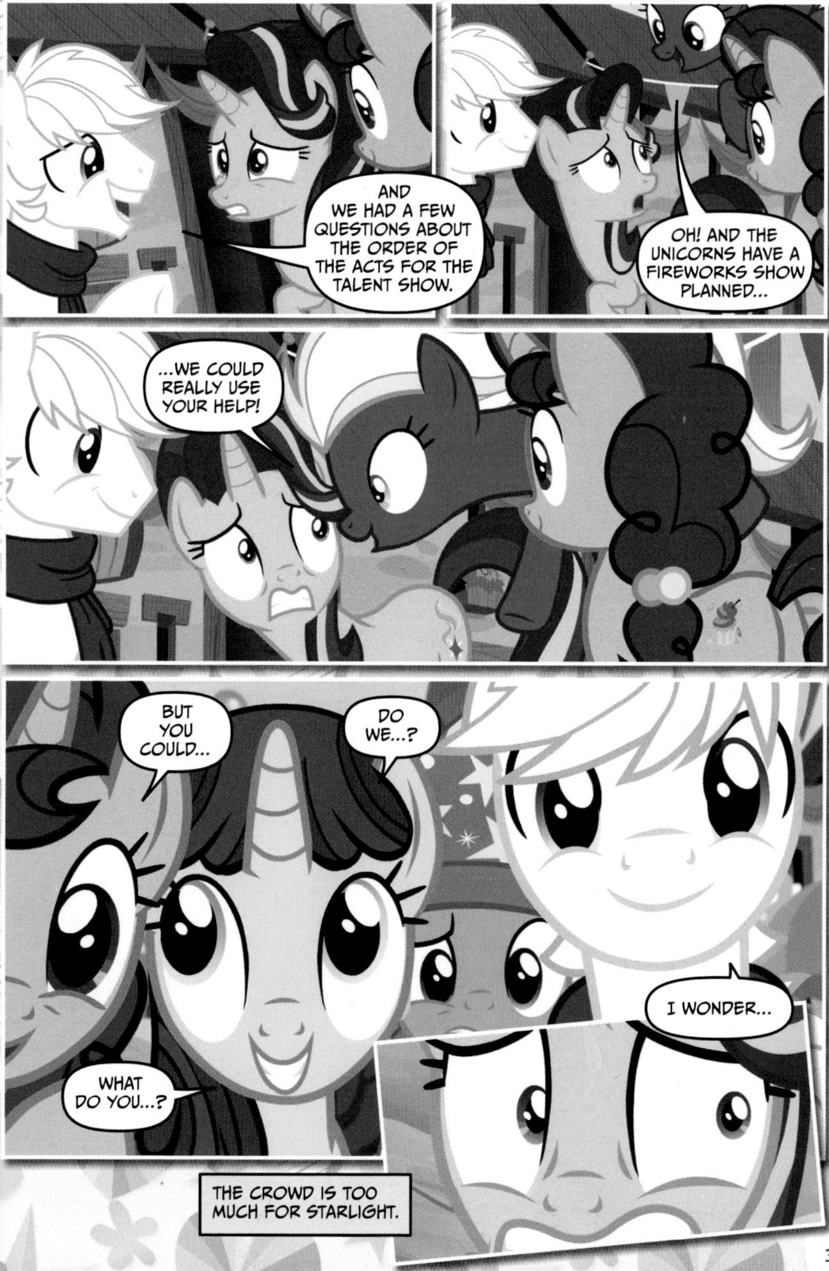
AND WE HAD A FEW QUESTIONS ABOUT THE ORDER OF THE ACTS FOR THE TALENT SHOW.
OH! AND THE UNICORNS HAVE A FIREWORKS SHOW PLANNED...
...WE COULD REALLY USE YOUR HELP!
BUT YOU COULD...
DO WE...?
WHAT DO YOU...?
I WONDER...
THE CROWD IS TOO MUCH FOR STARLIGHT.

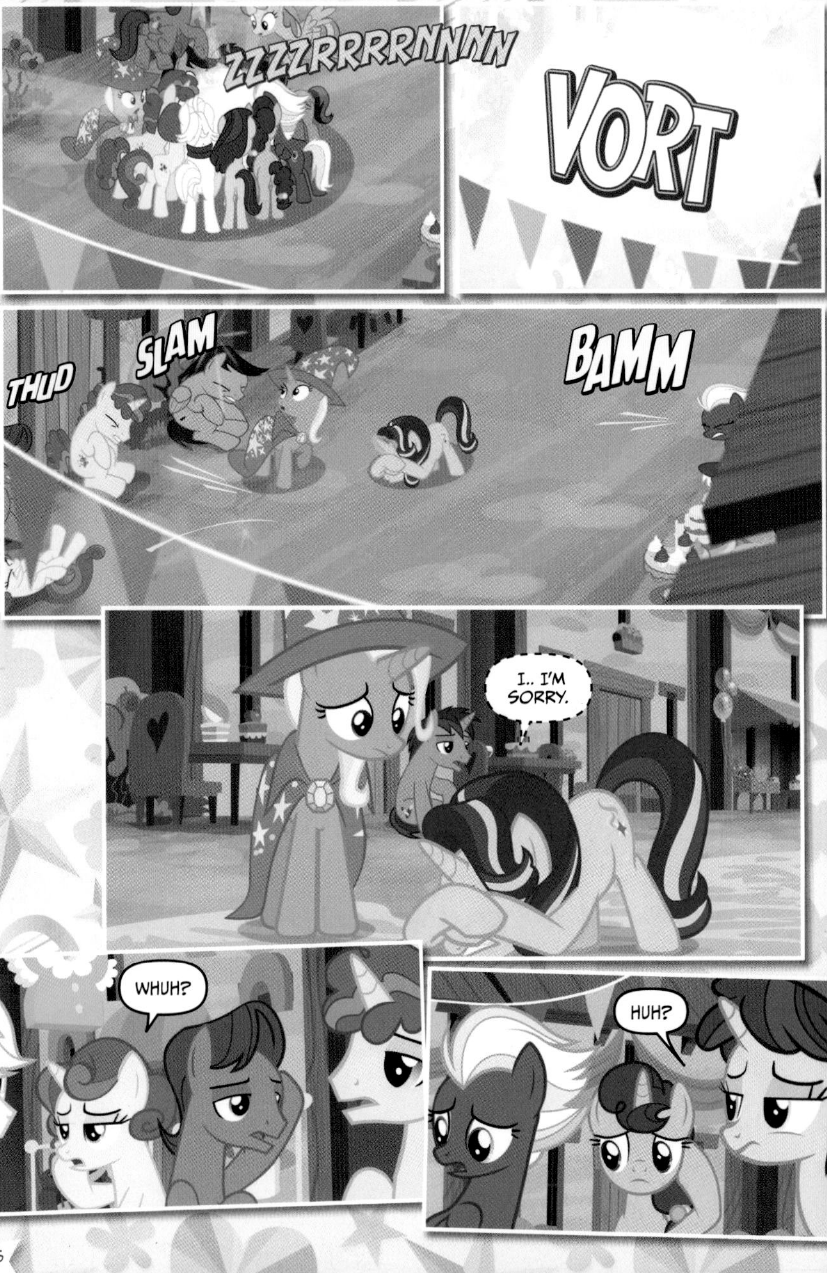
ZZZZRRRRRNNNN
VORT
THUD
SLAM
BAMM
I.. I'M SORRY.
WHUH?
HUH?

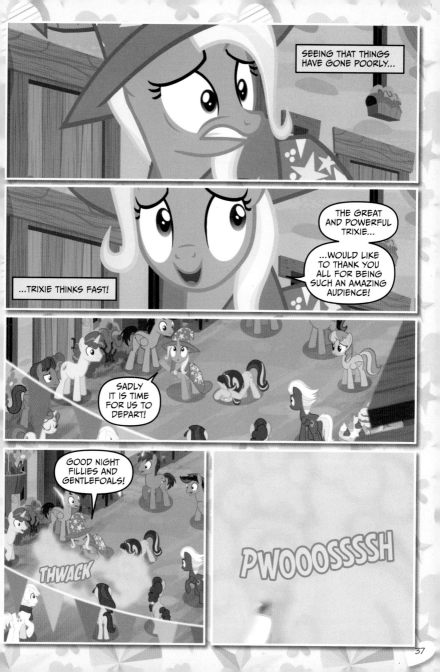

SEEING THAT THINGS HAVE GONE POORLY...

THE GREAT AND POWERFUL TRIXIE...

...WOULD LIKE TO THANK YOU ALL FOR BEING SUCH AN AMAZING AUDIENCE!

...TRIXIE THINKS FAST!

SADLY IT IS TIME FOR US TO DEPART!

GOOD NIGHT FILLIES AND GENTLEFOALS!

THWACK

PWOOOSSSSH

37

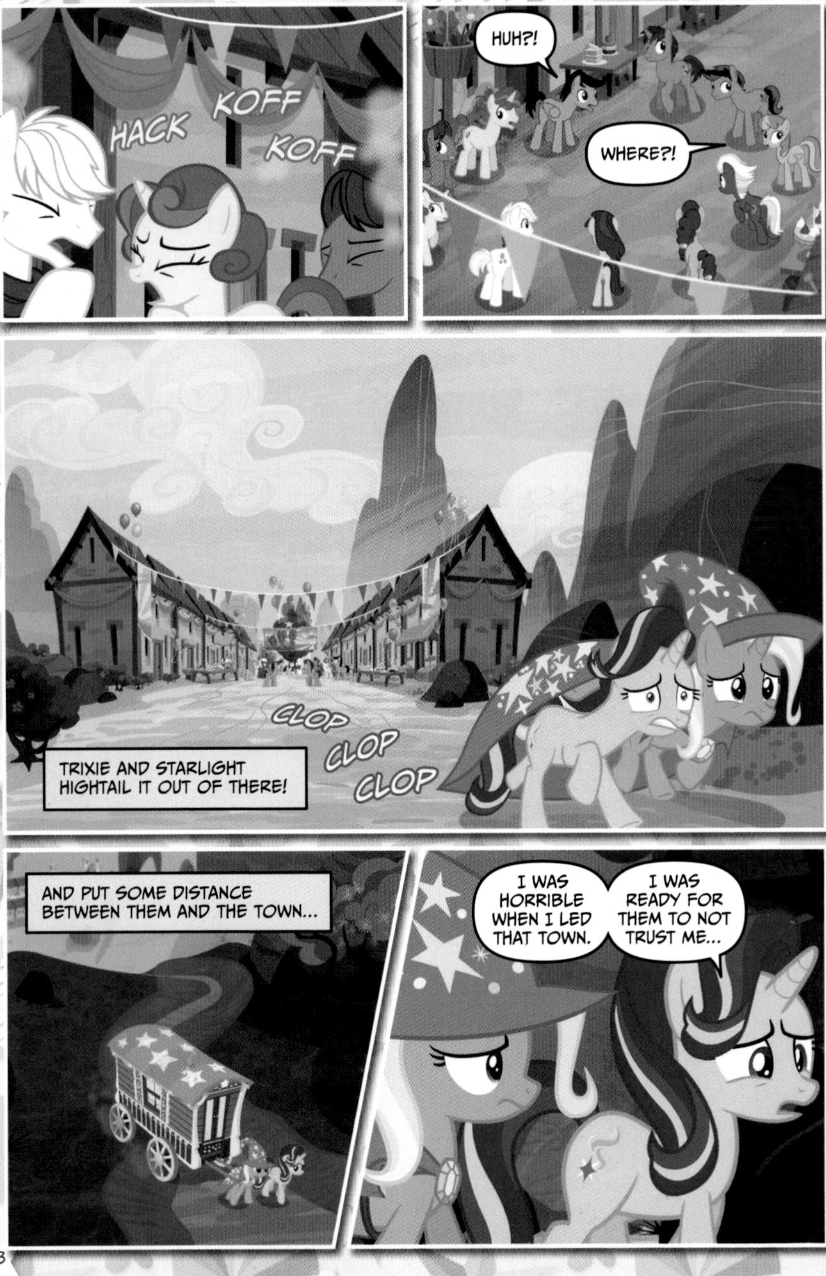
HACK
KOFF
KOFF
HUH?!
WHERE?!
CLOP
CLOP
CLOP
TRIXIE AND STARLIGHT HIGHTAIL IT OUT OF THERE!
AND PUT SOME DISTANCE BETWEEN THEM AND THE TOWN...
I WAS HORRIBLE WHEN I LED THAT TOWN.
I WAS READY FOR THEM TO NOT TRUST ME...

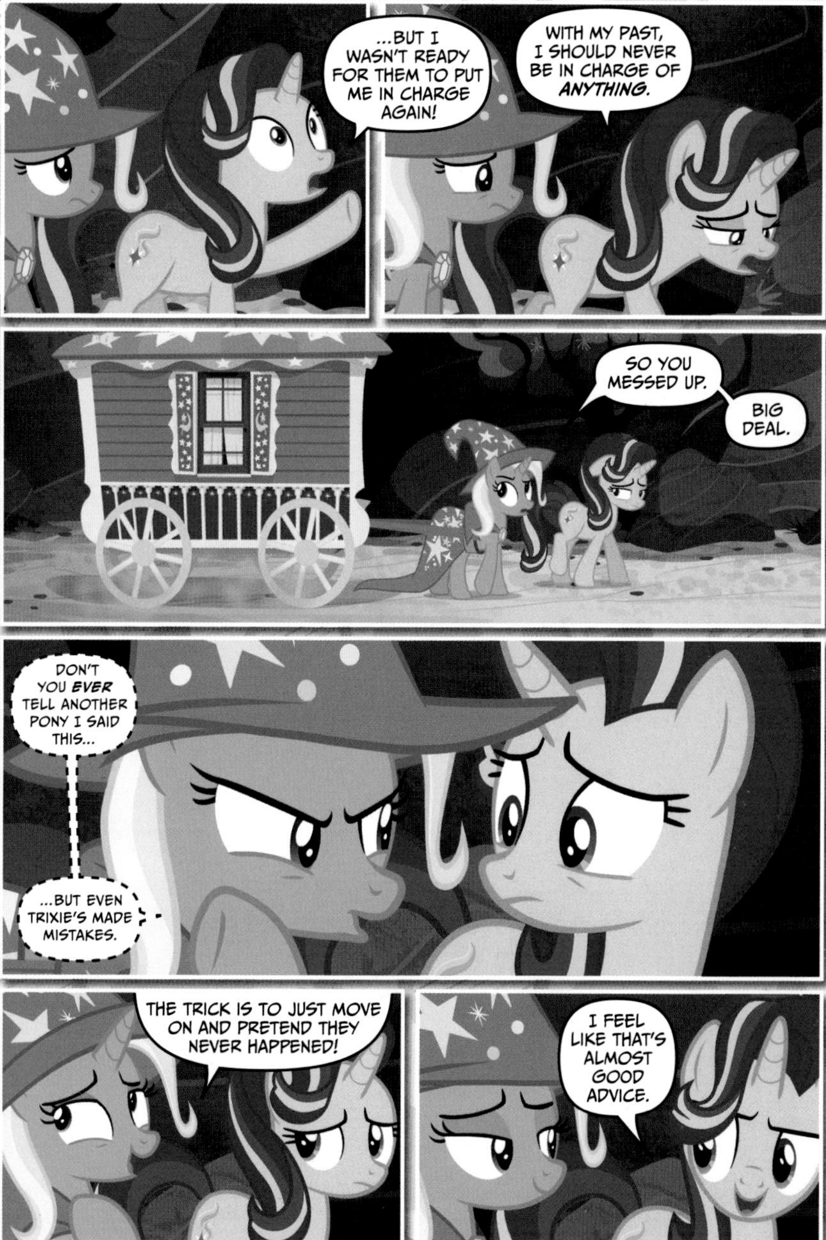
...BUT I WASN'T READY FOR THEM TO PUT ME IN CHARGE AGAIN!
WITH MY PAST, I SHOULD NEVER BE IN CHARGE OF *ANYTHING*.
SO YOU MESSED UP.
BIG DEAL.
DON'T YOU *EVER* TELL ANOTHER PONY I SAID THIS...
...BUT EVEN TRIXIE'S MADE MISTAKES.
THE TRICK IS TO JUST MOVE ON AND PRETEND THEY NEVER HAPPENED!
I FEEL LIKE THAT'S ALMOST GOOD ADVICE.

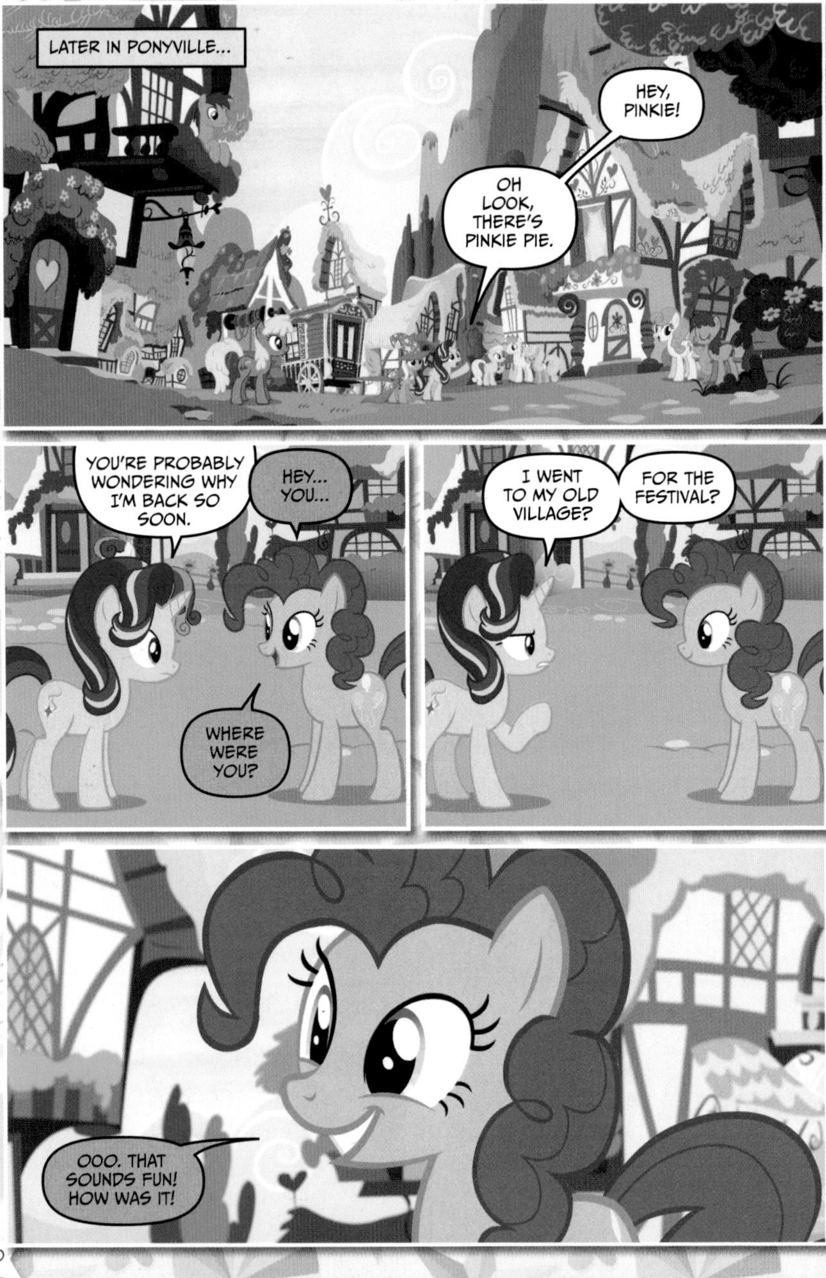
LATER IN PONYVILLE...
HEY, PINKIE!
OH LOOK, THERE'S PINKIE PIE.
YOU'RE PROBABLY WONDERING WHY I'M BACK SO SOON.
HEY... YOU...
WHERE WERE YOU?
I WENT TO MY OLD VILLAGE?
FOR THE FESTIVAL?
OOO. THAT SOUNDS FUN! HOW WAS IT!

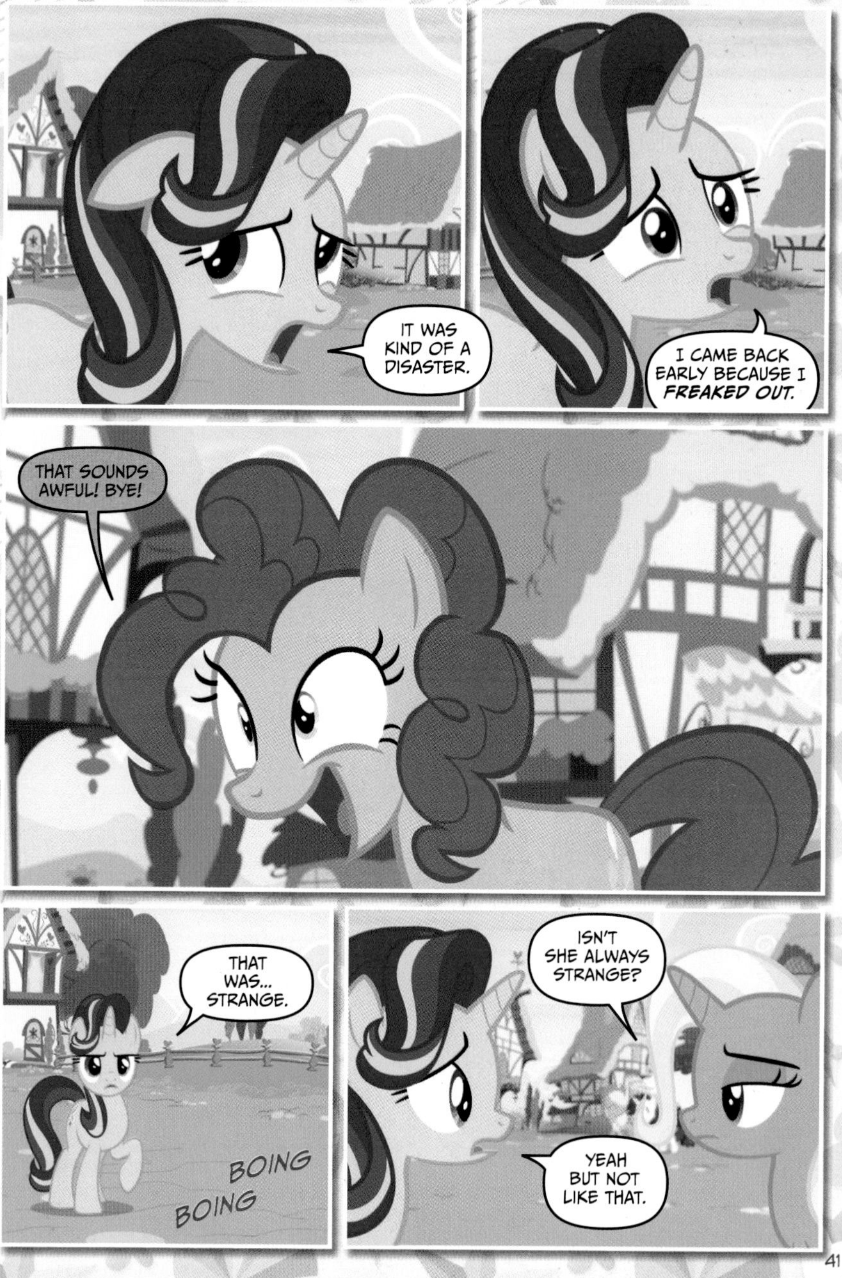
IT WAS KIND OF A DISASTER.
I CAME BACK EARLY BECAUSE I FREAKED OUT.
THAT SOUNDS AWFUL! BYE!
THAT WAS... STRANGE.
BOING
BOING
ISN'T SHE ALWAYS STRANGE?
YEAH BUT NOT LIKE THAT.

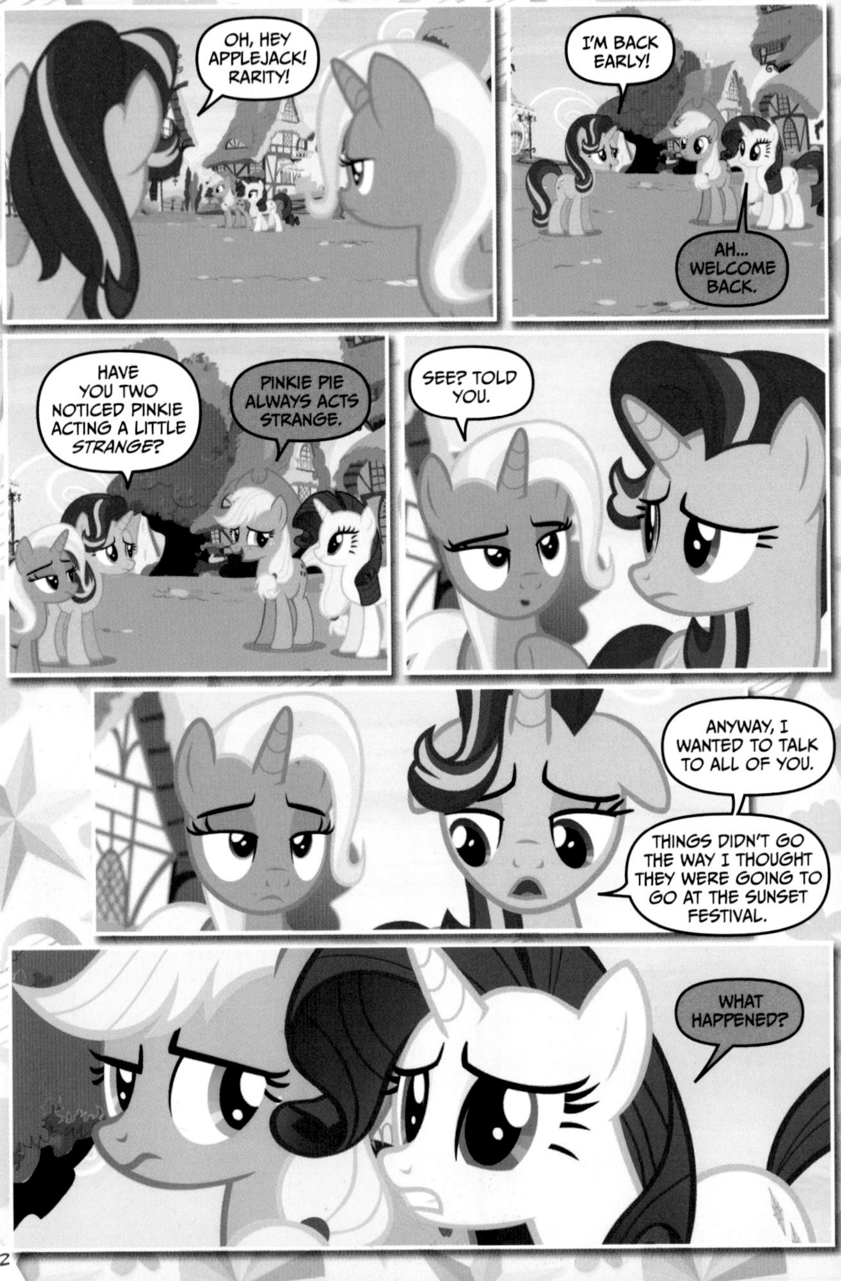
OH, HEY APPLEJACK! RARITY!
I'M BACK EARLY!
AH... WELCOME BACK.
HAVE YOU TWO NOTICED PINKIE ACTING A LITTLE STRANGE?
PINKIE PIE ALWAYS ACTS STRANGE.
SEE? TOLD YOU.
ANYWAY, I WANTED TO TALK TO ALL OF YOU.
THINGS DIDN'T GO THE WAY I THOUGHT THEY WERE GOING TO GO AT THE SUNSET FESTIVAL.
WHAT HAPPENED?

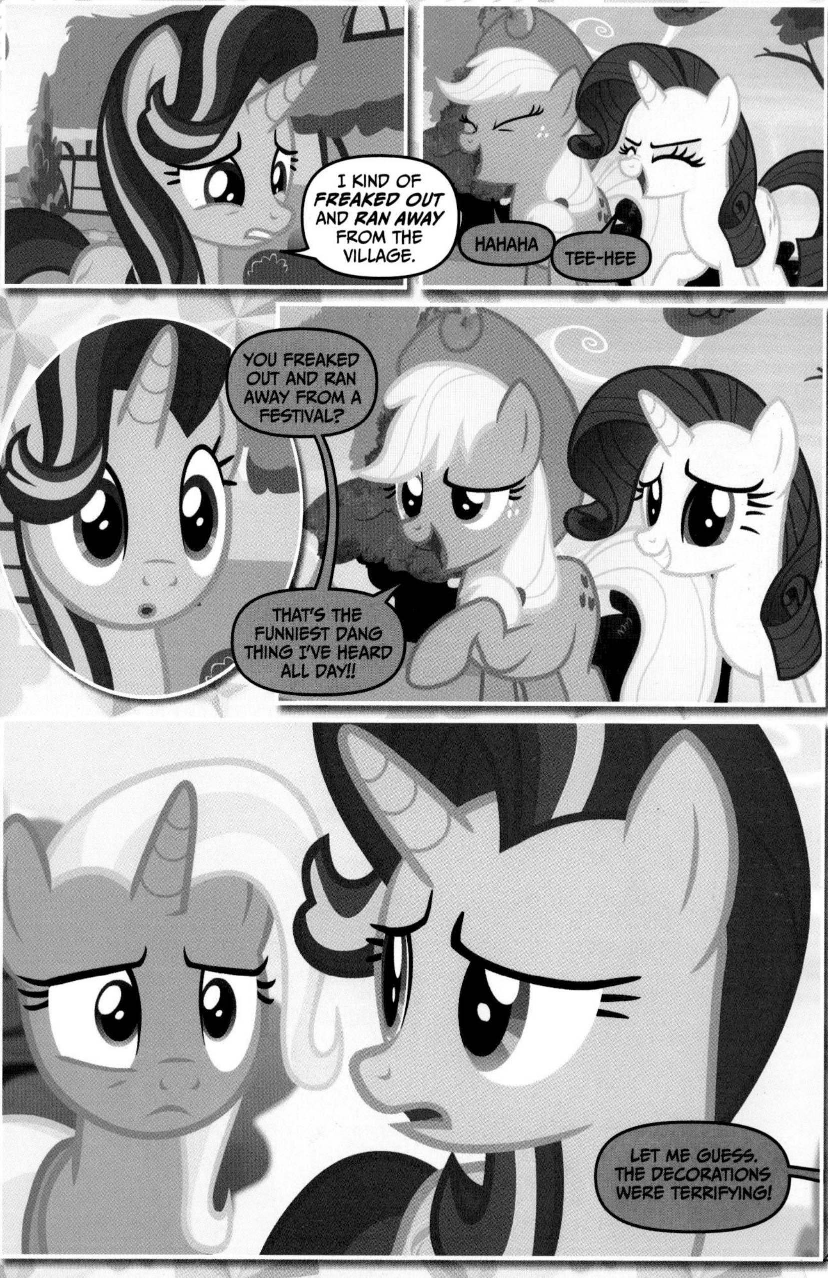
I KIND OF FREAKED OUT AND RAN AWAY FROM THE VILLAGE.
HAHAHA
TEE-HEE
YOU FREAKED OUT AND RAN AWAY FROM A FESTIVAL?
THAT'S THE FUNNIEST DANG THING I'VE HEARD ALL DAY!!
LET ME GUESS. THE DECORATIONS WERE TERRIFYING!

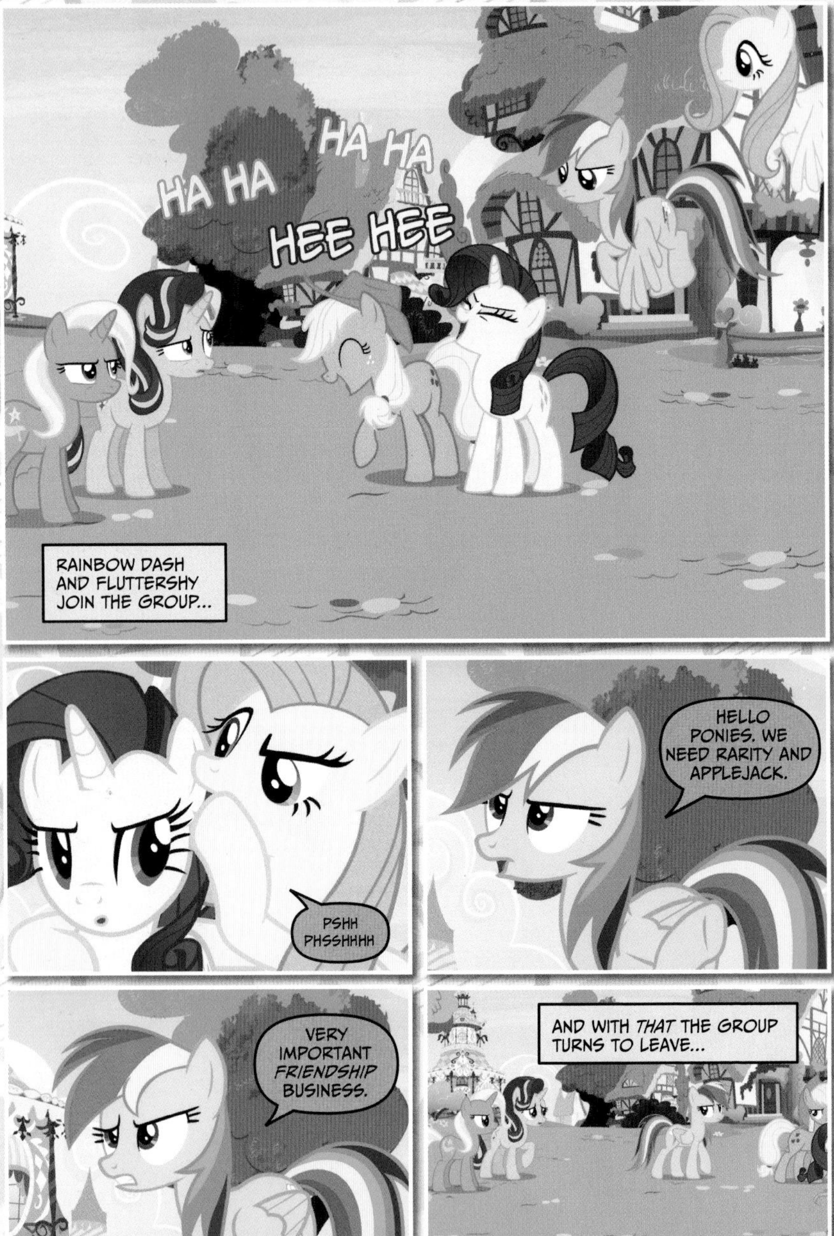
HA HA
HA HA
HEE HEE
RAINBOW DASH AND FLUTTERSHY JOIN THE GROUP...
PSHH PHSSHHHH
HELLO PONIES. WE NEED RARITY AND APPLEJACK.
VERY IMPORTANT *FRIENDSHIP* BUSINESS.
AND WITH *THAT* THE GROUP TURNS TO LEAVE...

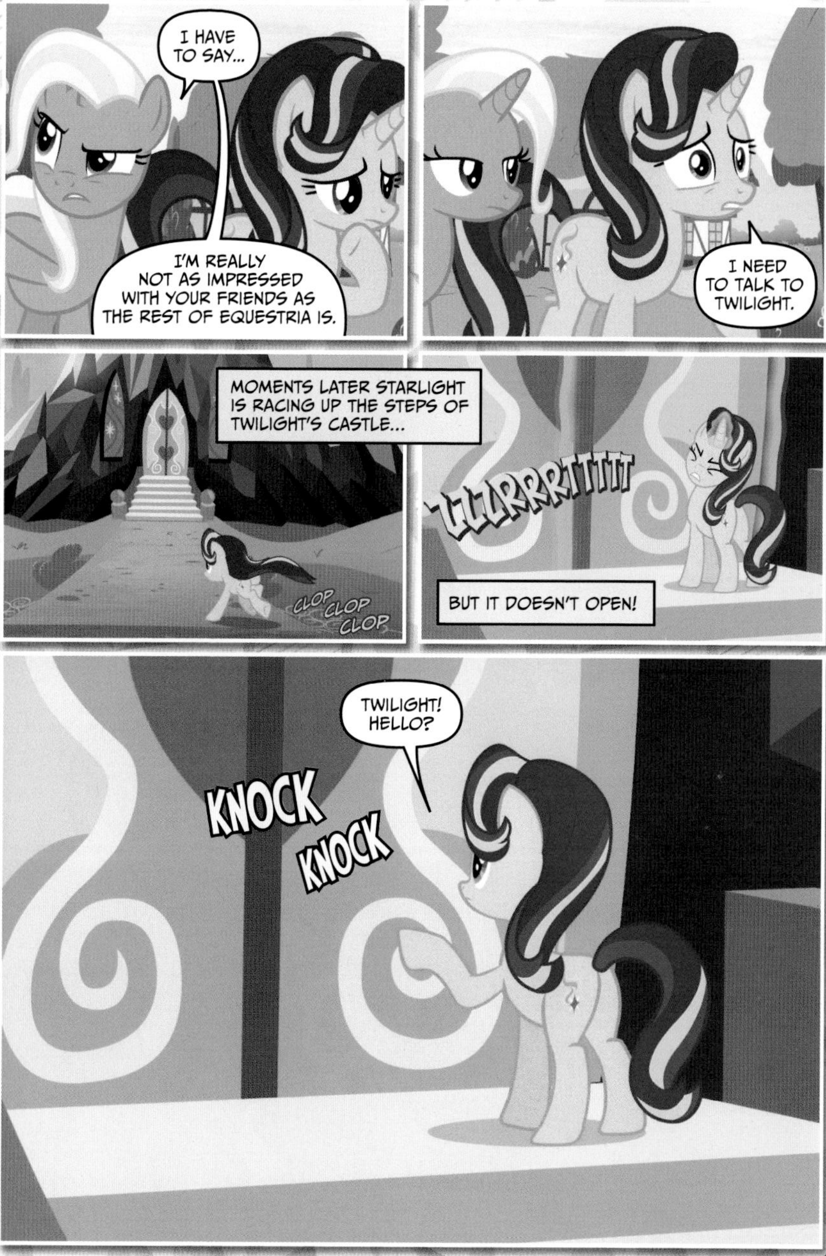

I HAVE TO SAY...
I'M REALLY NOT AS IMPRESSED WITH YOUR FRIENDS AS THE REST OF EQUESTRIA IS.
I NEED TO TALK TO TWILIGHT.
MOMENTS LATER STARLIGHT IS RACING UP THE STEPS OF TWILIGHT'S CASTLE...
CLOP CLOP CLOP
ZZZRRRTTTTT
BUT IT DOESN'T OPEN!
TWILIGHT! HELLO?
KNOCK
KNOCK

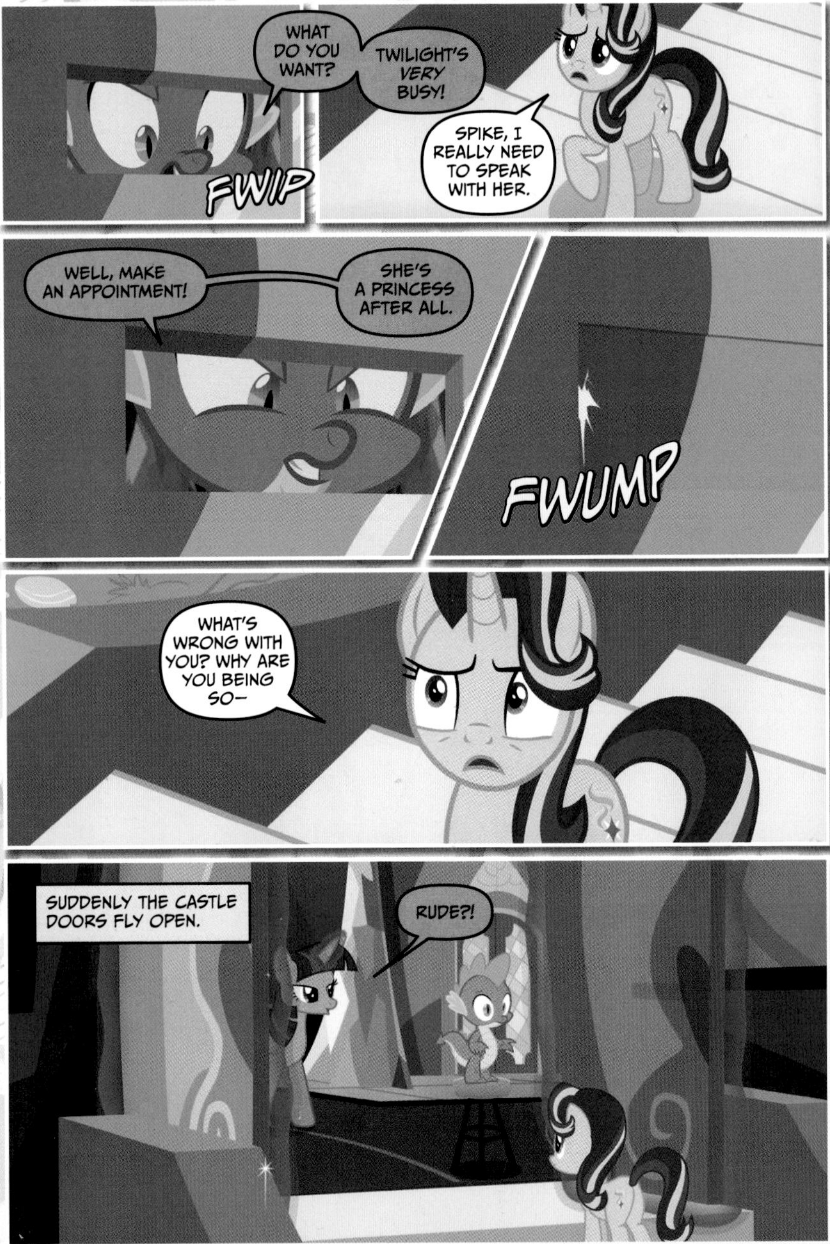
WHAT DO YOU WANT?
TWILIGHT'S VERY BUSY!
FWIP
SPIKE, I REALLY NEED TO SPEAK WITH HER.
WELL, MAKE AN APPOINTMENT!
SHE'S A PRINCESS AFTER ALL.
FWUMP
WHAT'S WRONG WITH YOU? WHY ARE YOU BEING SO–
SUDDENLY THE CASTLE DOORS FLY OPEN.
RUDE?!

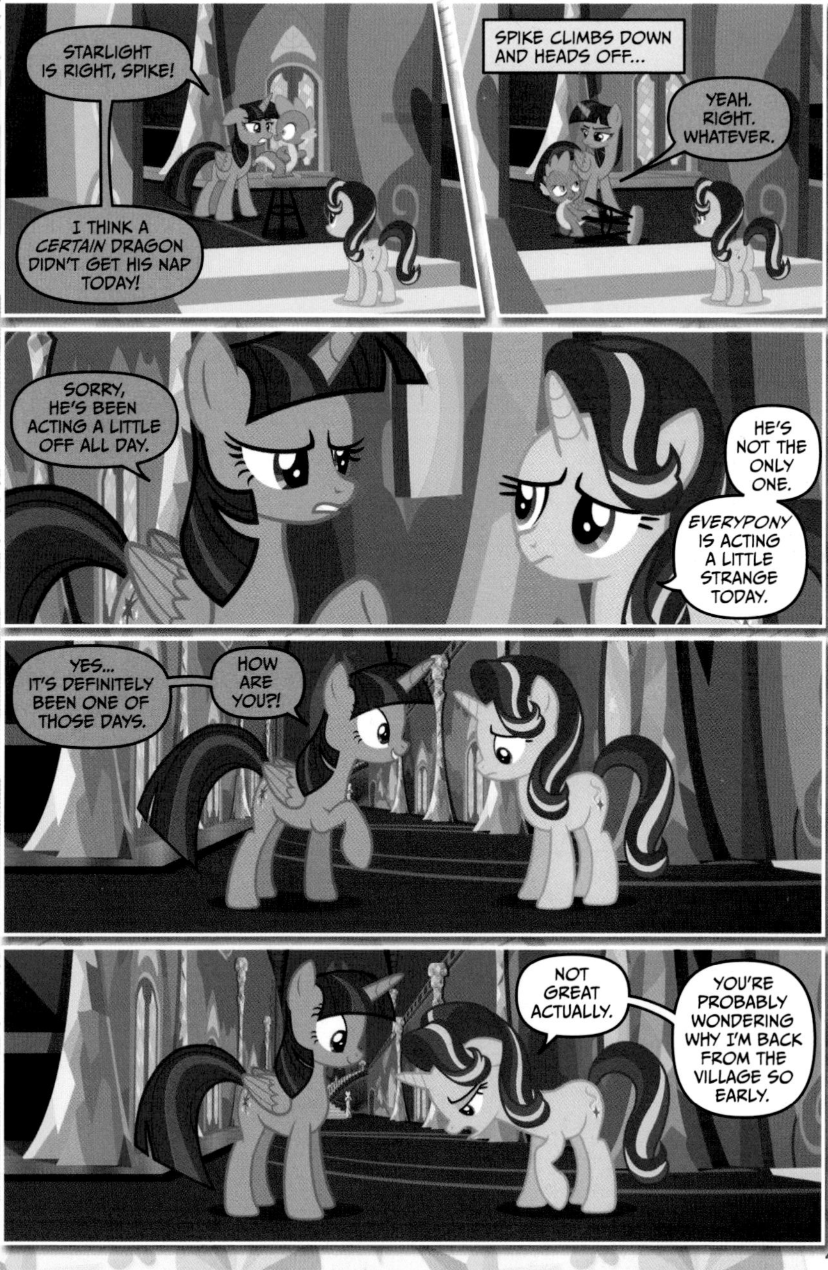
STARLIGHT IS RIGHT, SPIKE!
I THINK A *CERTAIN* DRAGON DIDN'T GET HIS NAP TODAY!
SPIKE CLIMBS DOWN AND HEADS OFF...
YEAH. RIGHT. WHATEVER.
SORRY, HE'S BEEN ACTING A LITTLE OFF ALL DAY.
HE'S NOT THE ONLY ONE.
EVERYPONY IS ACTING A LITTLE STRANGE TODAY.
YES... IT'S DEFINITELY BEEN ONE OF THOSE DAYS.
HOW ARE YOU?!
NOT GREAT ACTUALLY.
YOU'RE PROBABLY WONDERING WHY I'M BACK FROM THE VILLAGE SO EARLY.

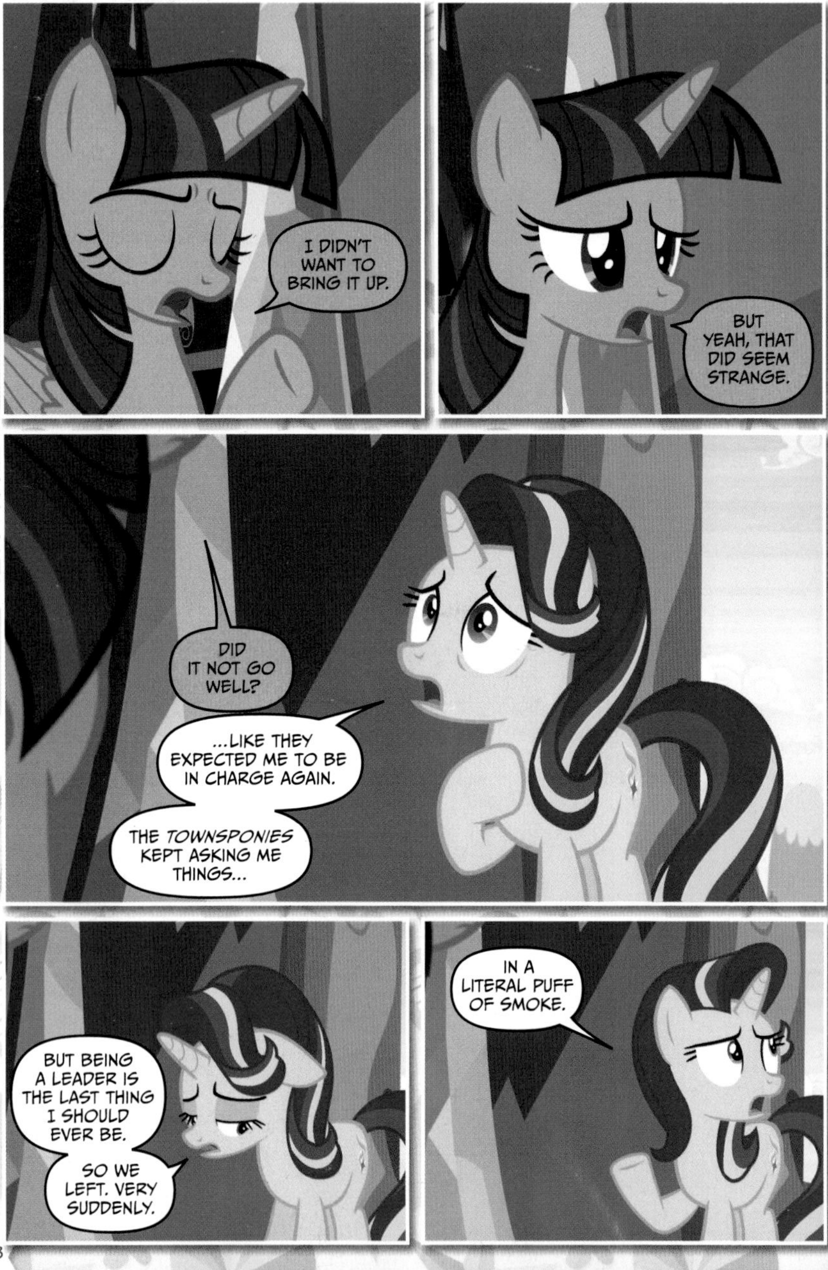
I DIDN'T WANT TO BRING IT UP.
BUT YEAH, THAT DID SEEM STRANGE.
DID IT NOT GO WELL?
THE *TOWNSPONIES* KEPT ASKING ME THINGS...
...LIKE THEY EXPECTED ME TO BE IN CHARGE AGAIN.
BUT BEING A LEADER IS THE LAST THING I SHOULD EVER BE.
SO WE LEFT. VERY SUDDENLY.
IN A LITERAL PUFF OF SMOKE.

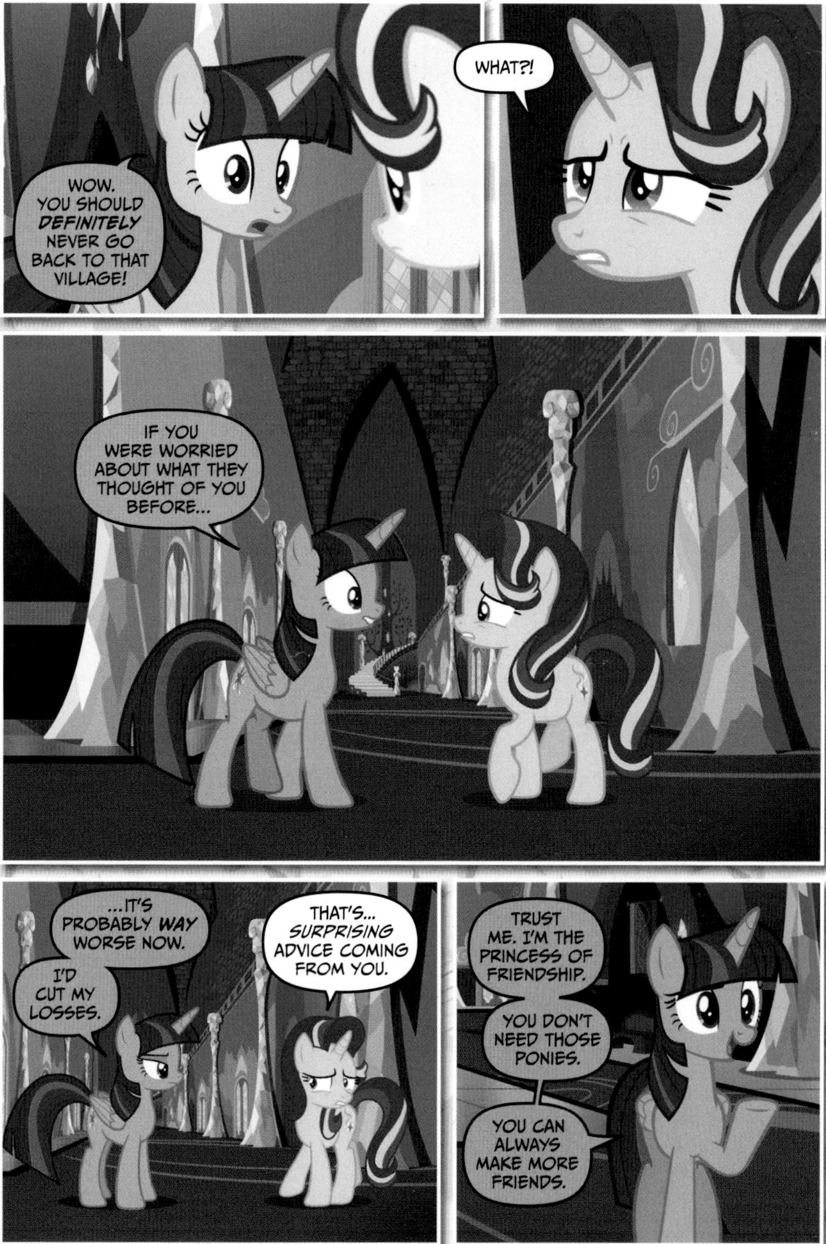
WOW. YOU SHOULD *DEFINITELY* NEVER GO BACK TO THAT VILLAGE!
WHAT?!
IF YOU WERE WORRIED ABOUT WHAT THEY THOUGHT OF YOU BEFORE...
...IT'S PROBABLY **WAY** WORSE NOW.
I'D CUT MY LOSSES.
THAT'S... *SURPRISING* ADVICE COMING FROM YOU.
TRUST ME. I'M THE PRINCESS OF FRIENDSHIP.
YOU DON'T NEED THOSE PONIES.
YOU CAN ALWAYS MAKE MORE FRIENDS.

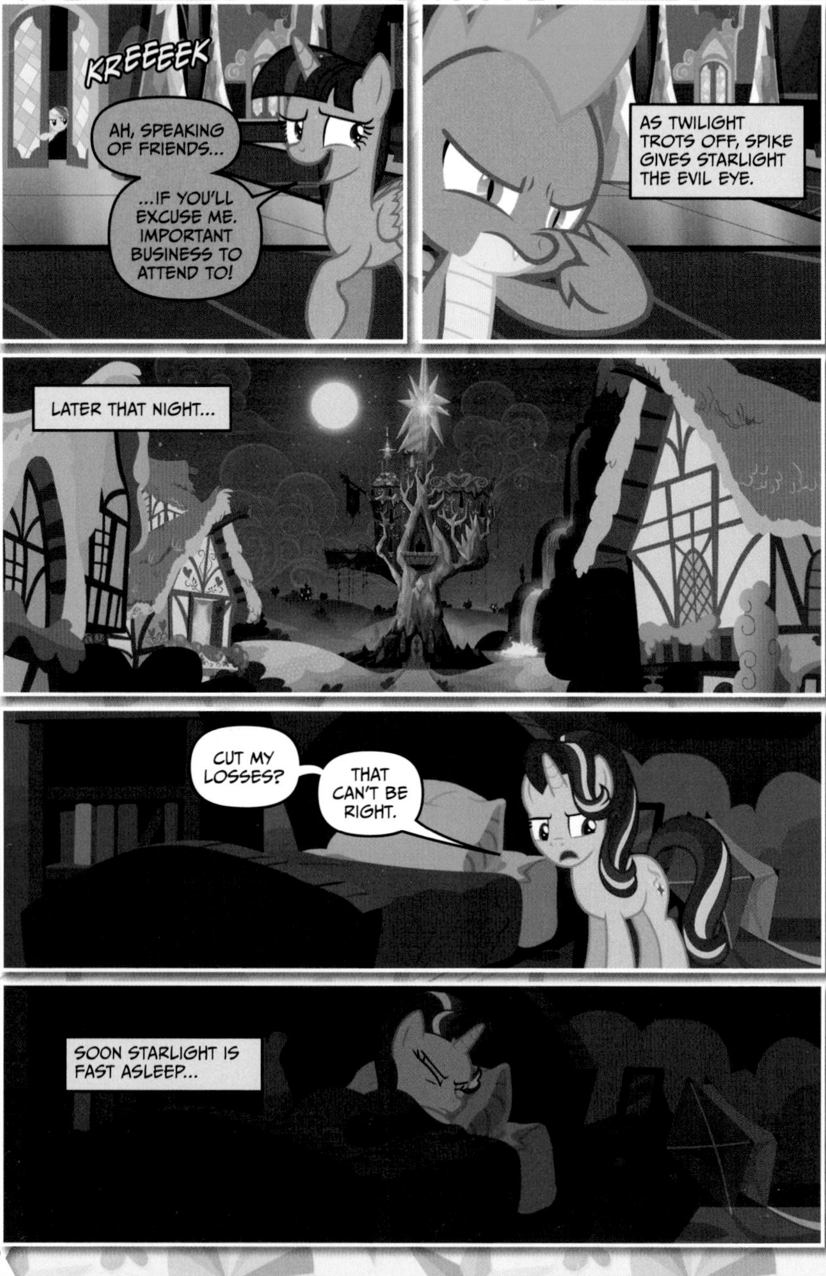
KREEEEK
AH, SPEAKING OF FRIENDS...
...IF YOU'LL EXCUSE ME. IMPORTANT BUSINESS TO ATTEND TO!
AS TWILIGHT TROTS OFF, SPIKE GIVES STARLIGHT THE EVIL EYE.
LATER THAT NIGHT...
CUT MY LOSSES?
THAT CAN'T BE RIGHT.
SOON STARLIGHT IS FAST ASLEEP...

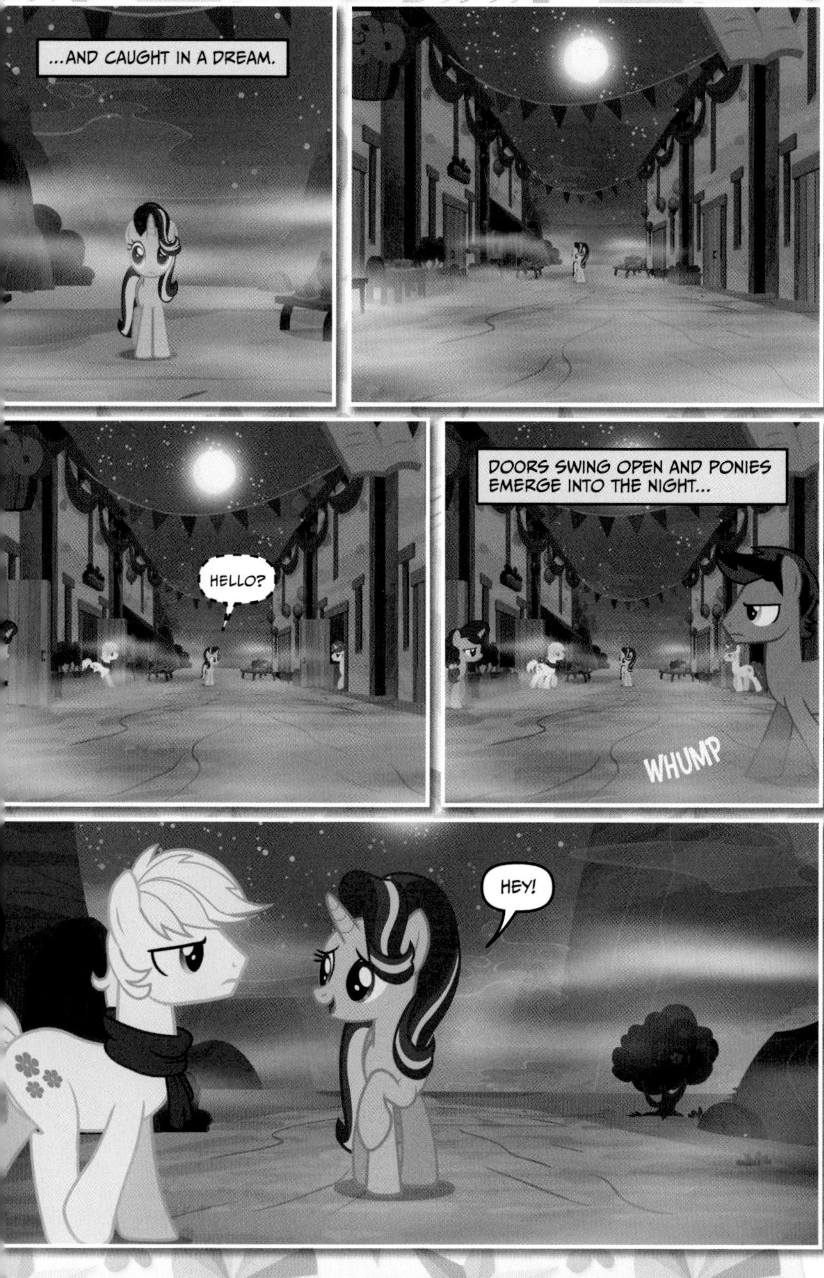
...AND CAUGHT IN A DREAM.
HELLO?
DOORS SWING OPEN AND PONIES EMERGE INTO THE NIGHT...
WHUMP
HEY!

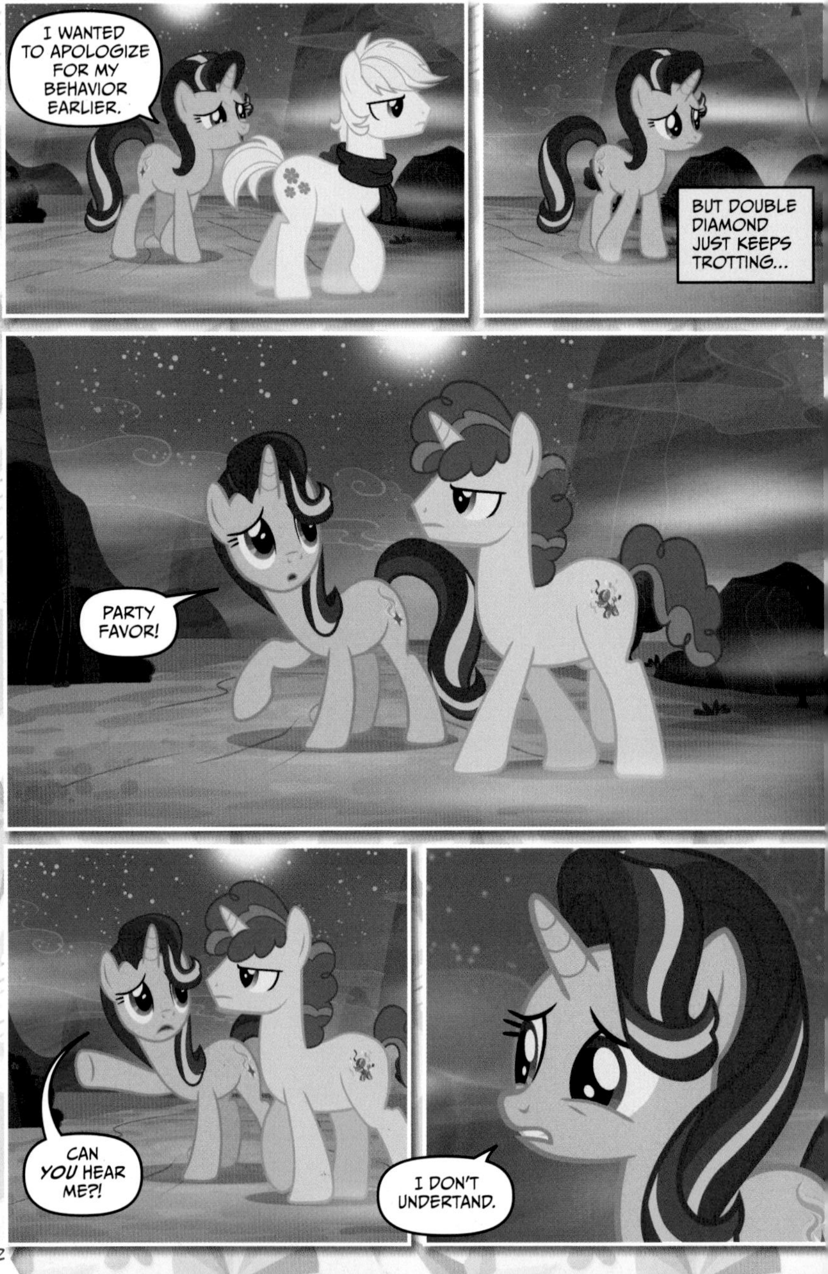
I WANTED TO APOLOGIZE FOR MY BEHAVIOR EARLIER.
BUT DOUBLE DIAMOND JUST KEEPS TROTTING...
PARTY FAVOR!
CAN *YOU* HEAR ME?!
I DON'T UNDERTAND.

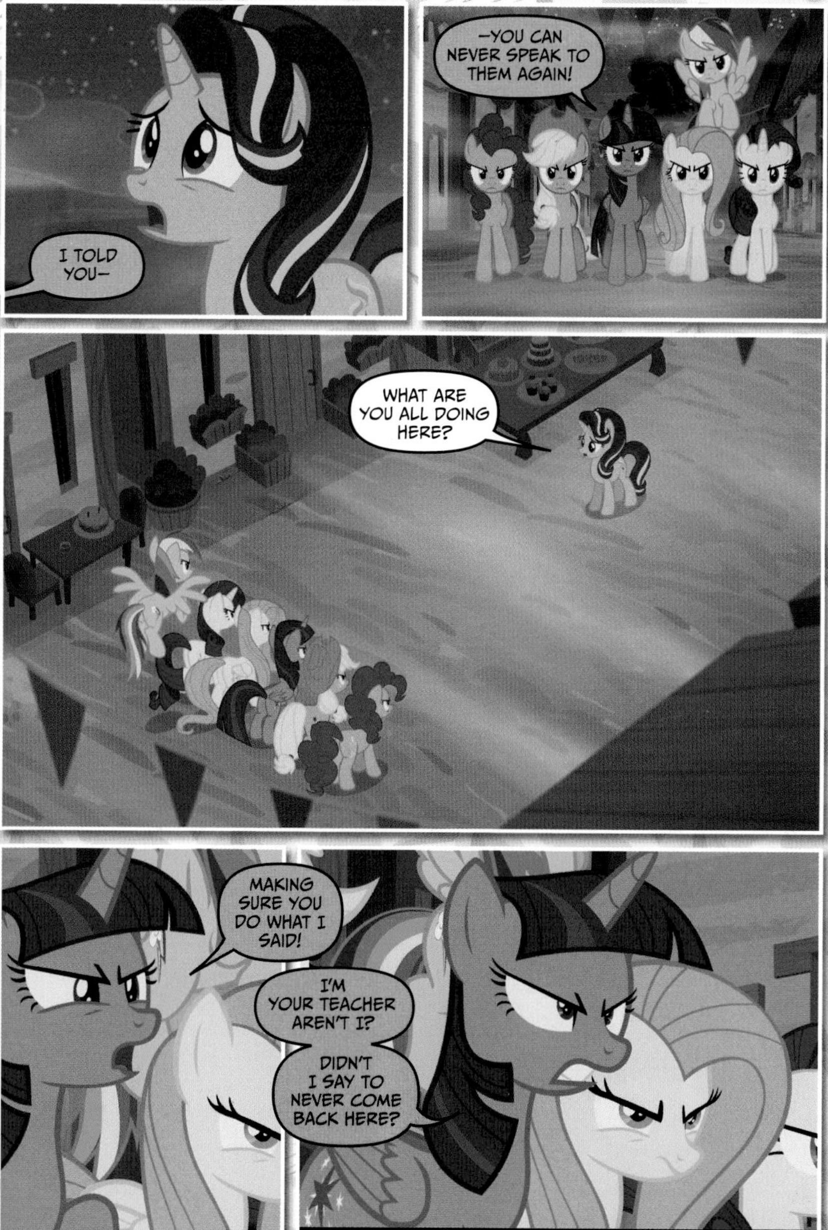
I TOLD YOU—
—YOU CAN NEVER SPEAK TO THEM AGAIN!
WHAT ARE YOU ALL DOING HERE?
MAKING SURE YOU DO WHAT I SAID!
I'M YOUR TEACHER AREN'T I?
DIDN'T I SAY TO NEVER COME BACK HERE?

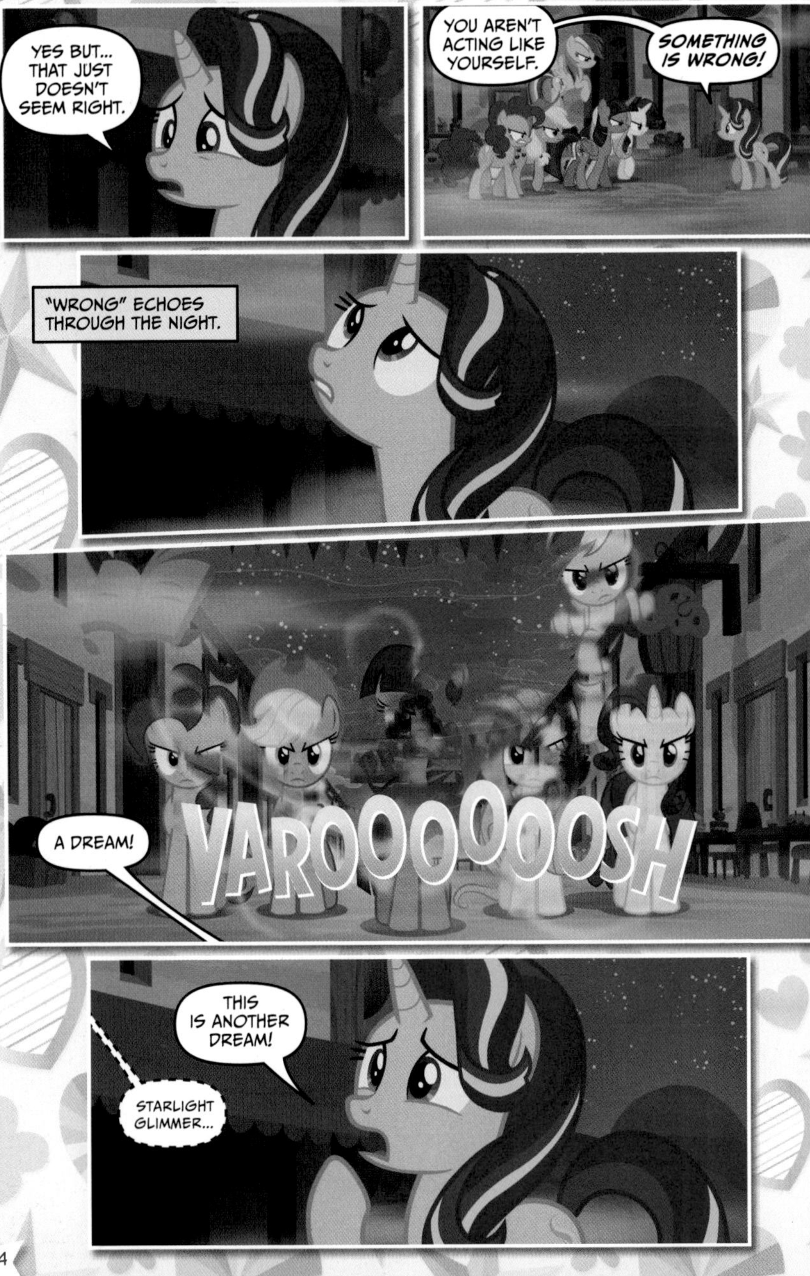
YES BUT... THAT JUST DOESN'T SEEM RIGHT.
YOU AREN'T ACTING LIKE YOURSELF.
SOMETHING IS WRONG!
"WRONG" ECHOES THROUGH THE NIGHT.
YAROOOOOOOSH
A DREAM!
THIS IS ANOTHER DREAM!
STARLIGHT GLIMMER...

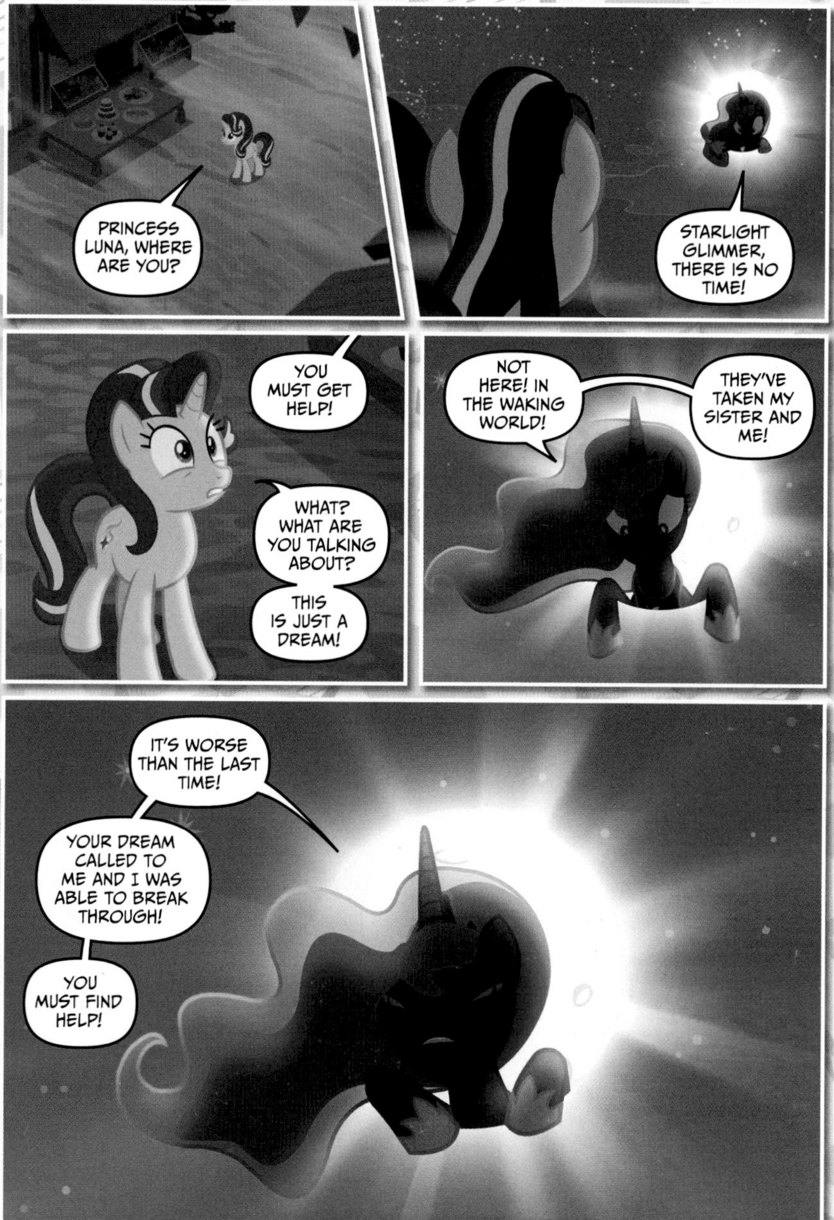
PRINCESS LUNA, WHERE ARE YOU?
STARLIGHT GLIMMER, THERE IS NO TIME!
YOU MUST GET HELP!
WHAT? WHAT ARE YOU TALKING ABOUT?
THIS IS JUST A DREAM!
NOT HERE! IN THE WAKING WORLD!
THEY'VE TAKEN MY SISTER AND ME!
IT'S WORSE THAN THE LAST TIME!
YOUR DREAM CALLED TO ME AND I WAS ABLE TO BREAK THROUGH!
YOU MUST FIND HELP!

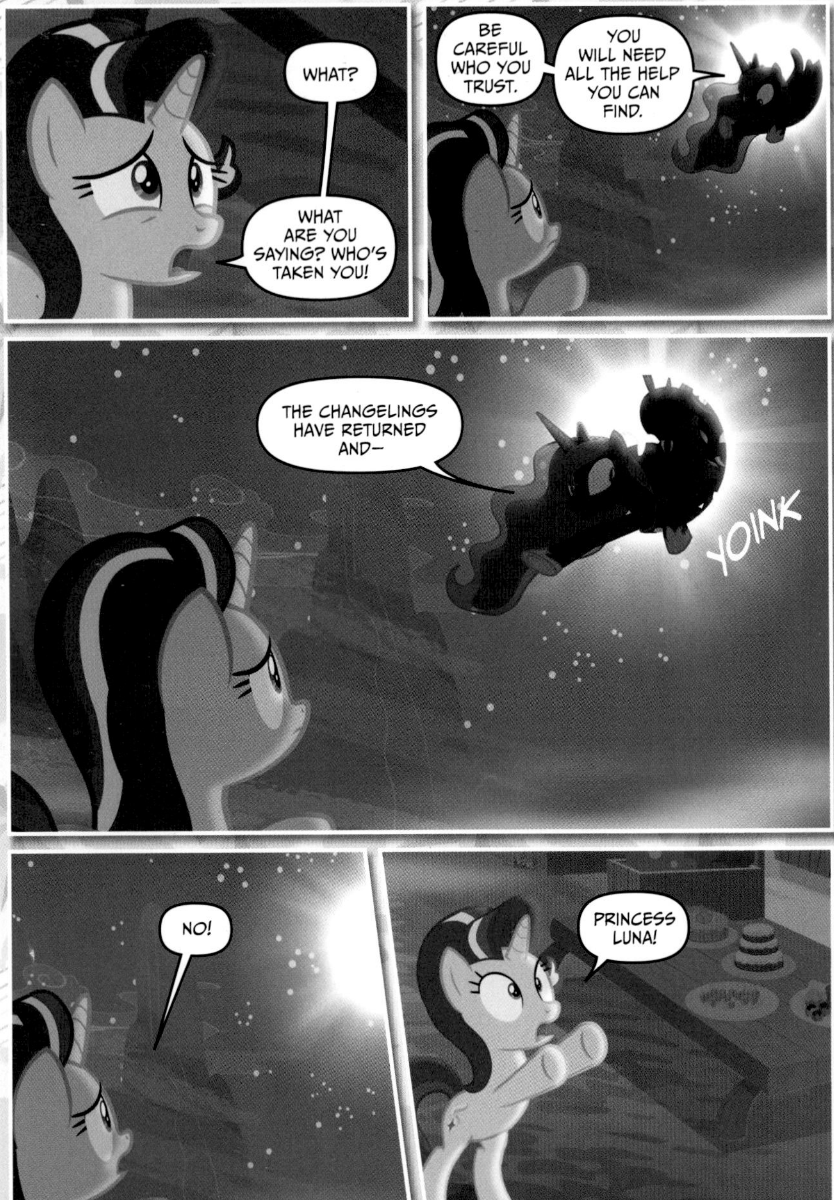
WHAT?
WHAT ARE YOU SAYING? WHO'S TAKEN YOU!
BE CAREFUL WHO YOU TRUST.
YOU WILL NEED ALL THE HELP YOU CAN FIND.
THE CHANGELINGS HAVE RETURNED AND—
YOINK
NO!
PRINCESS LUNA!

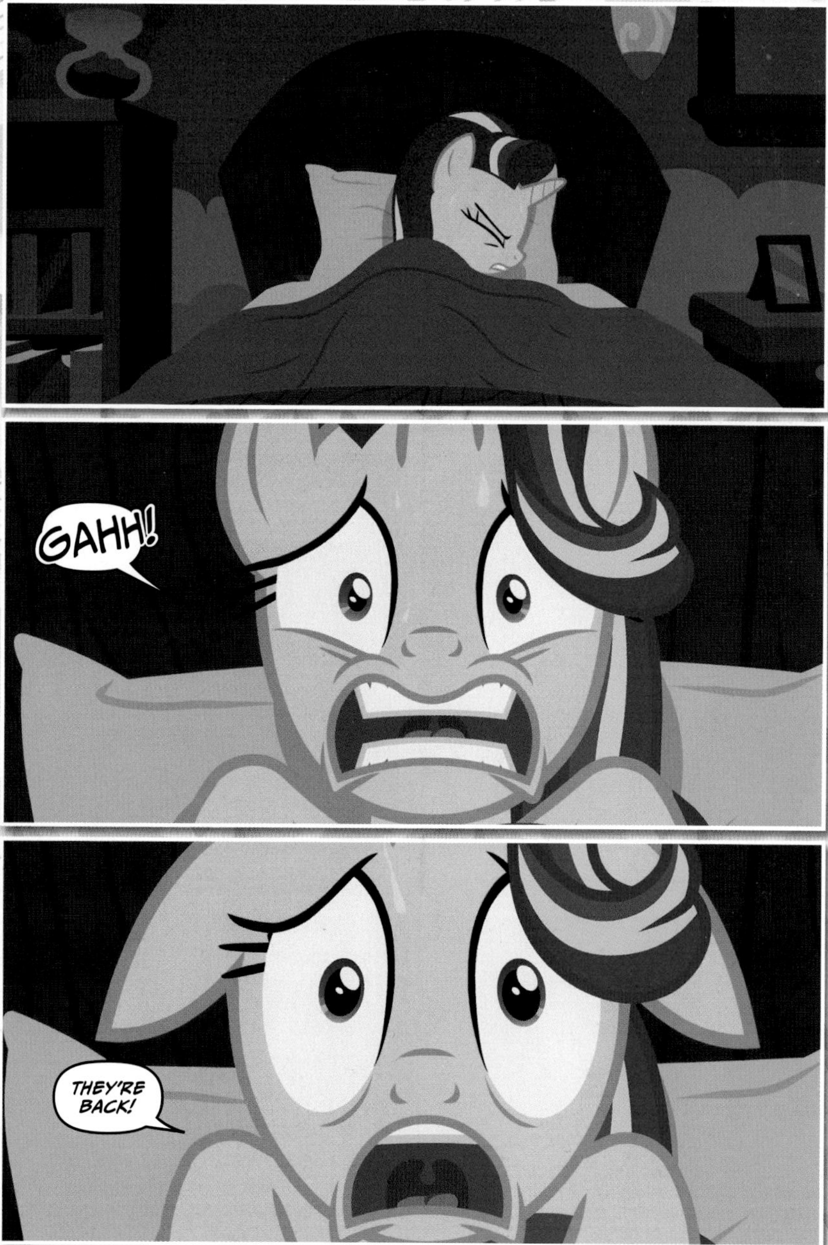
GAHH!
THEY'RE BACK!

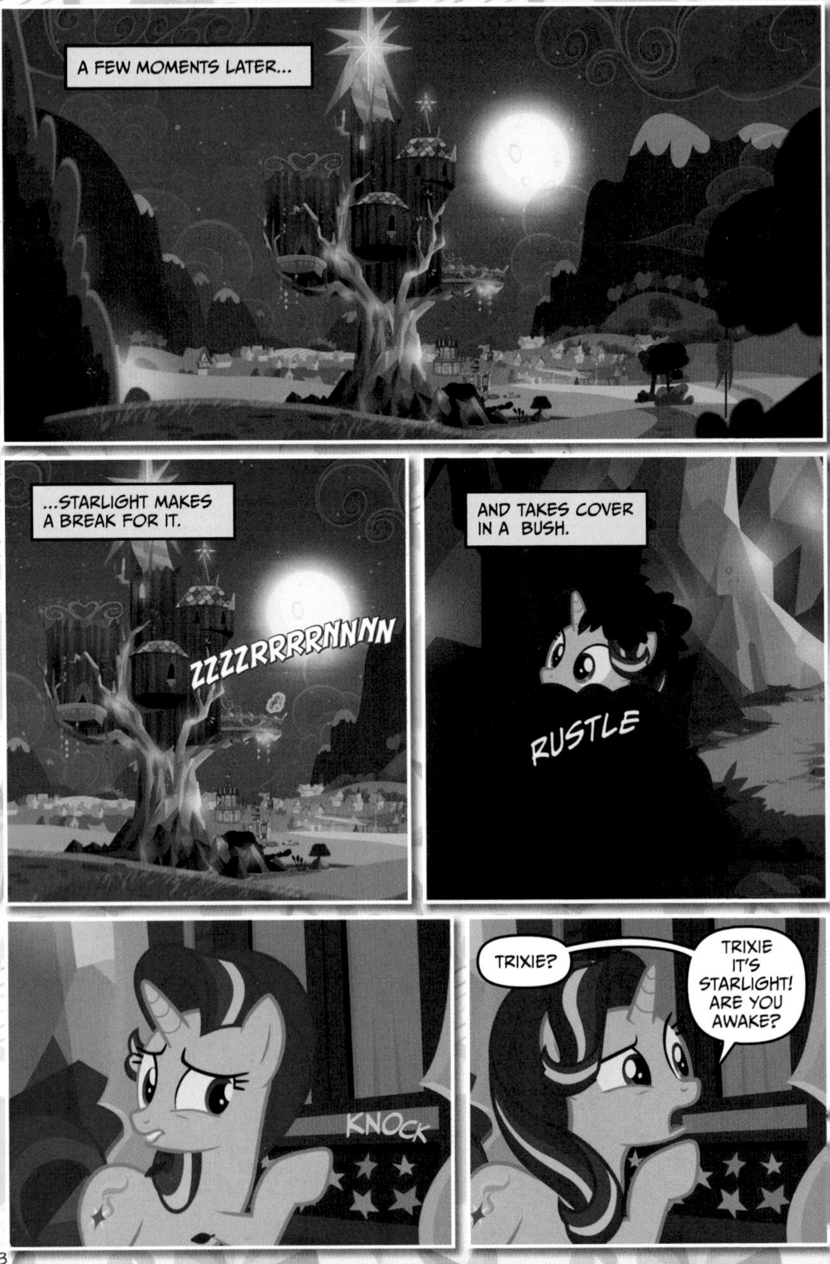
A FEW MOMENTS LATER...
...STARLIGHT MAKES A BREAK FOR IT.
ZZZZRRRRNNNN
AND TAKES COVER IN A BUSH.
RUSTLE
KNOCK
TRIXIE?
TRIXIE IT'S STARLIGHT! ARE YOU AWAKE?

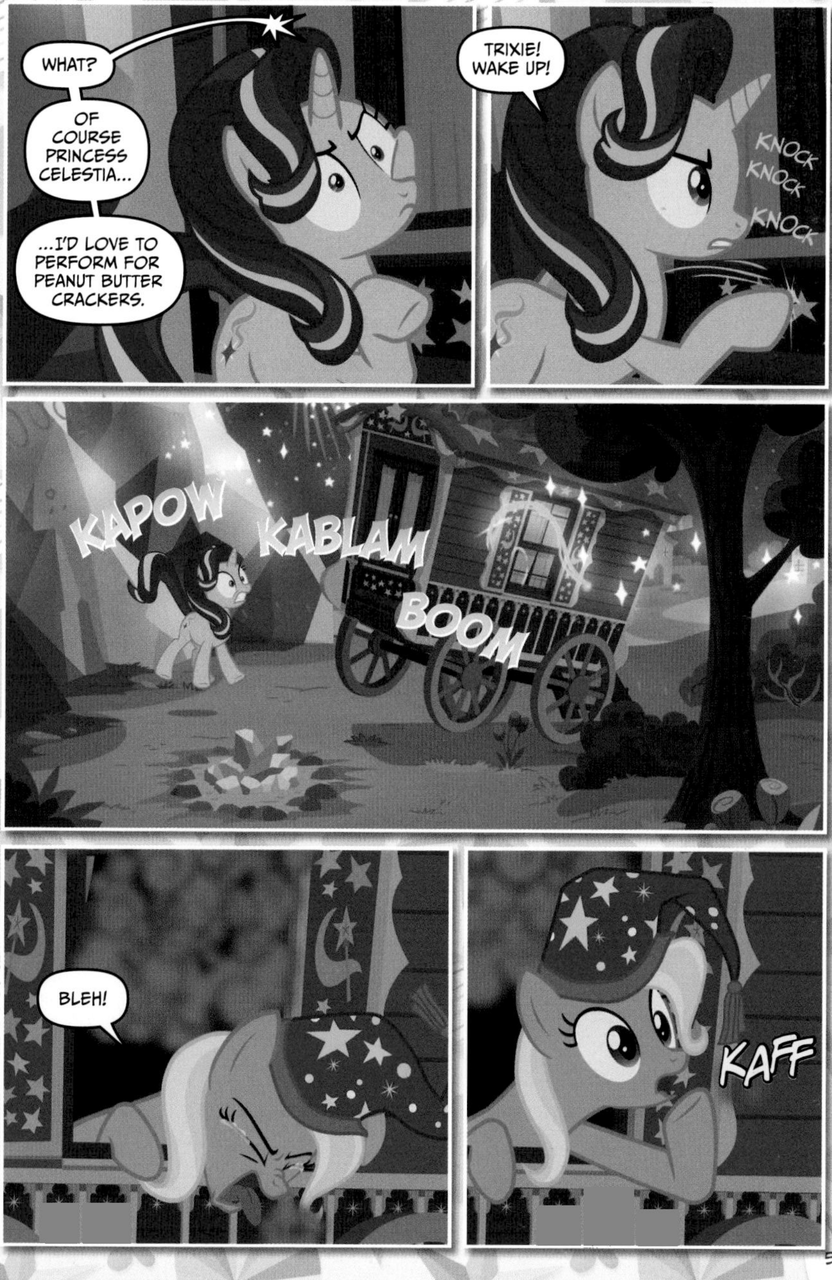
WHAT?
OF COURSE PRINCESS CELESTIA...
...I'D LOVE TO PERFORM FOR PEANUT BUTTER CRACKERS.
TRIXIE! WAKE UP!
KNOCK
KNOCK
KNOCK
KAPOW
KABLAM
BOOM
BLEH!
KAFF

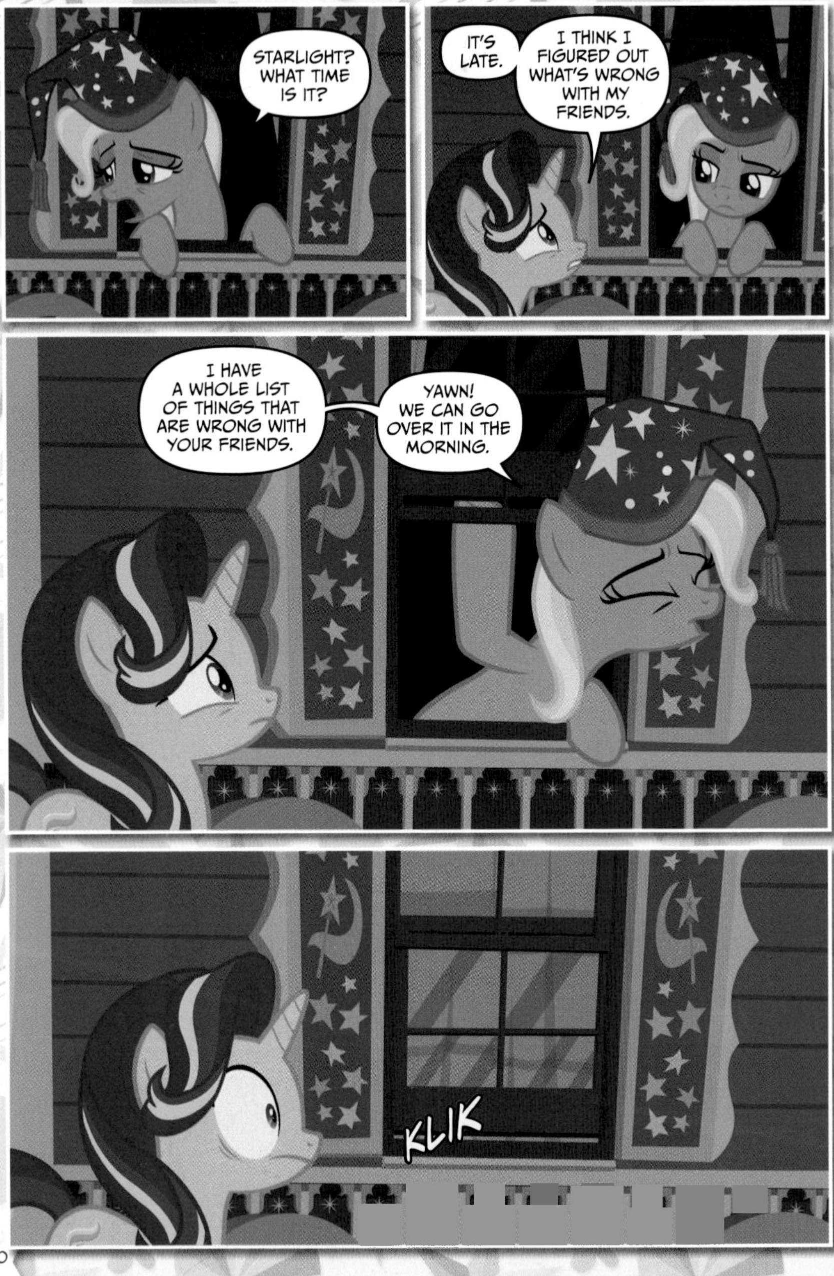
STARLIGHT? WHAT TIME IS IT?
IT'S LATE.
I THINK I FIGURED OUT WHAT'S WRONG WITH MY FRIENDS.
I HAVE A WHOLE LIST OF THINGS THAT ARE WRONG WITH YOUR FRIENDS.
YAWN! WE CAN GO OVER IT IN THE MORNING.
KLIK

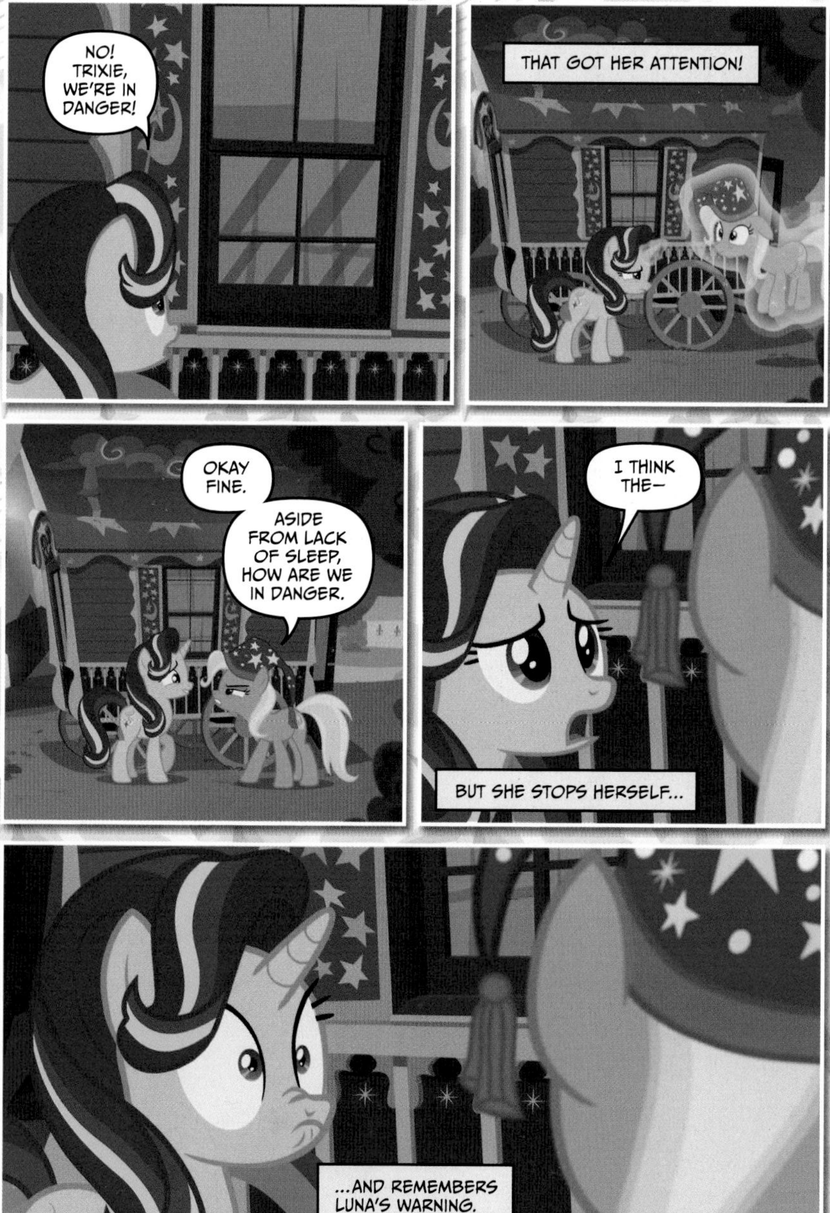
NO! TRIXIE, WE'RE IN DANGER!
THAT GOT HER ATTENTION!
OKAY FINE.
ASIDE FROM LACK OF SLEEP, HOW ARE WE IN DANGER.
I THINK THE—
BUT SHE STOPS HERSELF...
...AND REMEMBERS LUNA'S WARNING.

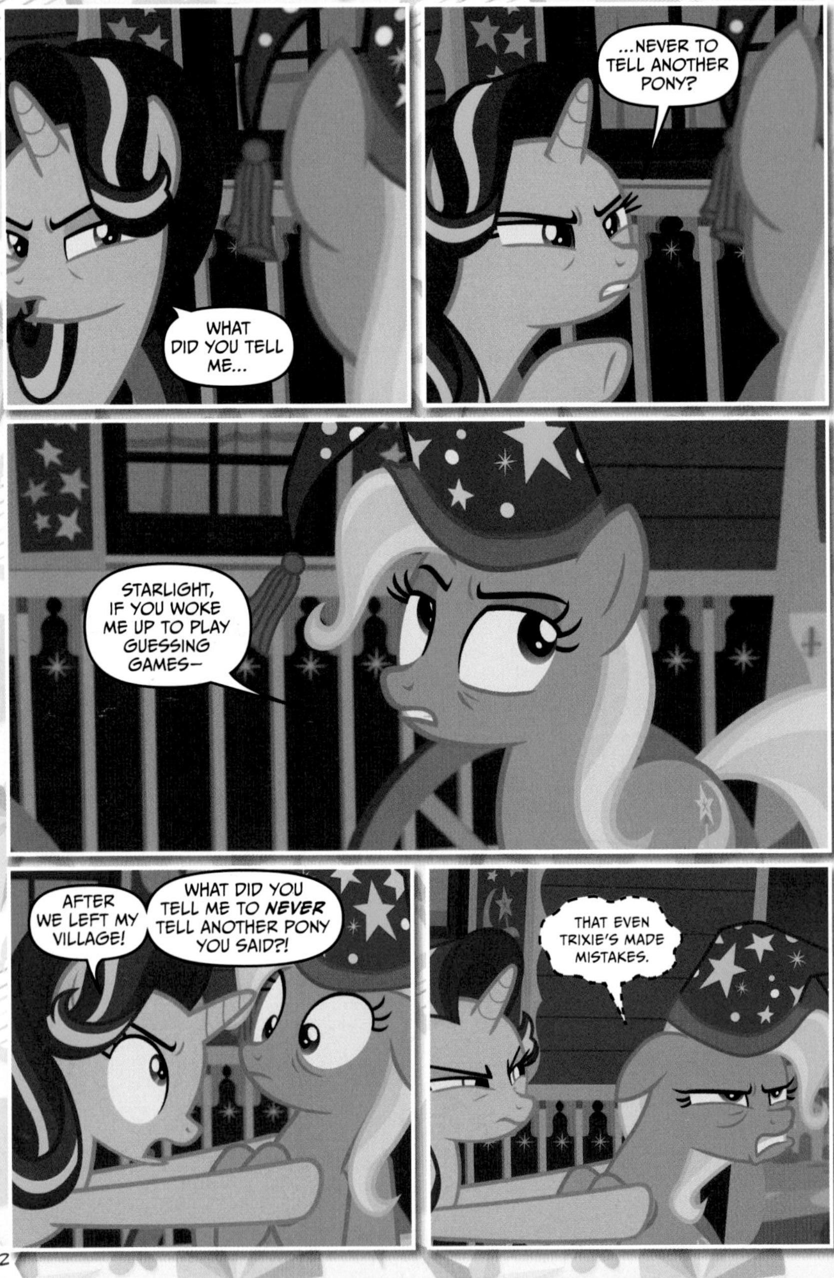
WHAT DID YOU TELL ME...
...NEVER TO TELL ANOTHER PONY?
STARLIGHT, IF YOU WOKE ME UP TO PLAY GUESSING GAMES—
AFTER WE LEFT MY VILLAGE!
WHAT DID YOU TELL ME TO *NEVER* TELL ANOTHER PONY YOU SAID?!
THAT EVEN TRIXIE'S MADE MISTAKES.

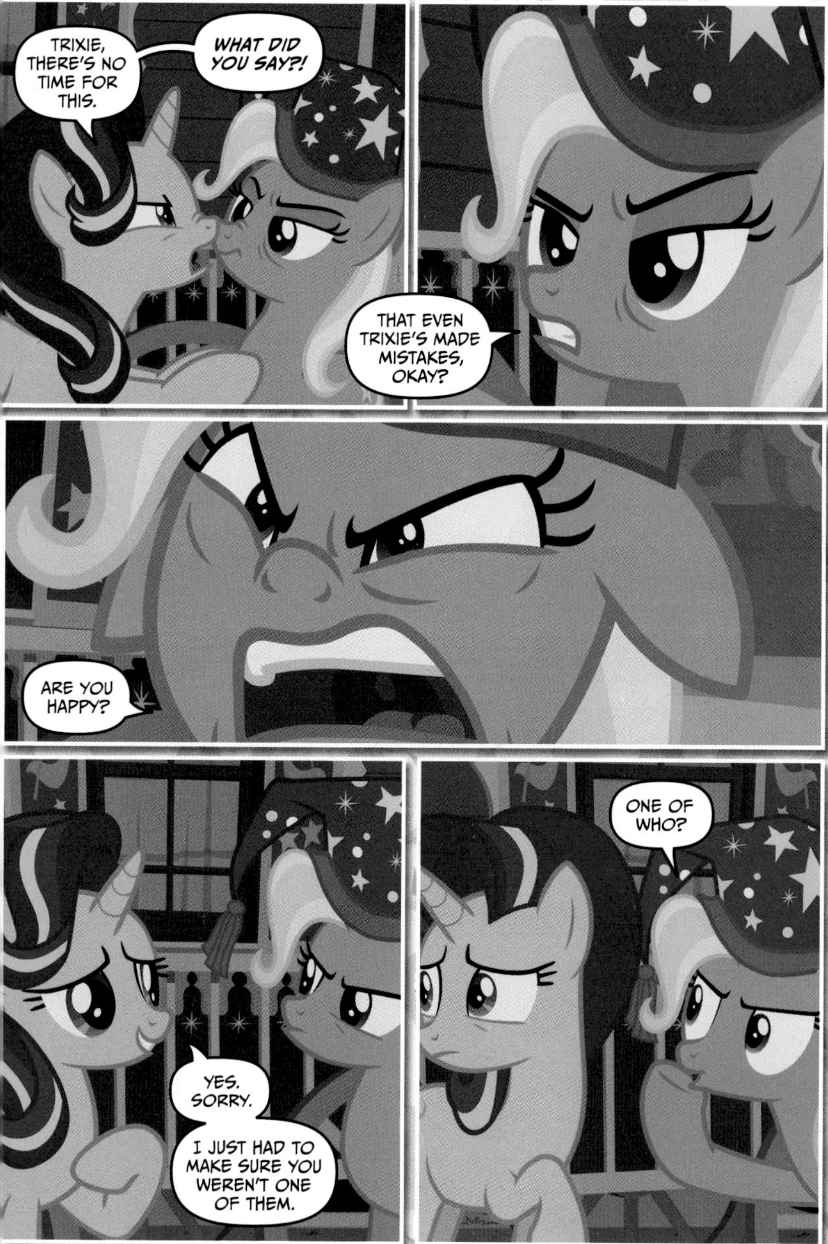
TRIXIE, THERE'S NO TIME FOR THIS.
WHAT DID YOU SAY?!
THAT EVEN TRIXIE'S MADE MISTAKES, OKAY?
ARE YOU HAPPY?
YES. SORRY.
I JUST HAD TO MAKE SURE YOU WEREN'T ONE OF THEM.
ONE OF WHO?

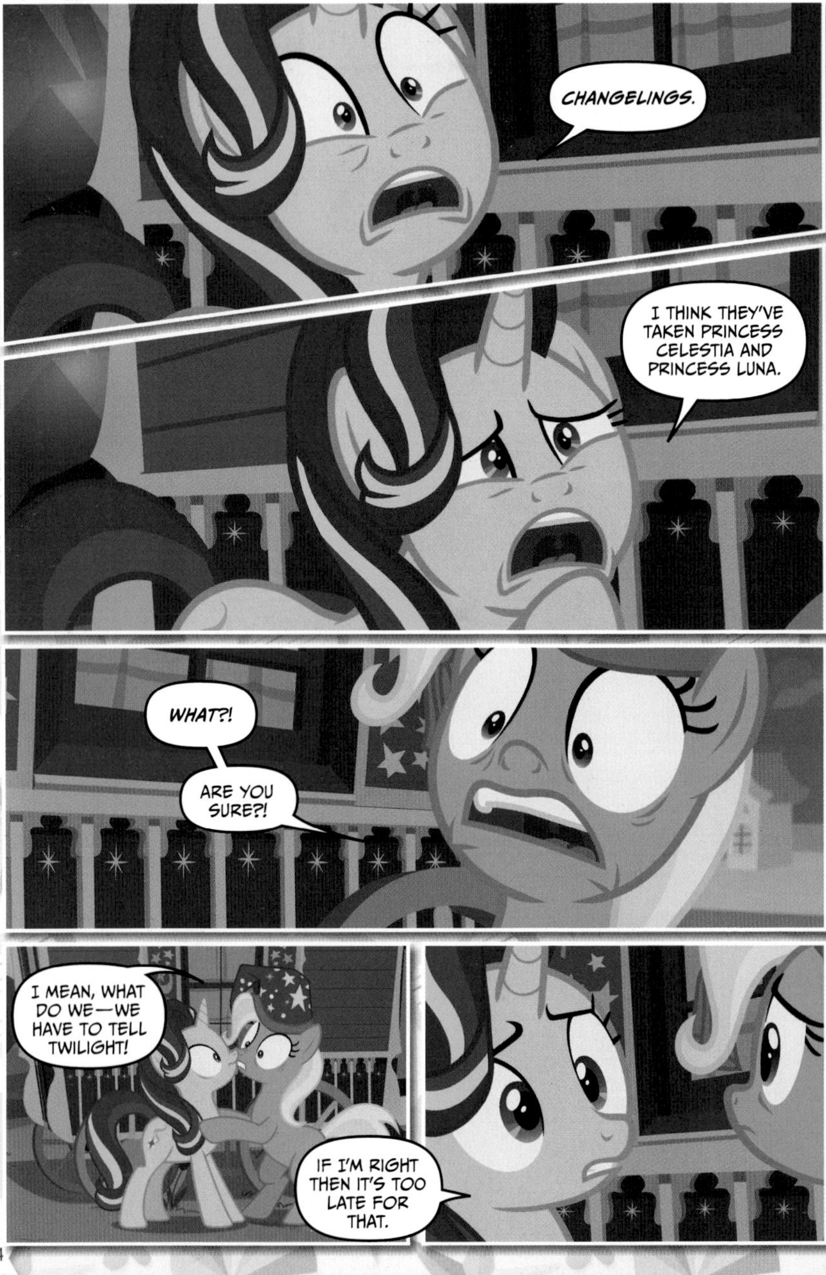
CHANGELINGS.
I THINK THEY'VE TAKEN PRINCESS CELESTIA AND PRINCESS LUNA.
WHAT?!
ARE YOU SURE?!
I MEAN, WHAT DO WE—WE HAVE TO TELL TWILIGHT!
IF I'M RIGHT THEN IT'S TOO LATE FOR THAT.

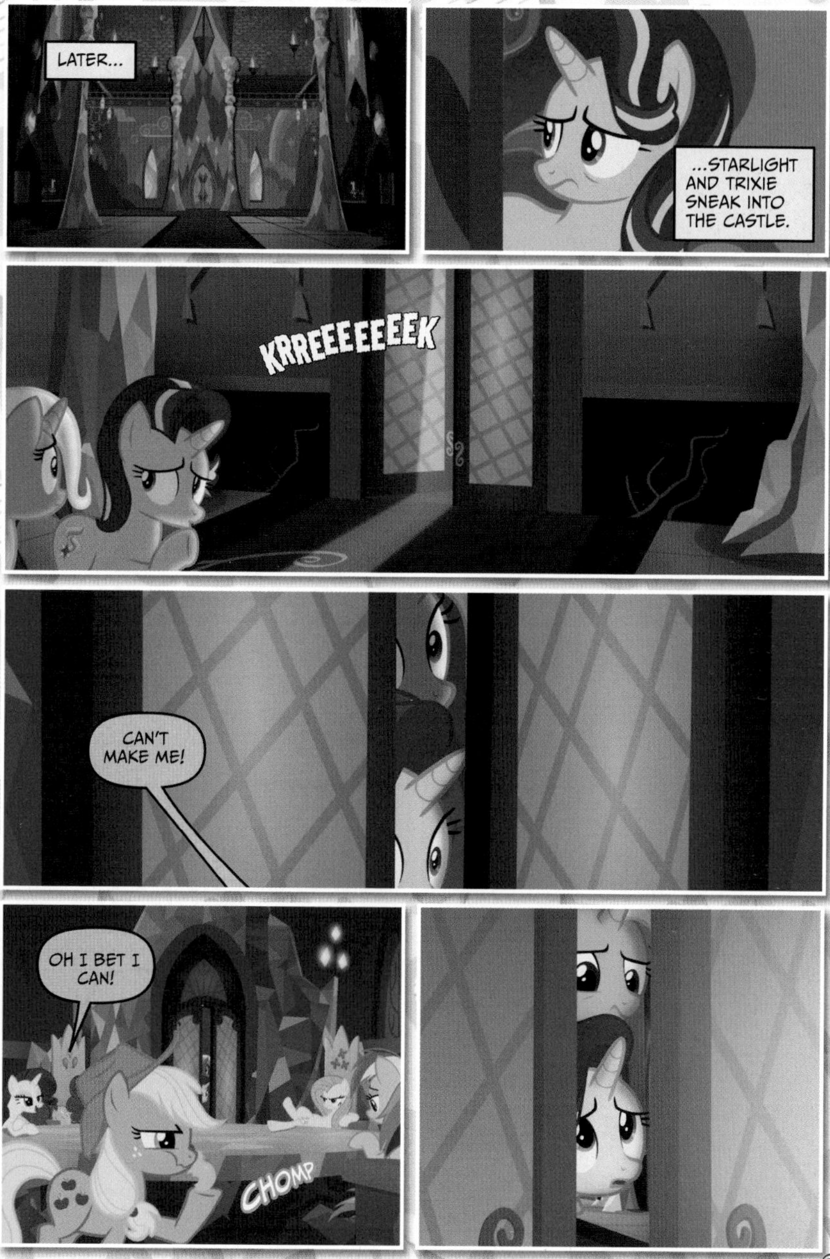
LATER...
...STARLIGHT AND TRIXIE SNEAK INTO THE CASTLE.
KRREEEEEEEK
CAN'T MAKE ME!
OH I BET I CAN!
CHOMP

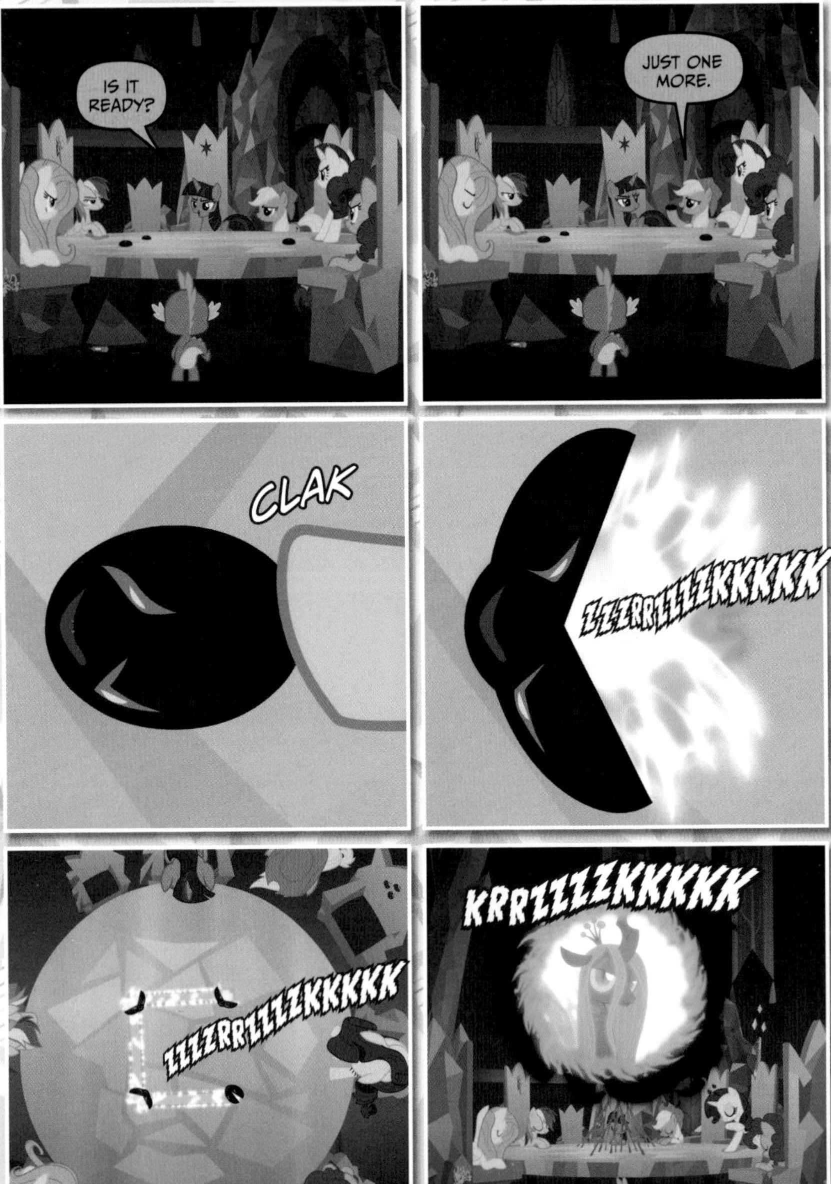
IS IT READY?
JUST ONE MORE.
CLAK
ZZZRRZZZZKKKKK
ZZZZRRZZZZKKKKK
KRRZZZZZKKKKK

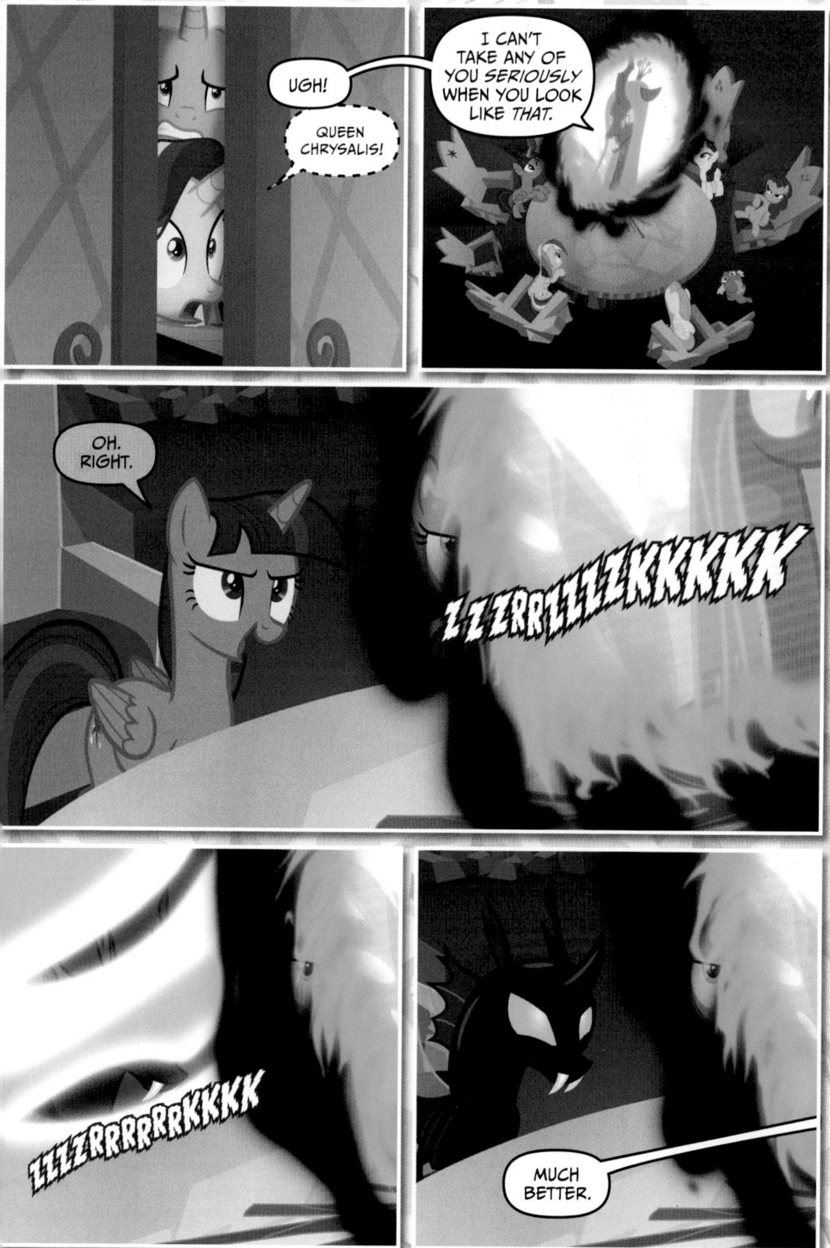
UGH!
QUEEN CHRYSALIS!
I CAN'T TAKE ANY OF YOU *SERIOUSLY* WHEN YOU LOOK LIKE *THAT*.
OH. RIGHT.
Z Z ZRRZZZZZKKKKKK
ZZZZRRRRRRKKKK
MUCH BETTER.

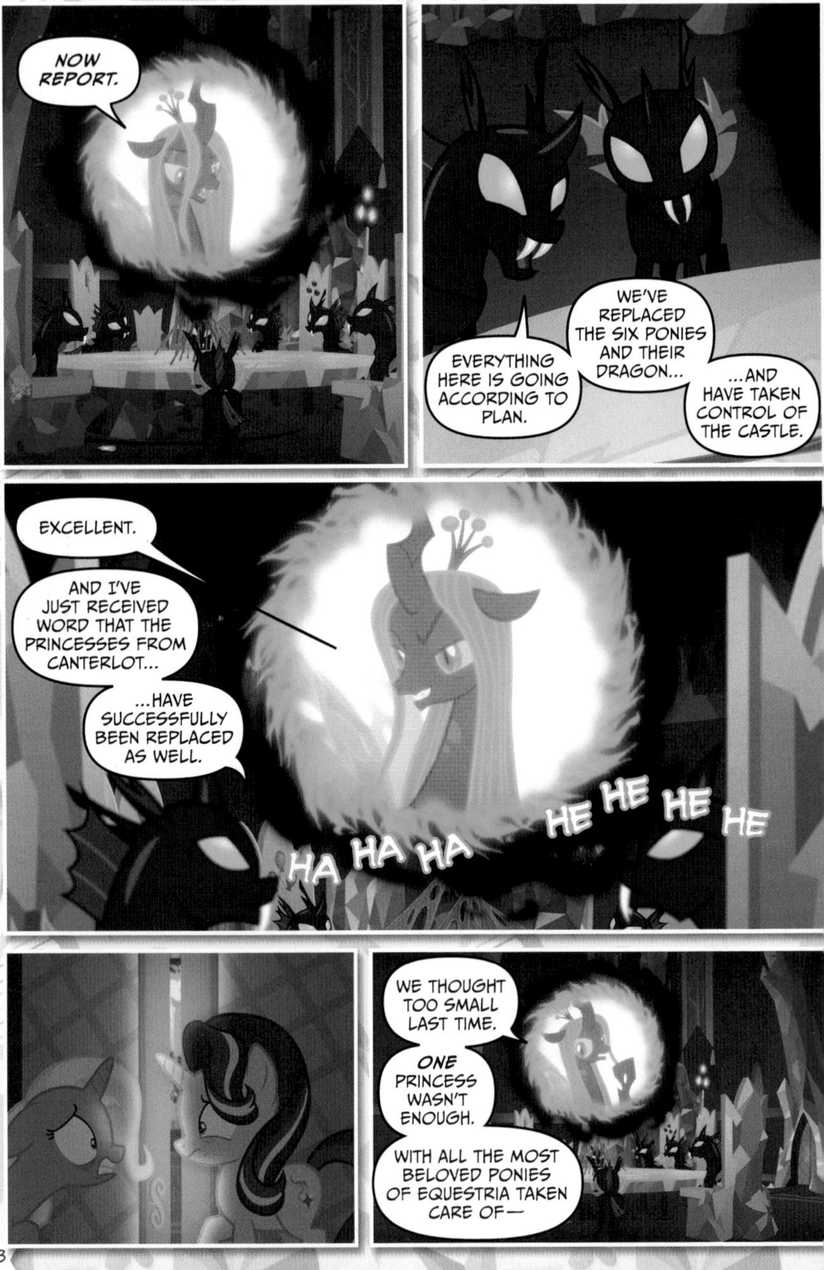

NOW REPORT.
EVERYTHING HERE IS GOING ACCORDING TO PLAN.
WE'VE REPLACED THE SIX PONIES AND THEIR DRAGON...
...AND HAVE TAKEN CONTROL OF THE CASTLE.
EXCELLENT.
AND I'VE JUST RECEIVED WORD THAT THE PRINCESSES FROM CANTERLOT...
...HAVE SUCCESSFULLY BEEN REPLACED AS WELL.
HA HA HA
HE HE HE HE
WE THOUGHT TOO SMALL LAST TIME.
ONE PRINCESS WASN'T ENOUGH.
WITH ALL THE MOST BELOVED PONIES OF EQUESTRIA TAKEN CARE OF—

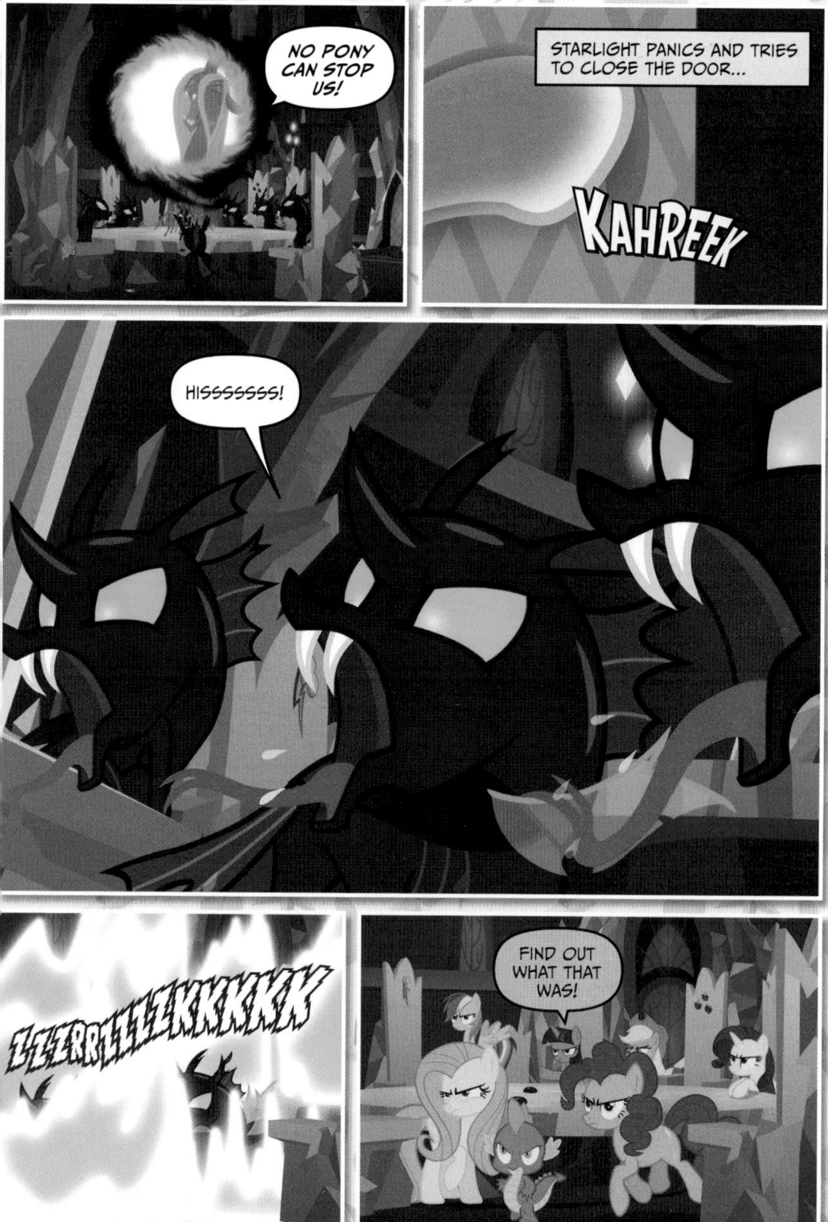
NO PONY CAN STOP US!
STARLIGHT PANICS AND TRIES TO CLOSE THE DOOR...
KAHREEK
HISSSSSSS!
ZZZRRZZZZKKKKK
FIND OUT WHAT THAT WAS!

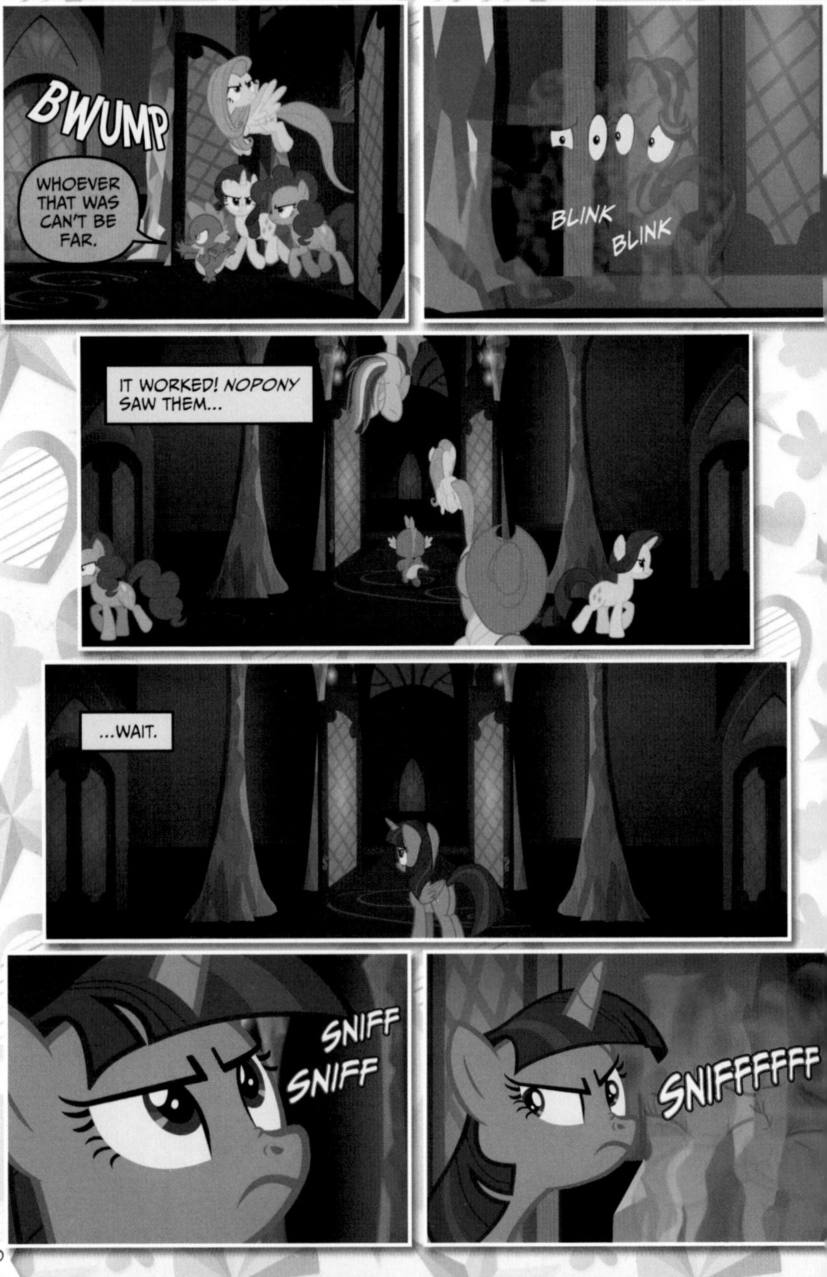

BWUMP
WHOEVER THAT WAS CAN'T BE FAR.
BLINK
BLINK
IT WORKED! NOPONY SAW THEM...
...WAIT.
SNIFF
SNIFF
SNIFFFFFF

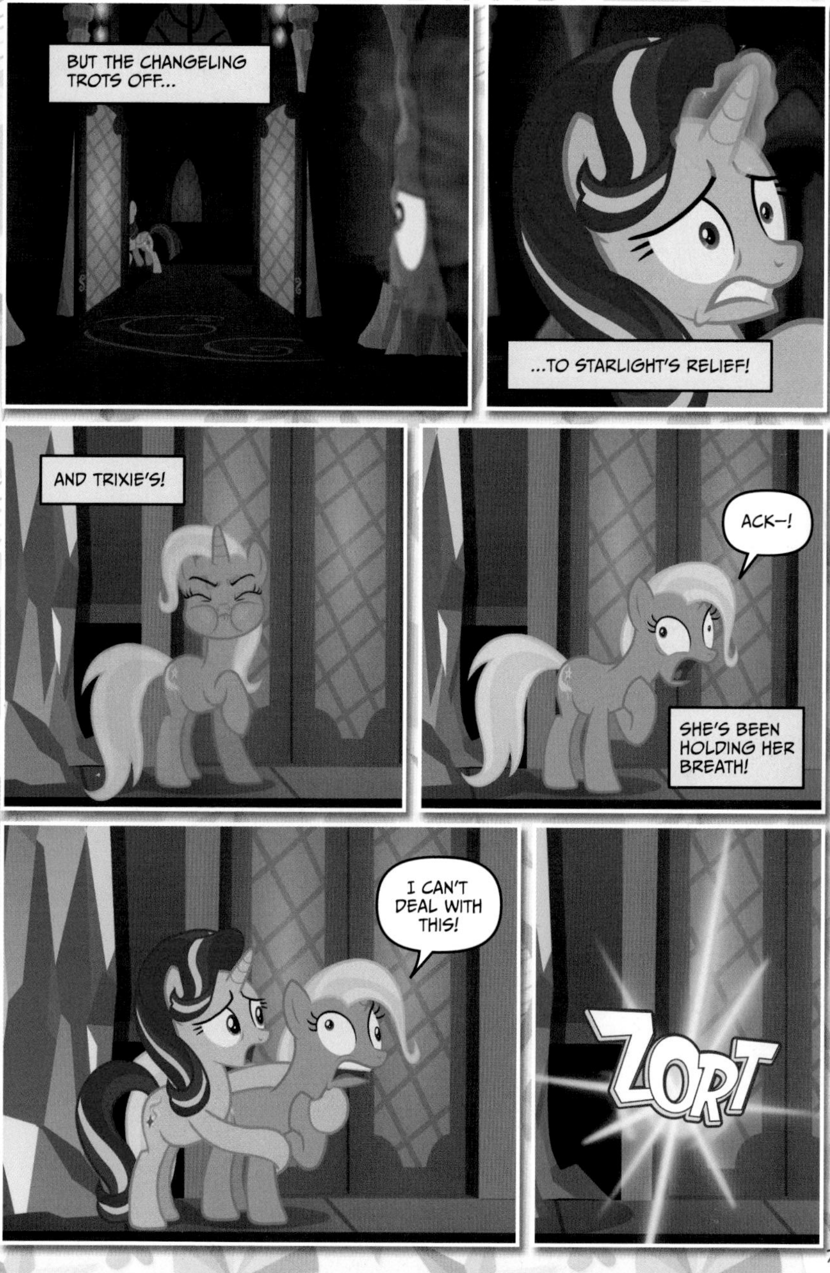
BUT THE CHANGELING TROTS OFF...
...TO STARLIGHT'S RELIEF!
AND TRIXIE'S!
ACK–!
SHE'S BEEN HOLDING HER BREATH!
I CAN'T DEAL WITH THIS!
ZORT

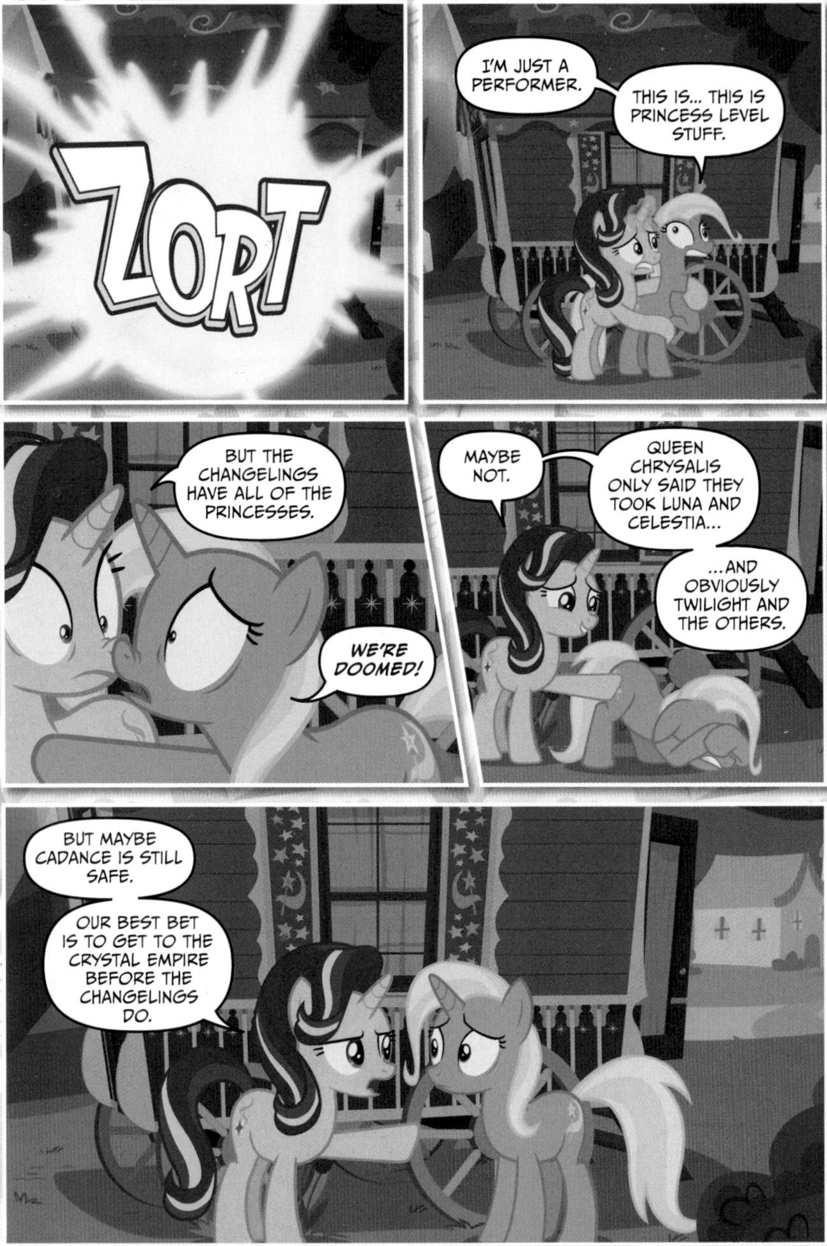
ZORT
I'M JUST A PERFORMER.
THIS IS... THIS IS PRINCESS LEVEL STUFF.
BUT THE CHANGELINGS HAVE ALL OF THE PRINCESSES.
WE'RE DOOMED!
MAYBE NOT.
QUEEN CHRYSALIS ONLY SAID THEY TOOK LUNA AND CELESTIA...
...AND OBVIOUSLY TWILIGHT AND THE OTHERS.
BUT MAYBE CADANCE IS STILL SAFE.
OUR BEST BET IS TO GET TO THE CRYSTAL EMPIRE BEFORE THE CHANGELINGS DO.

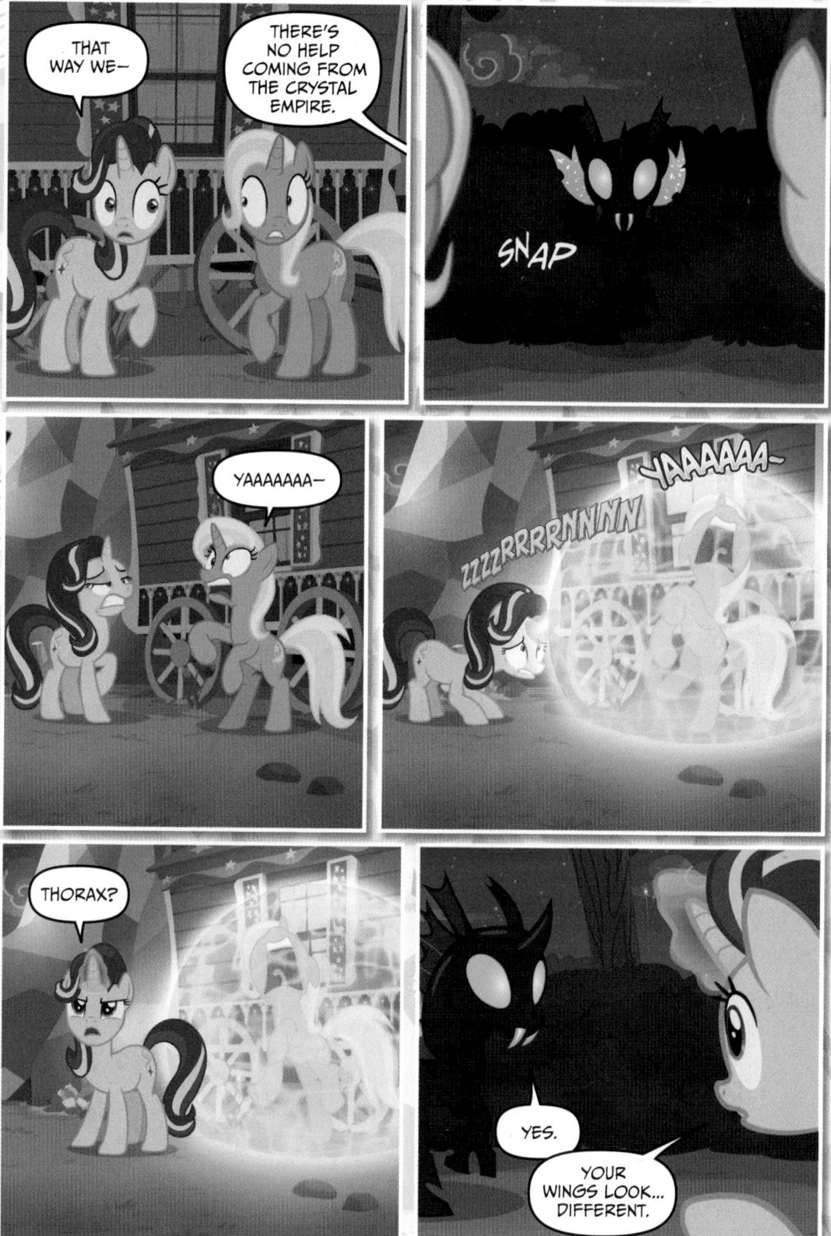
THAT WAY WE–
THERE'S NO HELP COMING FROM THE CRYSTAL EMPIRE.
SNAP
YAAAAAAA–
YAAAAAA–
ZZZZRRRRNNNN
THORAX?
YES.
YOUR WINGS LOOK... DIFFERENT.

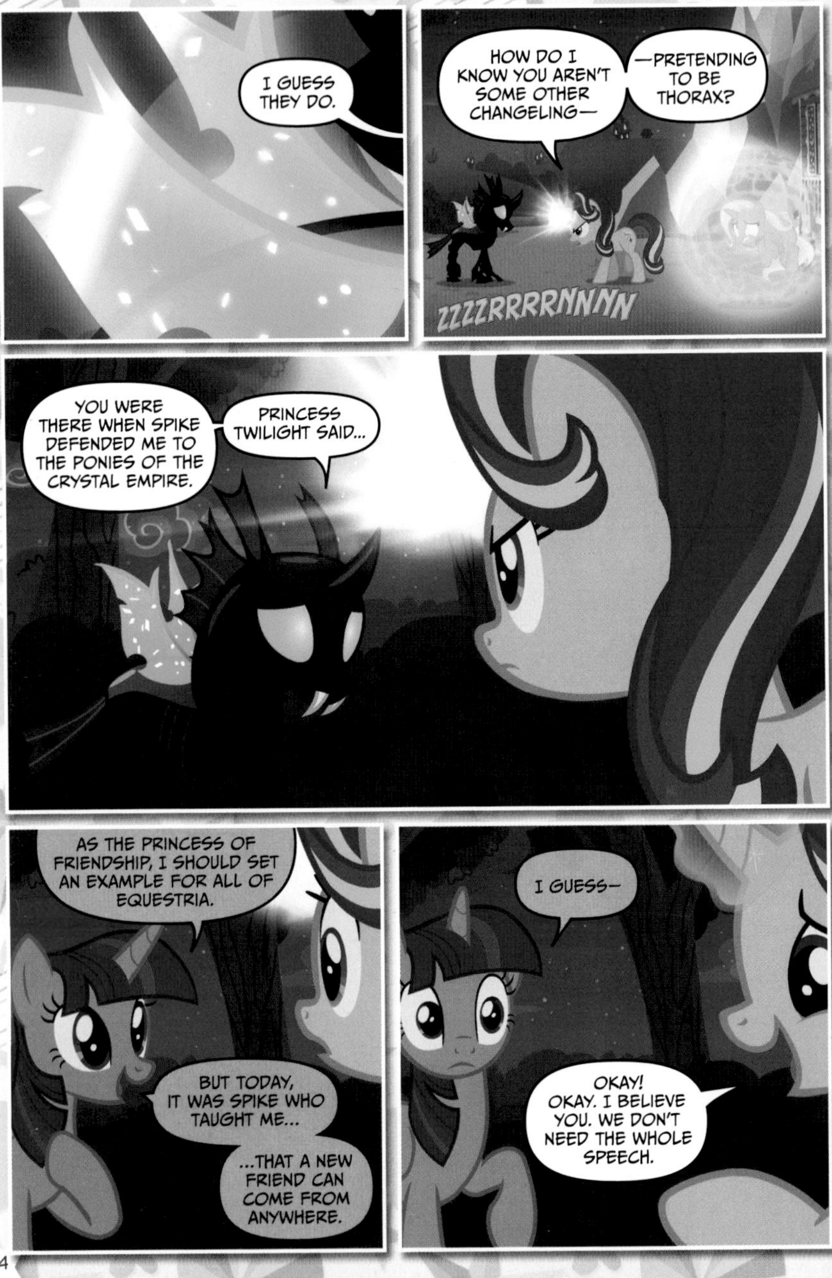
I GUESS THEY DO.
HOW DO I KNOW YOU AREN'T SOME OTHER CHANGELING—
—PRETENDING TO BE THORAX?
ZZZZRRRRNNNN
YOU WERE THERE WHEN SPIKE DEFENDED ME TO THE PONIES OF THE CRYSTAL EMPIRE.
PRINCESS TWILIGHT SAID...
AS THE PRINCESS OF FRIENDSHIP, I SHOULD SET AN EXAMPLE FOR ALL OF EQUESTRIA.
BUT TODAY, IT WAS SPIKE WHO TAUGHT ME...
...THAT A NEW FRIEND CAN COME FROM ANYWHERE.
I GUESS—
OKAY! OKAY. I BELIEVE YOU. WE DON'T NEED THE WHOLE SPEECH.

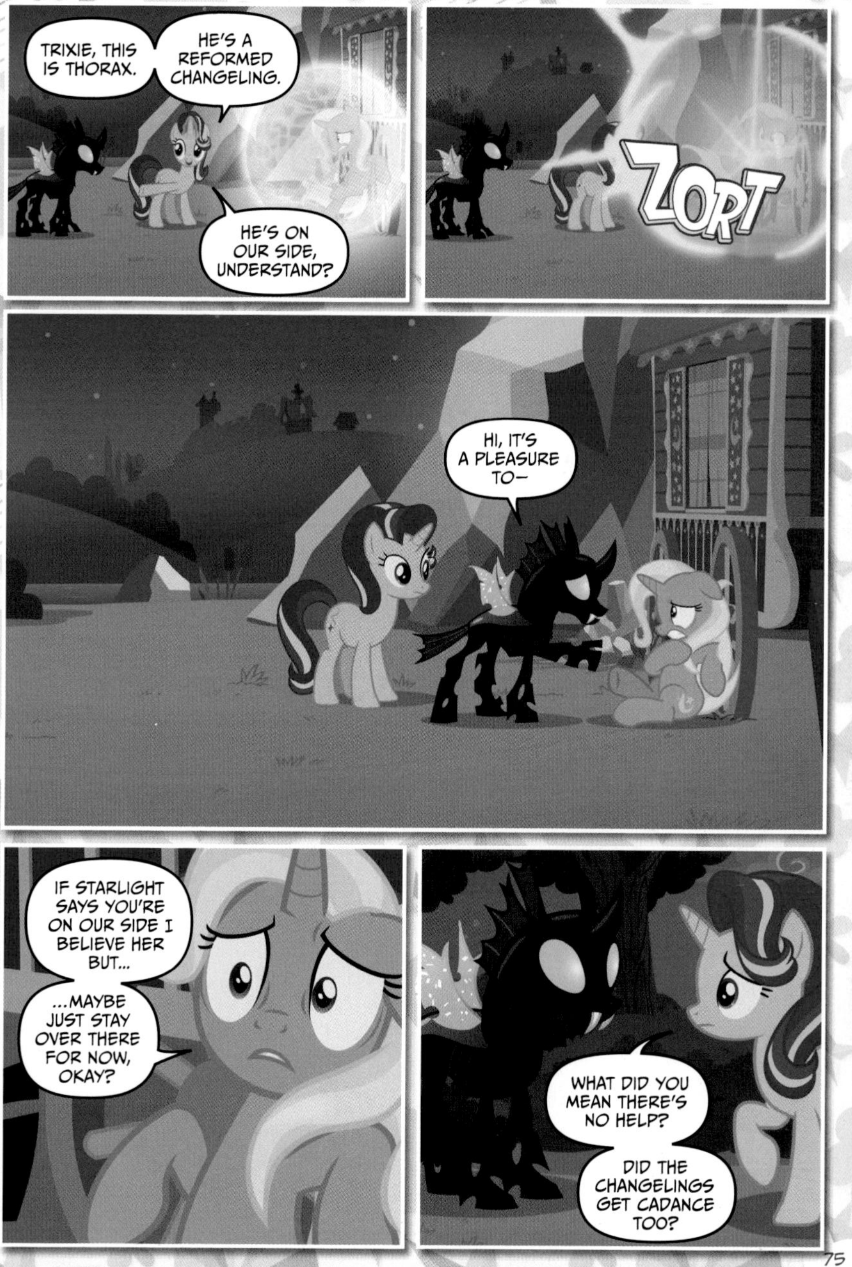

TRIXIE, THIS IS THORAX.
HE'S A REFORMED CHANGELING.
HE'S ON OUR SIDE, UNDERSTAND?
ZORT
HI, IT'S A PLEASURE TO—
IF STARLIGHT SAYS YOU'RE ON OUR SIDE I BELIEVE HER BUT...
...MAYBE JUST STAY OVER THERE FOR NOW, OKAY?
WHAT DID YOU MEAN THERE'S NO HELP?
DID THE CHANGELINGS GET CADANCE TOO?

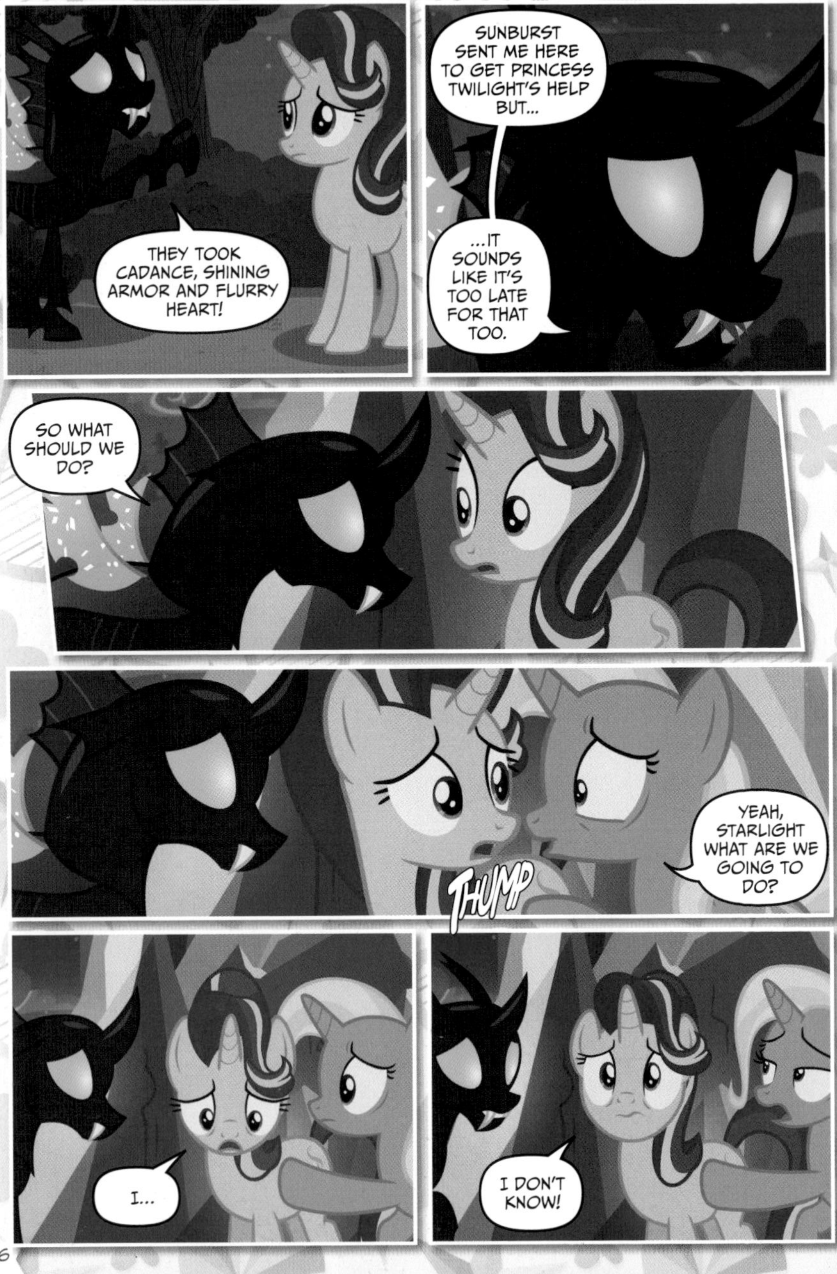

THEY TOOK CADANCE, SHINING ARMOR AND FLURRY HEART!
SUNBURST SENT ME HERE TO GET PRINCESS TWILIGHT'S HELP BUT...
...IT SOUNDS LIKE IT'S TOO LATE FOR THAT TOO.
SO WHAT SHOULD WE DO?
THUMP
YEAH, STARLIGHT WHAT ARE WE GOING TO DO?
I...
I DON'T KNOW!

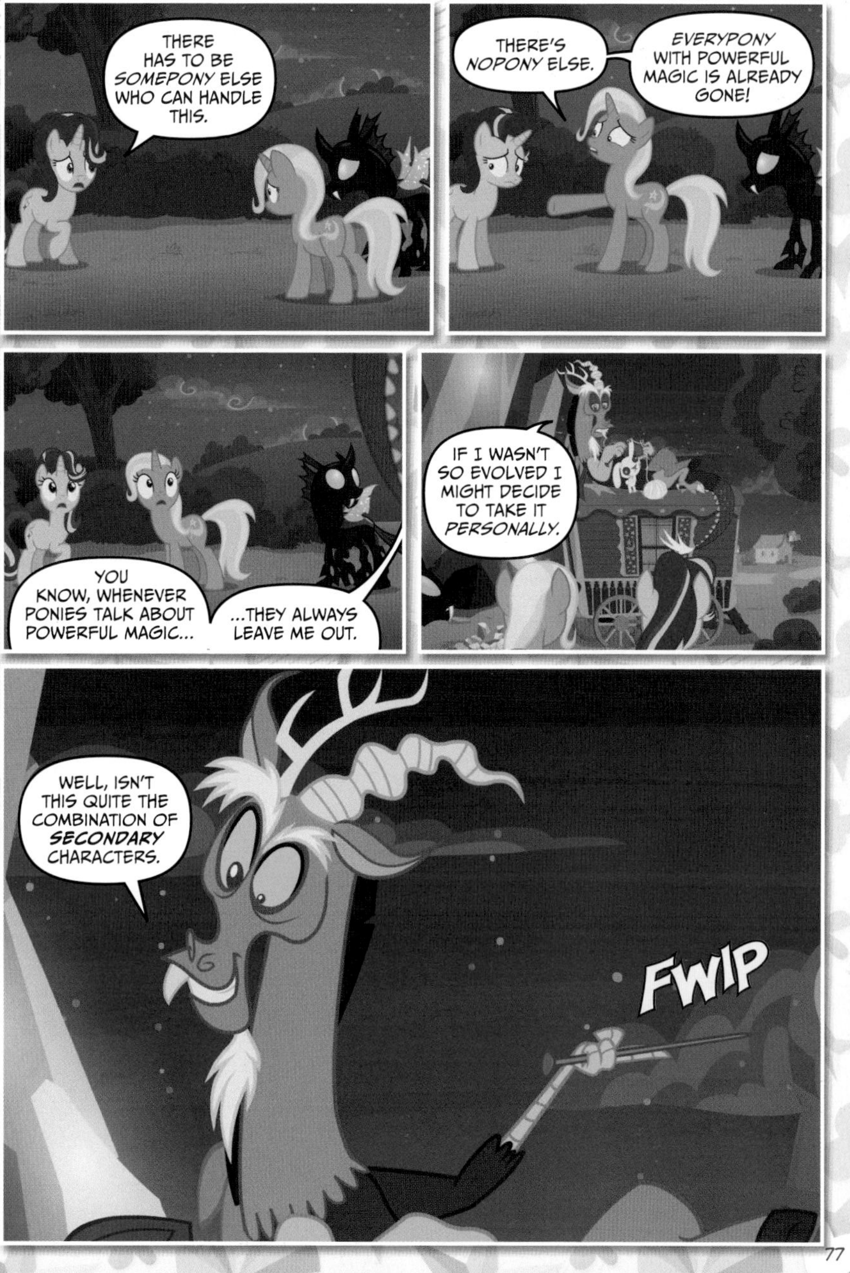
THERE HAS TO BE *SOMEPONY* ELSE WHO CAN HANDLE THIS.
THERE'S *NOPONY* ELSE.
EVERYPONY WITH POWERFUL MAGIC IS ALREADY GONE!
YOU KNOW, WHENEVER PONIES TALK ABOUT POWERFUL MAGIC...
...THEY ALWAYS LEAVE ME OUT.
IF I WASN'T SO EVOLVED I MIGHT DECIDE TO TAKE IT *PERSONALLY.*
WELL, ISN'T THIS QUITE THE COMBINATION OF ***SECONDARY*** CHARACTERS.
FWIP

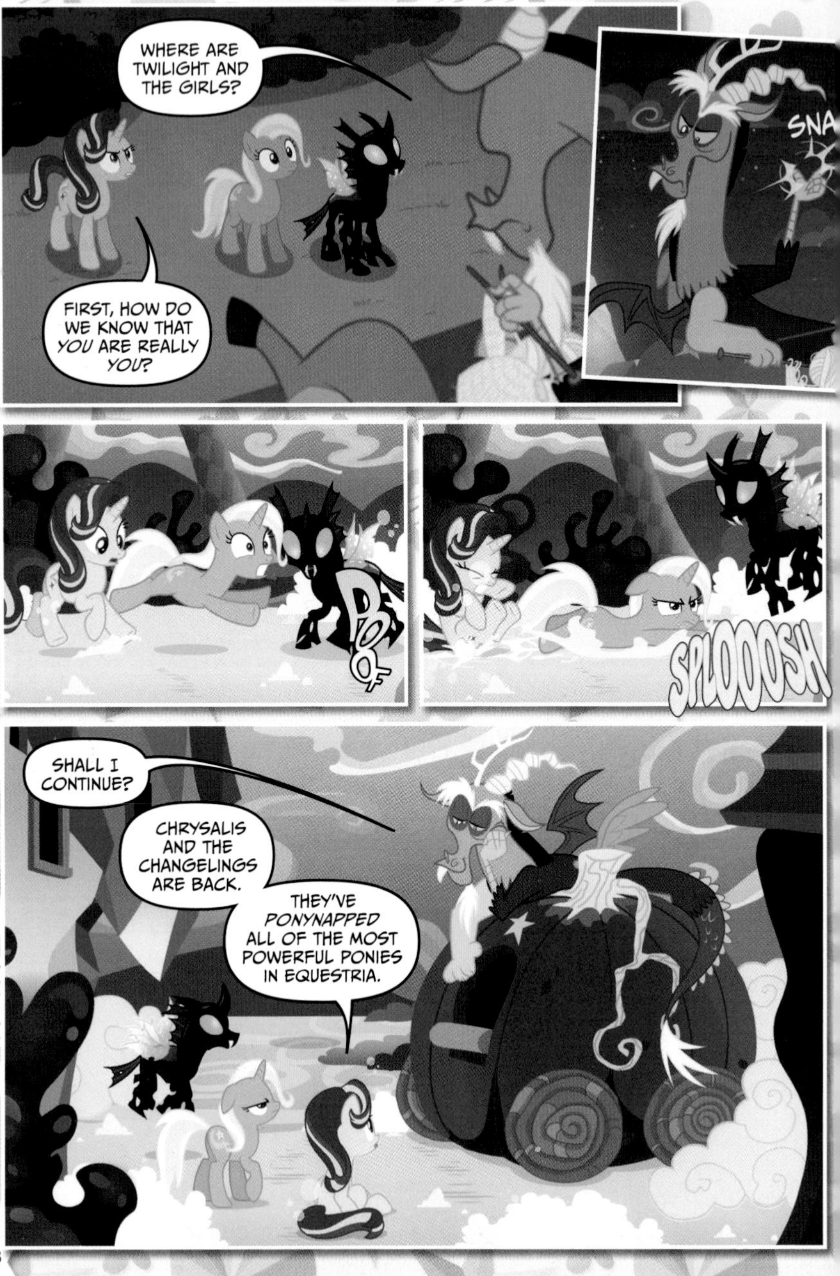

WHERE ARE TWILIGHT AND THE GIRLS?
FIRST, HOW DO WE KNOW THAT *YOU* ARE REALLY *YOU*?
SNA
POOF
SPLOOOSH
SHALL I CONTINUE?
CHRYSALIS AND THE CHANGELINGS ARE BACK.
THEY'VE *PONYNAPPED* ALL OF THE MOST POWERFUL PONIES IN EQUESTRIA.

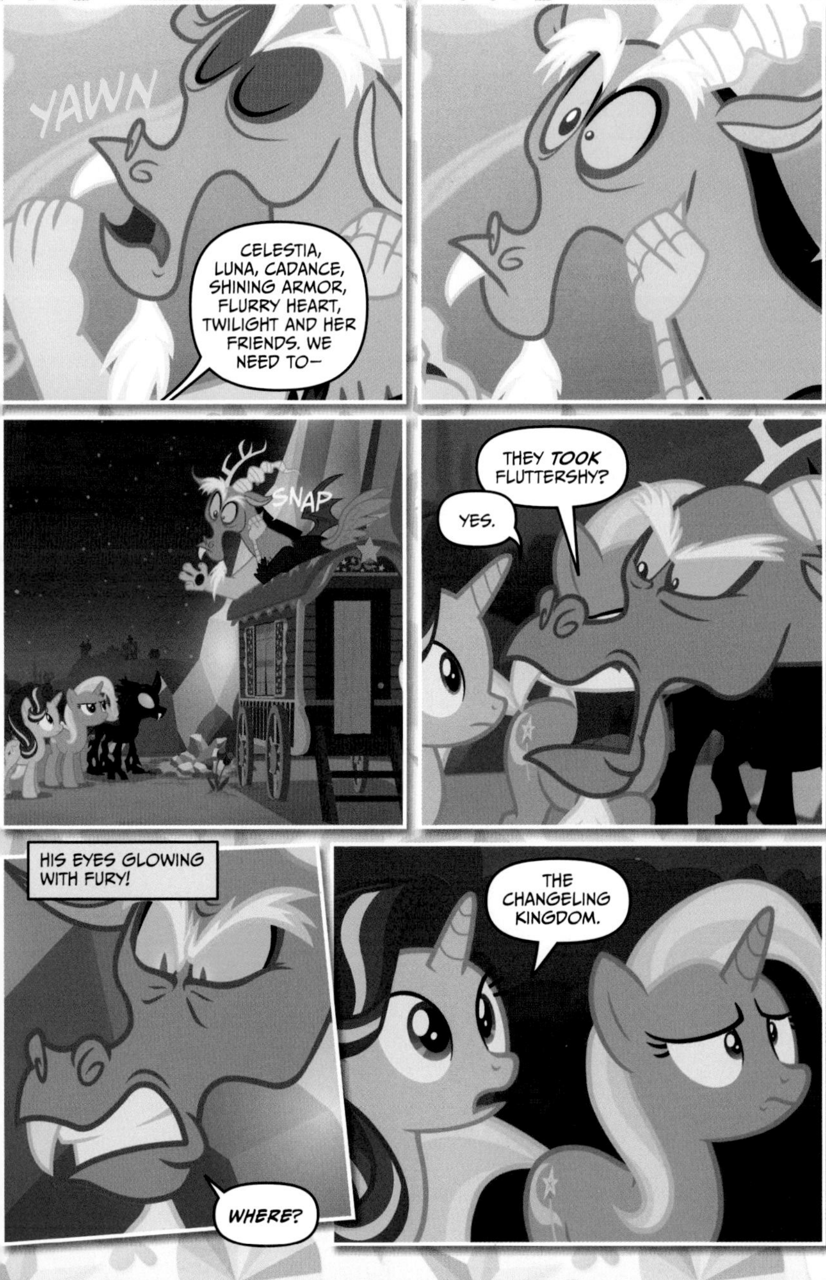
YAWN
CELESTIA, LUNA, CADANCE, SHINING ARMOR, FLURRY HEART, TWILIGHT AND HER FRIENDS. WE NEED TO—
SNAP
THEY *TOOK* FLUTTERSHY?
YES.
HIS EYES GLOWING WITH FURY!
WHERE?
THE CHANGELING KINGDOM.

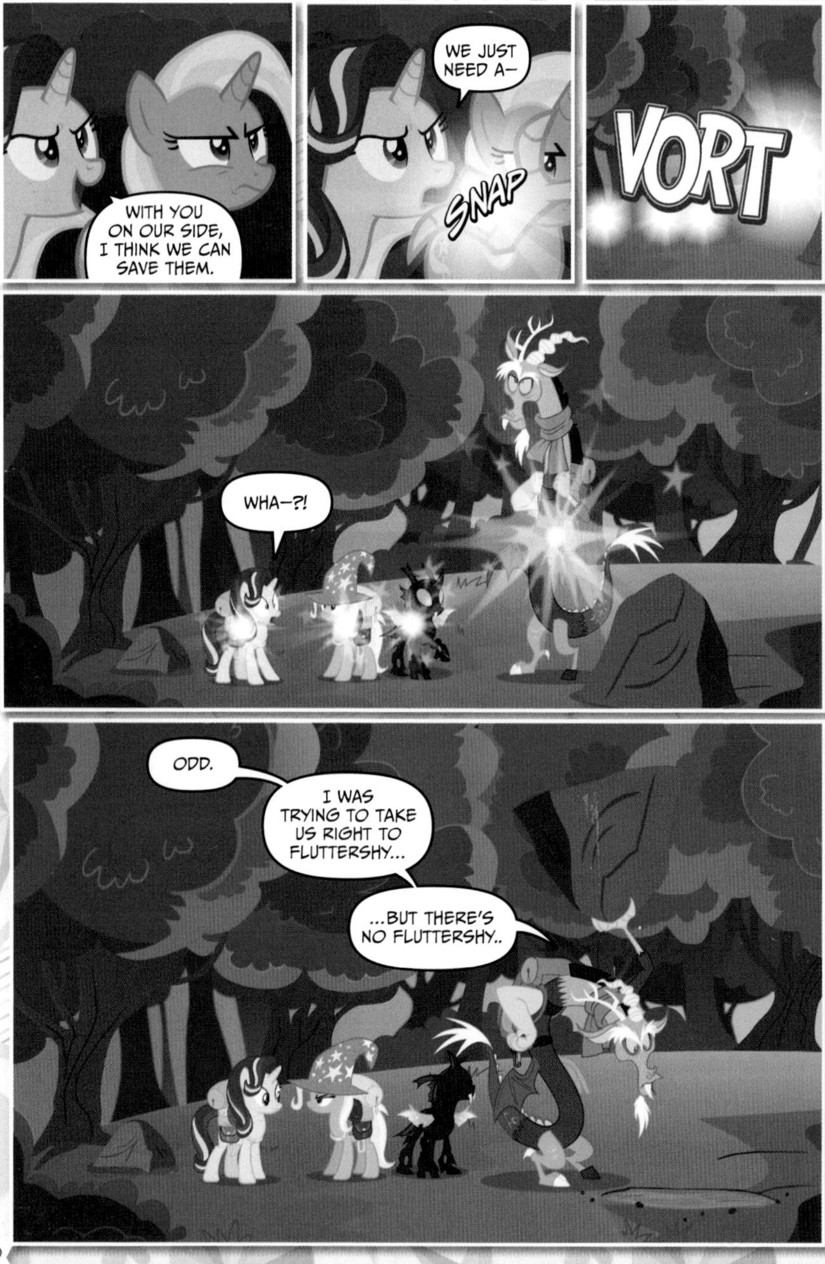
WITH YOU ON OUR SIDE, I THINK WE CAN SAVE THEM.
WE JUST NEED A—
SNAP
VORT
WHA—?!
ODD.
I WAS TRYING TO TAKE US RIGHT TO FLUTTERSHY...
...BUT THERE'S NO FLUTTERSHY..

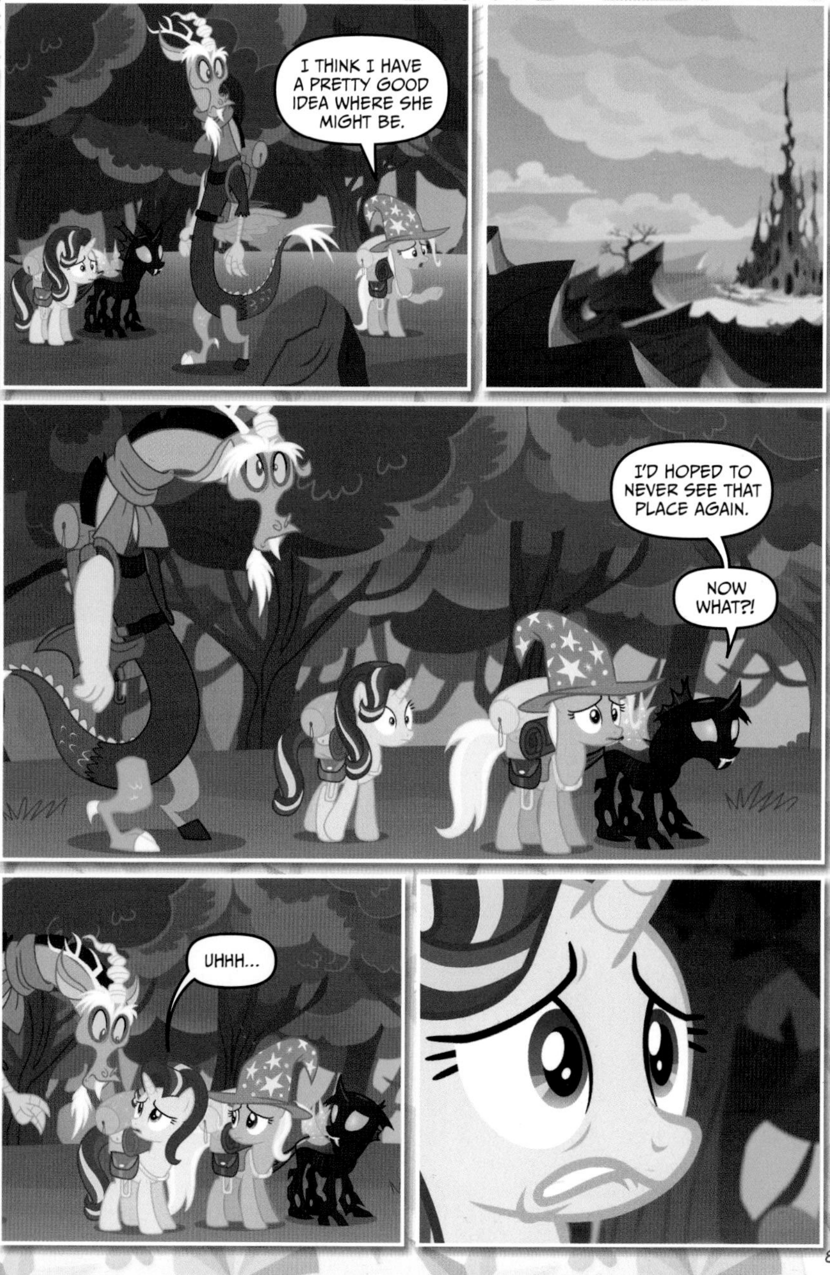
I THINK I HAVE A PRETTY GOOD IDEA WHERE SHE MIGHT BE.
I'D HOPED TO NEVER SEE THAT PLACE AGAIN.
NOW WHAT?!
UHHH...

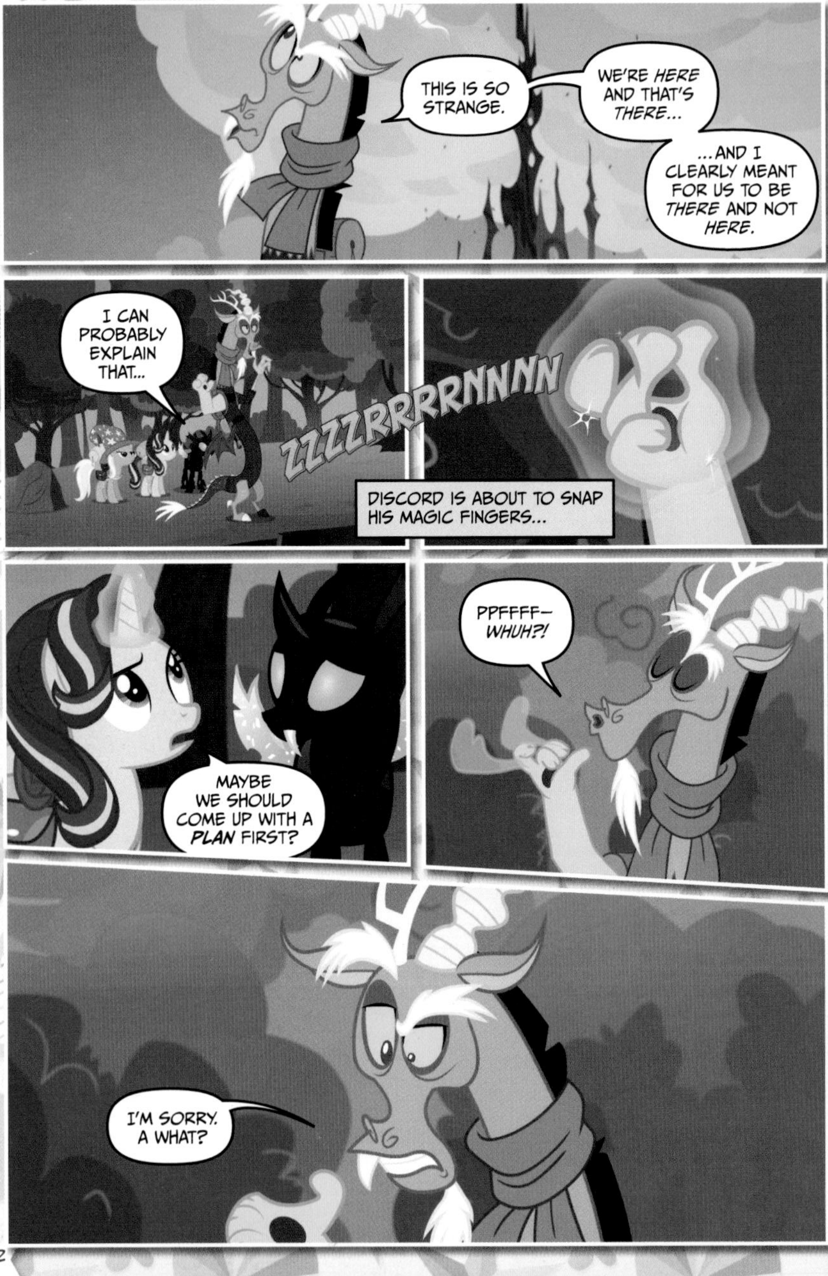
THIS IS SO STRANGE.
WE'RE *HERE* AND THAT'S *THERE*...
...AND I CLEARLY MEANT FOR US TO BE *THERE* AND NOT *HERE*.
I CAN PROBABLY EXPLAIN THAT...
ZZZZRRRRRNNNN
DISCORD IS ABOUT TO SNAP HIS MAGIC FINGERS...
MAYBE WE SHOULD COME UP WITH A ***PLAN*** FIRST?
PPFFFF— *WHUH?!*
I'M SORRY. A WHAT?

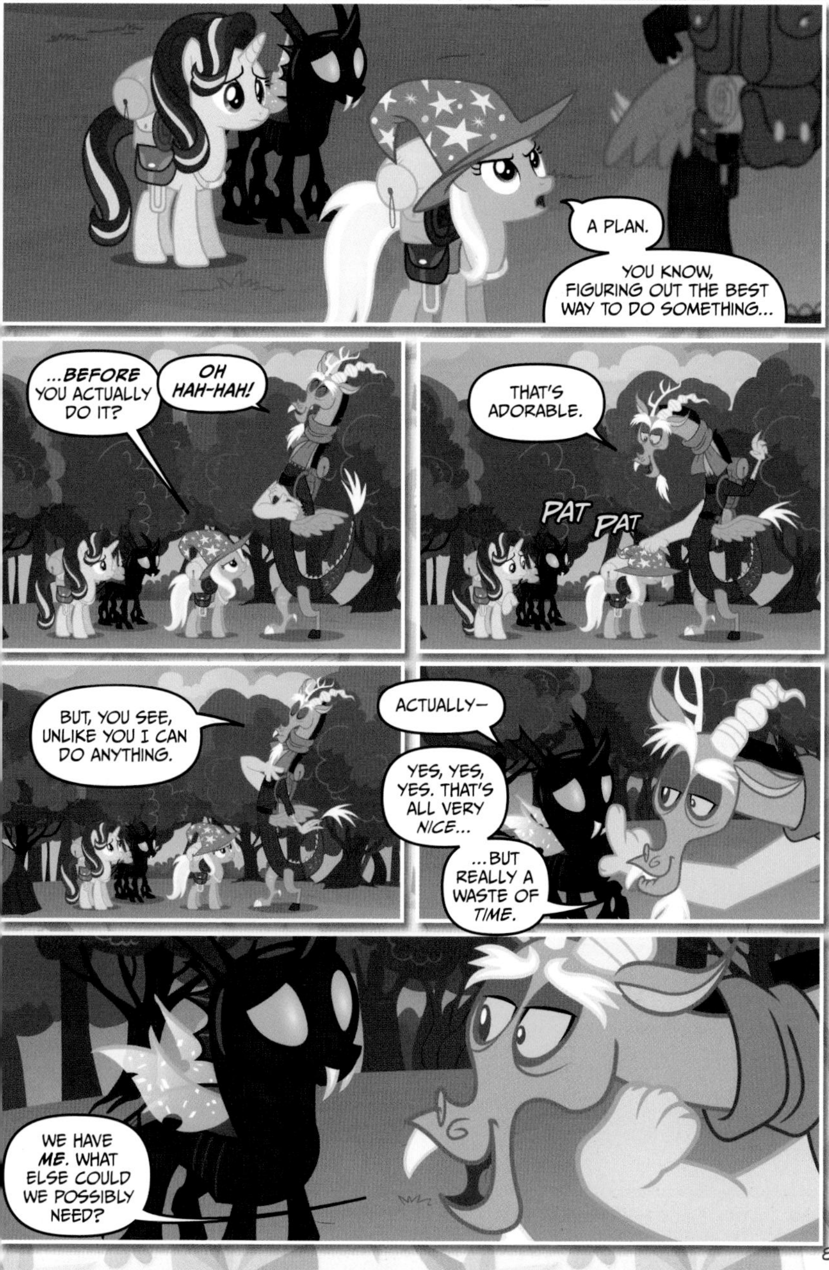
A PLAN.
YOU KNOW, FIGURING OUT THE BEST WAY TO DO SOMETHING...
...BEFORE YOU ACTUALLY DO IT?
OH HAH-HAH!
THAT'S ADORABLE.
PAT PAT
BUT, YOU SEE, UNLIKE YOU I CAN DO ANYTHING.
ACTUALLY—
YES, YES, YES. THAT'S ALL VERY NICE...
...BUT REALLY A WASTE OF TIME.
WE HAVE ME. WHAT ELSE COULD WE POSSIBLY NEED?

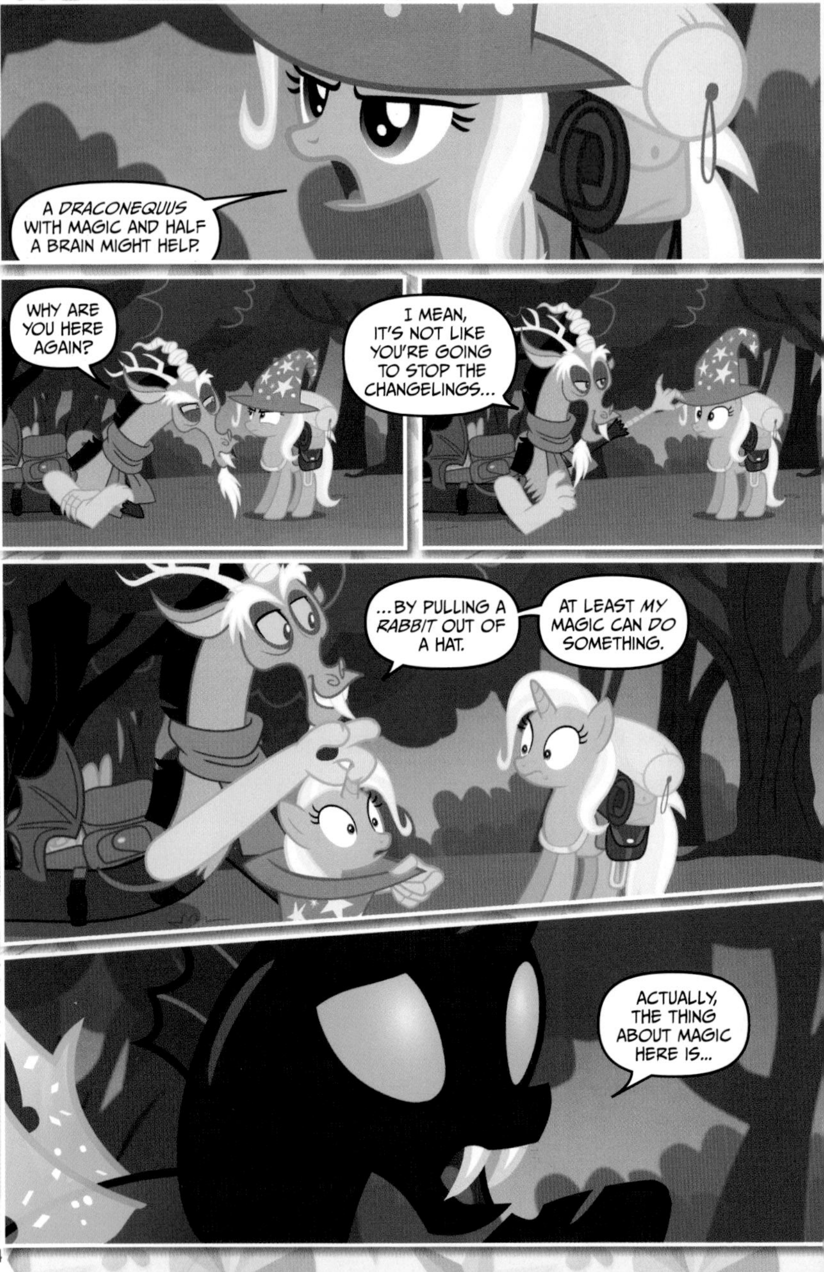
A *DRACONEQUUS* WITH MAGIC AND HALF A BRAIN MIGHT HELP.
WHY ARE YOU HERE AGAIN?
I MEAN, IT'S NOT LIKE YOU'RE GOING TO STOP THE CHANGELINGS...
...BY PULLING A *RABBIT* OUT OF A HAT.
AT LEAST *MY* MAGIC CAN *DO* SOMETHING.
ACTUALLY, THE THING ABOUT MAGIC HERE IS...

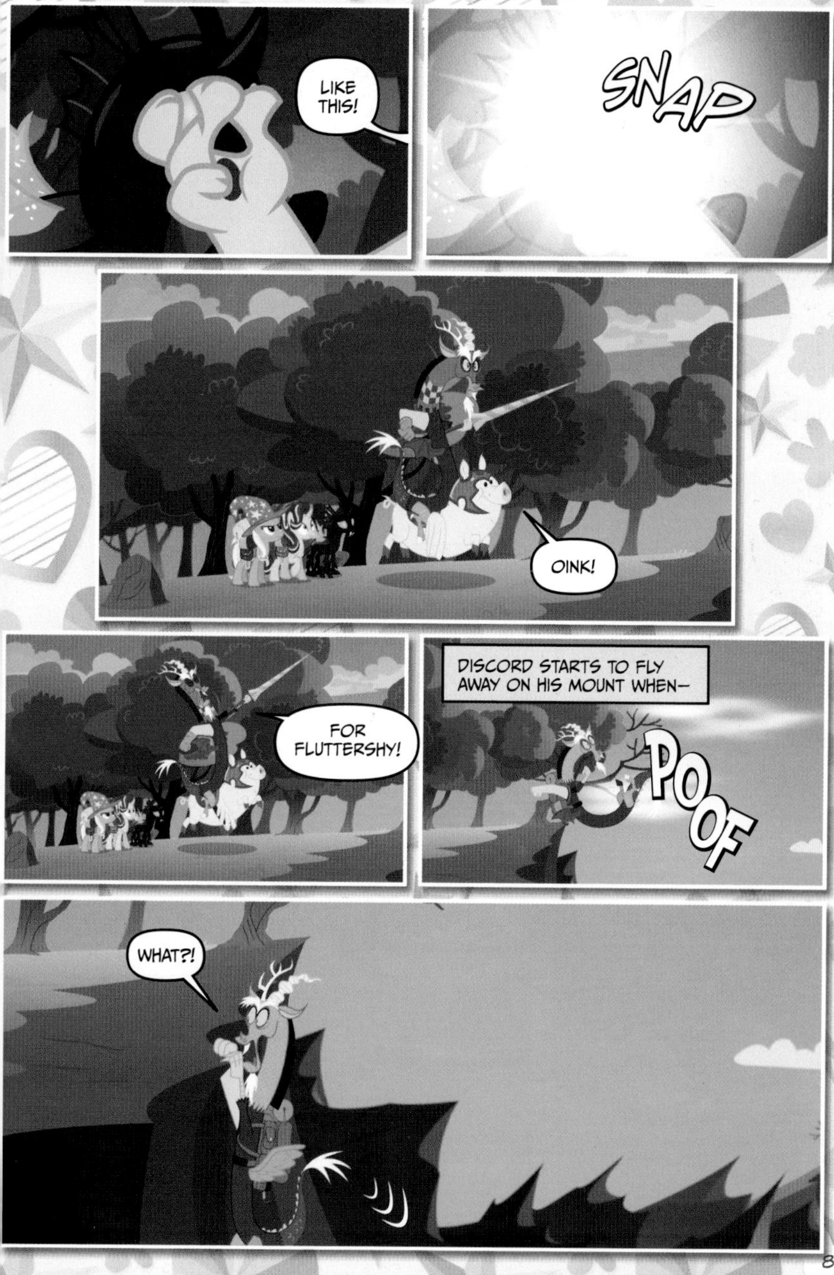
LIKE THIS!
SNAP
OINK!
FOR FLUTTERSHY!
DISCORD STARTS TO FLY AWAY ON HIS MOUNT WHEN—
POOF
WHAT?!

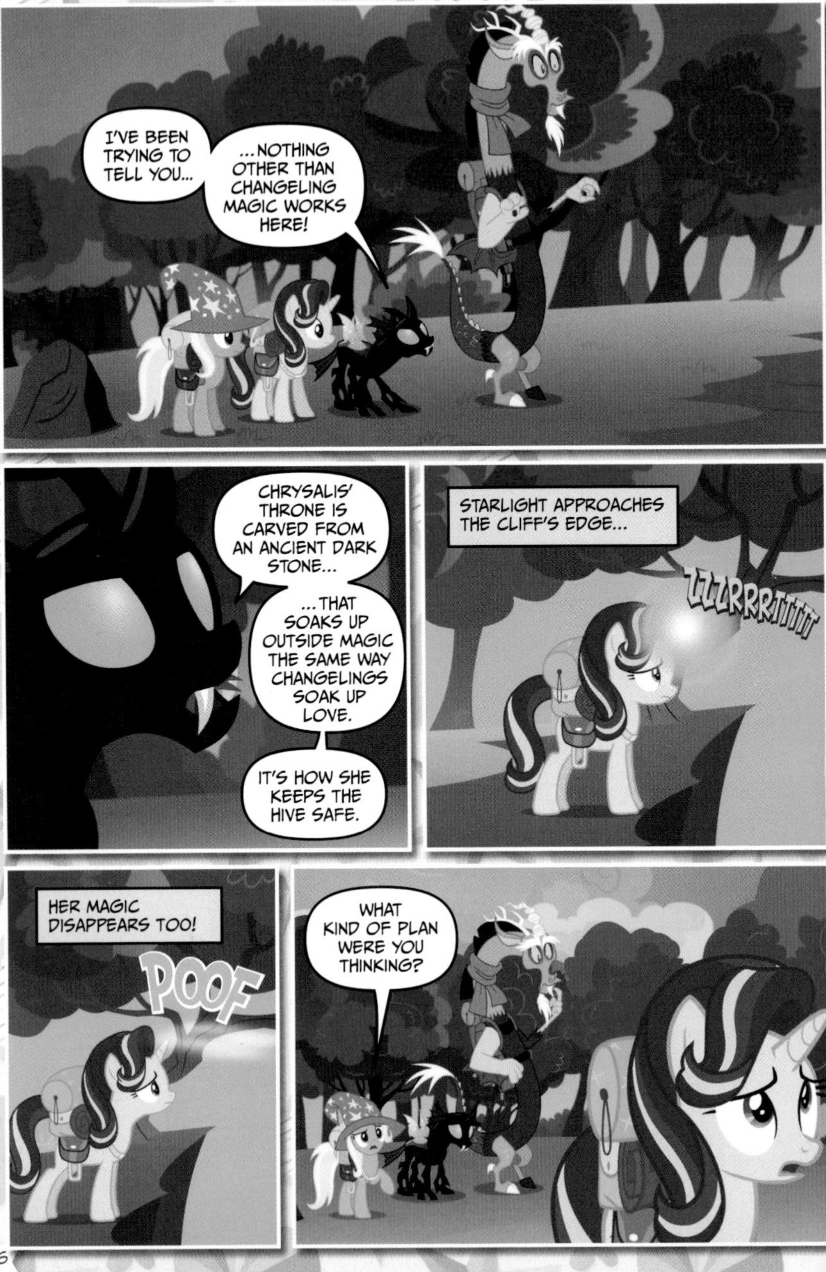
I'VE BEEN TRYING TO TELL YOU...
...NOTHING OTHER THAN CHANGELING MAGIC WORKS HERE!
CHRYSALIS' THRONE IS CARVED FROM AN ANCIENT DARK STONE...
...THAT SOAKS UP OUTSIDE MAGIC THE SAME WAY CHANGELINGS SOAK UP LOVE.
IT'S HOW SHE KEEPS THE HIVE SAFE.
STARLIGHT APPROACHES THE CLIFF'S EDGE...
ZZZRRRTTTTT
HER MAGIC DISAPPEARS TOO!
POOF
WHAT KIND OF PLAN WERE YOU THINKING?

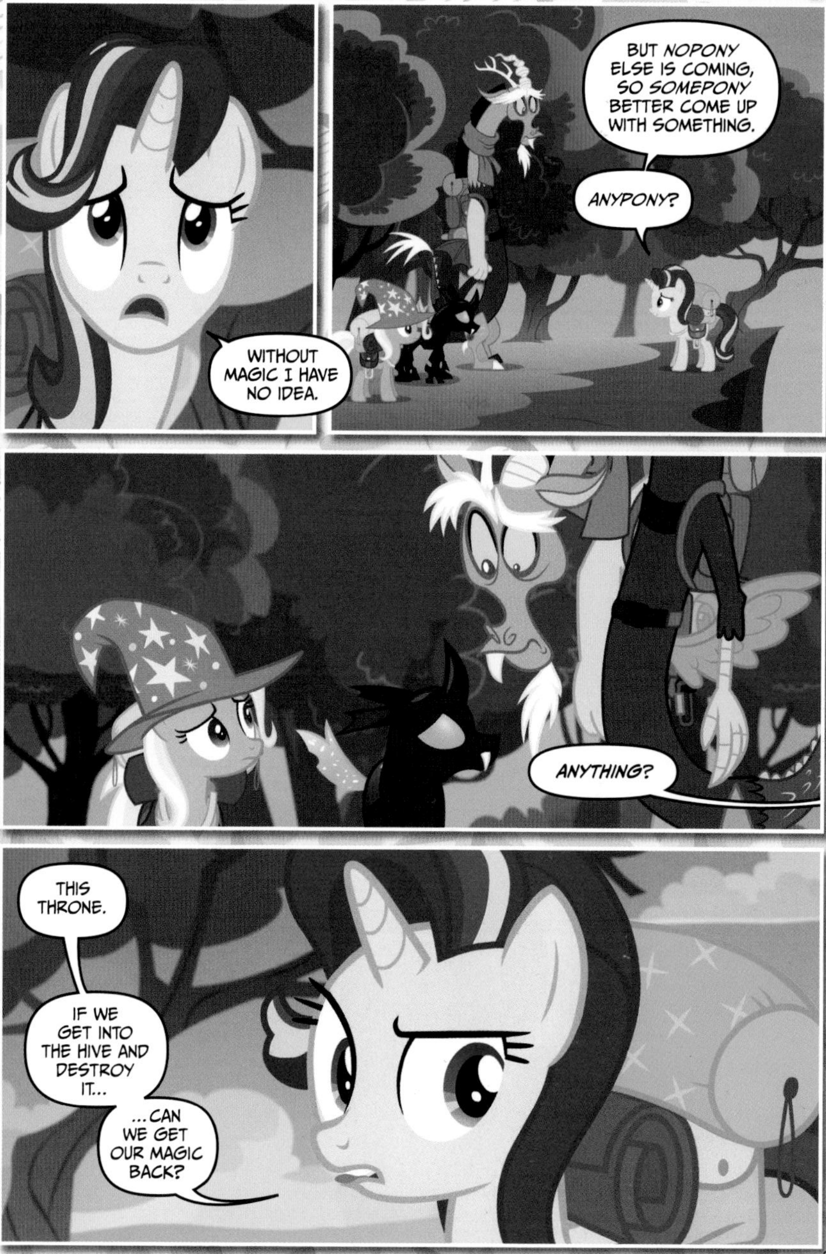
WITHOUT MAGIC I HAVE NO IDEA.
BUT NOPONY ELSE IS COMING, SO SOMEPONY BETTER COME UP WITH SOMETHING.
ANYPONY?
ANYTHING?
THIS THRONE.
IF WE GET INTO THE HIVE AND DESTROY IT...
...CAN WE GET OUR MAGIC BACK?

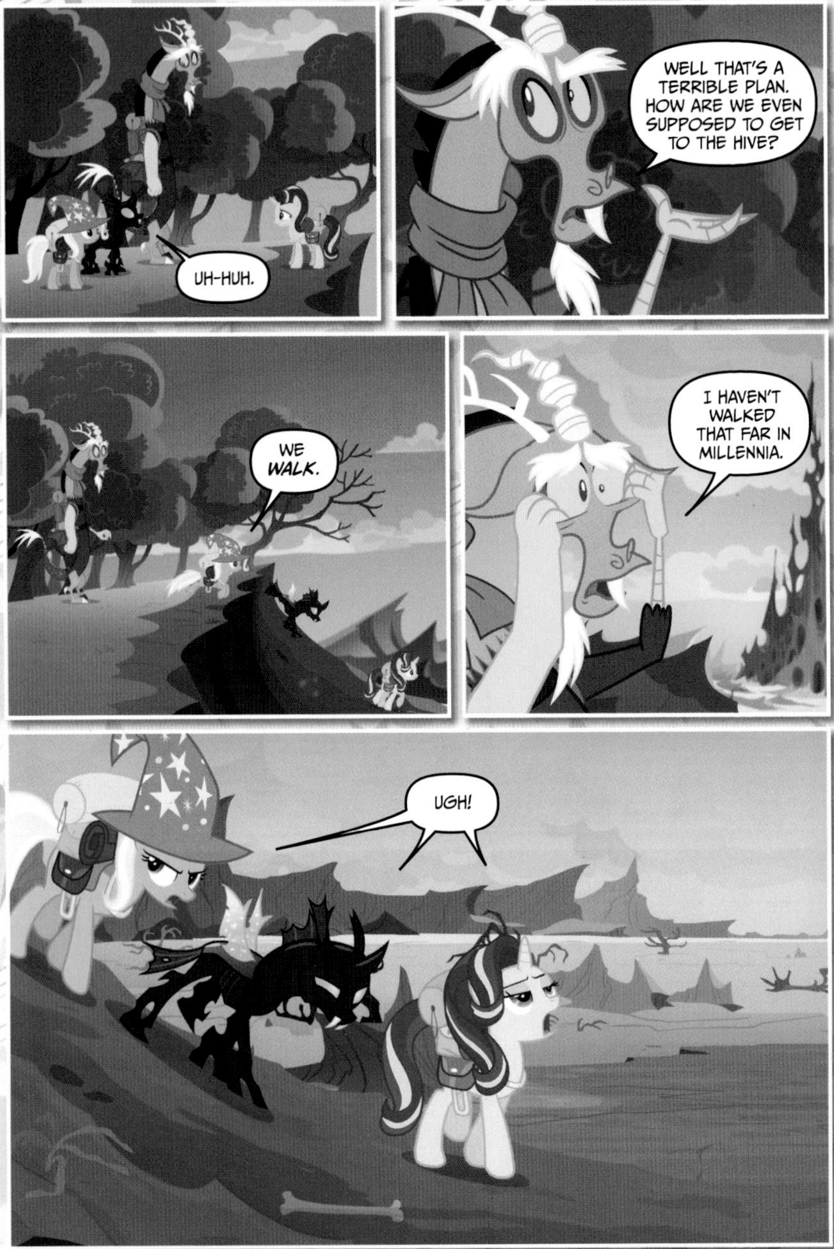
UH-HUH.
WELL THAT'S A TERRIBLE PLAN. HOW ARE WE EVEN SUPPOSED TO GET TO THE HIVE?
WE *WALK.*
I HAVEN'T WALKED THAT FAR IN MILLENNIA.
UGH!

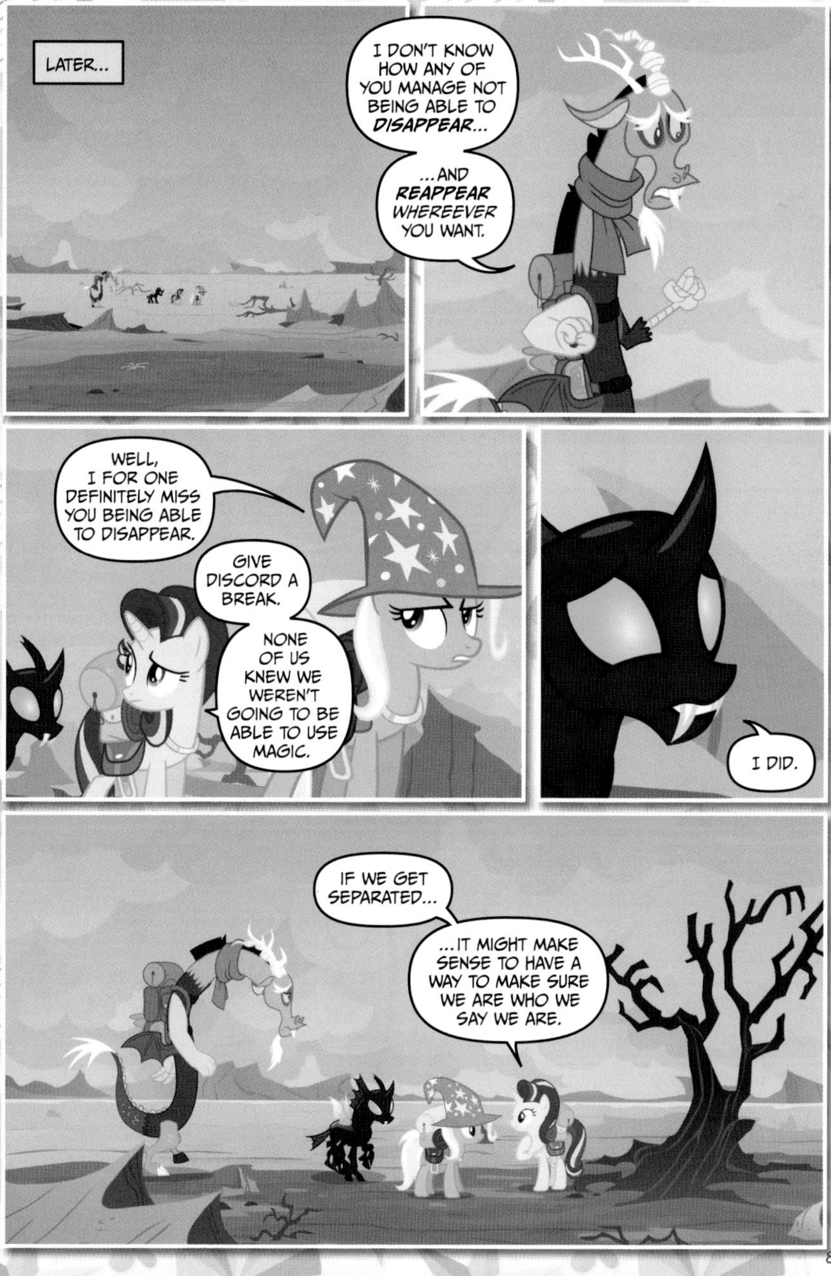
LATER...
I DON'T KNOW HOW ANY OF YOU MANAGE NOT BEING ABLE TO *DISAPPEAR*...
...AND *REAPPEAR* WHEREEVER YOU WANT.
WELL, I FOR ONE DEFINITELY MISS YOU BEING ABLE TO DISAPPEAR.
GIVE DISCORD A BREAK.
NONE OF US KNEW WE WEREN'T GOING TO BE ABLE TO USE MAGIC.
I DID.
IF WE GET SEPARATED...
...IT MIGHT MAKE SENSE TO HAVE A WAY TO MAKE SURE WE ARE WHO WE SAY WE ARE.

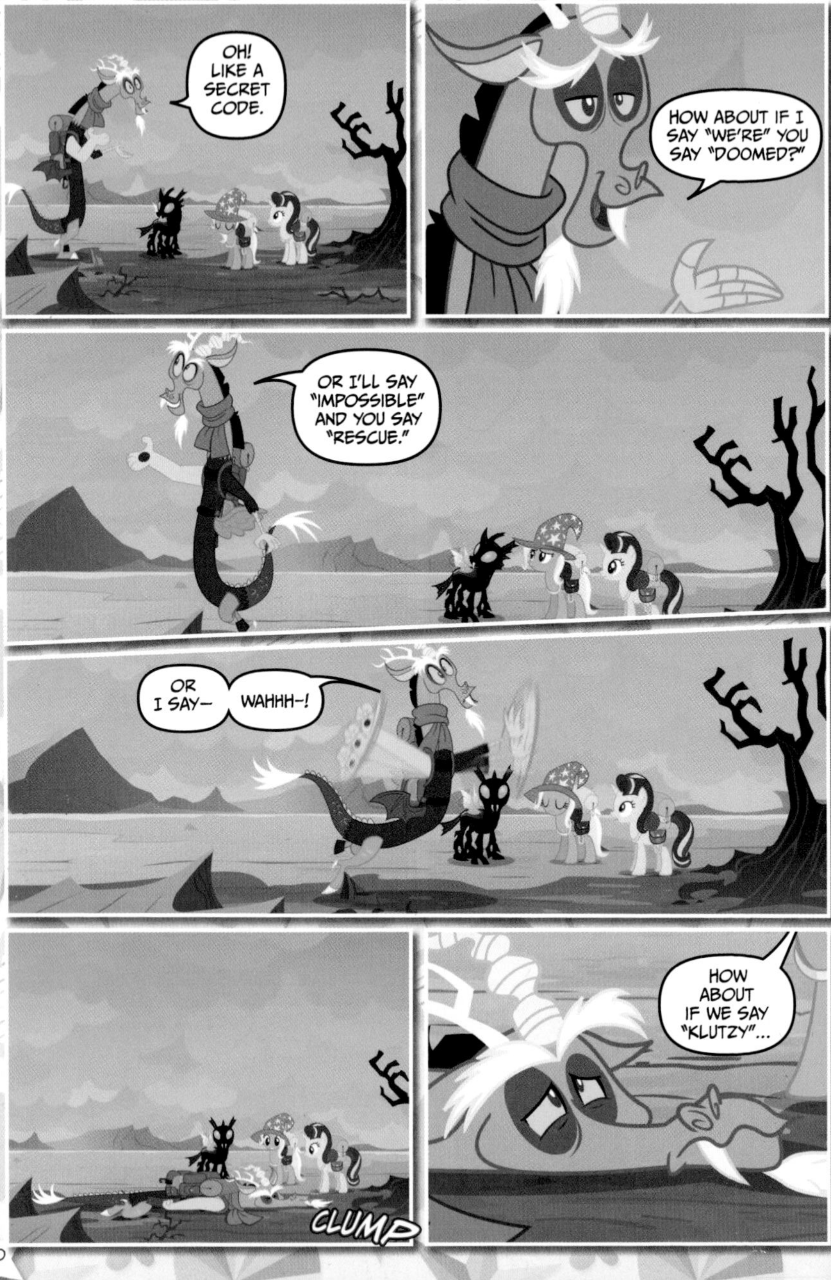
OH! LIKE A SECRET CODE.
HOW ABOUT IF I SAY "WE'RE" YOU SAY "DOOMED?"
OR I'LL SAY "IMPOSSIBLE" AND YOU SAY "RESCUE."
OR I SAY—
WAHHH—!
CLUMP
HOW ABOUT IF WE SAY "KLUTZY"...

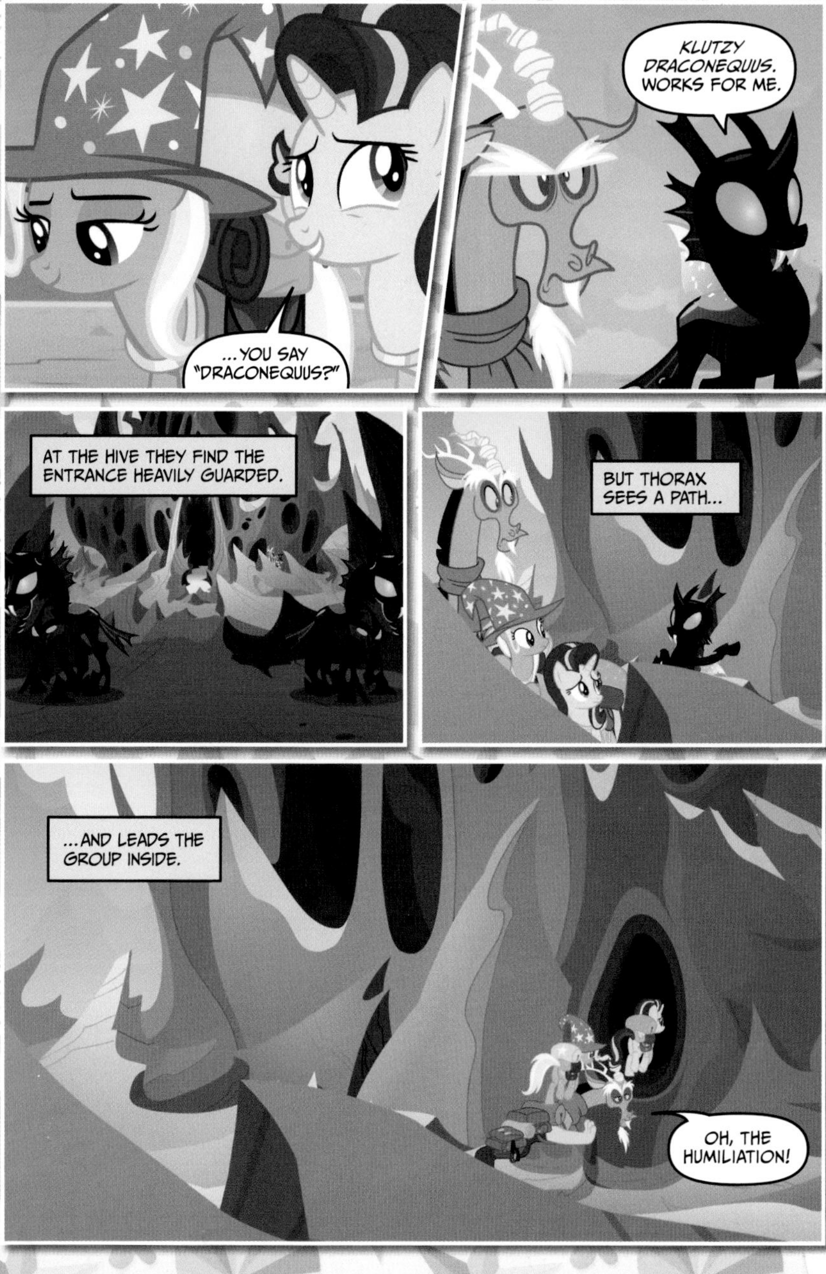
...YOU SAY "DRACONEQUUS?"
KLUTZY DRACONEQUUS. WORKS FOR ME.
AT THE HIVE THEY FIND THE ENTRANCE HEAVILY GUARDED.
BUT THORAX SEES A PATH...
...AND LEADS THE GROUP INSIDE.
OH, THE HUMILIATION!

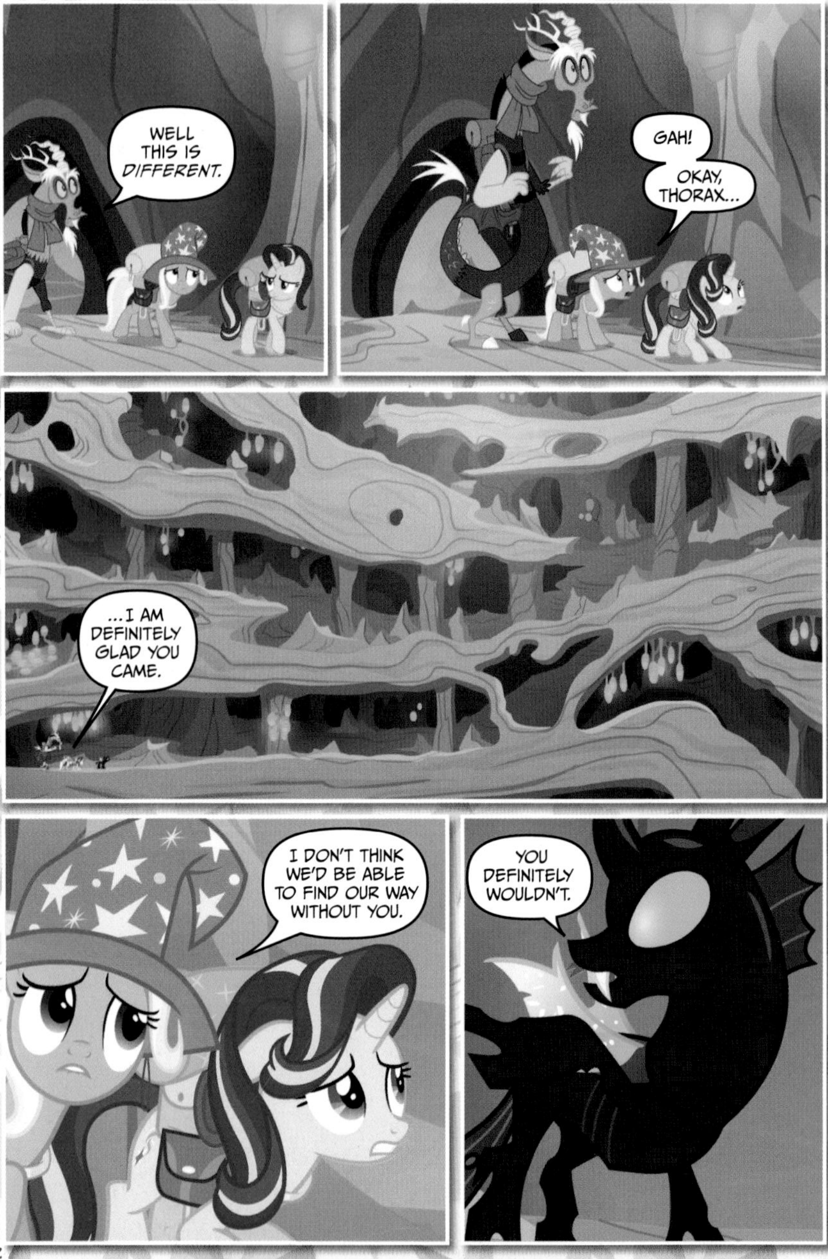
WELL THIS IS DIFFERENT.
GAH!
OKAY, THORAX...
...I AM DEFINITELY GLAD YOU CAME.
I DON'T THINK WE'D BE ABLE TO FIND OUR WAY WITHOUT YOU.
YOU DEFINITELY WOULDN'T.

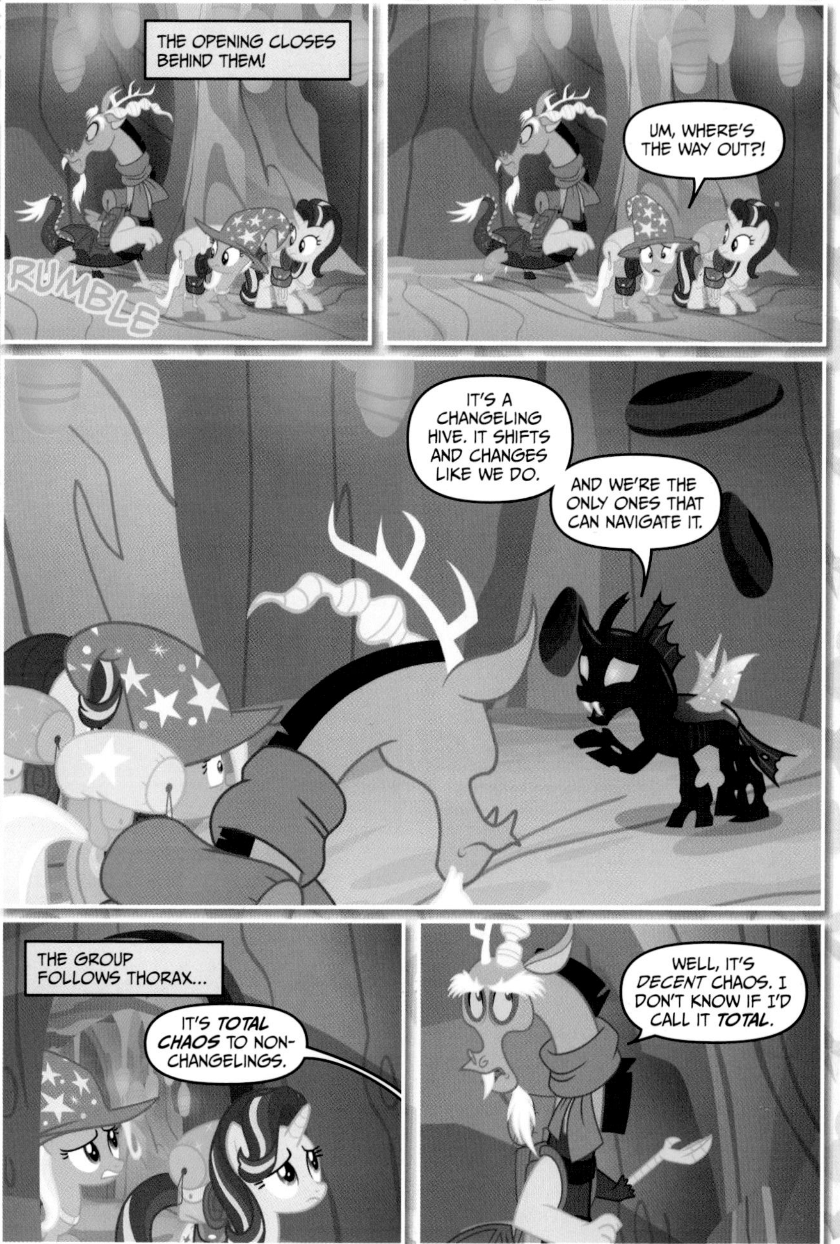
THE OPENING CLOSES BEHIND THEM!
RUMBLE
UM, WHERE'S THE WAY OUT?!
IT'S A CHANGELING HIVE. IT SHIFTS AND CHANGES LIKE WE DO.
AND WE'RE THE ONLY ONES THAT CAN NAVIGATE IT.
THE GROUP FOLLOWS THORAX...
IT'S **TOTAL CHAOS** TO NON-CHANGELINGS.
WELL, IT'S *DECENT* CHAOS. I DON'T KNOW IF I'D CALL IT ***TOTAL***.

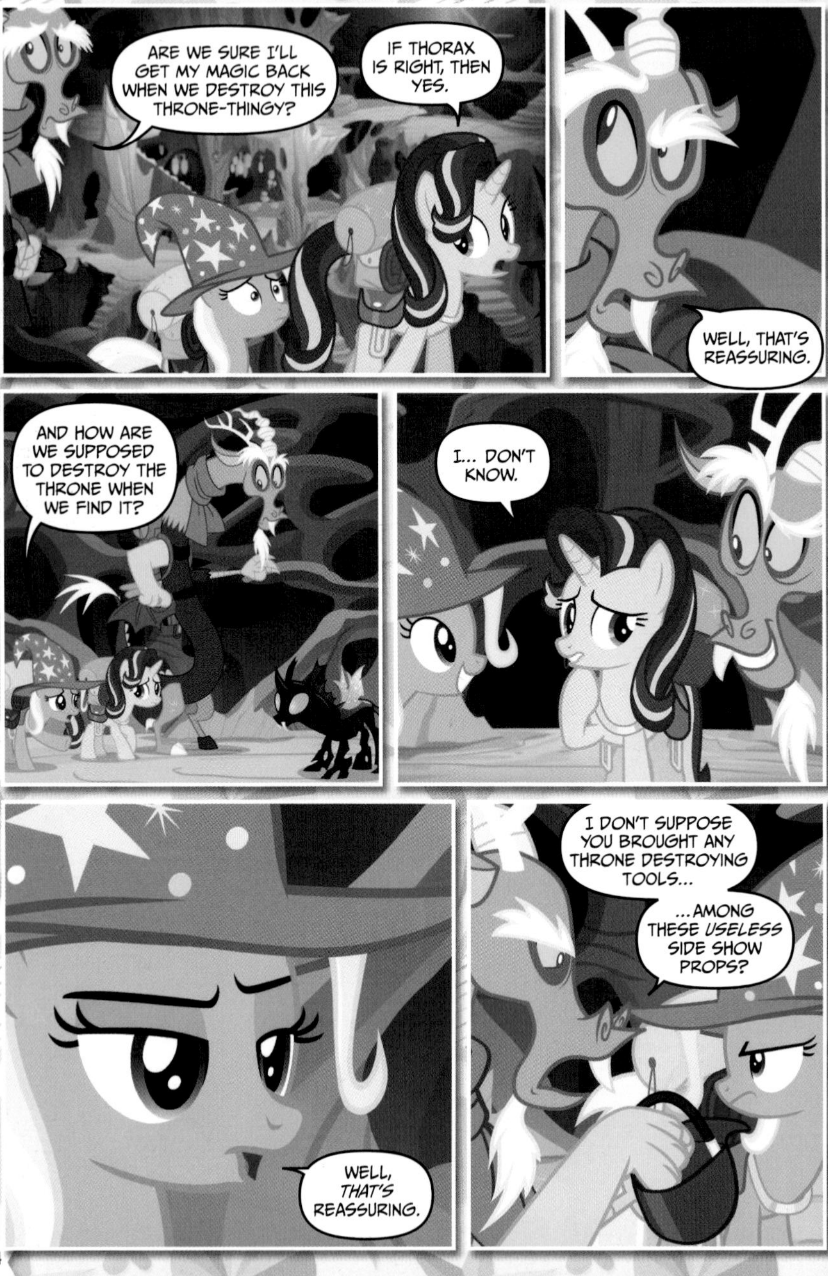
ARE WE SURE I'LL GET MY MAGIC BACK WHEN WE DESTROY THIS THRONE-THINGY?
IF THORAX IS RIGHT, THEN YES.
WELL, THAT'S REASSURING.
AND HOW ARE WE SUPPOSED TO DESTROY THE THRONE WHEN WE FIND IT?
I... DON'T KNOW.
WELL, *THAT'S* REASSURING.
I DON'T SUPPOSE YOU BROUGHT ANY THRONE DESTROYING TOOLS...
...AMONG THESE *USELESS* SIDE SHOW PROPS?

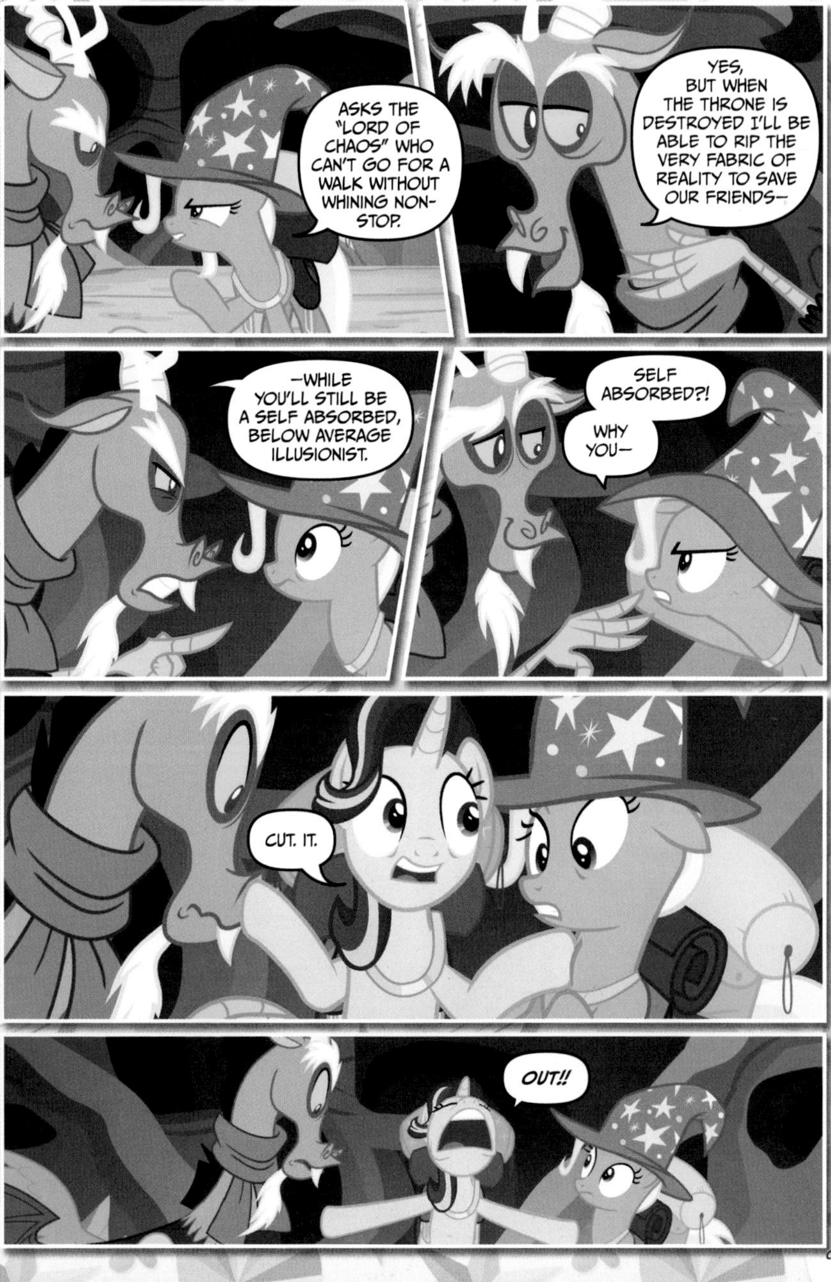
ASKS THE "LORD OF CHAOS" WHO CAN'T GO FOR A WALK WITHOUT WHINING NON-STOP.
YES, BUT WHEN THE THRONE IS DESTROYED I'LL BE ABLE TO RIP THE VERY FABRIC OF REALITY TO SAVE OUR FRIENDS—
—WHILE YOU'LL STILL BE A SELF ABSORBED, BELOW AVERAGE ILLUSIONIST.
SELF ABSORBED?!
WHY YOU—
CUT. IT.
OUT!!

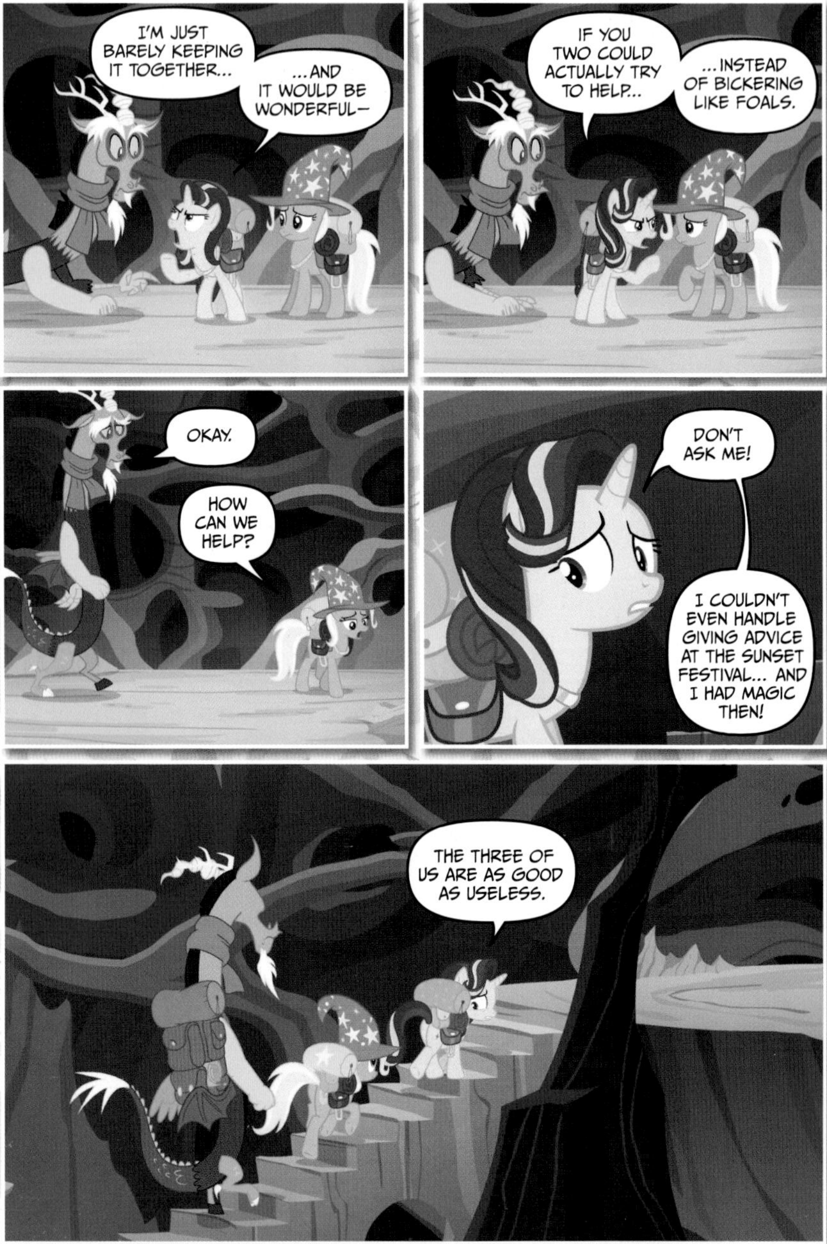

I'M JUST BARELY KEEPING IT TOGETHER...
...AND IT WOULD BE WONDERFUL—
IF YOU TWO COULD ACTUALLY TRY TO HELP...
...INSTEAD OF BICKERING LIKE FOALS.
OKAY.
HOW CAN WE HELP?
DON'T ASK ME!
I COULDN'T EVEN HANDLE GIVING ADVICE AT THE SUNSET FESTIVAL... AND I HAD MAGIC THEN!
THE THREE OF US ARE AS GOOD AS USELESS.

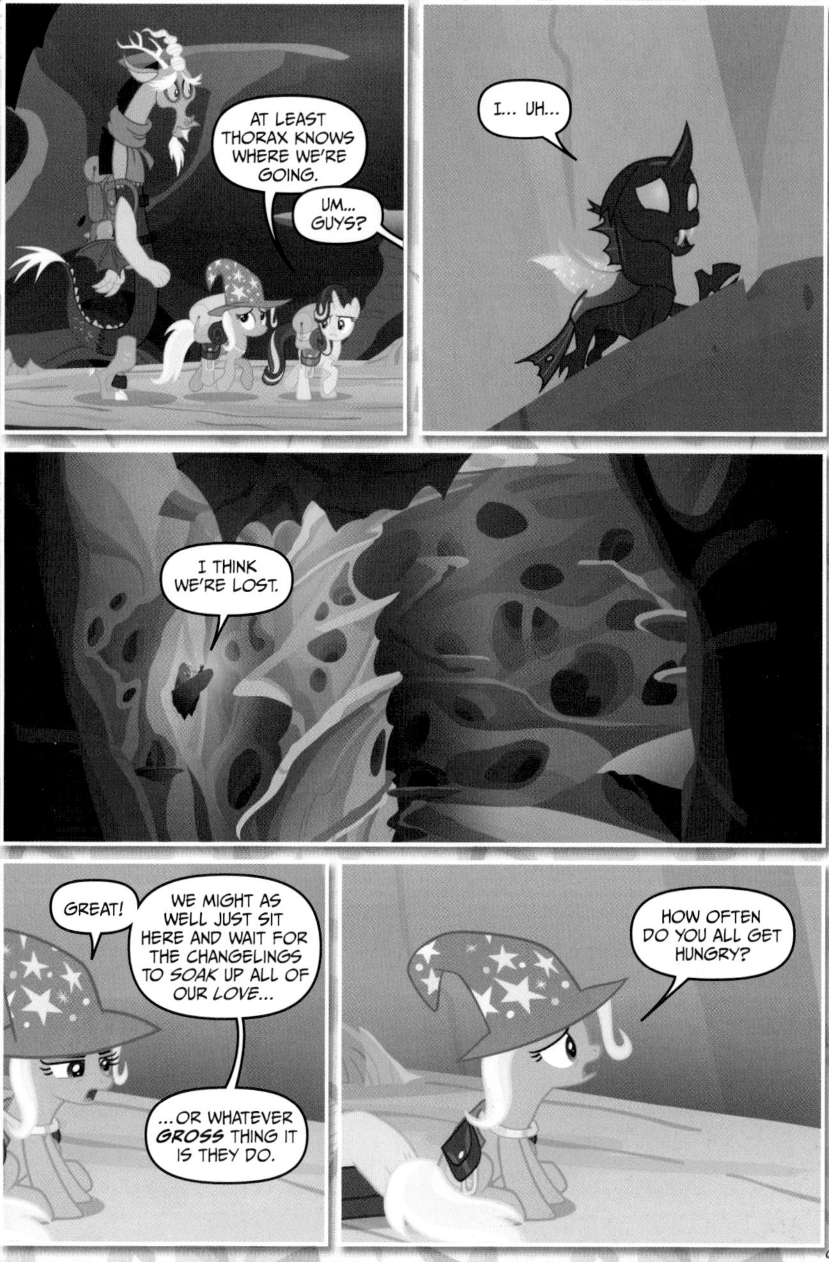
AT LEAST THORAX KNOWS WHERE WE'RE GOING.
UM... GUYS?
I... UH...
I THINK WE'RE LOST.
GREAT!
WE MIGHT AS WELL JUST SIT HERE AND WAIT FOR THE CHANGELINGS TO SOAK UP ALL OF OUR LOVE...
...OR WHATEVER GROSS THING IT IS THEY DO.
HOW OFTEN DO YOU ALL GET HUNGRY?

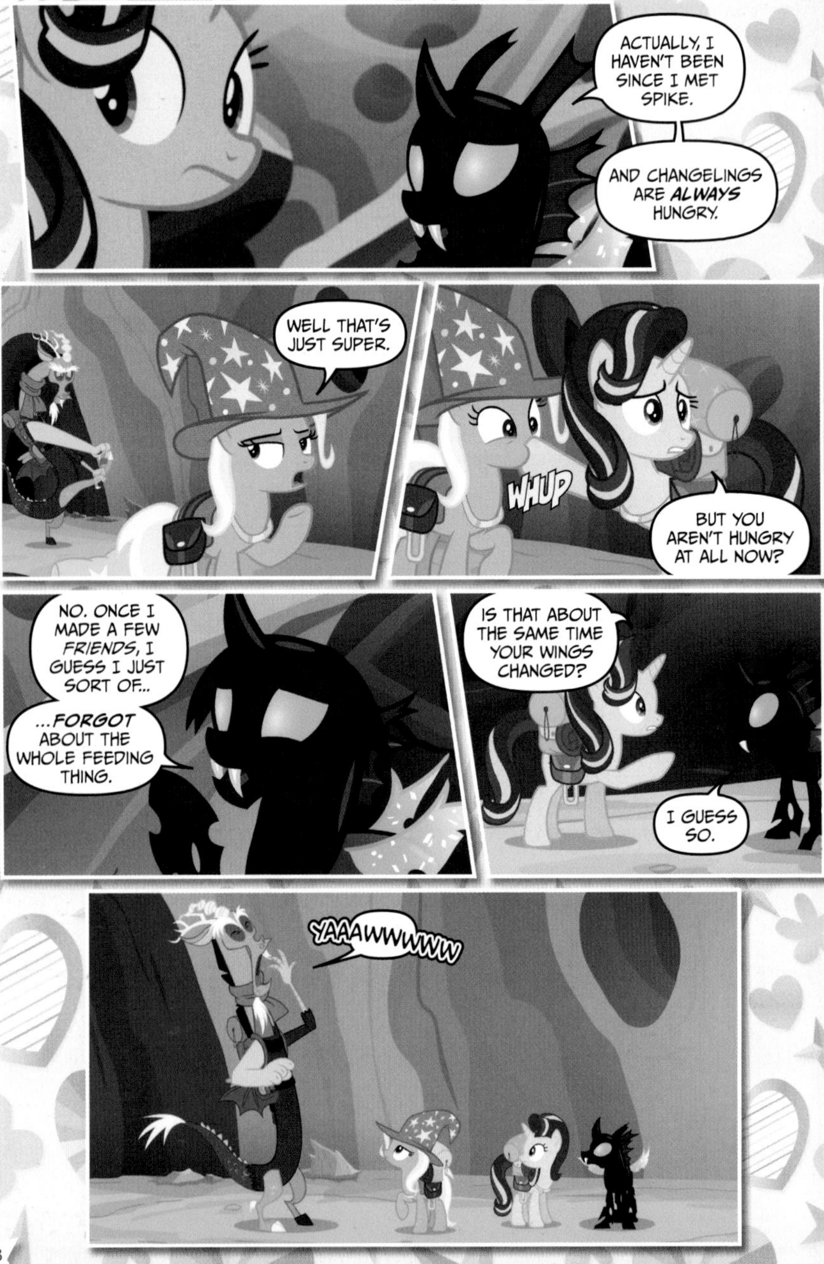
ACTUALLY, I HAVEN'T BEEN SINCE I MET SPIKE.
AND CHANGELINGS ARE *ALWAYS* HUNGRY.
WELL THAT'S JUST SUPER.
WHUP
BUT YOU AREN'T HUNGRY AT ALL NOW?
NO. ONCE I MADE A FEW *FRIENDS*, I GUESS I JUST SORT OF...
...*FORGOT* ABOUT THE WHOLE FEEDING THING.
IS THAT ABOUT THE SAME TIME YOUR WINGS CHANGED?
I GUESS SO.
YAAAWWWWW

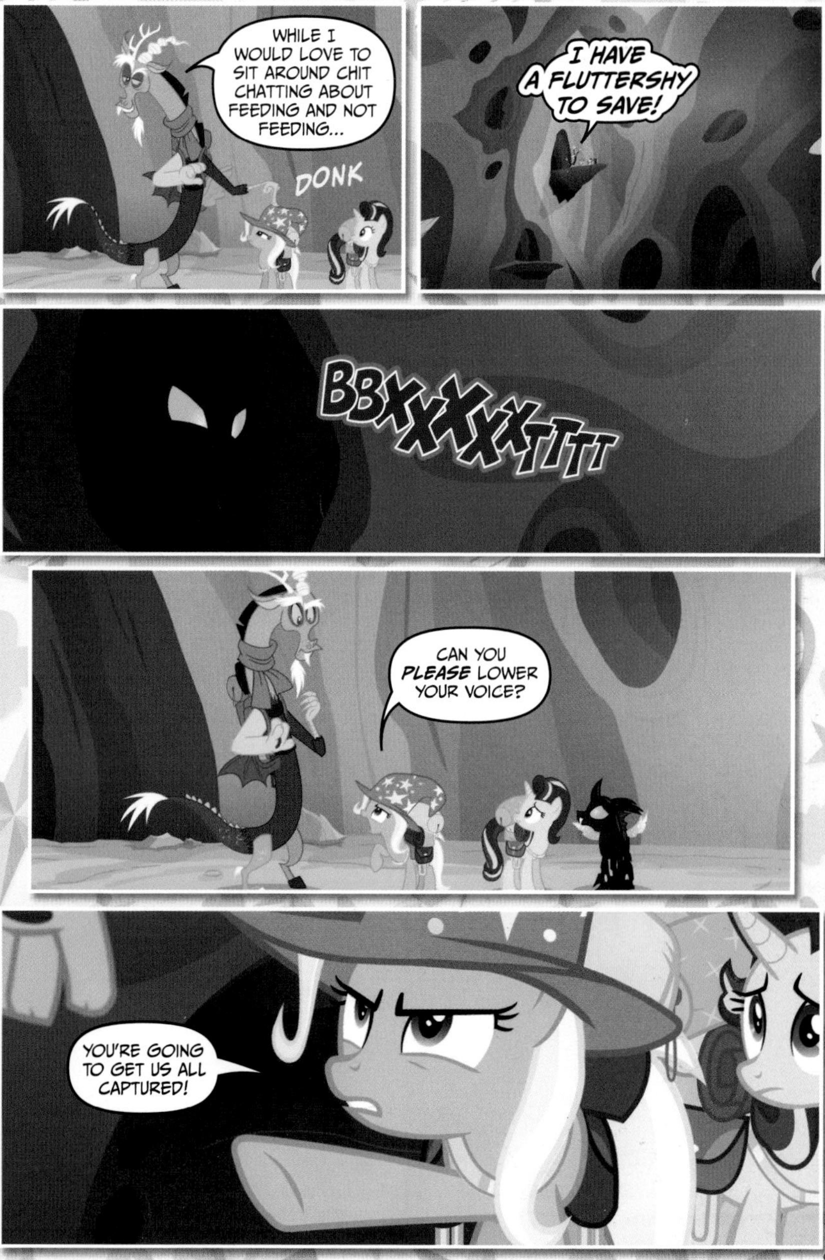
WHILE I WOULD LOVE TO SIT AROUND CHIT CHATTING ABOUT FEEDING AND NOT FEEDING...
DONK
I HAVE A FLUTTERSHY TO SAVE!
BBXXXXXTTTT
CAN YOU PLEASE LOWER YOUR VOICE?
YOU'RE GOING TO GET US ALL CAPTURED!

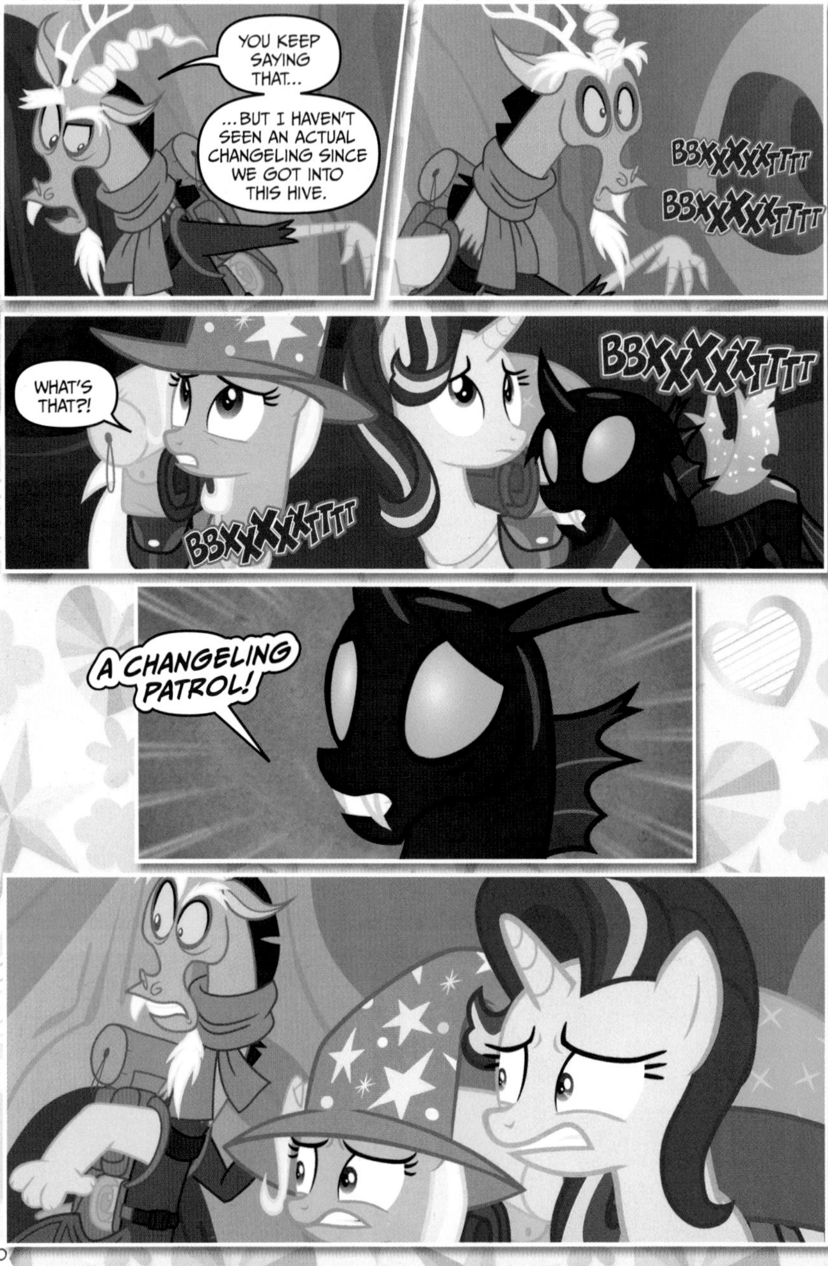
YOU KEEP SAYING THAT...
...BUT I HAVEN'T SEEN AN ACTUAL CHANGELING SINCE WE GOT INTO THIS HIVE.
BBXXXXXTTTT
BBXXXXXTTTT
WHAT'S THAT?!
BBXXXXXTTTT
BBXXXXXTTTT
A CHANGELING PATROL!

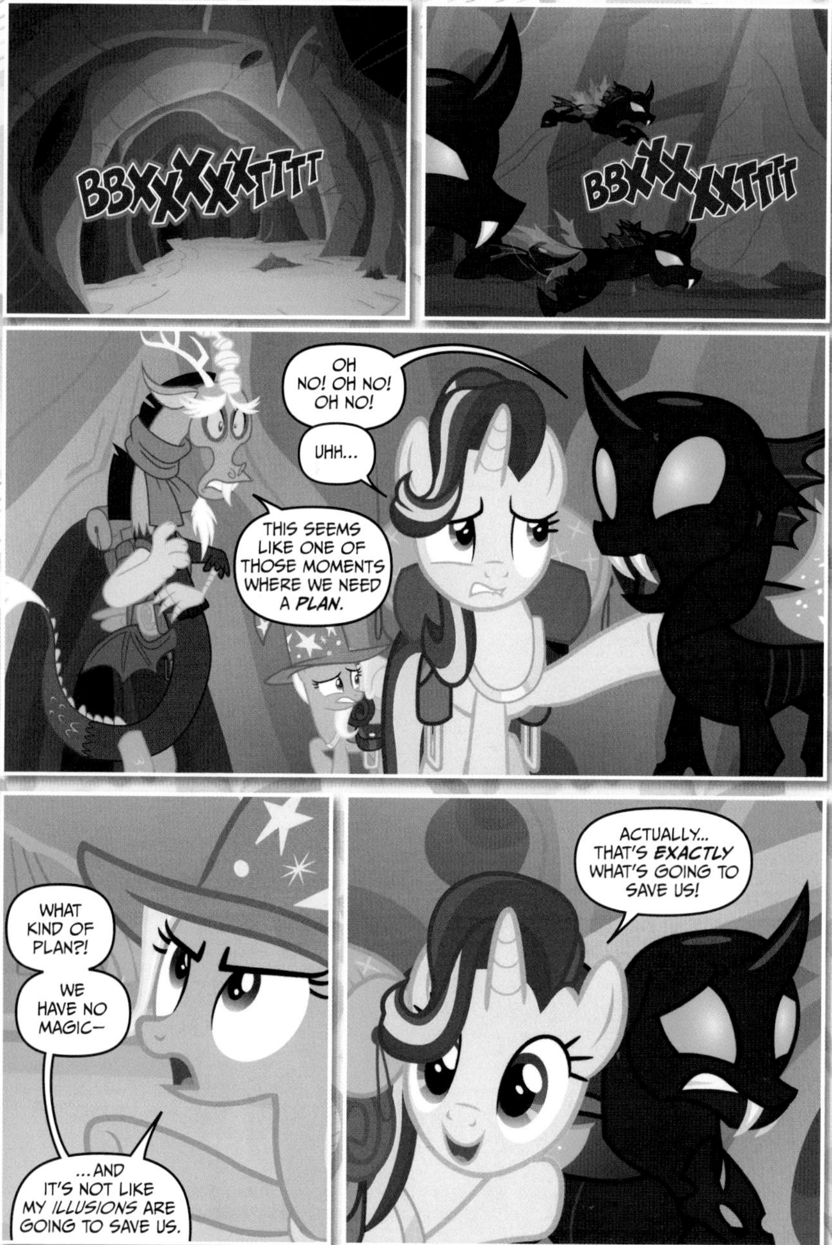
BBXXXXXTTTT
BBXXXXXTTTT
OH NO! OH NO! OH NO!
UHH...
THIS SEEMS LIKE ONE OF THOSE MOMENTS WHERE WE NEED A *PLAN.*
WHAT KIND OF PLAN?!
WE HAVE NO MAGIC–
...AND IT'S NOT LIKE MY *ILLUSIONS* ARE GOING TO SAVE US.
ACTUALLY... THAT'S *EXACTLY* WHAT'S GOING TO SAVE US!

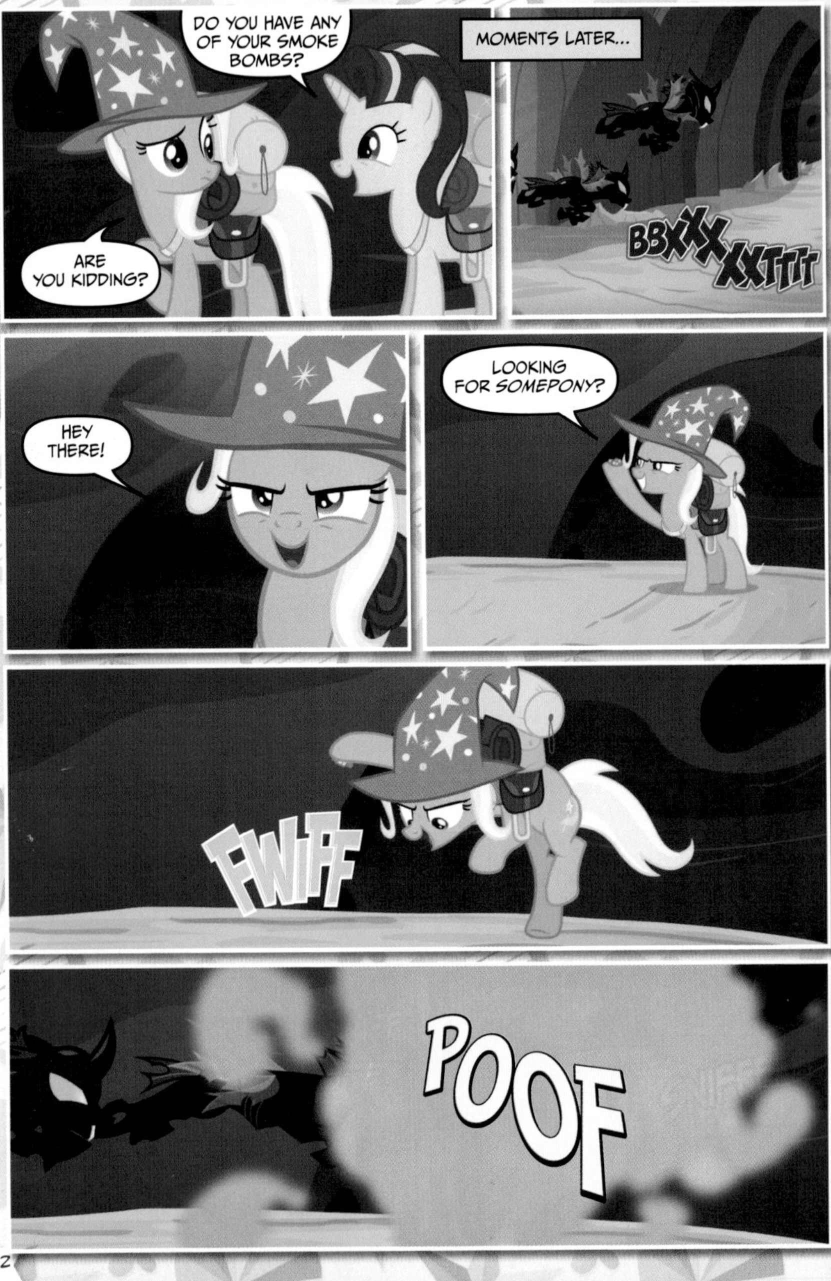
DO YOU HAVE ANY OF YOUR SMOKE BOMBS?
ARE YOU KIDDING?
MOMENTS LATER...
BBXXXXXTTTT
HEY THERE!
LOOKING FOR SOMEPONY?
FWIFF
POOF

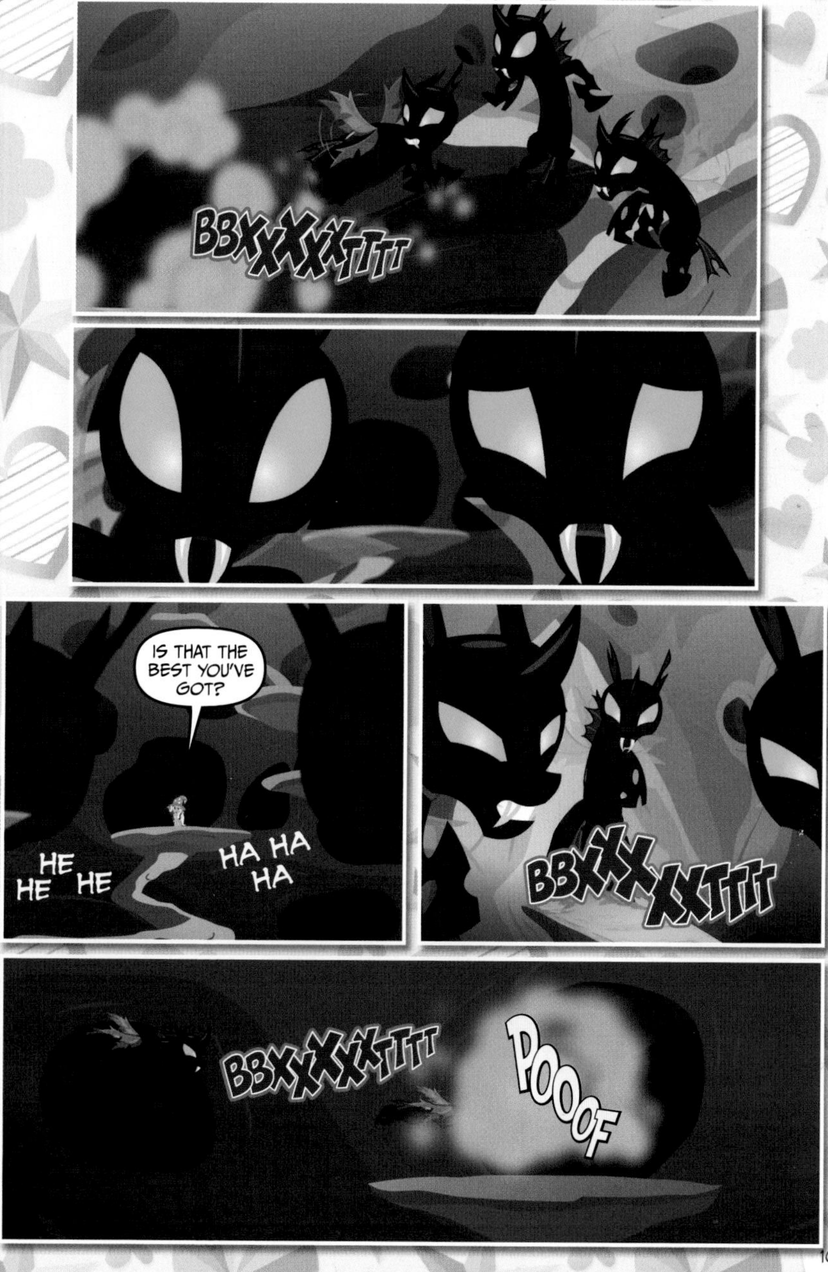
BBXXXXTTTT
IS THAT THE BEST YOU'VE GOT?
HE HE HE
HA HA HA
BBXXXXTTTT
BBXXXXTTTT
POOOF

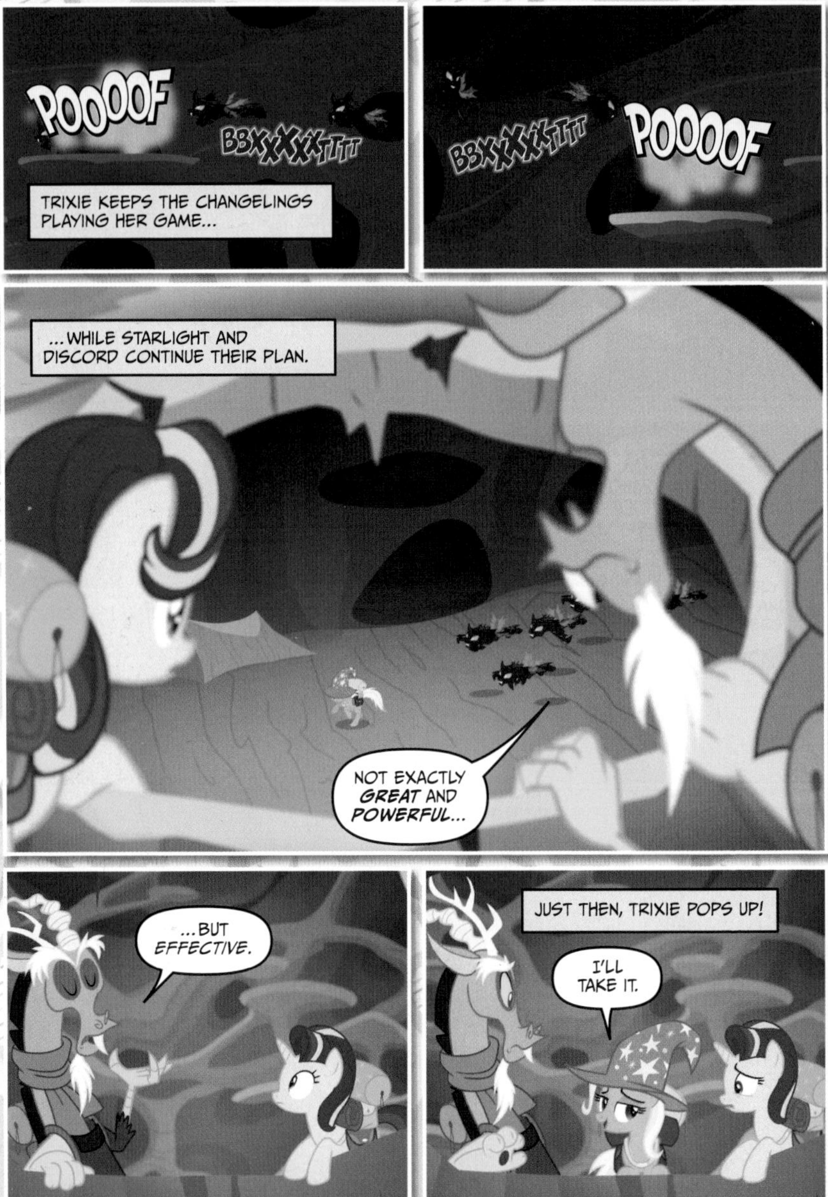
POOOOF
BBXXXXXTTTT
TRIXIE KEEPS THE CHANGELINGS PLAYING HER GAME...
BBXXXXXTTTT
POOOOF
...WHILE STARLIGHT AND DISCORD CONTINUE THEIR PLAN.
NOT EXACTLY GREAT AND POWERFUL...
...BUT EFFECTIVE.
JUST THEN, TRIXIE POPS UP!
I'LL TAKE IT.

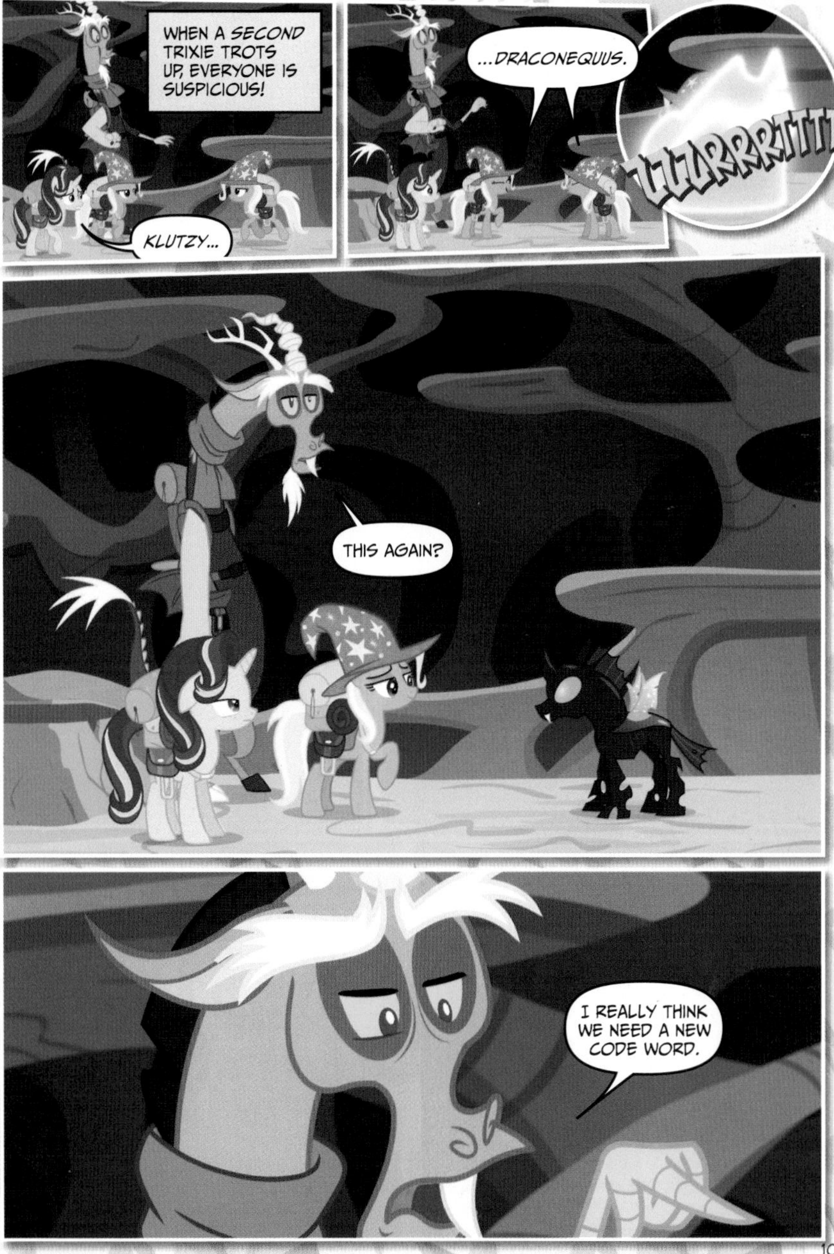
WHEN A SECOND TRIXIE TROTS UP, EVERYONE IS SUSPICIOUS!
KLUTZY...
...DRACONEQUUS.
ZZZARRRITTTT
THIS AGAIN?
I REALLY THINK WE NEED A NEW CODE WORD.

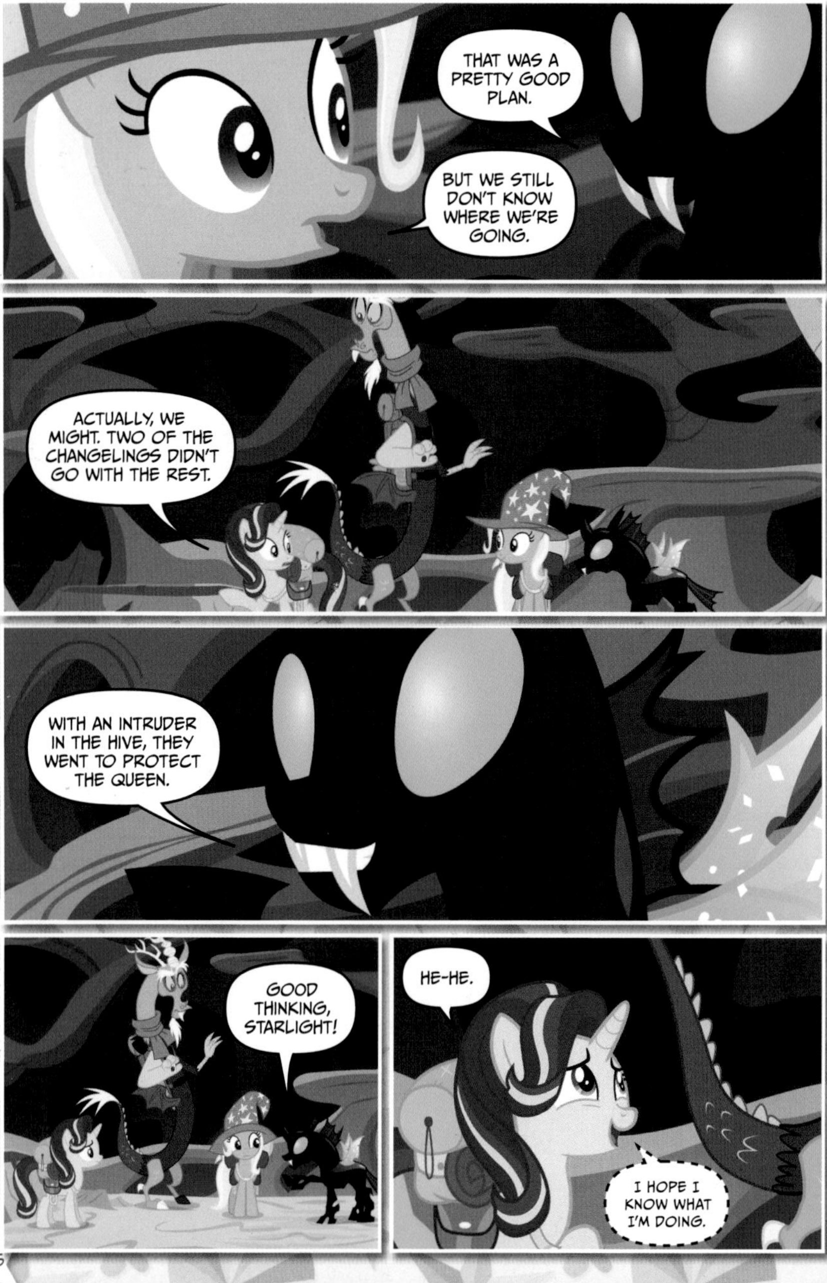
THAT WAS A PRETTY GOOD PLAN.
BUT WE STILL DON'T KNOW WHERE WE'RE GOING.
ACTUALLY, WE MIGHT. TWO OF THE CHANGELINGS DIDN'T GO WITH THE REST.
WITH AN INTRUDER IN THE HIVE, THEY WENT TO PROTECT THE QUEEN.
GOOD THINKING, STARLIGHT!
HE-HE.
I HOPE I KNOW WHAT I'M DOING.

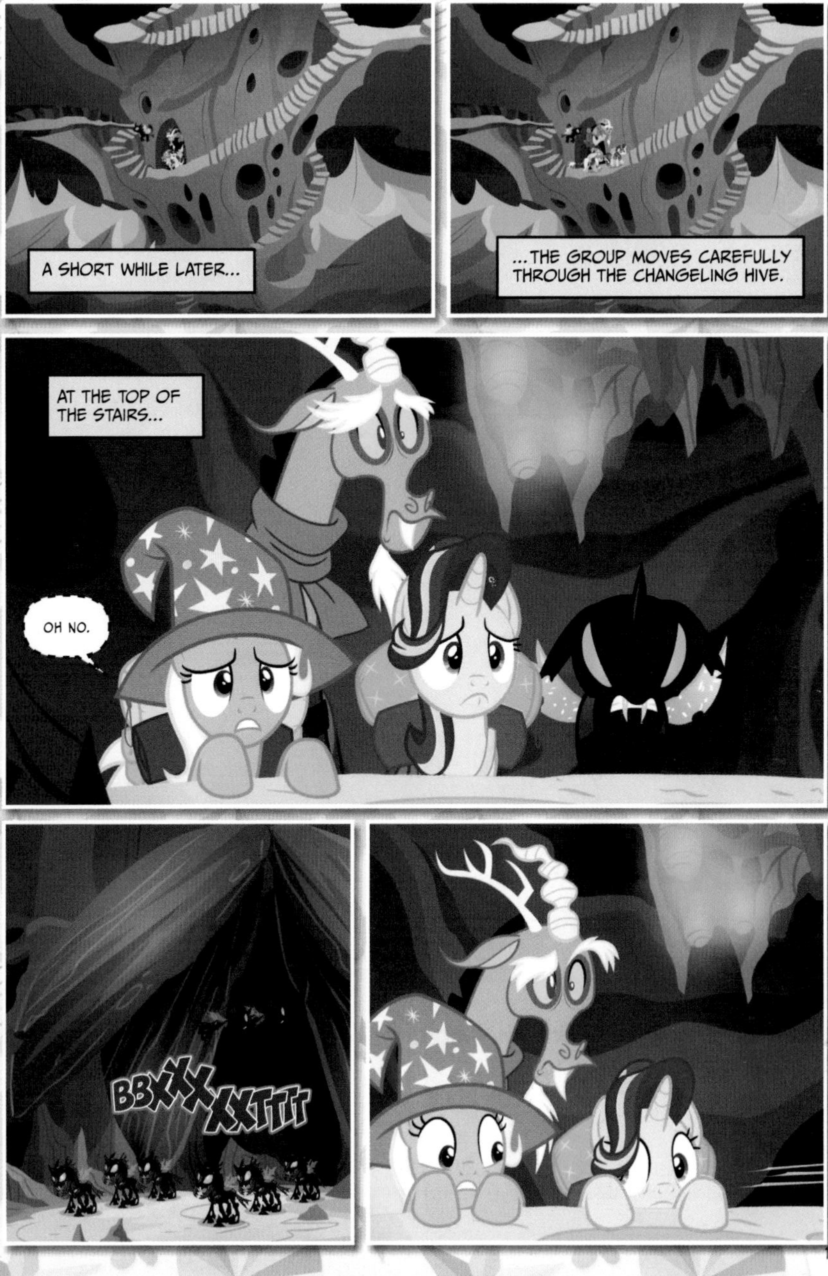
A SHORT WHILE LATER...
...THE GROUP MOVES CAREFULLY THROUGH THE CHANGELING HIVE.
AT THE TOP OF THE STAIRS...
OH NO.
BBXXXXXTTTT

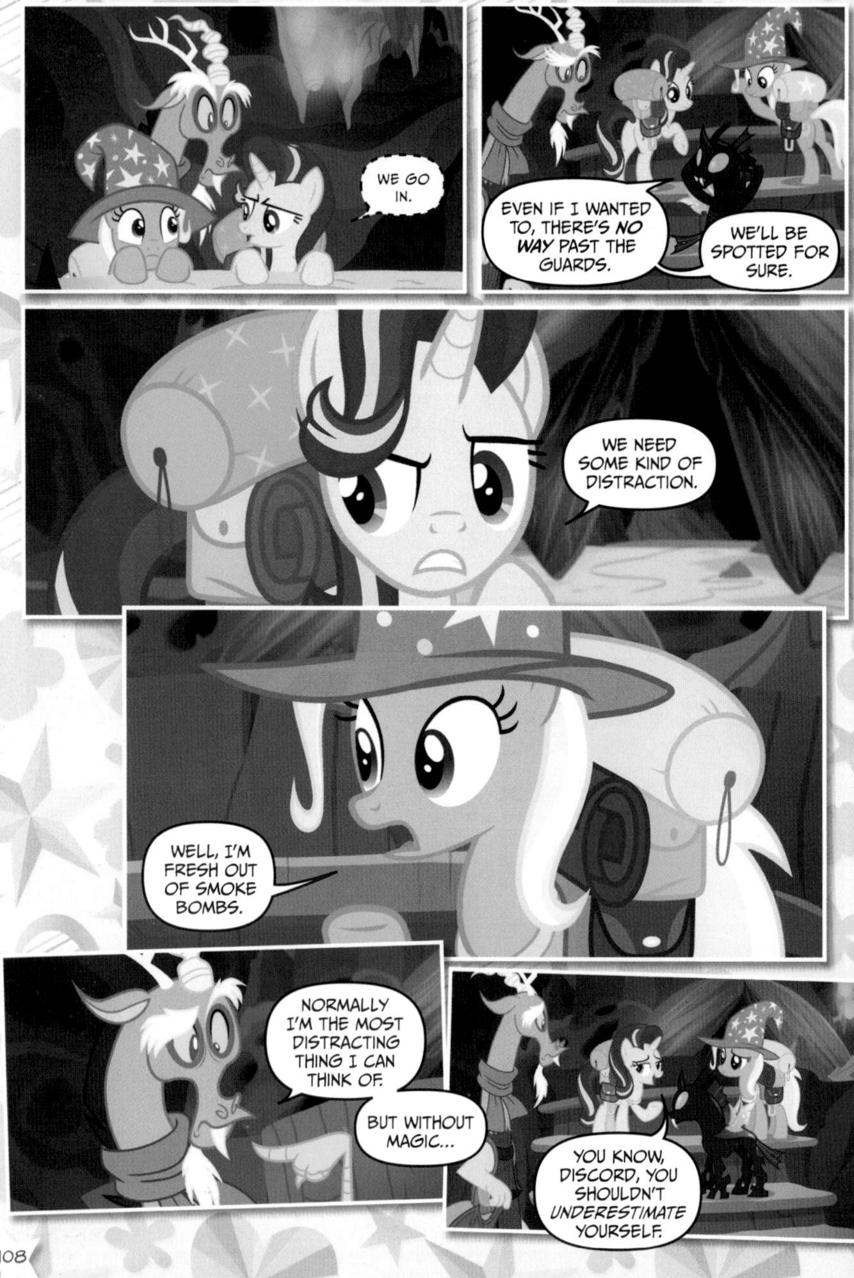
WE GO IN.
EVEN IF I WANTED TO, THERE'S NO WAY PAST THE GUARDS.
WE'LL BE SPOTTED FOR SURE.
WE NEED SOME KIND OF DISTRACTION.
WELL, I'M FRESH OUT OF SMOKE BOMBS.
NORMALLY I'M THE MOST DISTRACTING THING I CAN THINK OF.
BUT WITHOUT MAGIC...
YOU KNOW, DISCORD, YOU SHOULDN'T UNDERESTIMATE YOURSELF.

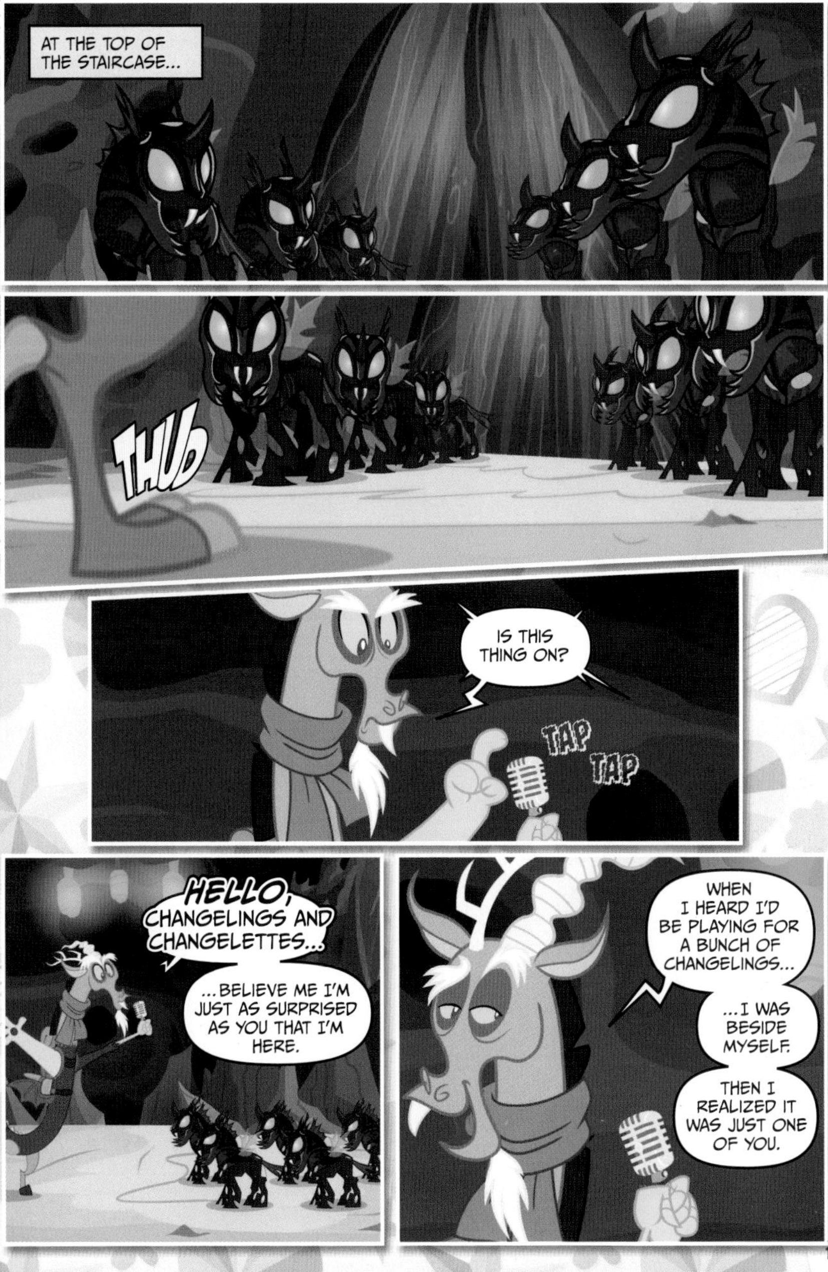
AT THE TOP OF THE STAIRCASE...
THUD
IS THIS THING ON?
TAP
TAP
HELLO, CHANGELINGS AND CHANGELETTES...
...BELIEVE ME I'M JUST AS SURPRISED AS YOU THAT I'M HERE.
WHEN I HEARD I'D BE PLAYING FOR A BUNCH OF CHANGELINGS...
...I WAS BESIDE MYSELF.
THEN I REALIZED IT WAS JUST ONE OF YOU.

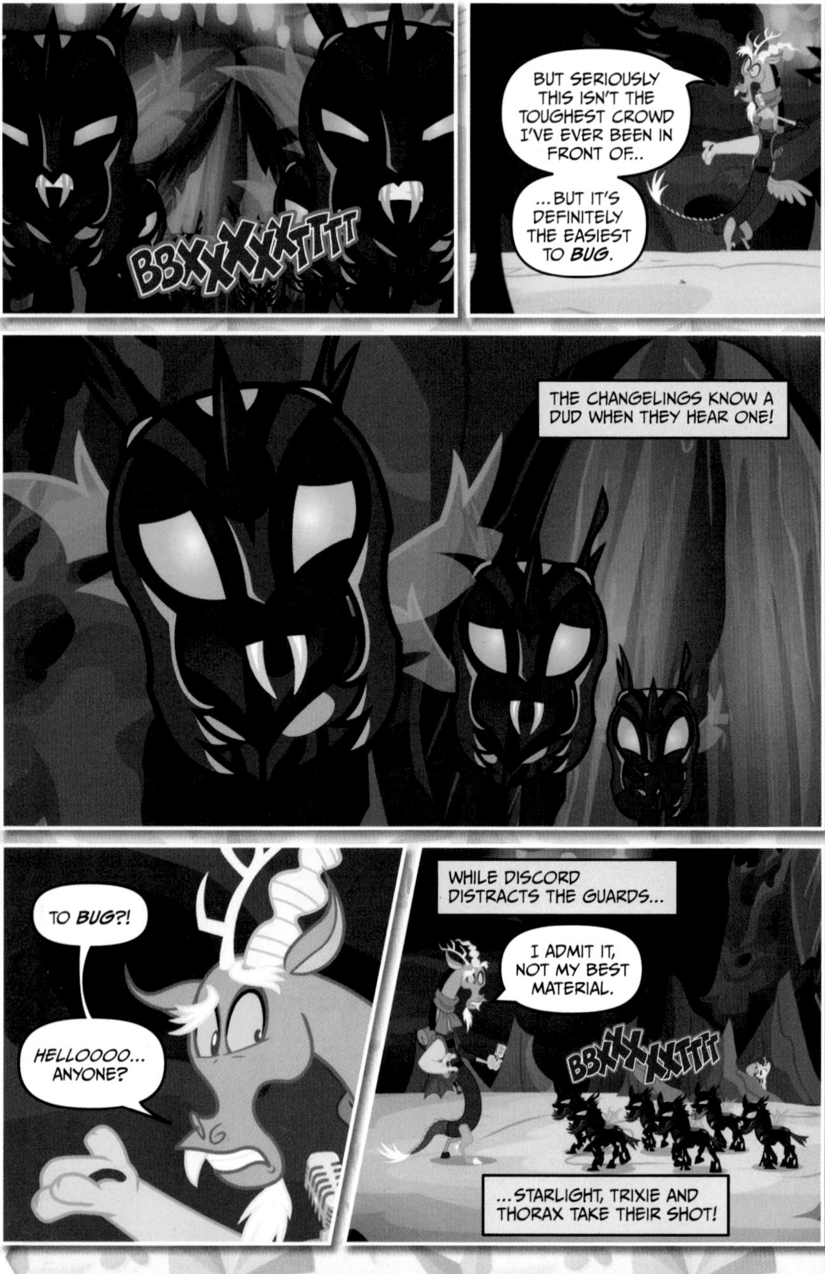
BBXXXXTTTT
BUT SERIOUSLY THIS ISN'T THE TOUGHEST CROWD I'VE EVER BEEN IN FRONT OF...
...BUT IT'S DEFINITELY THE EASIEST TO BUG.
THE CHANGELINGS KNOW A DUD WHEN THEY HEAR ONE!
TO BUG?!
HELLOOOO... ANYONE?
WHILE DISCORD DISTRACTS THE GUARDS...
I ADMIT IT, NOT MY BEST MATERIAL.
BBXXXXTTTT
...STARLIGHT, TRIXIE AND THORAX TAKE THEIR SHOT!

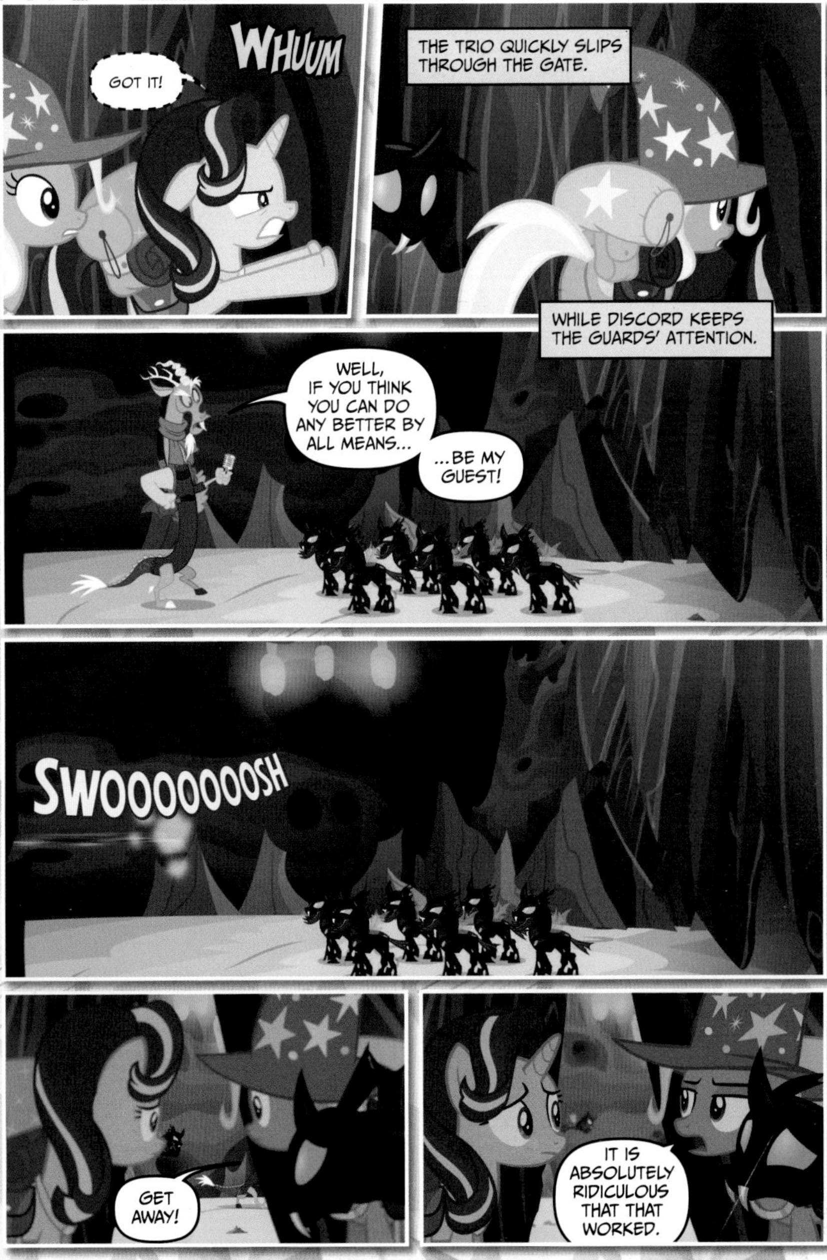
WHUUM
GOT IT!
THE TRIO QUICKLY SLIPS THROUGH THE GATE.
WHILE DISCORD KEEPS THE GUARDS' ATTENTION.
WELL, IF YOU THINK YOU CAN DO ANY BETTER BY ALL MEANS...
...BE MY GUEST!
SWOOOOOOOSH
GET AWAY!
IT IS ABSOLUTELY RIDICULOUS THAT THAT WORKED.

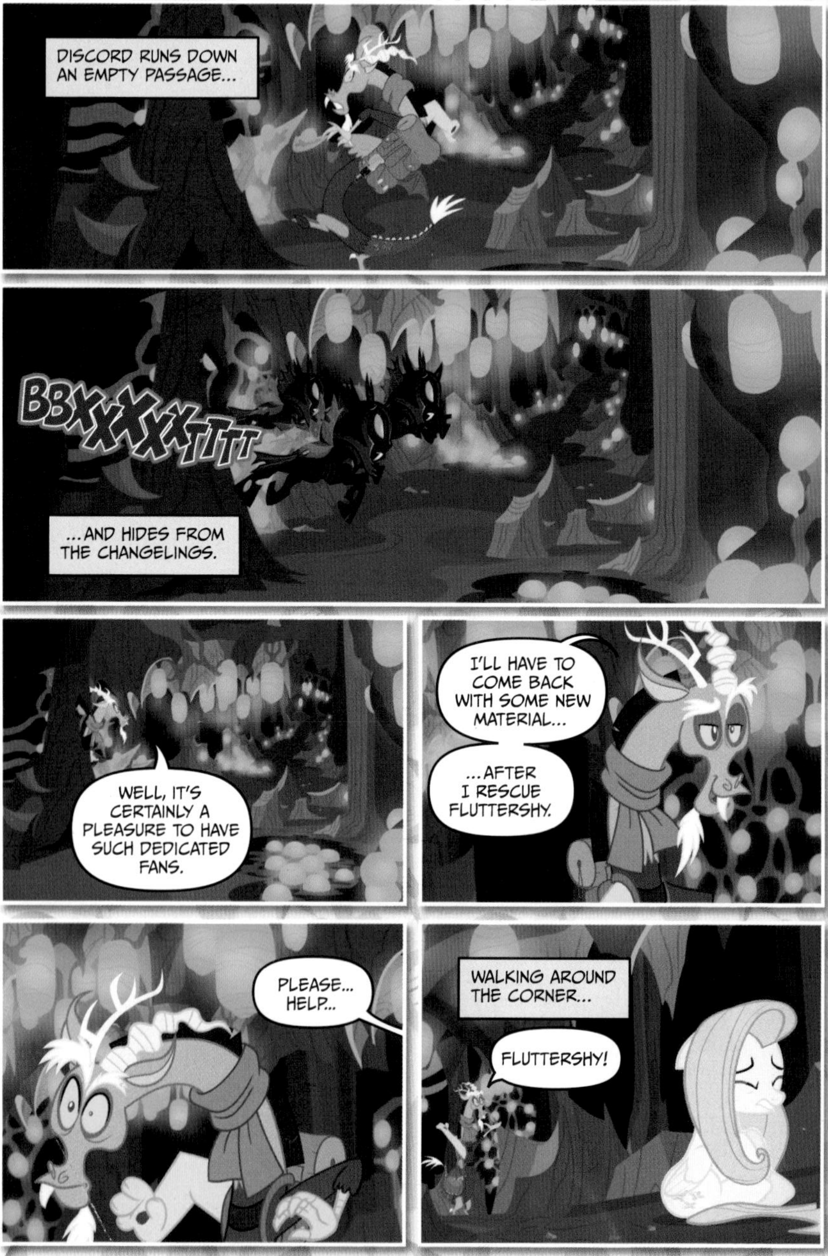
DISCORD RUNS DOWN AN EMPTY PASSAGE...
BBXXXXXTTTT
...AND HIDES FROM THE CHANGELINGS.
WELL, IT'S CERTAINLY A PLEASURE TO HAVE SUCH DEDICATED FANS.
I'LL HAVE TO COME BACK WITH SOME NEW MATERIAL...
...AFTER I RESCUE FLUTTERSHY.
PLEASE... HELP...
WALKING AROUND THE CORNER...
FLUTTERSHY!

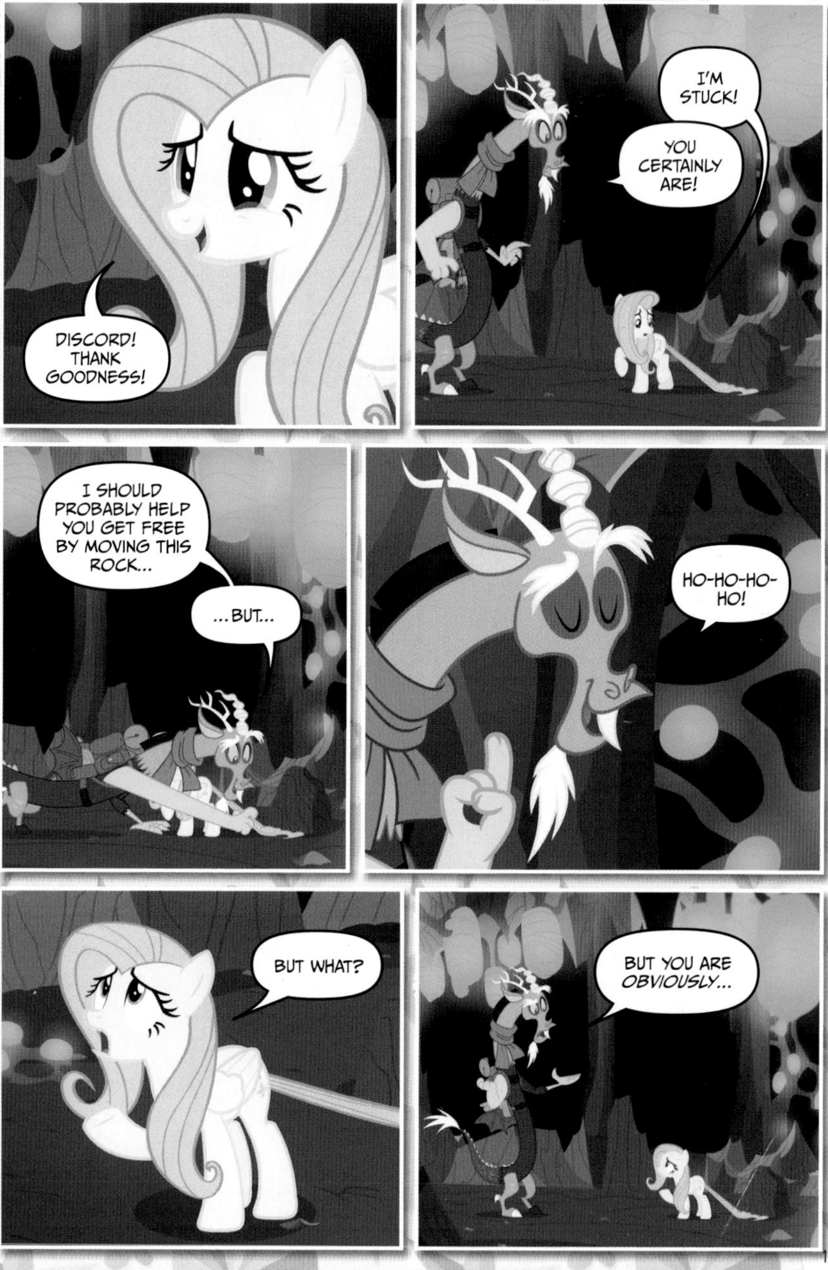
DISCORD! THANK GOODNESS!
I'M STUCK!
YOU CERTAINLY ARE!
I SHOULD PROBABLY HELP YOU GET FREE BY MOVING THIS ROCK...
...BUT...
HO-HO-HO-HO!
BUT WHAT?
BUT YOU ARE *OBVIOUSLY*...

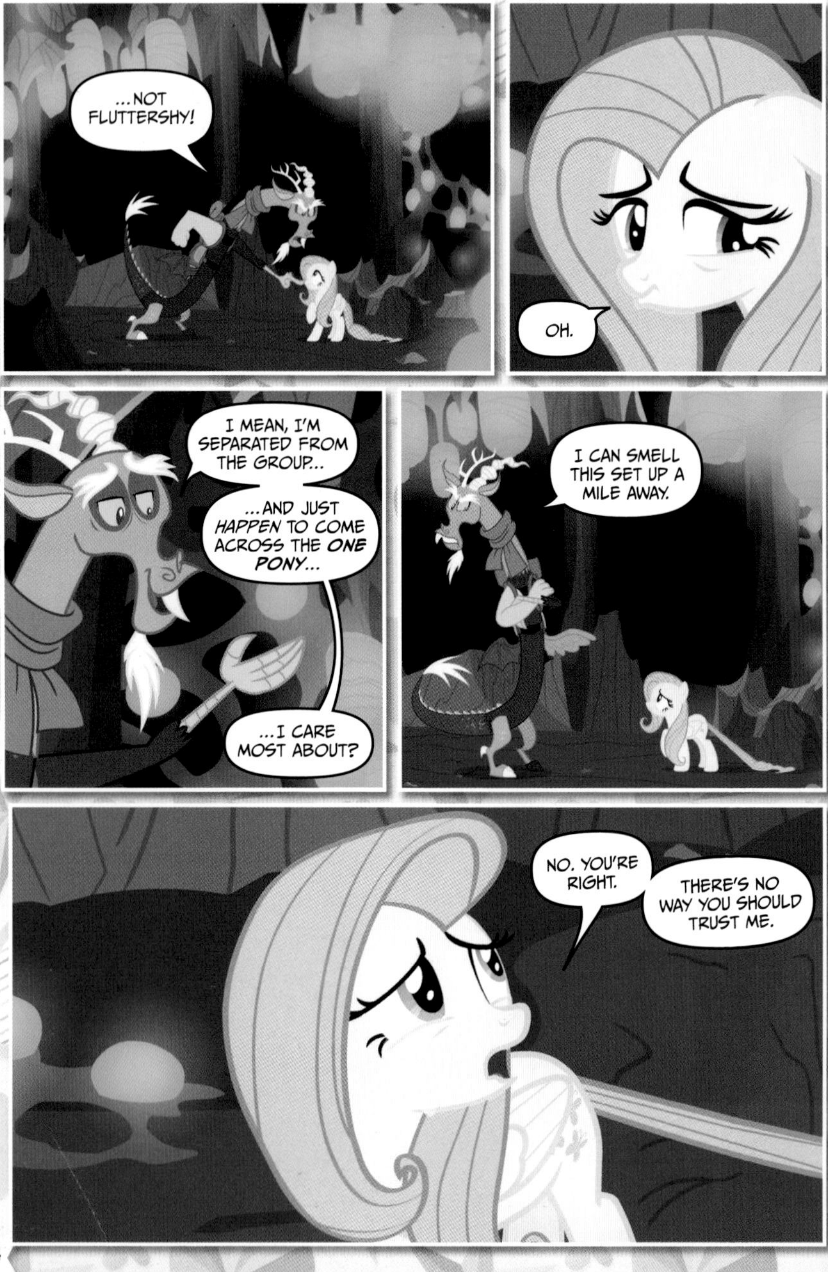
...NOT FLUTTERSHY!
OH.
I MEAN, I'M SEPARATED FROM THE GROUP...
...AND JUST *HAPPEN* TO COME ACROSS THE ***ONE PONY***...
...I CARE MOST ABOUT?
I CAN SMELL THIS SET UP A MILE AWAY.
NO. YOU'RE RIGHT.
THERE'S NO WAY YOU SHOULD TRUST ME.

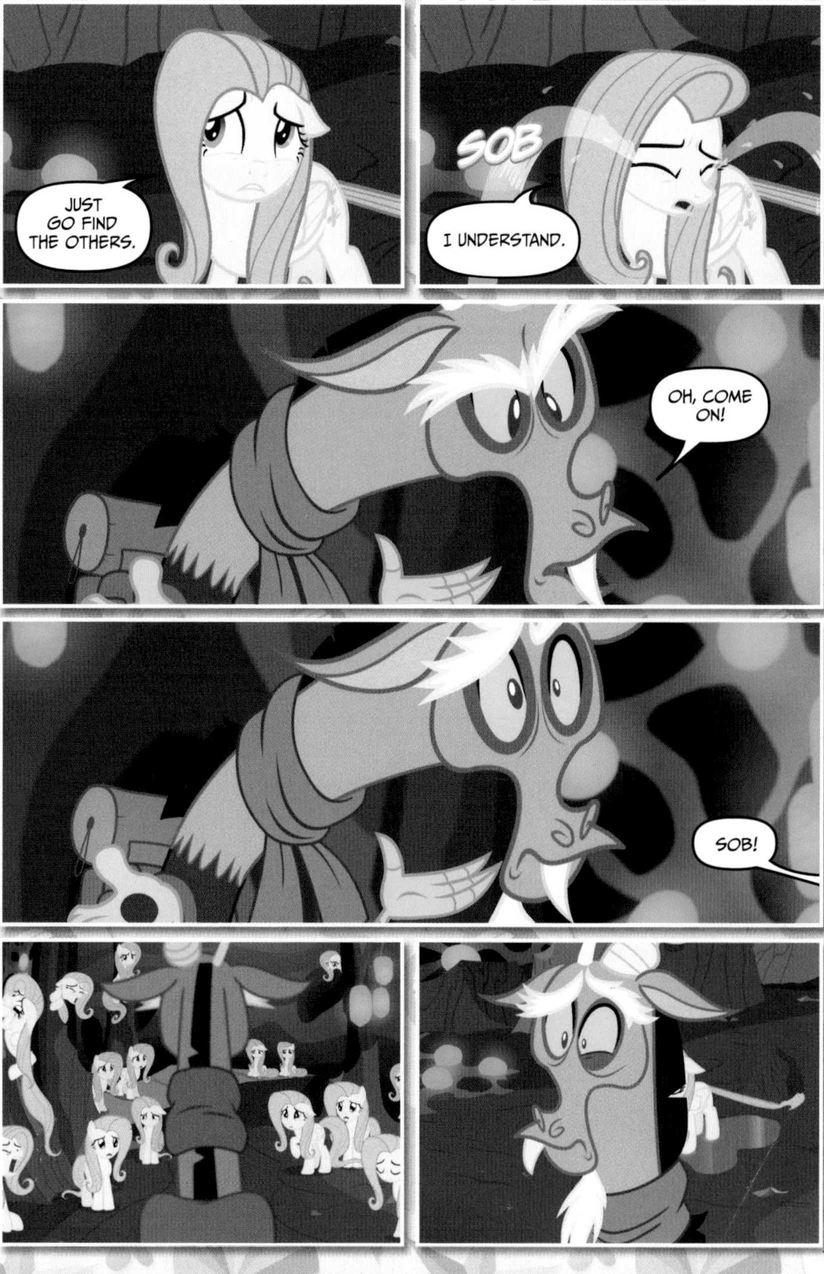
JUST GO FIND THE OTHERS.
SOB
I UNDERSTAND.
OH, COME ON!
SOB!

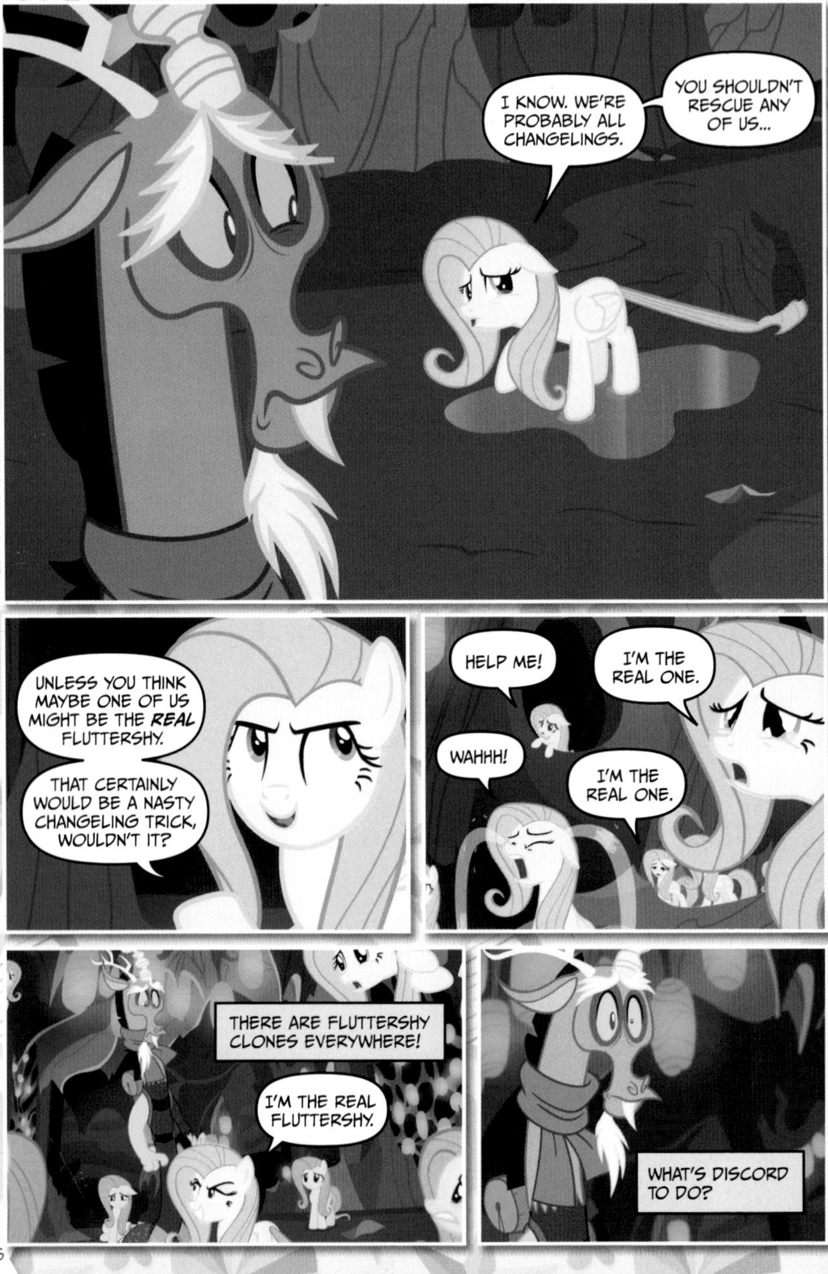

YOU SHOULDN'T RESCUE ANY OF US...
I KNOW. WE'RE PROBABLY ALL CHANGELINGS.
UNLESS YOU THINK MAYBE ONE OF US MIGHT BE THE *REAL* FLUTTERSHY.
THAT CERTAINLY WOULD BE A NASTY CHANGELING TRICK, WOULDN'T IT?
HELP ME!
I'M THE REAL ONE.
WAHHH!
I'M THE REAL ONE.
THERE ARE FLUTTERSHY CLONES EVERYWHERE!
I'M THE REAL FLUTTERSHY.
WHAT'S DISCORD TO DO?

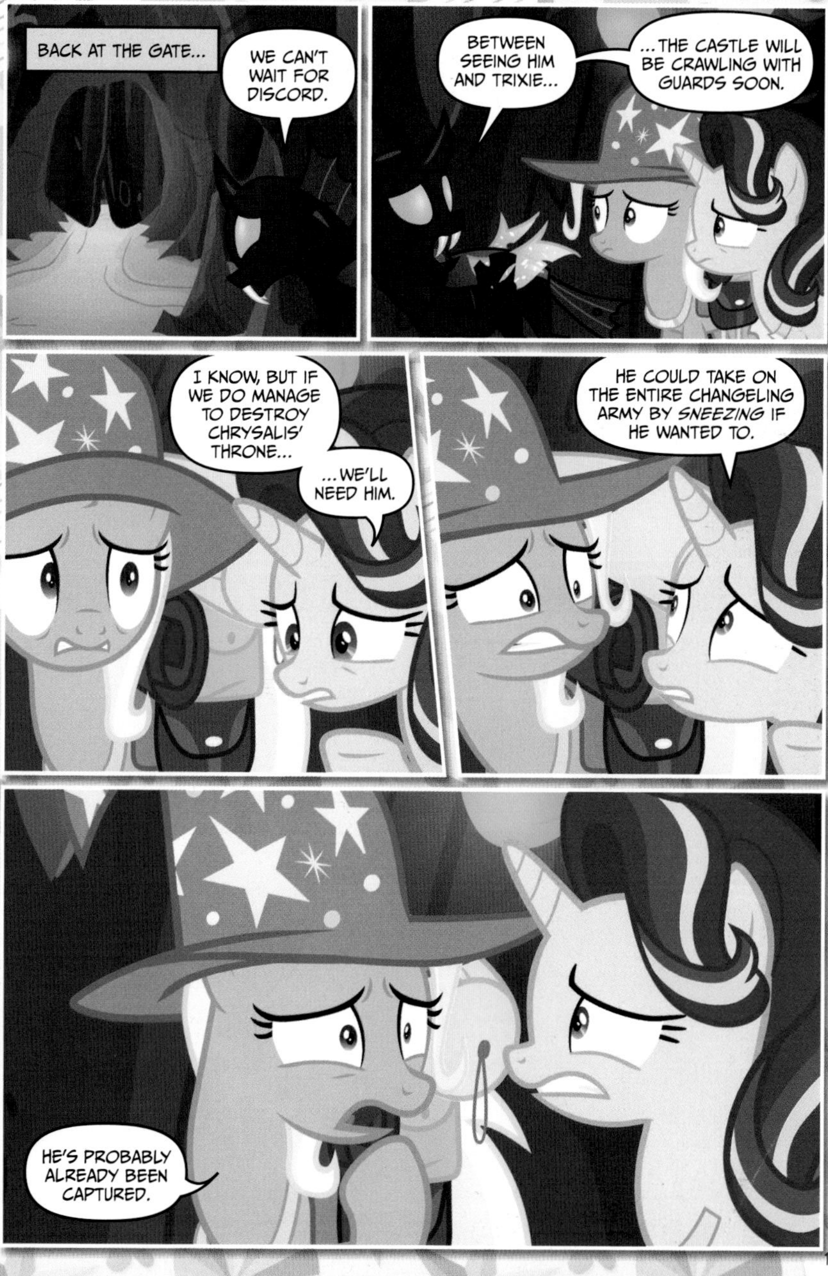
BACK AT THE GATE...
WE CAN'T WAIT FOR DISCORD.
BETWEEN SEEING HIM AND TRIXIE...
...THE CASTLE WILL BE CRAWLING WITH GUARDS SOON.
I KNOW, BUT IF WE DO MANAGE TO DESTROY CHRYSALIS' THRONE...
...WE'LL NEED HIM.
HE COULD TAKE ON THE ENTIRE CHANGELING ARMY BY *SNEEZING* IF HE WANTED TO.
HE'S PROBABLY ALREADY BEEN CAPTURED.

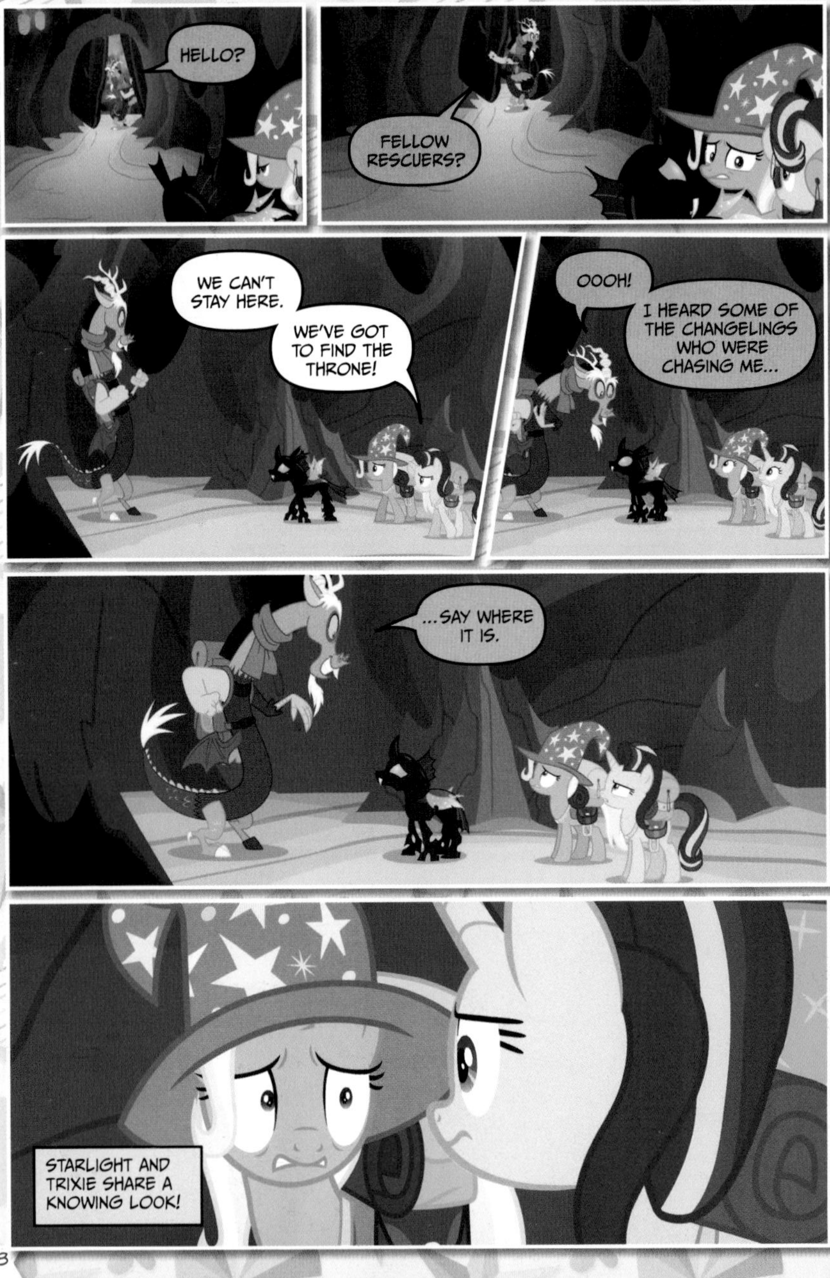

HELLO?
FELLOW RESCUERS?
WE CAN'T STAY HERE.
WE'VE GOT TO FIND THE THRONE!
OOOH!
I HEARD SOME OF THE CHANGELINGS WHO WERE CHASING ME...
...SAY WHERE IT IS.
STARLIGHT AND TRIXIE SHARE A KNOWING LOOK!

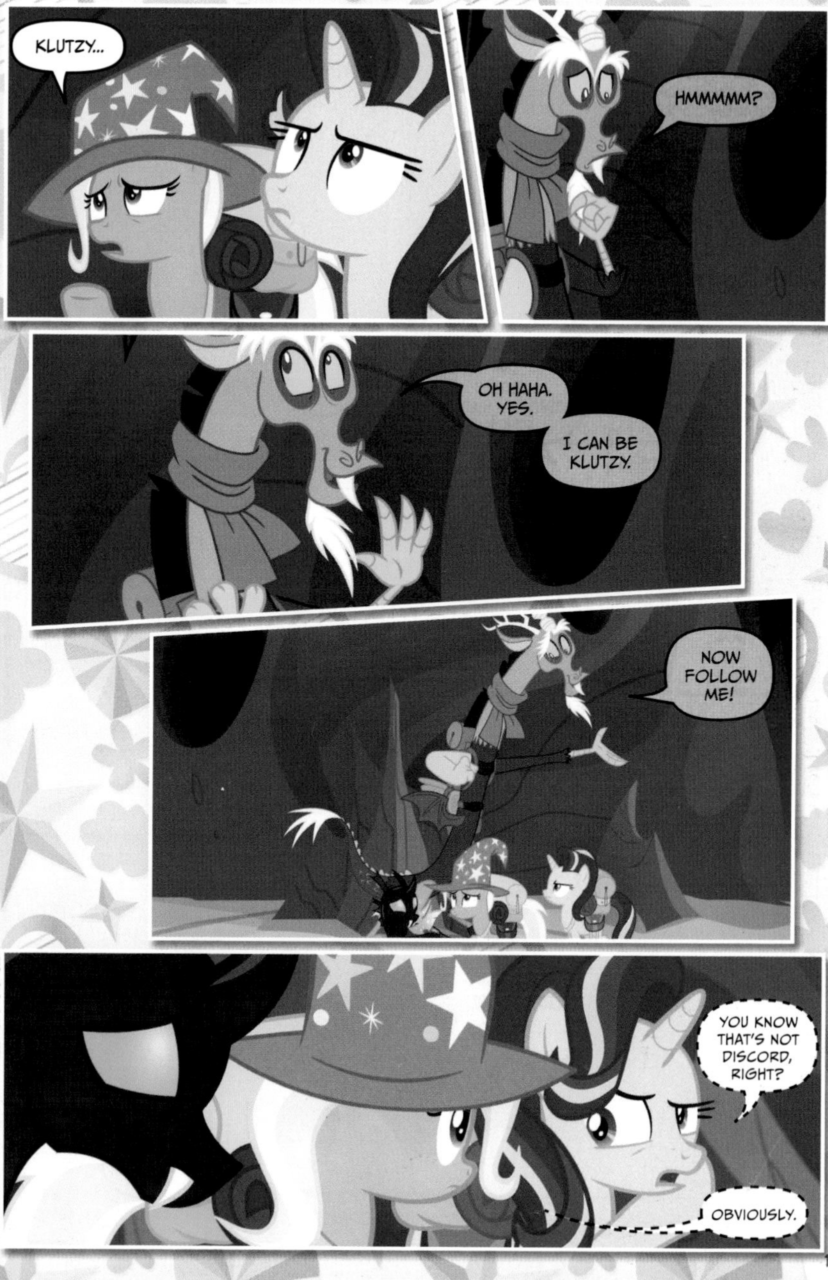
KLUTZY...
HMMMMM?
OH HAHA. YES.
I CAN BE KLUTZY.
NOW FOLLOW ME!
YOU KNOW THAT'S NOT DISCORD, RIGHT?
OBVIOUSLY.

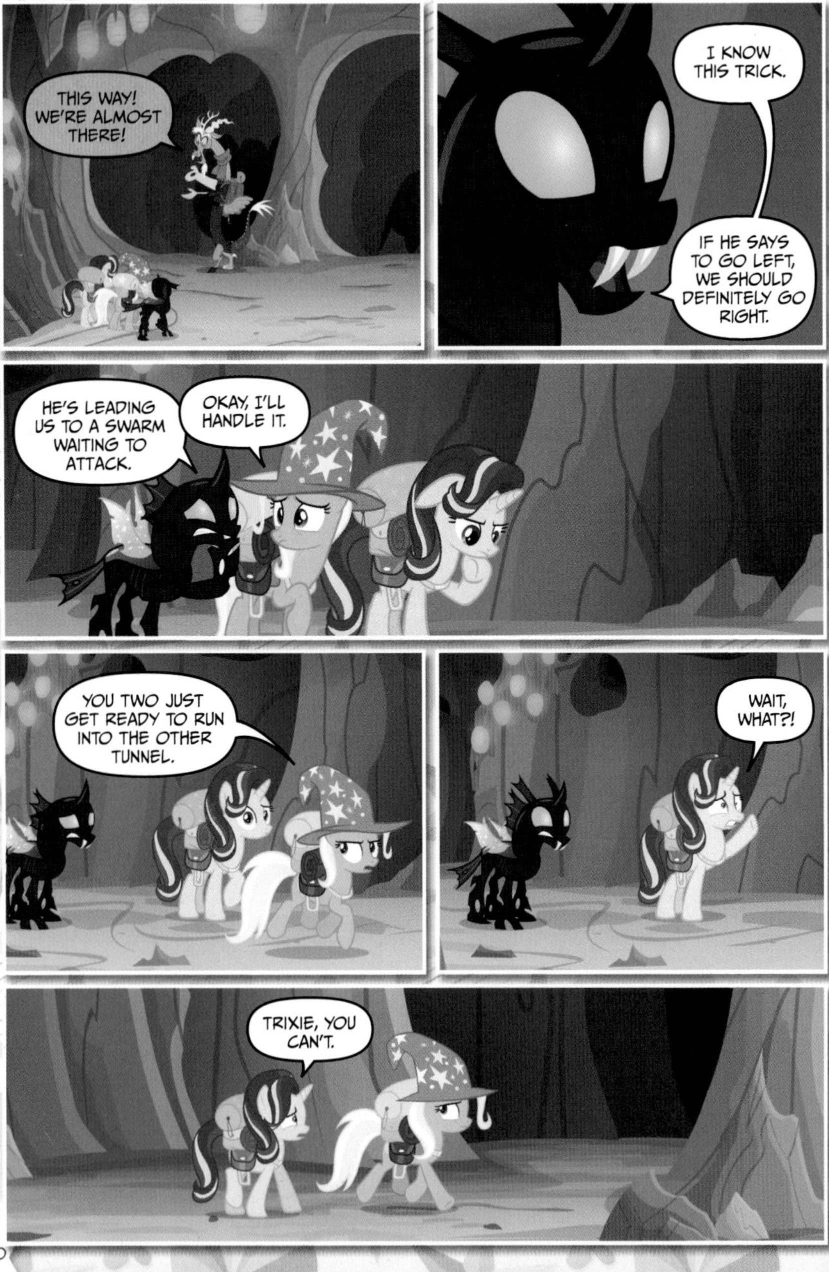
THIS WAY! WE'RE ALMOST THERE!
I KNOW THIS TRICK.
IF HE SAYS TO GO LEFT, WE SHOULD DEFINITELY GO RIGHT.
HE'S LEADING US TO A SWARM WAITING TO ATTACK.
OKAY, I'LL HANDLE IT.
YOU TWO JUST GET READY TO RUN INTO THE OTHER TUNNEL.
WAIT, WHAT?!
TRIXIE, YOU CAN'T.

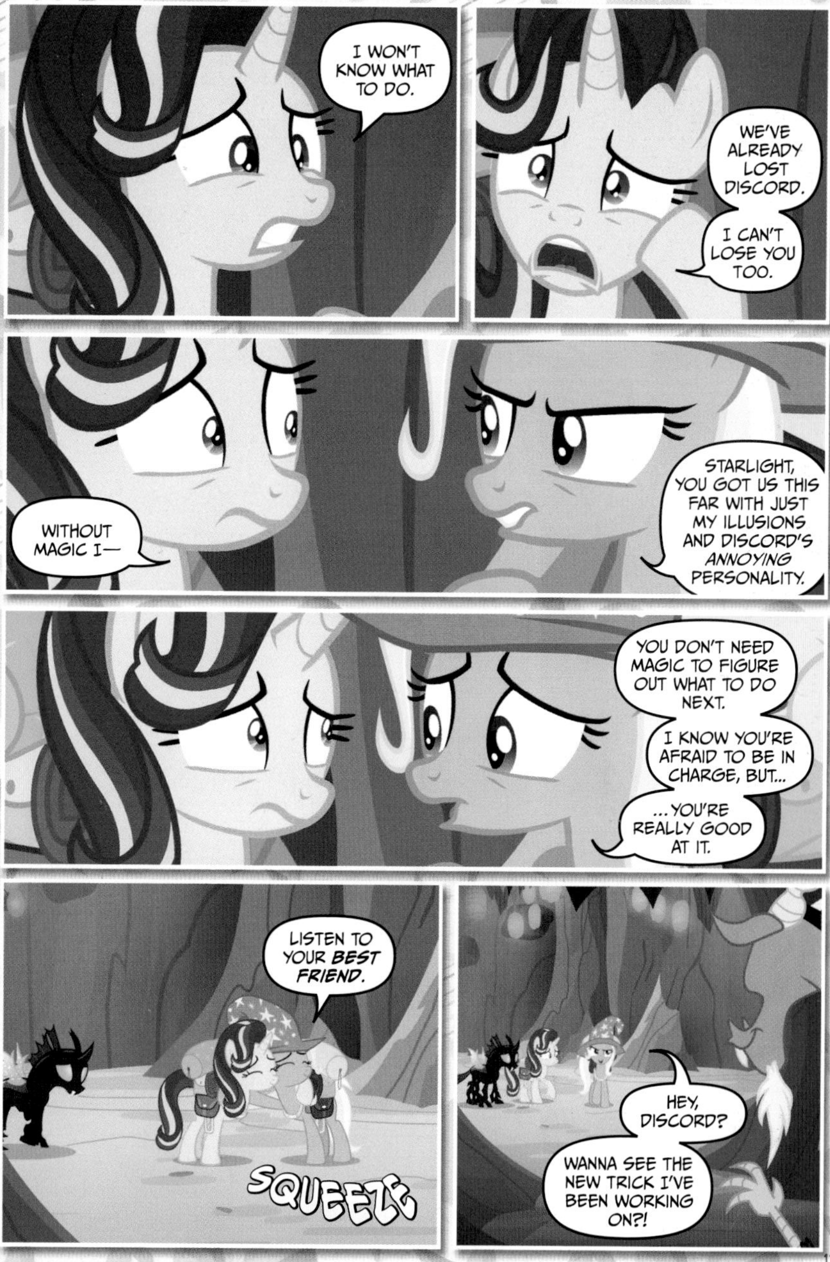
I WON'T KNOW WHAT TO DO.
WE'VE ALREADY LOST DISCORD.
I CAN'T LOSE YOU TOO.
WITHOUT MAGIC I—
STARLIGHT, YOU GOT US THIS FAR WITH JUST MY ILLUSIONS AND DISCORD'S *ANNOYING* PERSONALITY.
YOU DON'T NEED MAGIC TO FIGURE OUT WHAT TO DO NEXT.
I KNOW YOU'RE AFRAID TO BE IN CHARGE, BUT...
...YOU'RE REALLY GOOD AT IT.
LISTEN TO YOUR ***BEST FRIEND***.
SQUEEZE
HEY, DISCORD?
WANNA SEE THE NEW TRICK I'VE BEEN WORKING ON?!

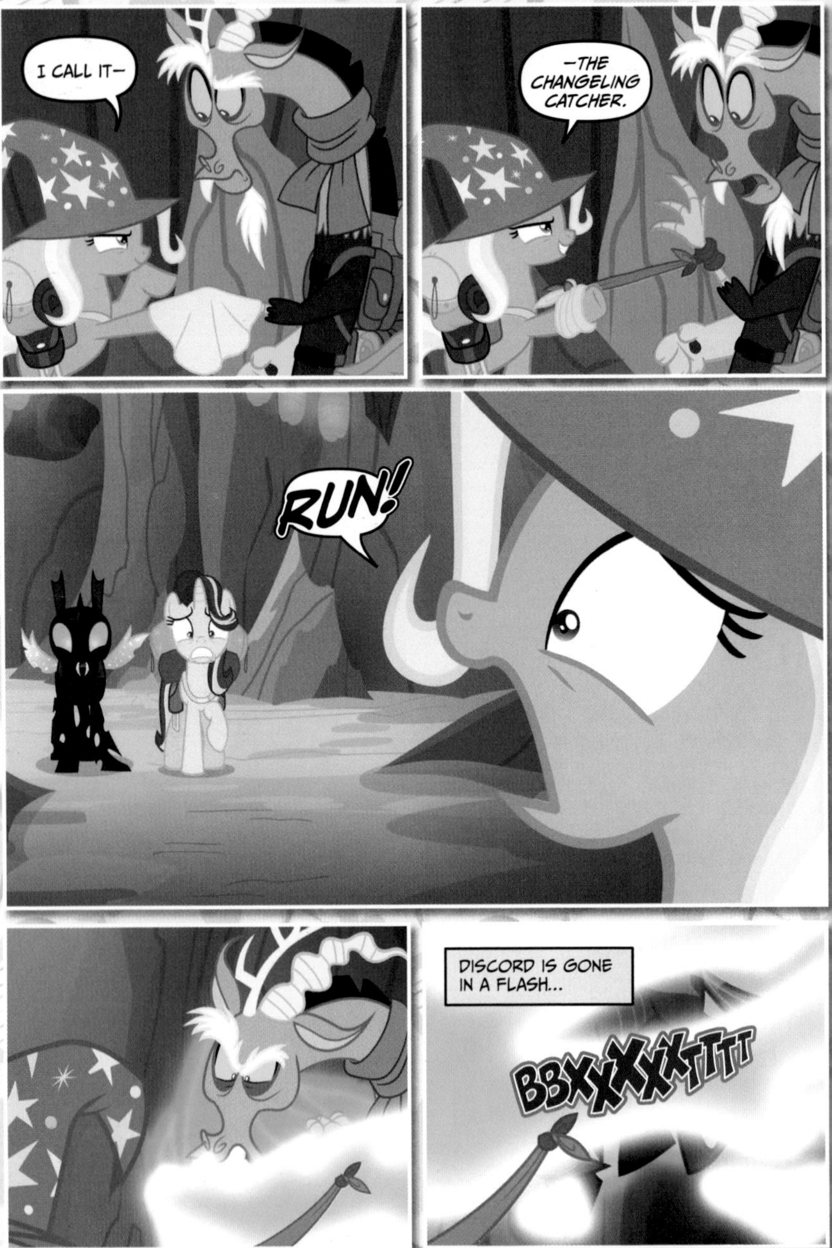
I CALL IT—
—THE CHANGELING CATCHER.
RUN!
DISCORD IS GONE IN A FLASH...
BBXXXXXTTTT

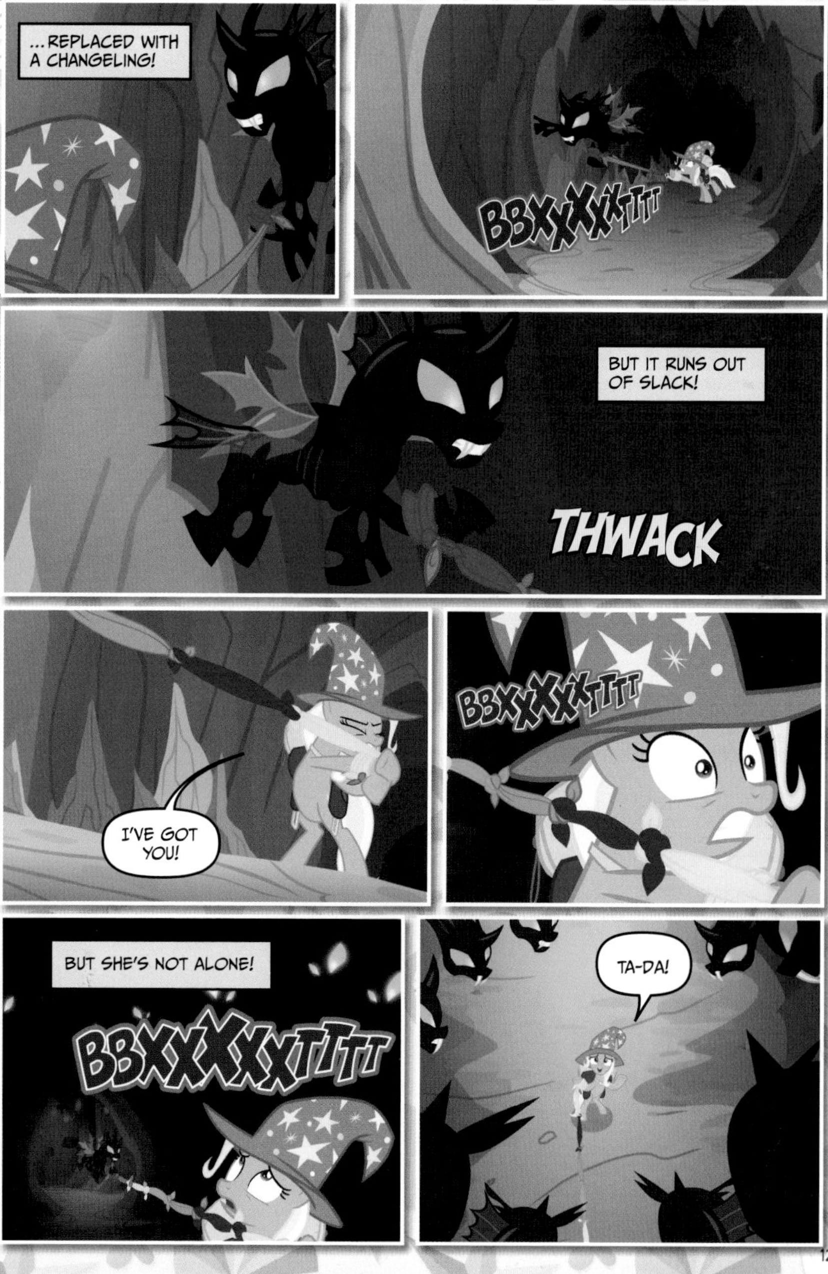

...REPLACED WITH A CHANGELING!
BBXXXXXTTTT
BUT IT RUNS OUT OF SLACK!
THWACK
I'VE GOT YOU!
BBXXXXXTTTT
BUT SHE'S NOT ALONE!
BBXXXXXTTTT
TA-DA!

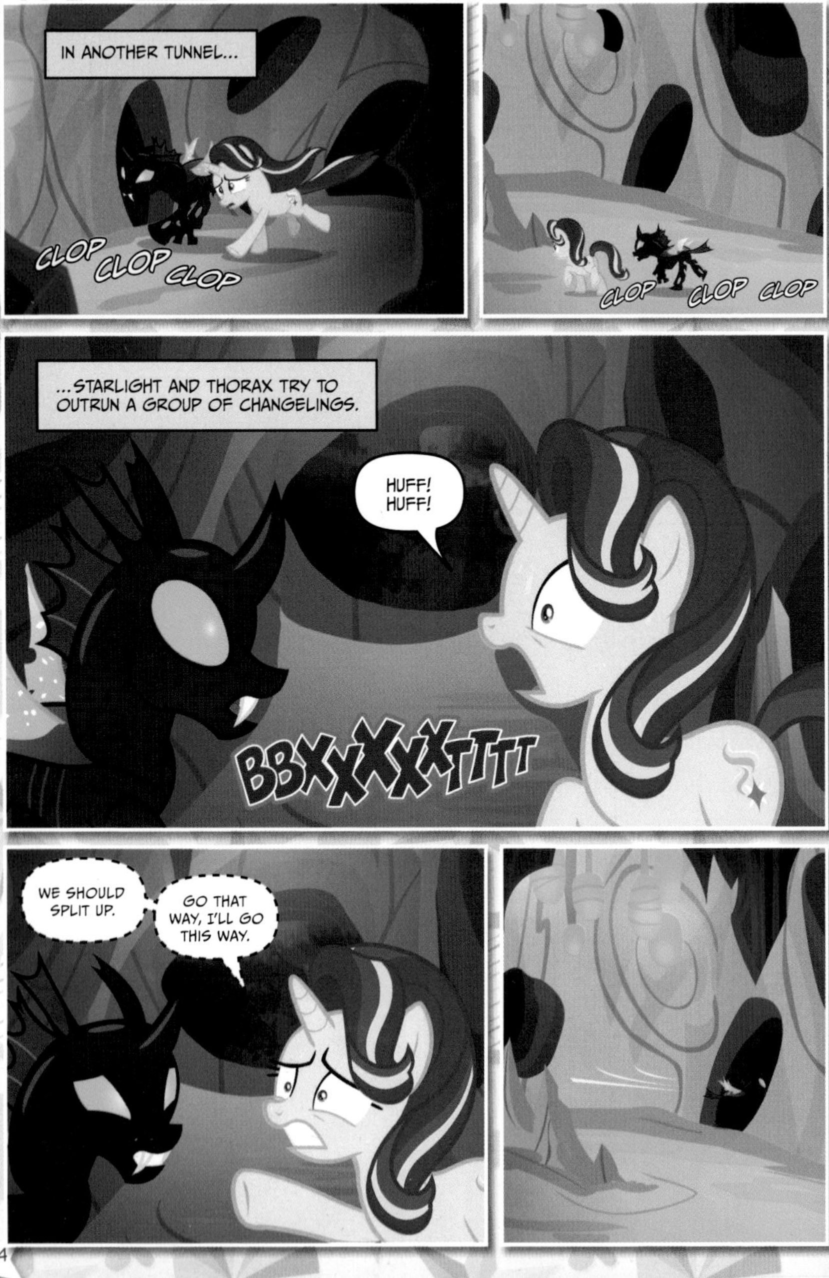

IN ANOTHER TUNNEL...
CLOP CLOP CLOP
CLOP CLOP CLOP
...STARLIGHT AND THORAX TRY TO OUTRUN A GROUP OF CHANGELINGS.
HUFF! HUFF!
BBXXXXTTTT
WE SHOULD SPLIT UP.
GO THAT WAY, I'LL GO THIS WAY.

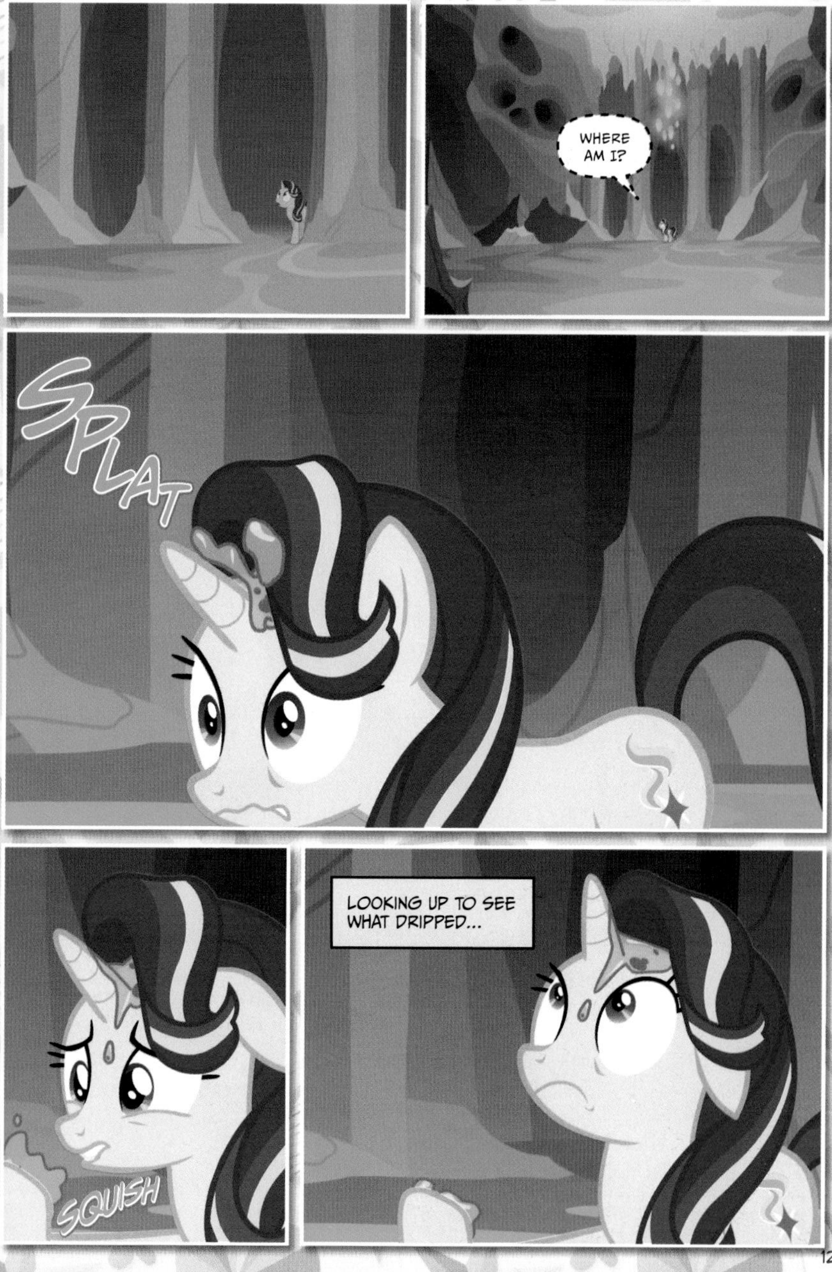
WHERE AM I?
SPLAT
LOOKING UP TO SEE WHAT DRIPPED...
SQUISH

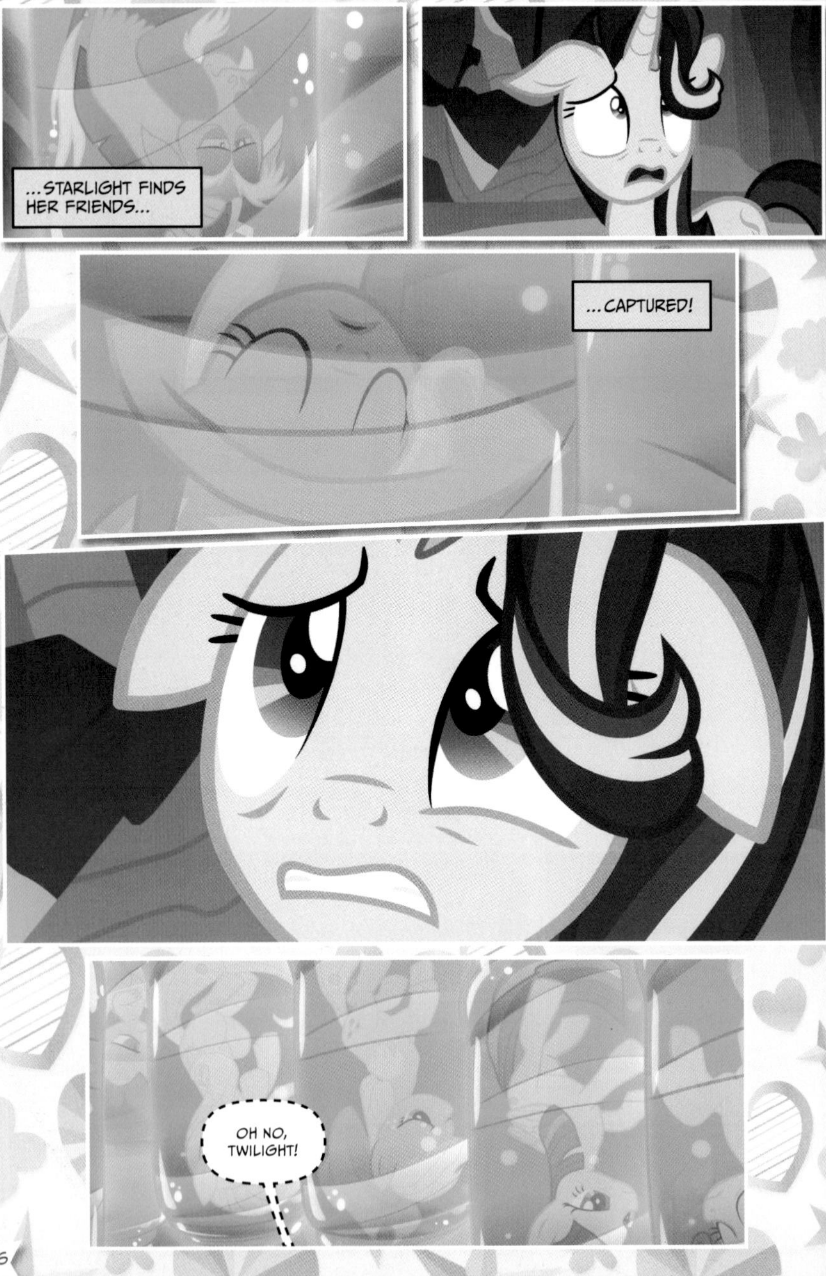
...STARLIGHT FINDS HER FRIENDS...
...CAPTURED!
OH NO, TWILIGHT!

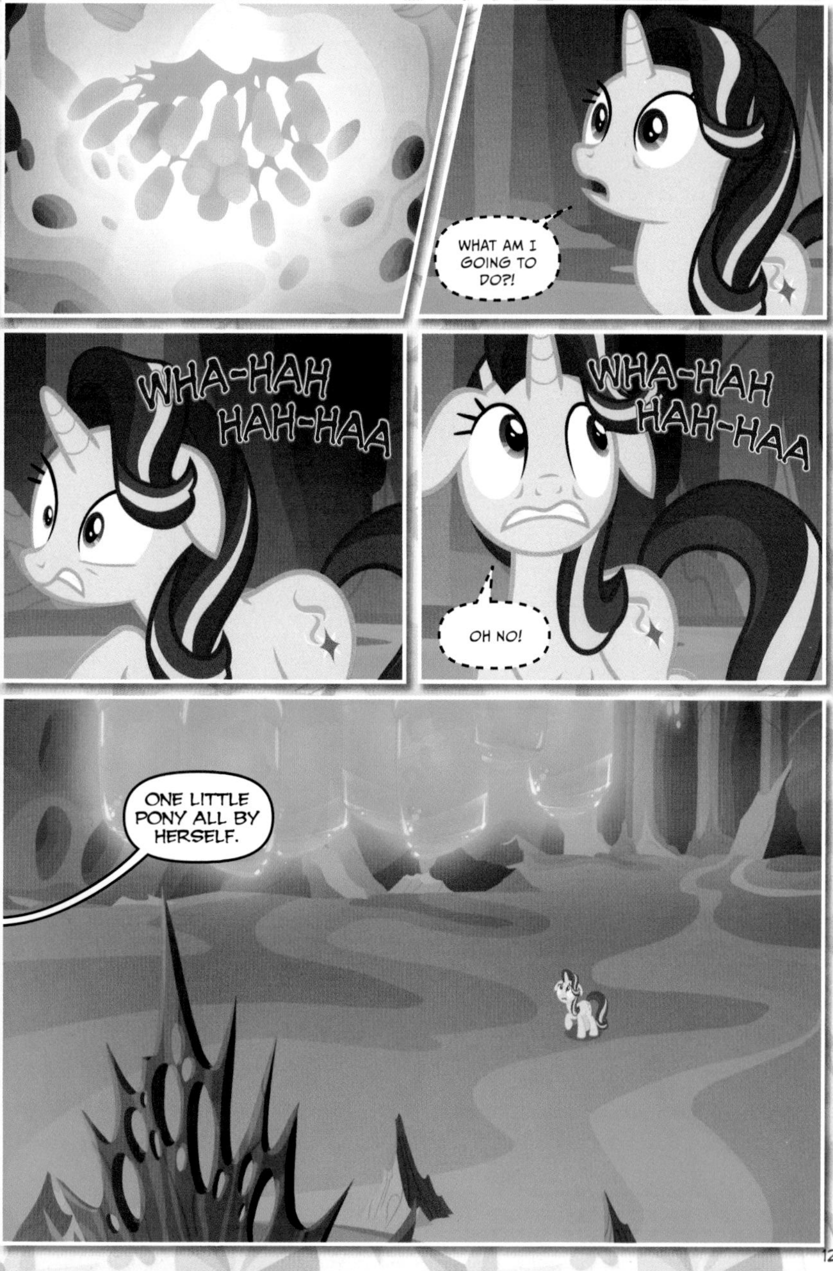
WHAT AM I GOING TO DO?!
WHA-HAH HAH-HAA
WHA-HAH HAH-HAA
OH NO!
ONE LITTLE PONY ALL BY HERSELF.

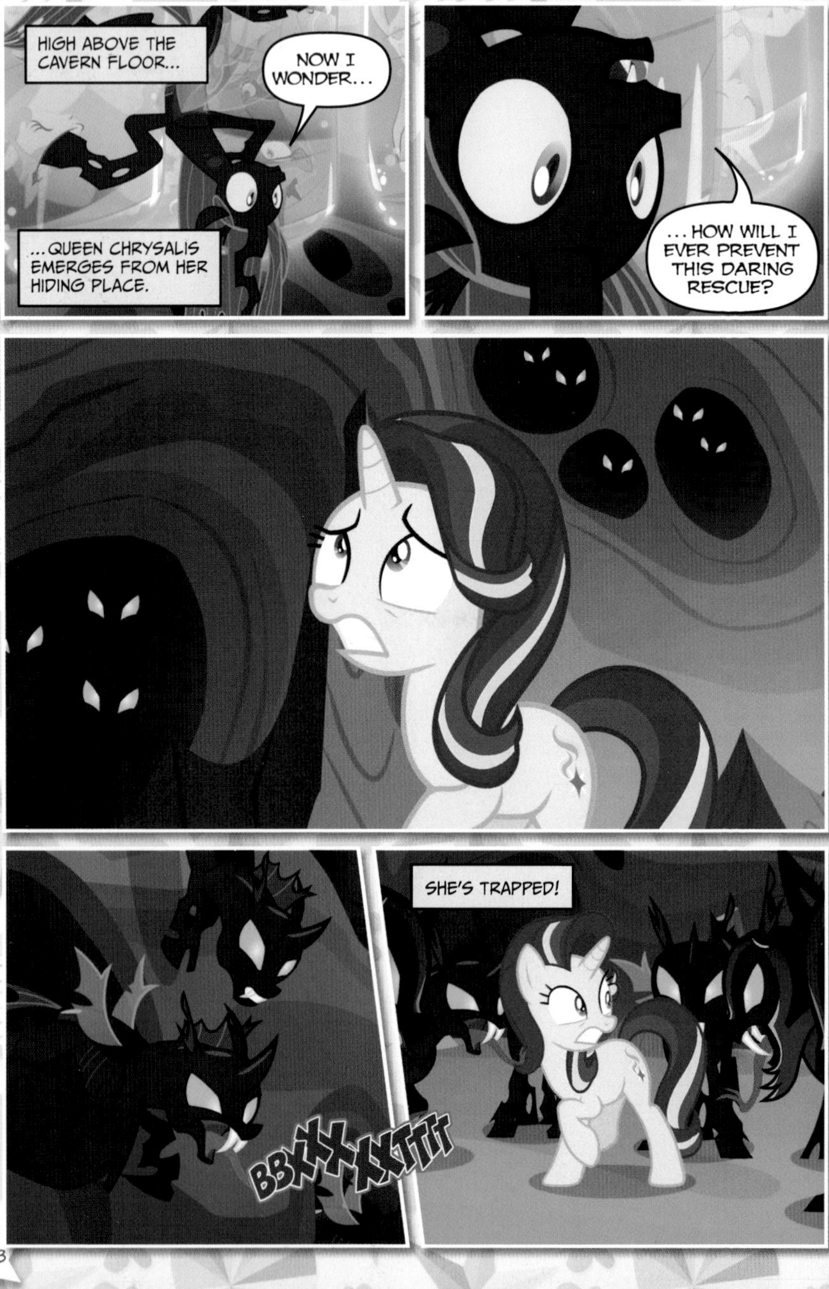
HIGH ABOVE THE CAVERN FLOOR...
NOW I WONDER...
...QUEEN CHRYSALIS EMERGES FROM HER HIDING PLACE.
...HOW WILL I EVER PREVENT THIS DARING RESCUE?
SHE'S TRAPPED!
BBXXXXXTTTT

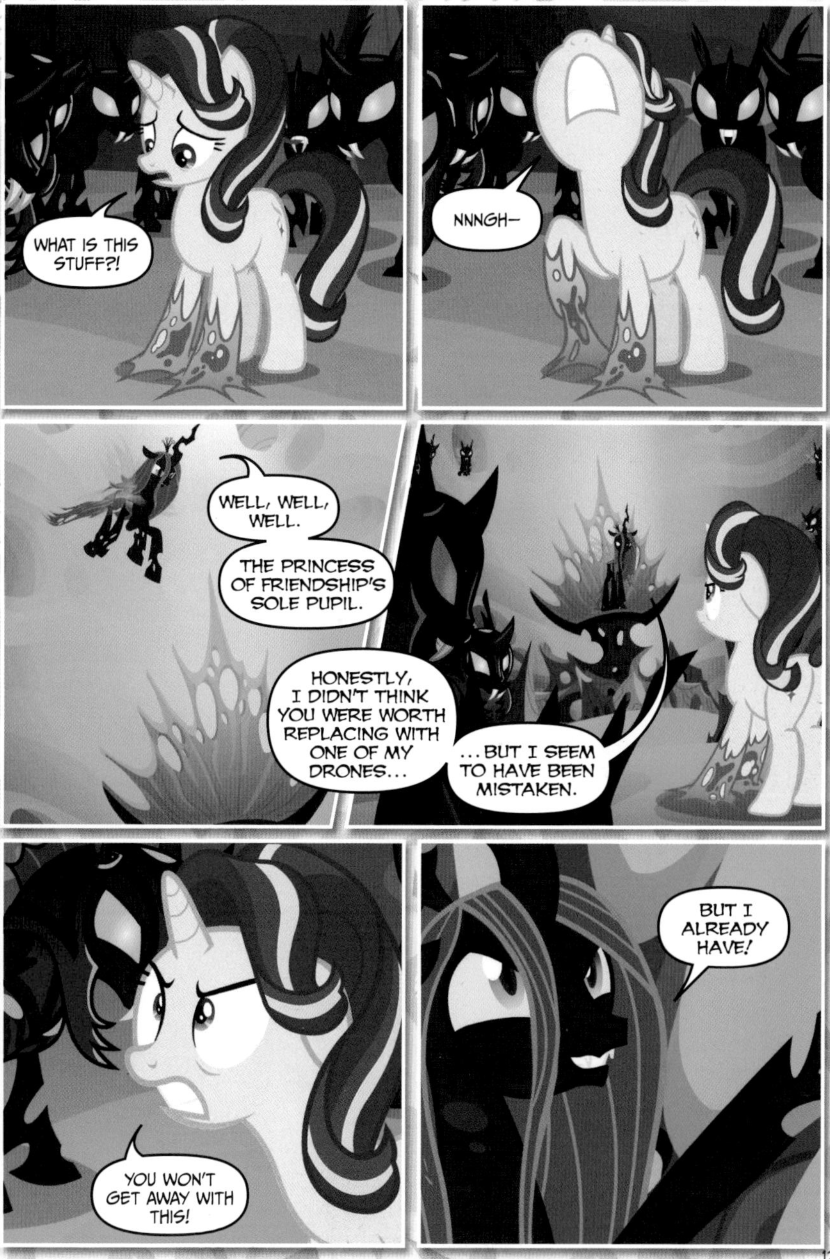
WHAT IS THIS STUFF?!
NNNGH—
WELL, WELL, WELL.
THE PRINCESS OF FRIENDSHIP'S SOLE PUPIL.
HONESTLY, I DIDN'T THINK YOU WERE WORTH REPLACING WITH ONE OF MY DRONES...
...BUT I SEEM TO HAVE BEEN MISTAKEN.
YOU WON'T GET AWAY WITH THIS!
BUT I ALREADY HAVE!

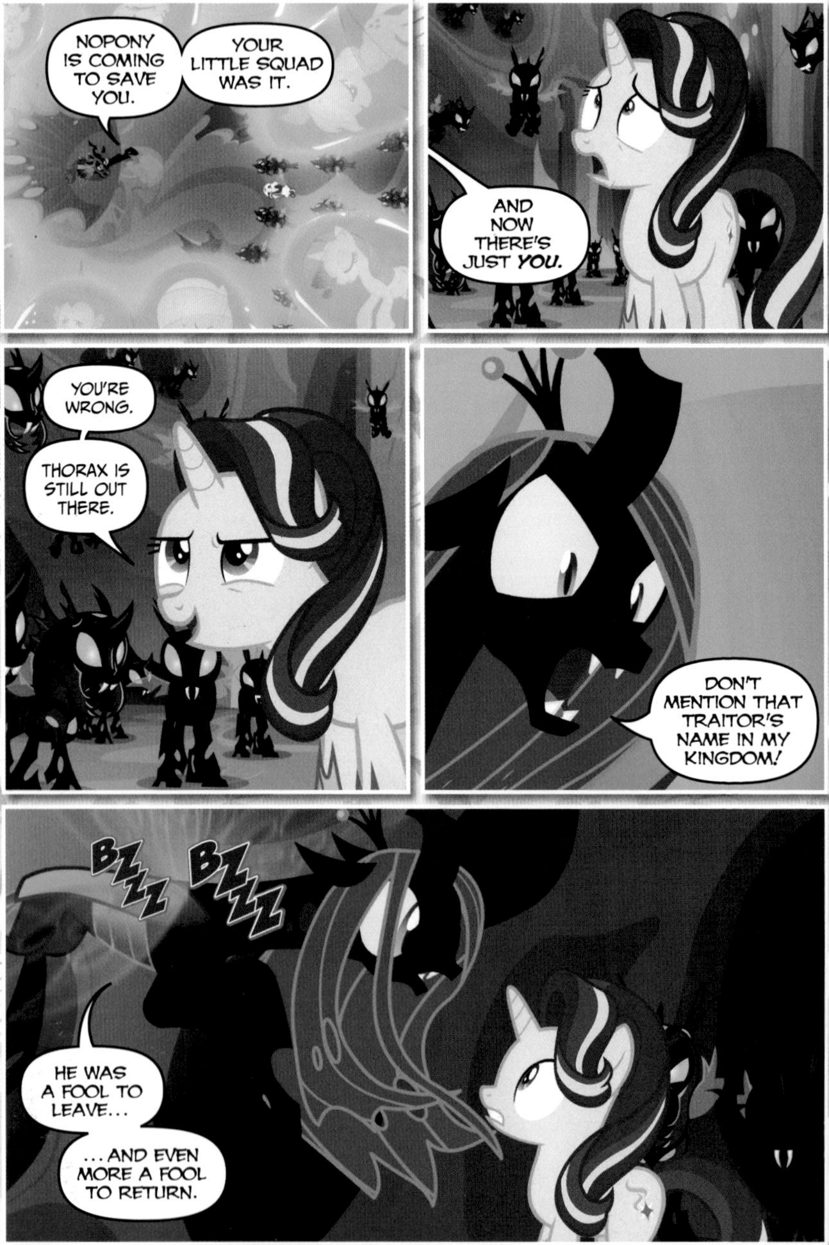
NOPONY IS COMING TO SAVE YOU.
YOUR LITTLE SQUAD WAS IT.
AND NOW THERE'S JUST *YOU.*
YOU'RE WRONG.
THORAX IS STILL OUT THERE.
DON'T MENTION THAT TRAITOR'S NAME IN MY KINGDOM!
BZZZ BZZZ
HE WAS A FOOL TO LEAVE...
...AND EVEN MORE A FOOL TO RETURN.

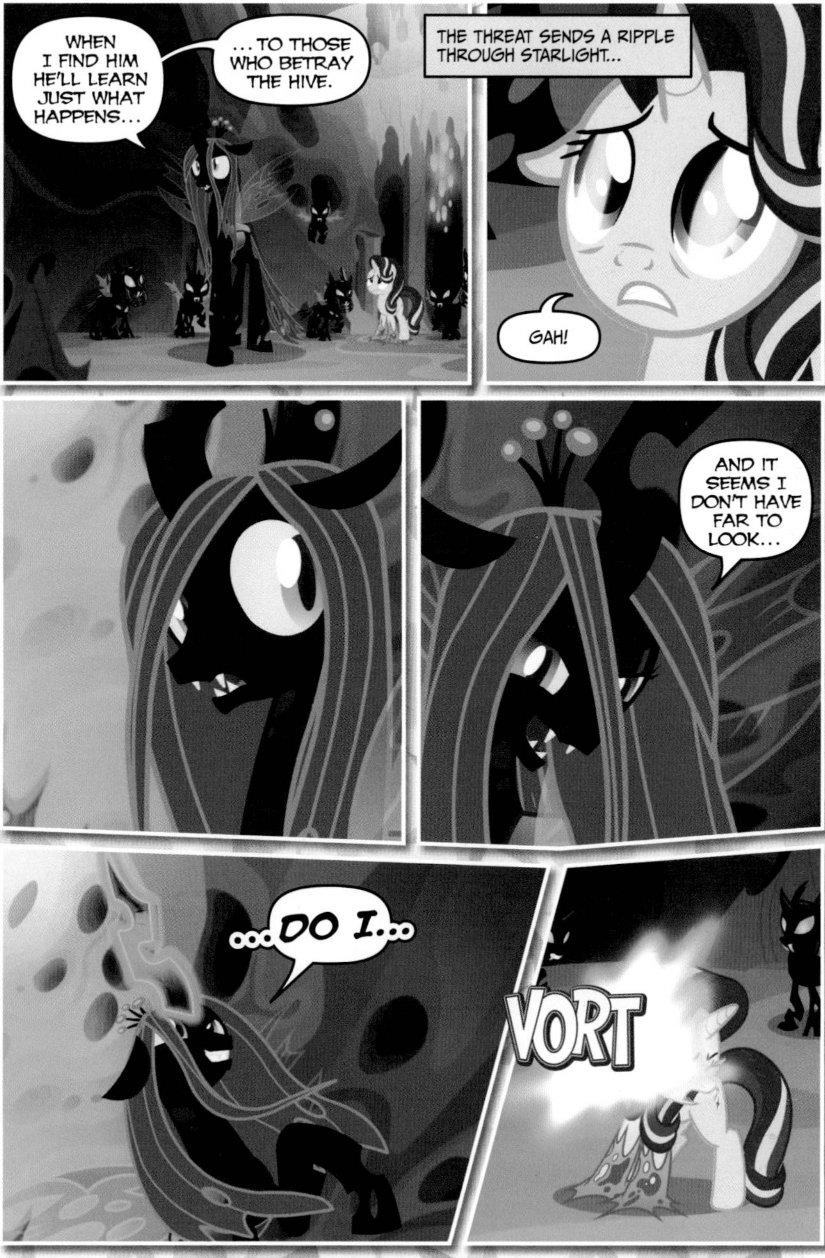
WHEN I FIND HIM HE'LL LEARN JUST WHAT HAPPENS...
...TO THOSE WHO BETRAY THE HIVE.
THE THREAT SENDS A RIPPLE THROUGH STARLIGHT...
GAH!
AND IT SEEMS I DON'T HAVE FAR TO LOOK...
...DO I...
VORT

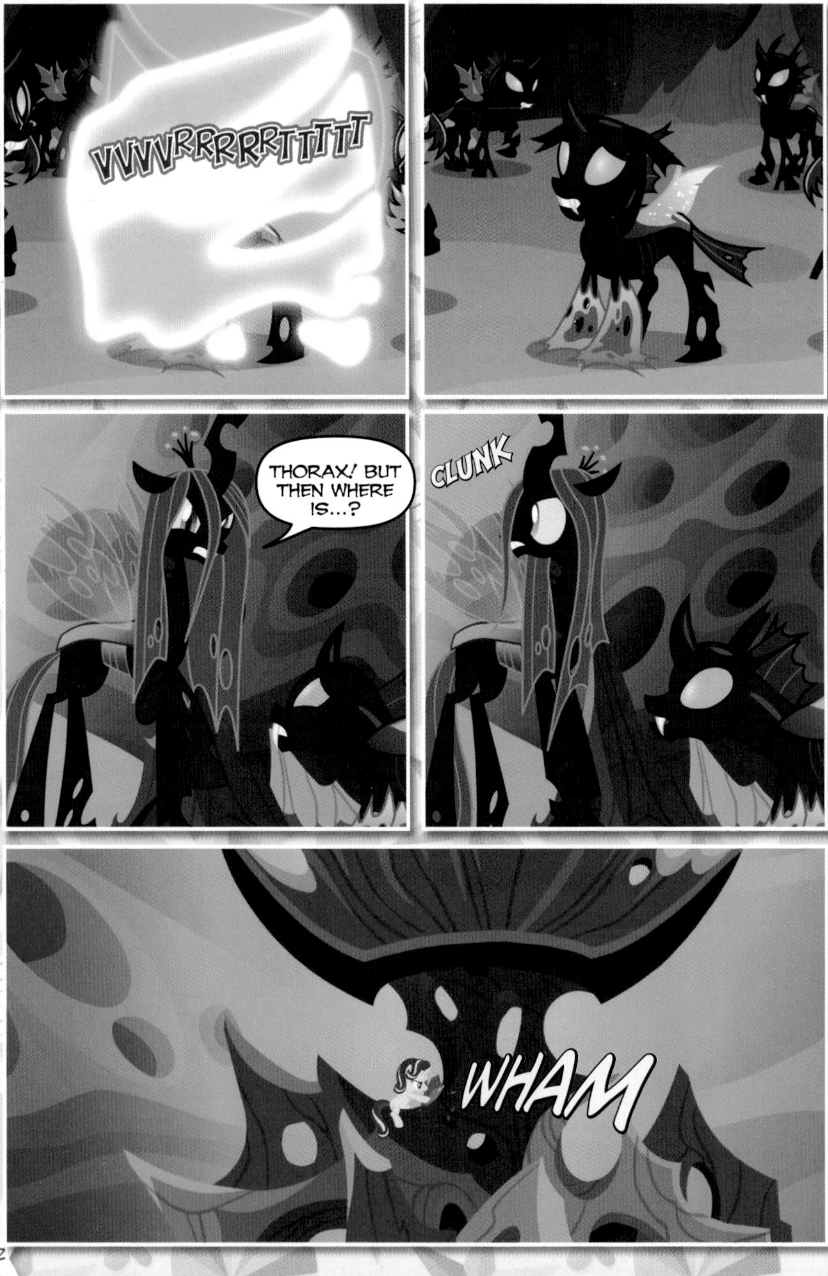

VVVVRRRRRTTTTT
THORAX! BUT THEN WHERE IS...?
CLUNK
WHAM

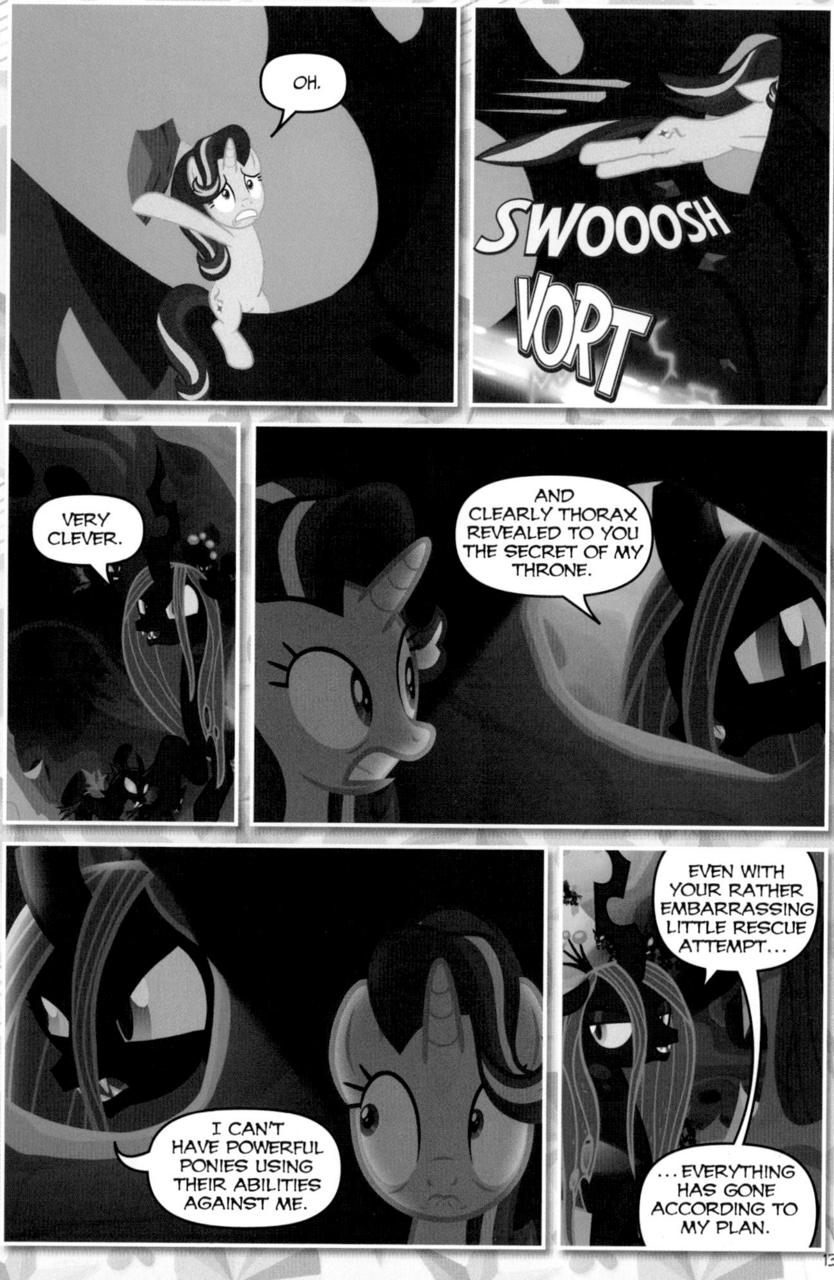
OH.
SWOOOSH
VORT
VERY CLEVER.
AND CLEARLY THORAX REVEALED TO YOU THE SECRET OF MY THRONE.
I CAN'T HAVE POWERFUL PONIES USING THEIR ABILITIES AGAINST ME.
EVEN WITH YOUR RATHER EMBARRASSING LITTLE RESCUE ATTEMPT...
...EVERYTHING HAS GONE ACCORDING TO MY PLAN.

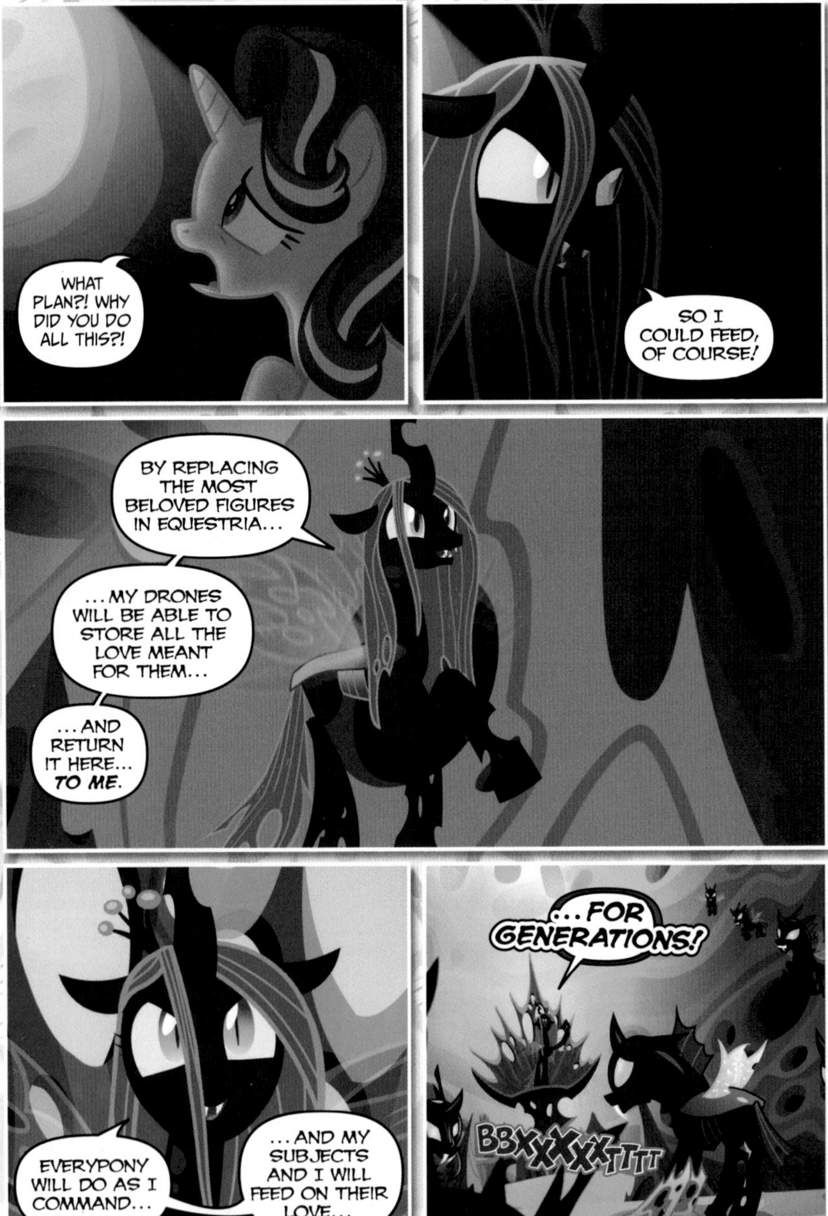
WHAT PLAN?! WHY DID YOU DO ALL THIS?!
SO I COULD FEED, OF COURSE!
BY REPLACING THE MOST BELOVED FIGURES IN EQUESTRIA...
...MY DRONES WILL BE ABLE TO STORE ALL THE LOVE MEANT FOR THEM...
...AND RETURN IT HERE... *TO ME*.
EVERYPONY WILL DO AS I COMMAND...
...AND MY SUBJECTS AND I WILL FEED ON THEIR LOVE...
...FOR GENERATIONS!
BBXXXXXTTTT

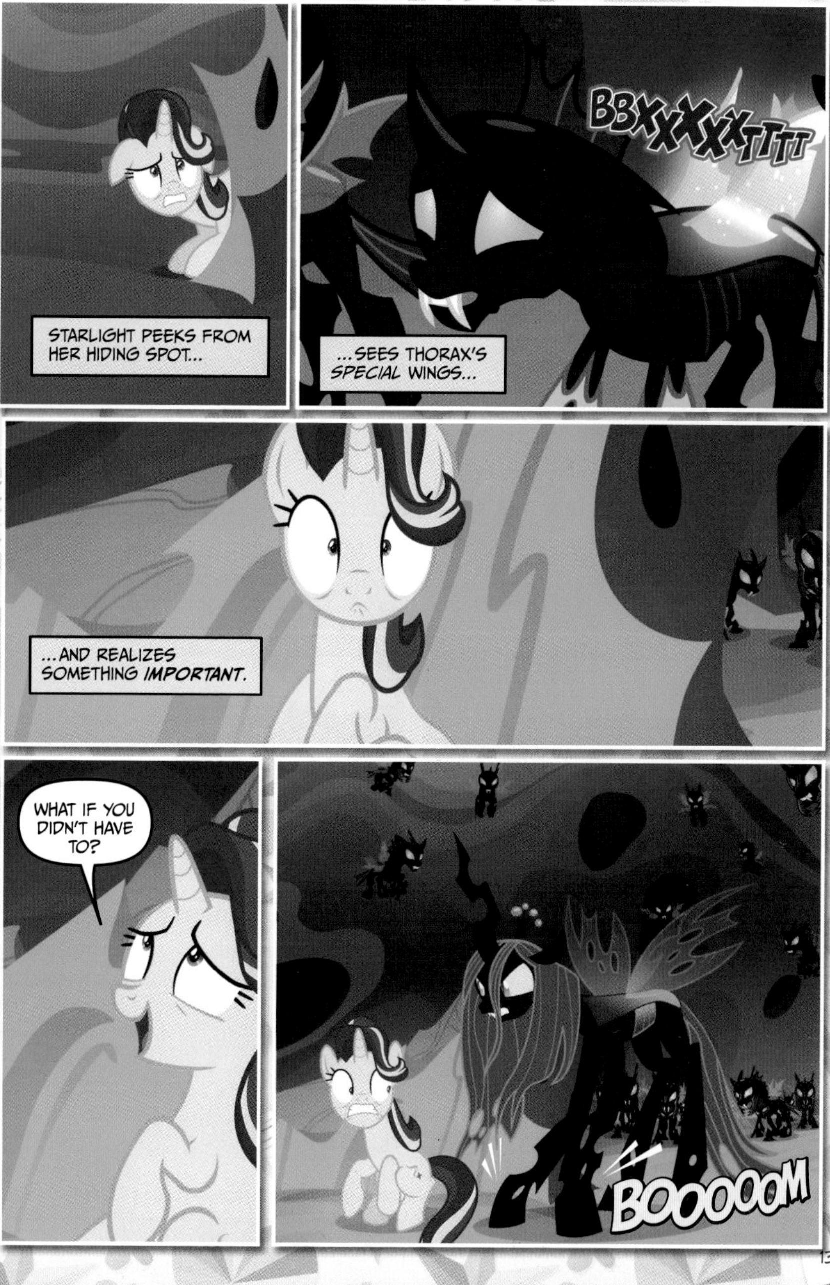
STARLIGHT PEEKS FROM HER HIDING SPOT...
BBXXXXXTTTT
...SEES THORAX'S SPECIAL WINGS...
...AND REALIZES SOMETHING IMPORTANT.
WHAT IF YOU DIDN'T HAVE TO?
BOOOOOM

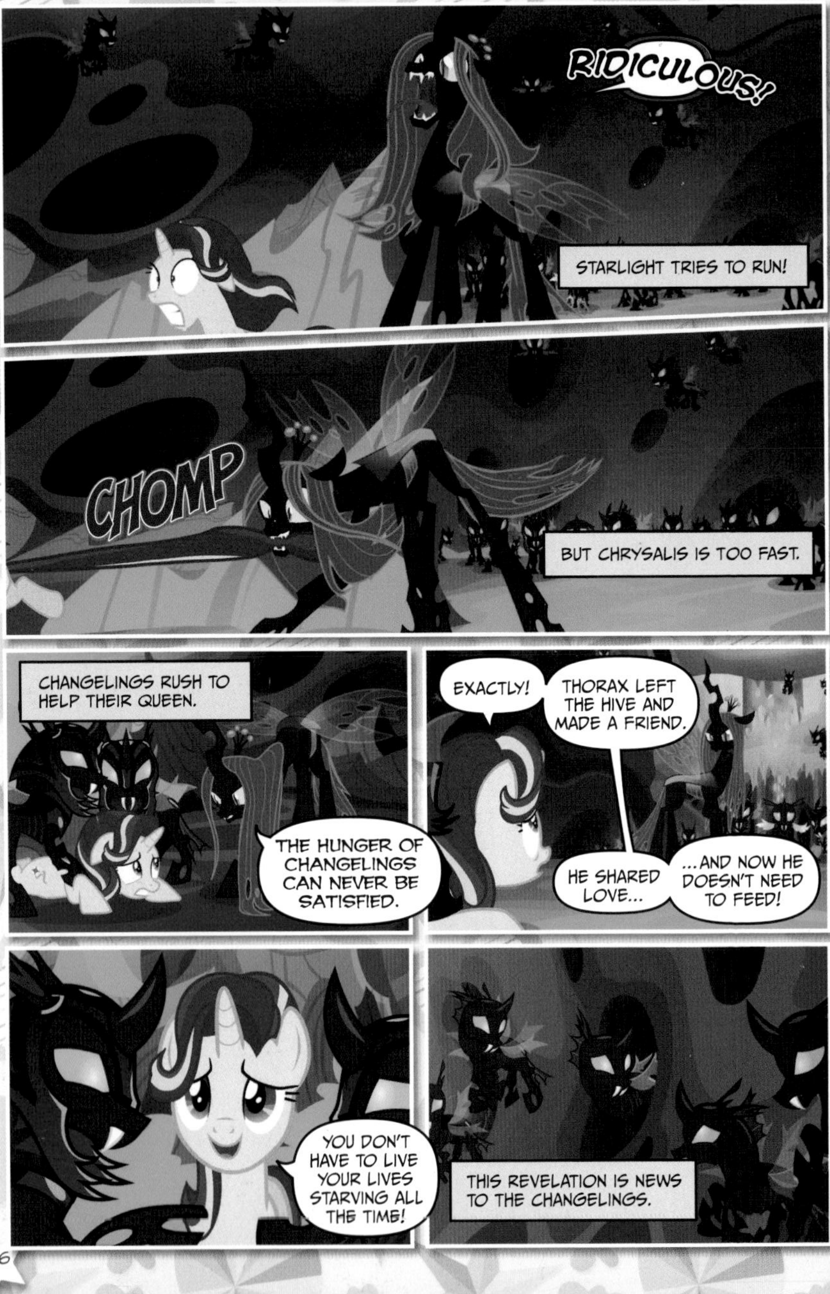
RIDICULOUS!
STARLIGHT TRIES TO RUN!
CHOMP
BUT CHRYSALIS IS TOO FAST.
CHANGELINGS RUSH TO HELP THEIR QUEEN.
THE HUNGER OF CHANGELINGS CAN NEVER BE SATISFIED.
EXACTLY!
THORAX LEFT THE HIVE AND MADE A FRIEND.
HE SHARED LOVE...
...AND NOW HE DOESN'T NEED TO FEED!
YOU DON'T HAVE TO LIVE YOUR LIVES STARVING ALL THE TIME!
THIS REVELATION IS NEWS TO THE CHANGELINGS.

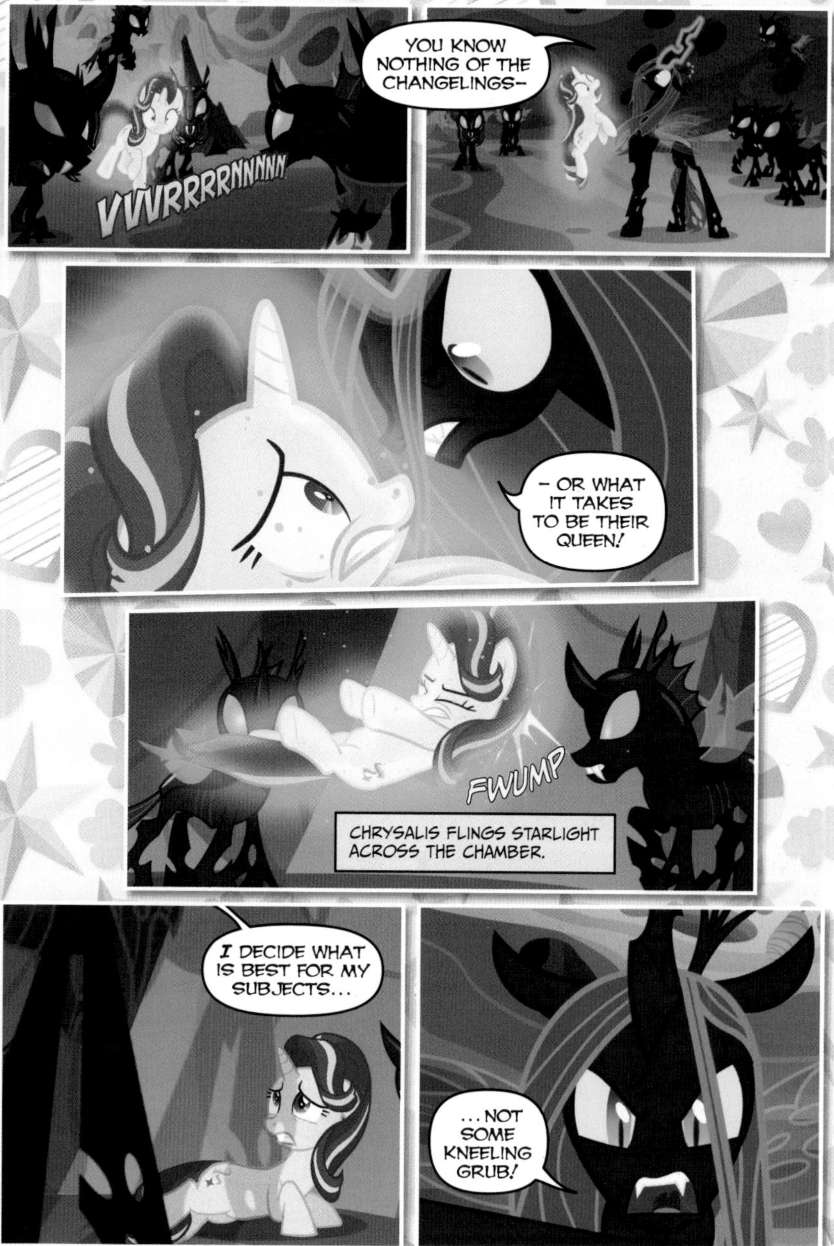
VVVRRRRNNNNN
YOU KNOW NOTHING OF THE CHANGELINGS–
– OR WHAT IT TAKES TO BE THEIR QUEEN!
FWUMP
CHRYSALIS FLINGS STARLIGHT ACROSS THE CHAMBER.
I DECIDE WHAT IS BEST FOR MY SUBJECTS...
...NOT SOME KNEELING GRUB!

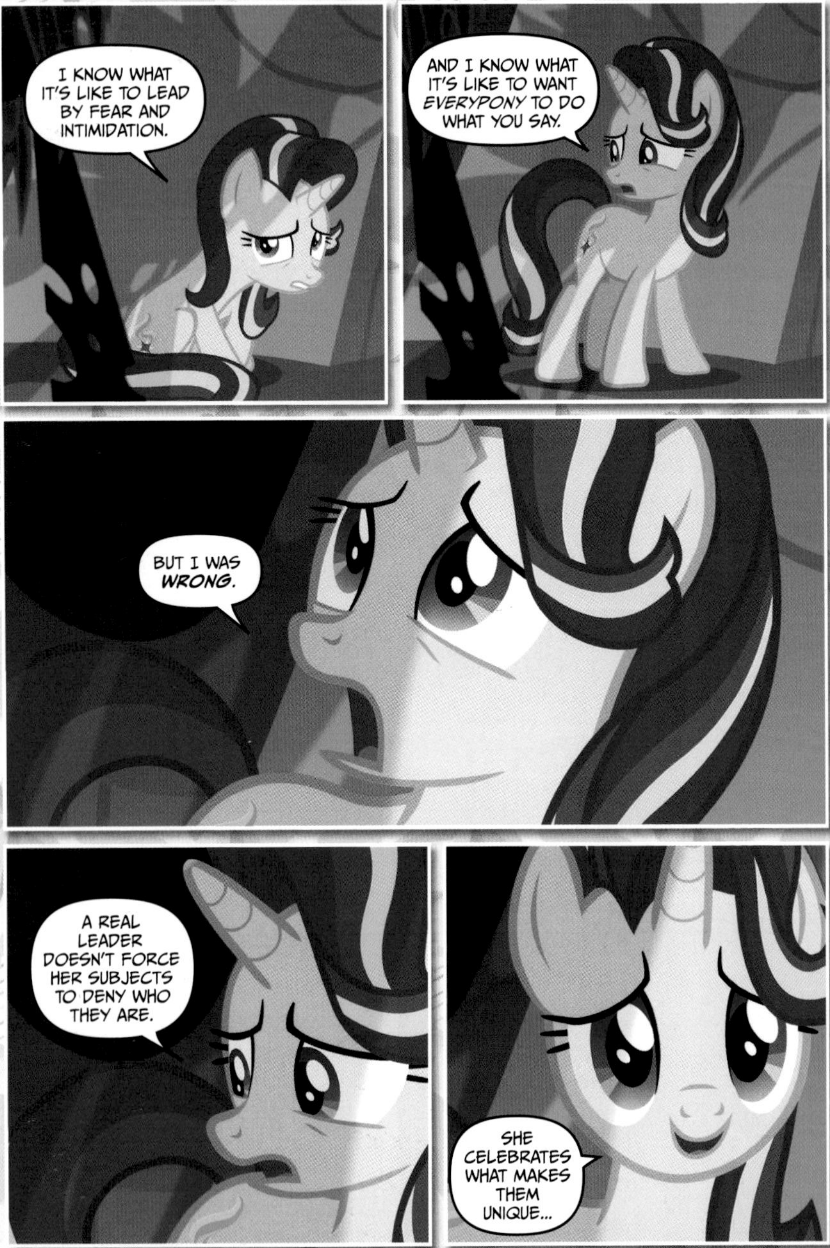

I KNOW WHAT IT'S LIKE TO LEAD BY FEAR AND INTIMIDATION.
AND I KNOW WHAT IT'S LIKE TO WANT *EVERYPONY* TO DO WHAT YOU SAY.
BUT I WAS ***WRONG***.
A REAL LEADER DOESN'T FORCE HER SUBJECTS TO DENY WHO THEY ARE.
SHE CELEBRATES WHAT MAKES THEM UNIQUE...

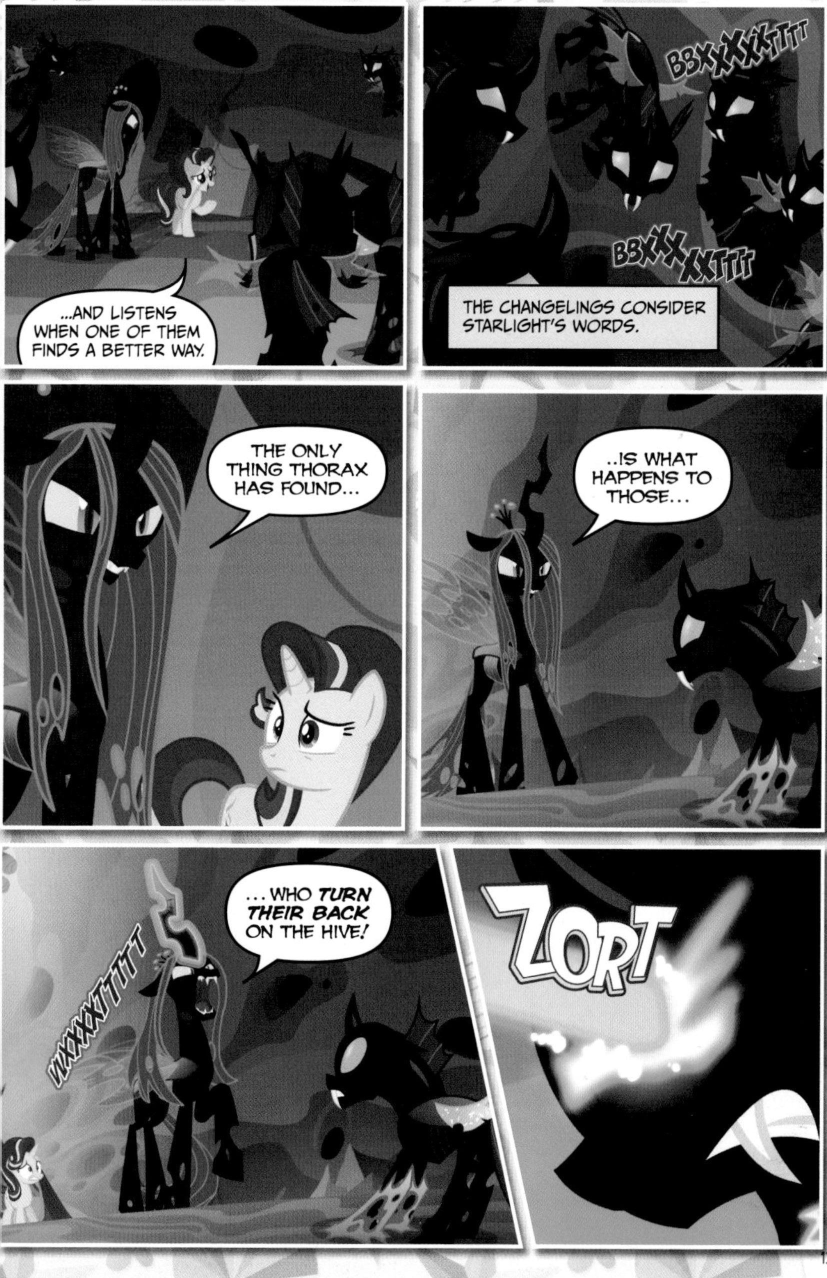
...AND LISTENS WHEN ONE OF THEM FINDS A BETTER WAY.
BBXXXXTTTT
BBXXXXXTTTT
THE CHANGELINGS CONSIDER STARLIGHT'S WORDS.
THE ONLY THING THORAX HAS FOUND...
..IS WHAT HAPPENS TO THOSE...
...WHO *TURN THEIR BACK* ON THE HIVE!
VVXXXXTTTTTT
ZORT

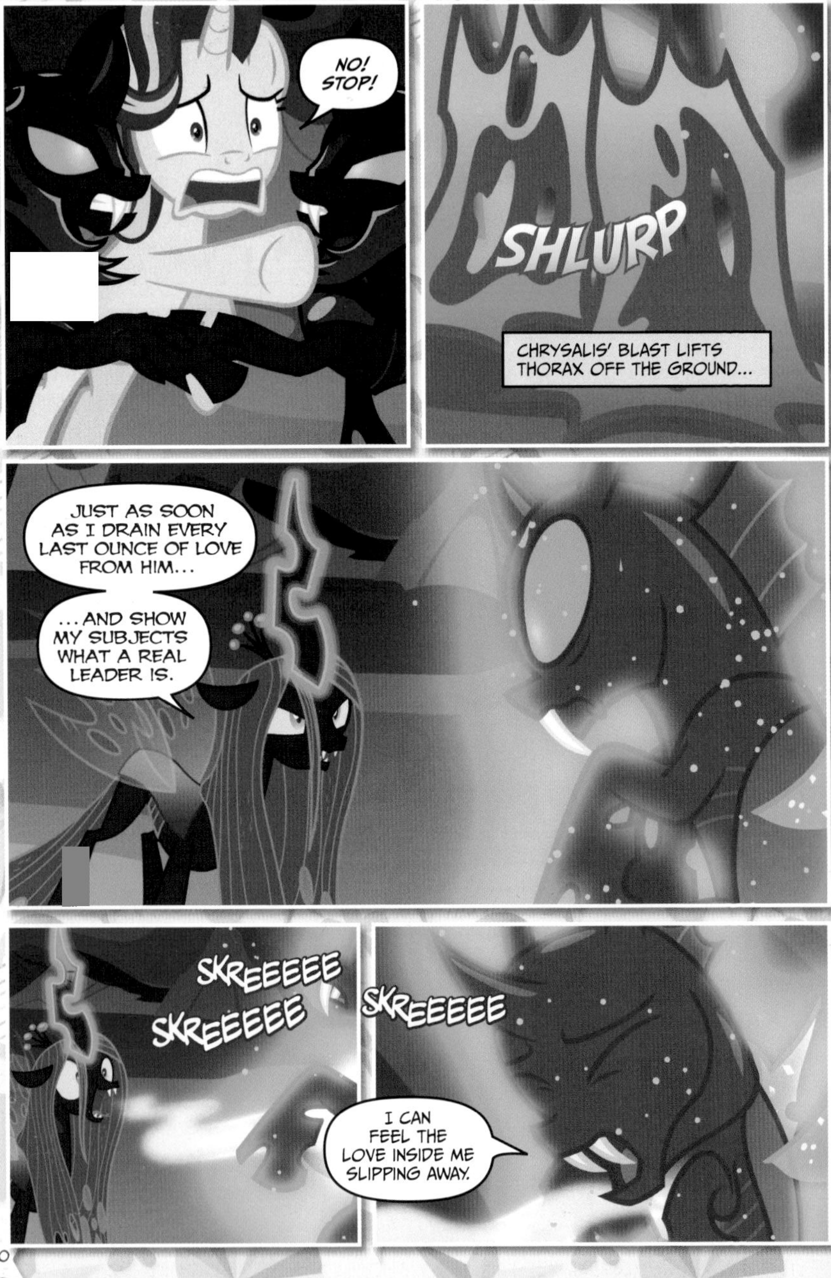
NO! STOP!
SHLURP
CHRYSALIS' BLAST LIFTS THORAX OFF THE GROUND...
JUST AS SOON AS I DRAIN EVERY LAST OUNCE OF LOVE FROM HIM...
...AND SHOW MY SUBJECTS WHAT A REAL LEADER IS.
SKREEEEEE
SKREEEEEE
SKREEEEEE
I CAN FEEL THE LOVE INSIDE ME SLIPPING AWAY.

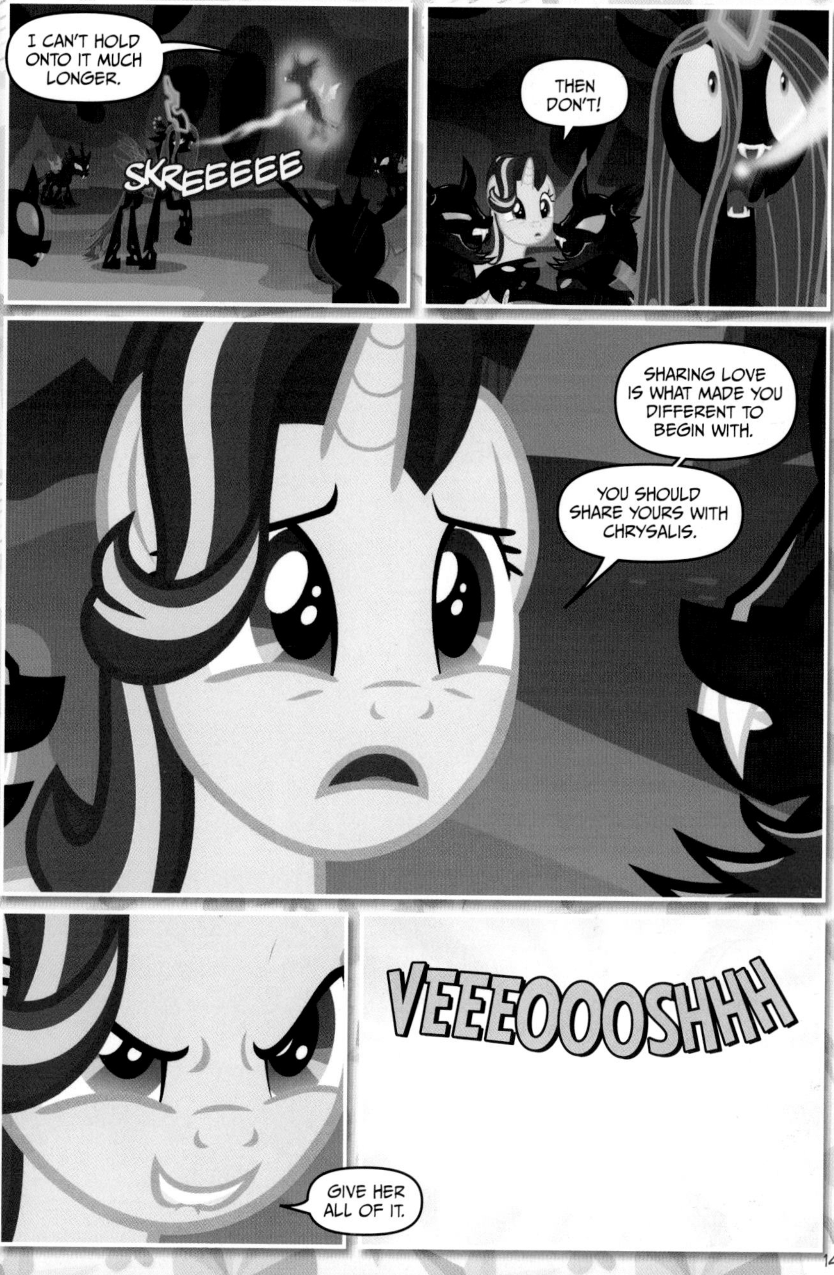
I CAN'T HOLD ONTO IT MUCH LONGER.
SKREEEEEE
THEN DON'T!
SHARING LOVE IS WHAT MADE YOU DIFFERENT TO BEGIN WITH.
YOU SHOULD SHARE YOURS WITH CHRYSALIS.
GIVE HER ALL OF IT.
VEEEOOOSHHH

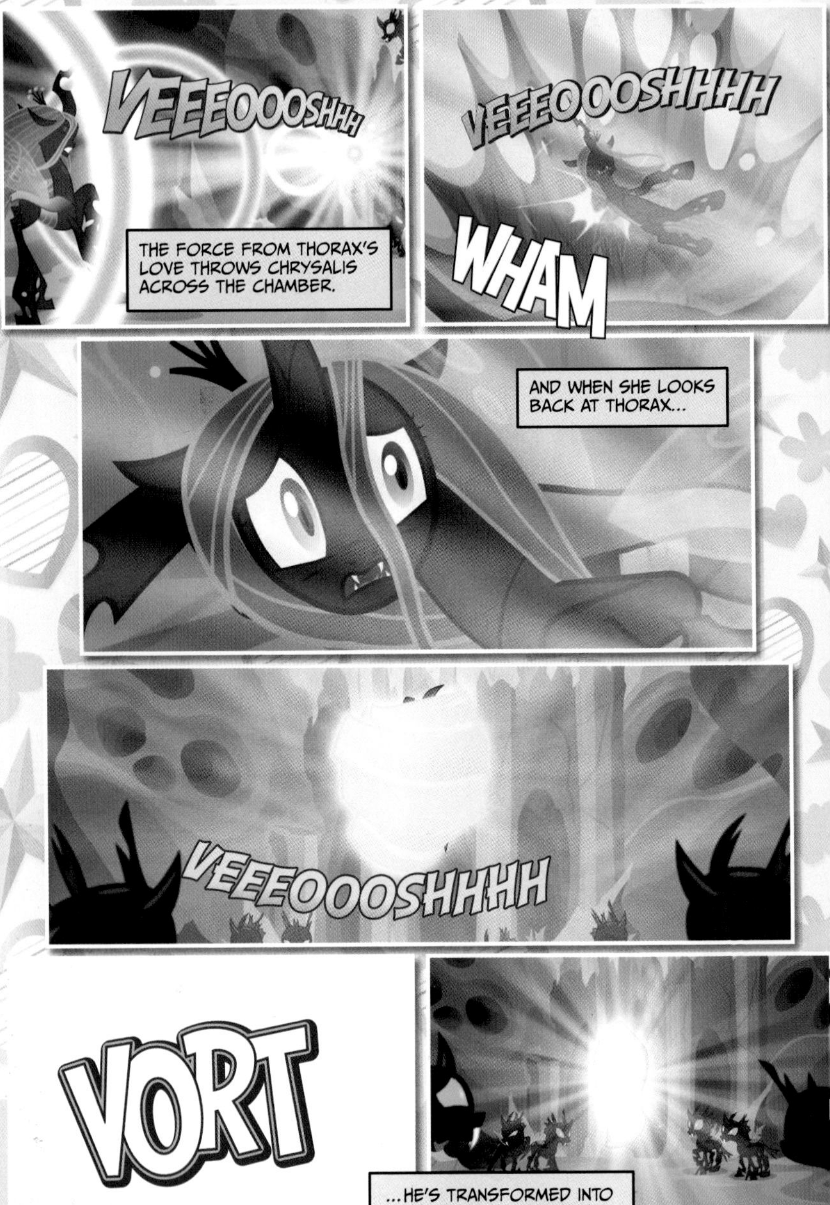
VEEEOOOSHHH
THE FORCE FROM THORAX'S LOVE THROWS CHRYSALIS ACROSS THE CHAMBER.
VEEEOOOSHHHH
WHAM
AND WHEN SHE LOOKS BACK AT THORAX...
VEEEOOOSHHHH
VORT
...HE'S TRANSFORMED INTO A SHIMMERING COCOON!

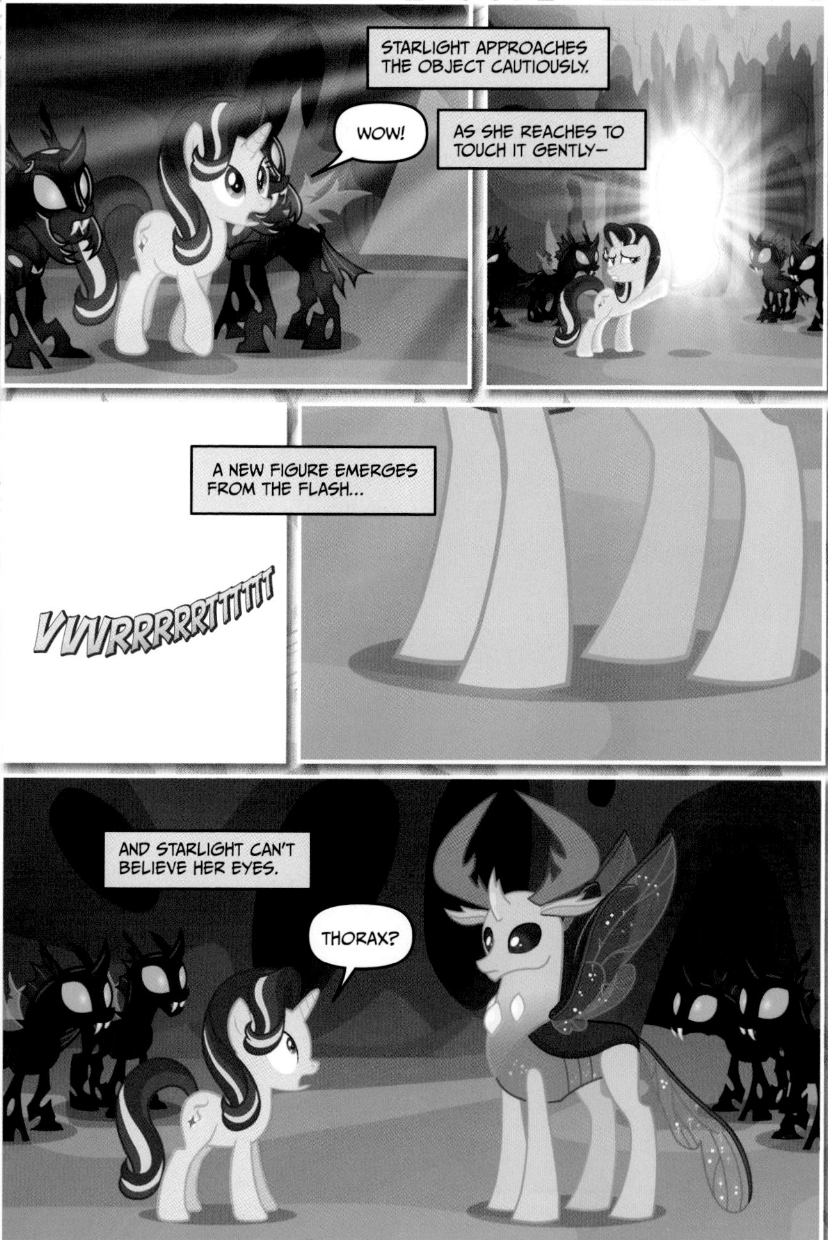
STARLIGHT APPROACHES THE OBJECT CAUTIOUSLY.
WOW!
AS SHE REACHES TO TOUCH IT GENTLY—
A NEW FIGURE EMERGES FROM THE FLASH...
VVVRRRRRRTTTTTT
AND STARLIGHT CAN'T BELIEVE HER EYES.
THORAX?

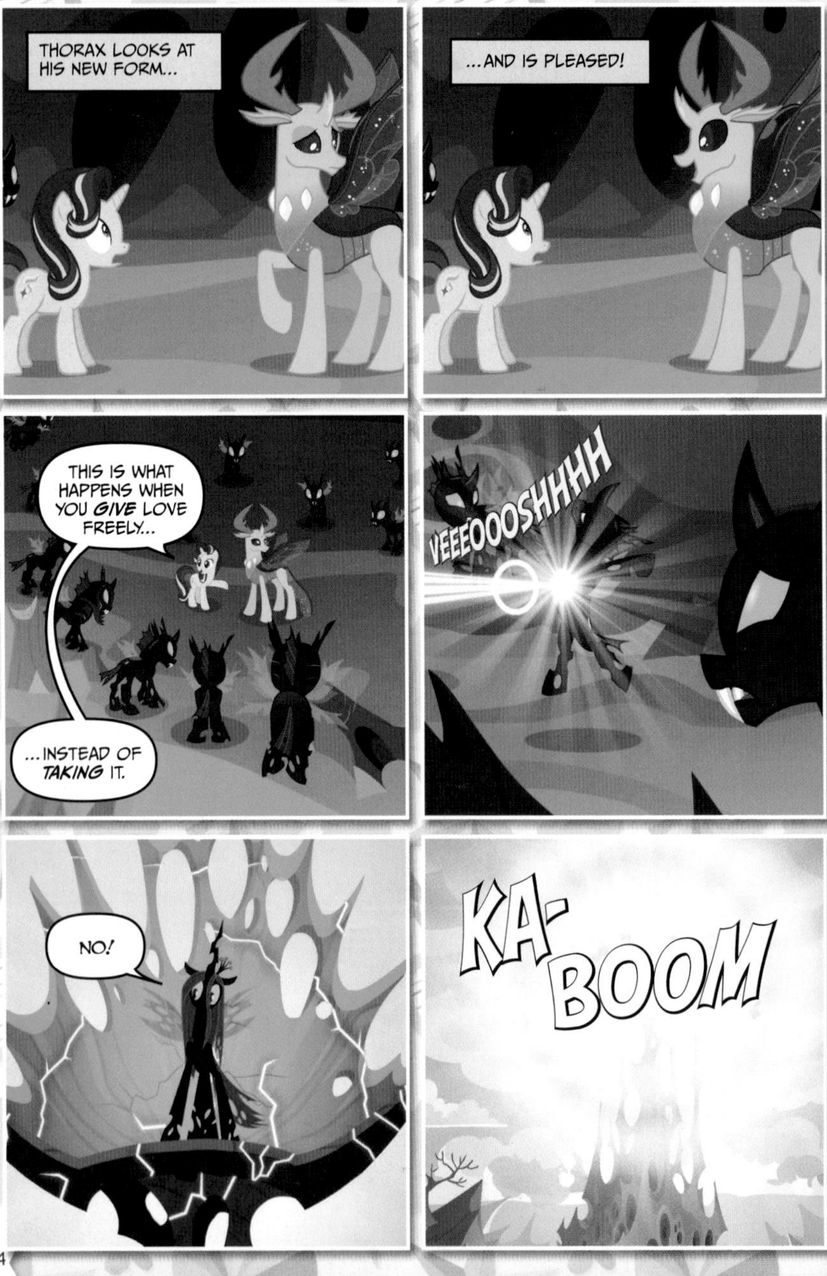
THORAX LOOKS AT HIS NEW FORM...
...AND IS PLEASED!
THIS IS WHAT HAPPENS WHEN YOU *GIVE* LOVE FREELY...
...INSTEAD OF *TAKING* IT.
VEEEOOOSHHHH
NO!
KA-BOOM

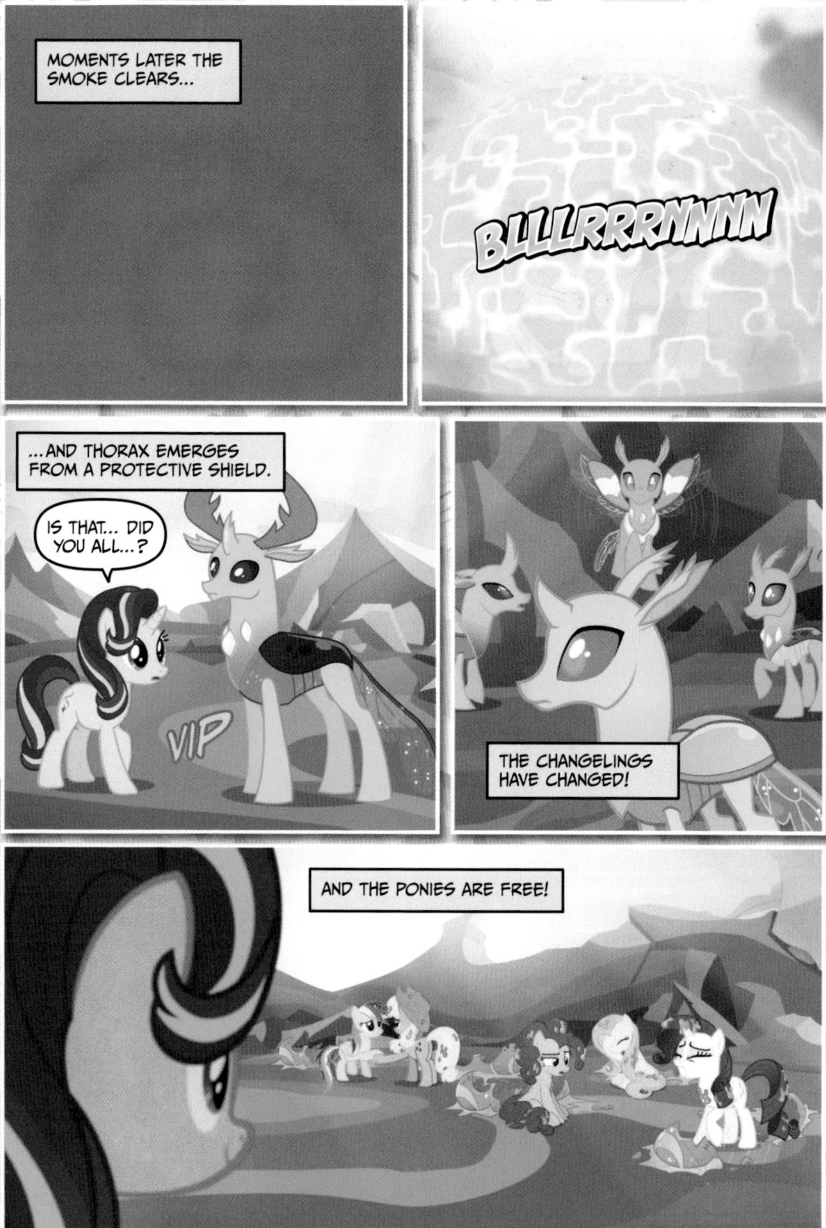
MOMENTS LATER THE SMOKE CLEARS...
BLLLRRRRNNNN
...AND THORAX EMERGES FROM A PROTECTIVE SHIELD.
IS THAT... DID YOU ALL...?
VIP
THE CHANGELINGS HAVE CHANGED!
AND THE PONIES ARE FREE!

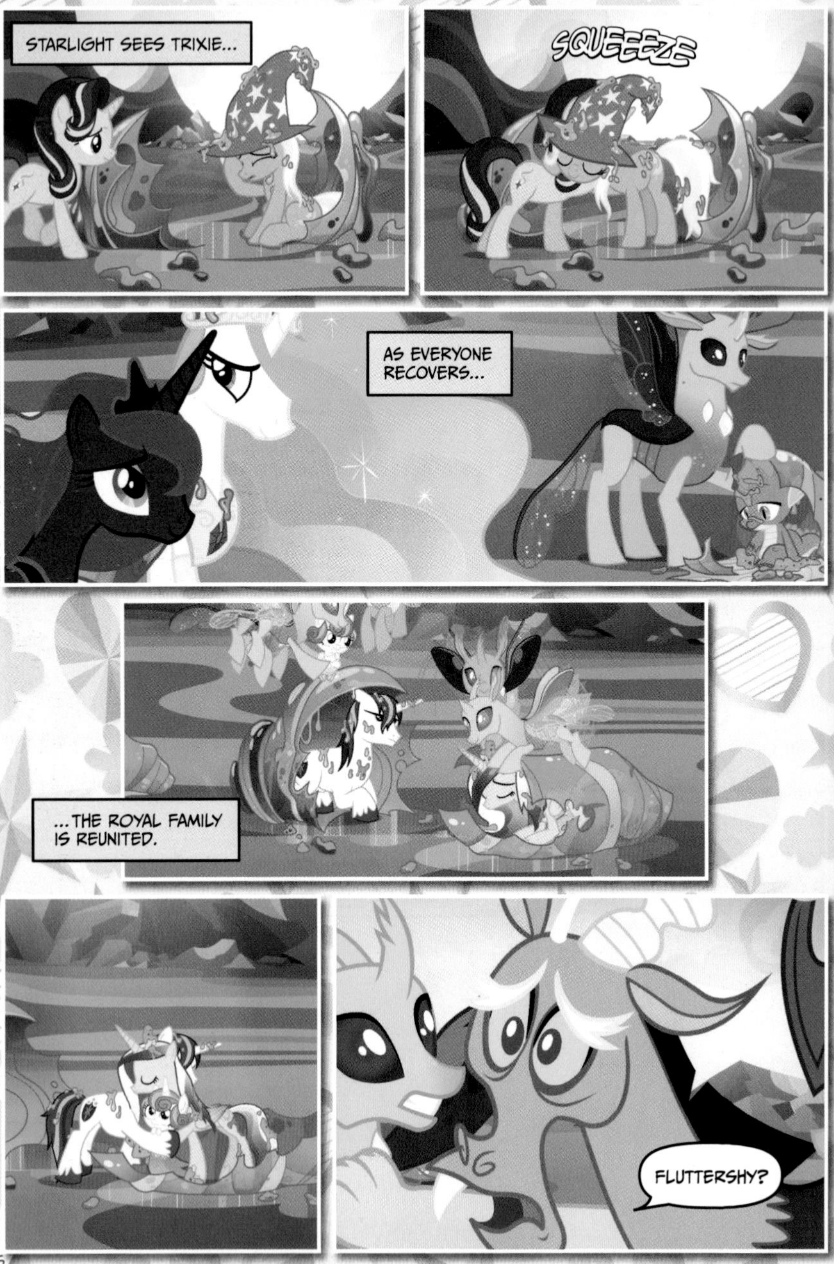
STARLIGHT SEES TRIXIE...
SQUEEEEZE
AS EVERYONE RECOVERS...
...THE ROYAL FAMILY IS REUNITED.
FLUTTERSHY?

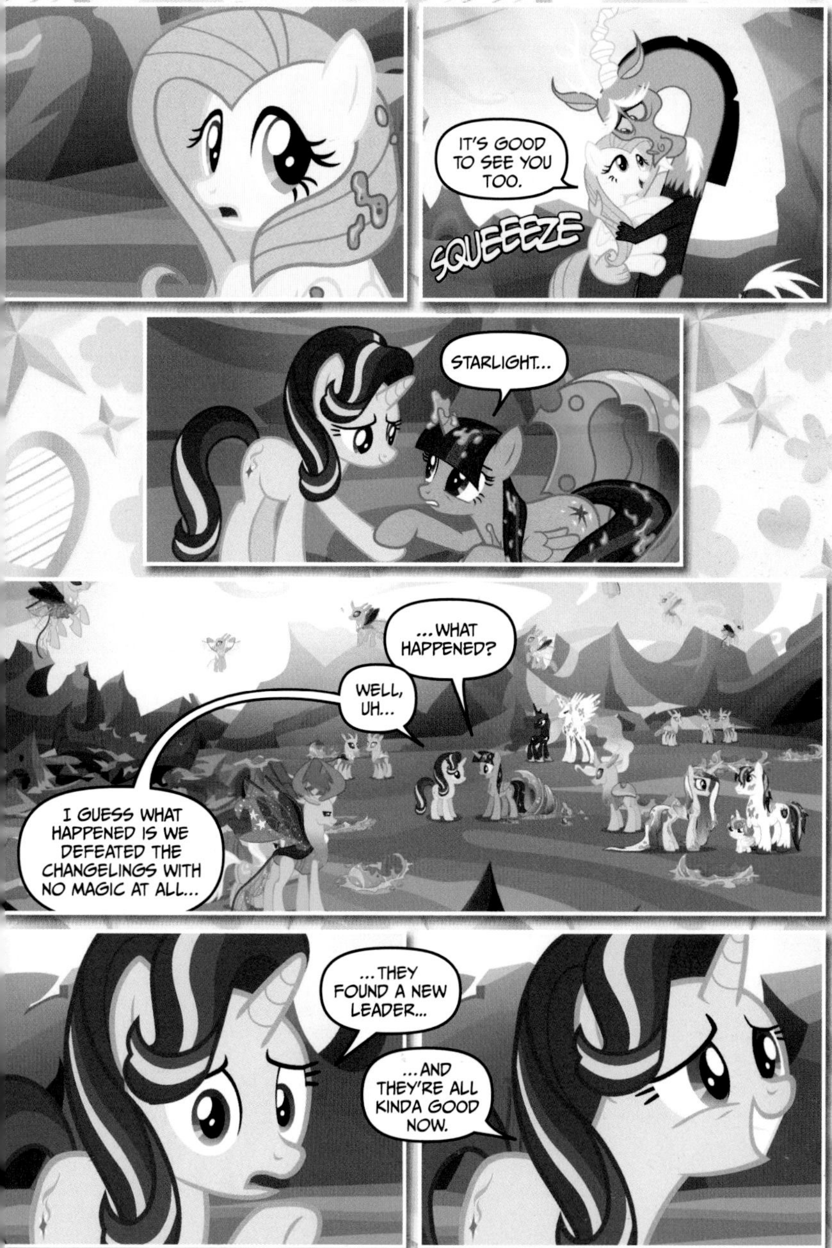
IT'S GOOD TO SEE YOU TOO.
SQUEEEEZE
STARLIGHT...
...WHAT HAPPENED?
WELL, UH...
I GUESS WHAT HAPPENED IS WE DEFEATED THE CHANGELINGS WITH NO MAGIC AT ALL...
...THEY FOUND A NEW LEADER...
...AND THEY'RE ALL KINDA GOOD NOW.

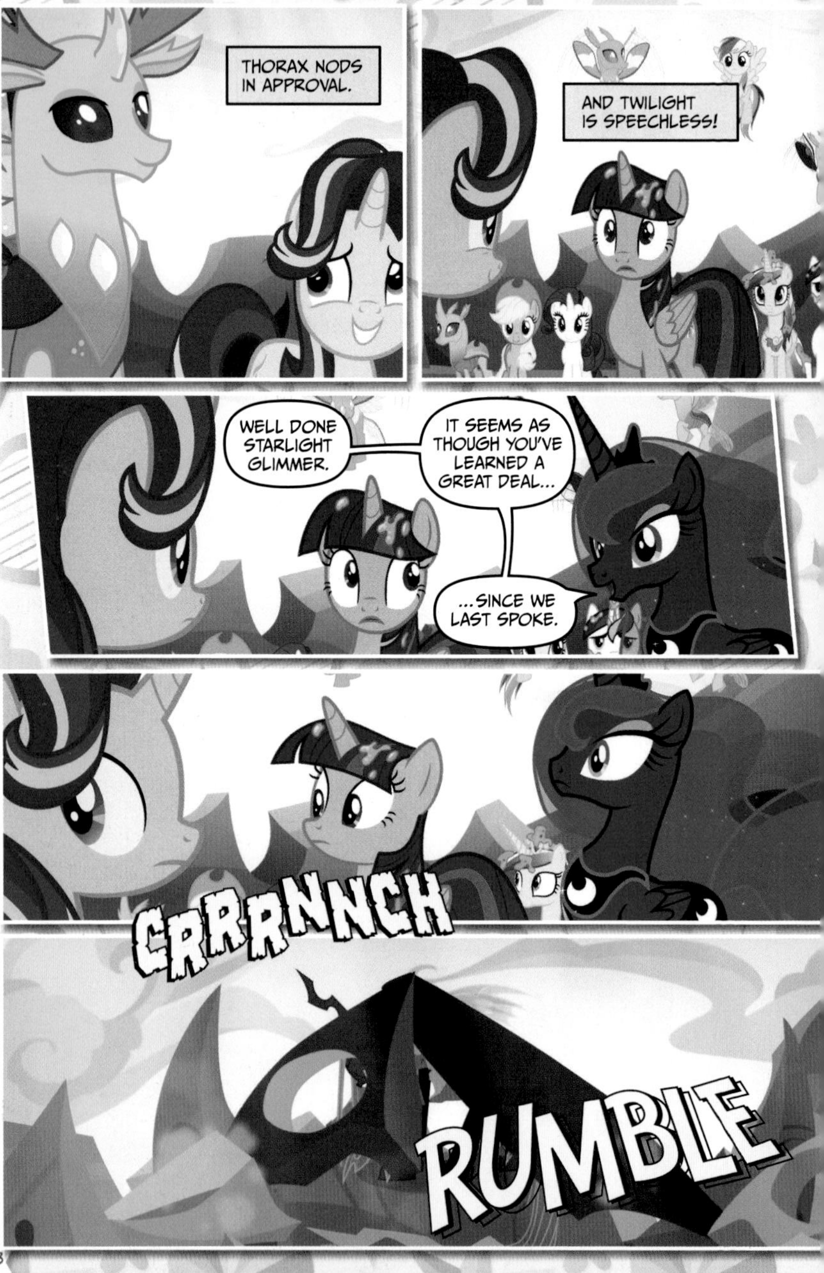
THORAX NODS IN APPROVAL.
AND TWILIGHT IS SPEECHLESS!
WELL DONE STARLIGHT GLIMMER.
IT SEEMS AS THOUGH YOU'VE LEARNED A GREAT DEAL...
...SINCE WE LAST SPOKE.
CRRRNNCH
RUMBLE

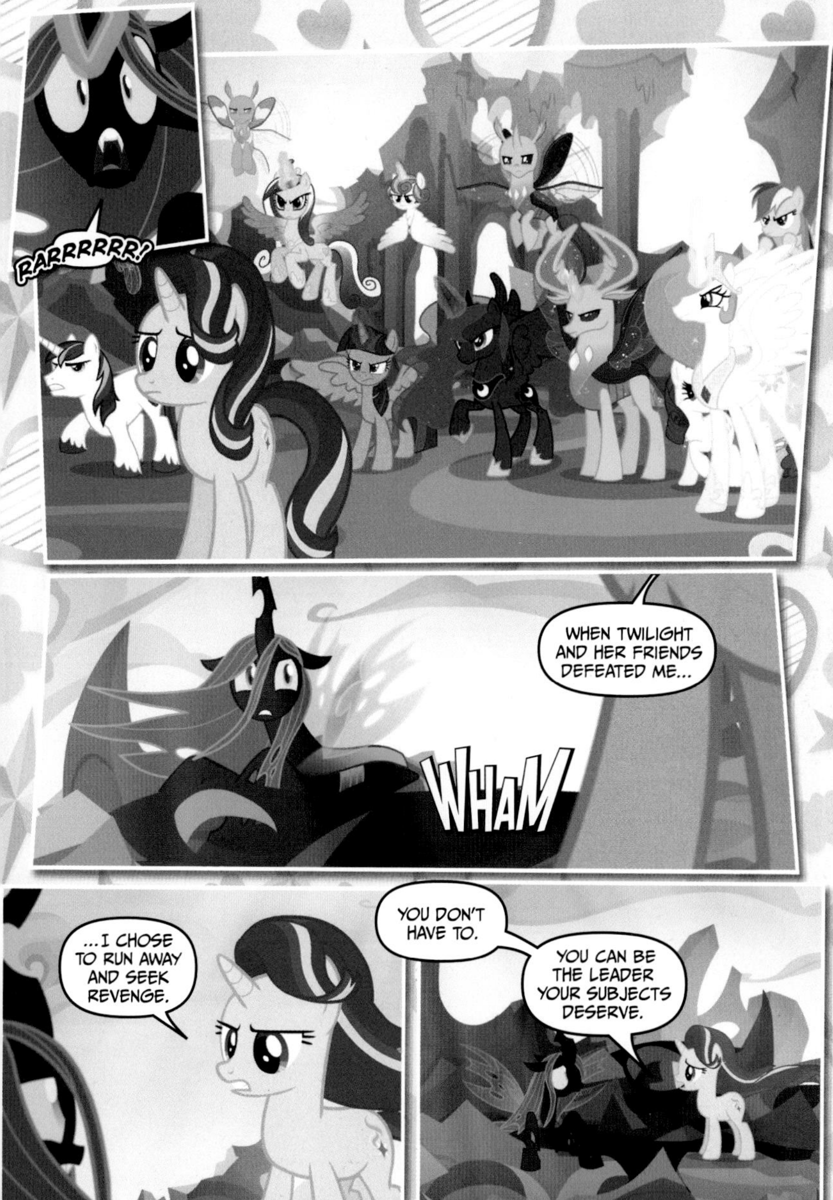
RARRRRRR!
WHEN TWILIGHT AND HER FRIENDS DEFEATED ME...
WHAM
...I CHOSE TO RUN AWAY AND SEEK REVENGE.
YOU DON'T HAVE TO.
YOU CAN BE THE LEADER YOUR SUBJECTS DESERVE.

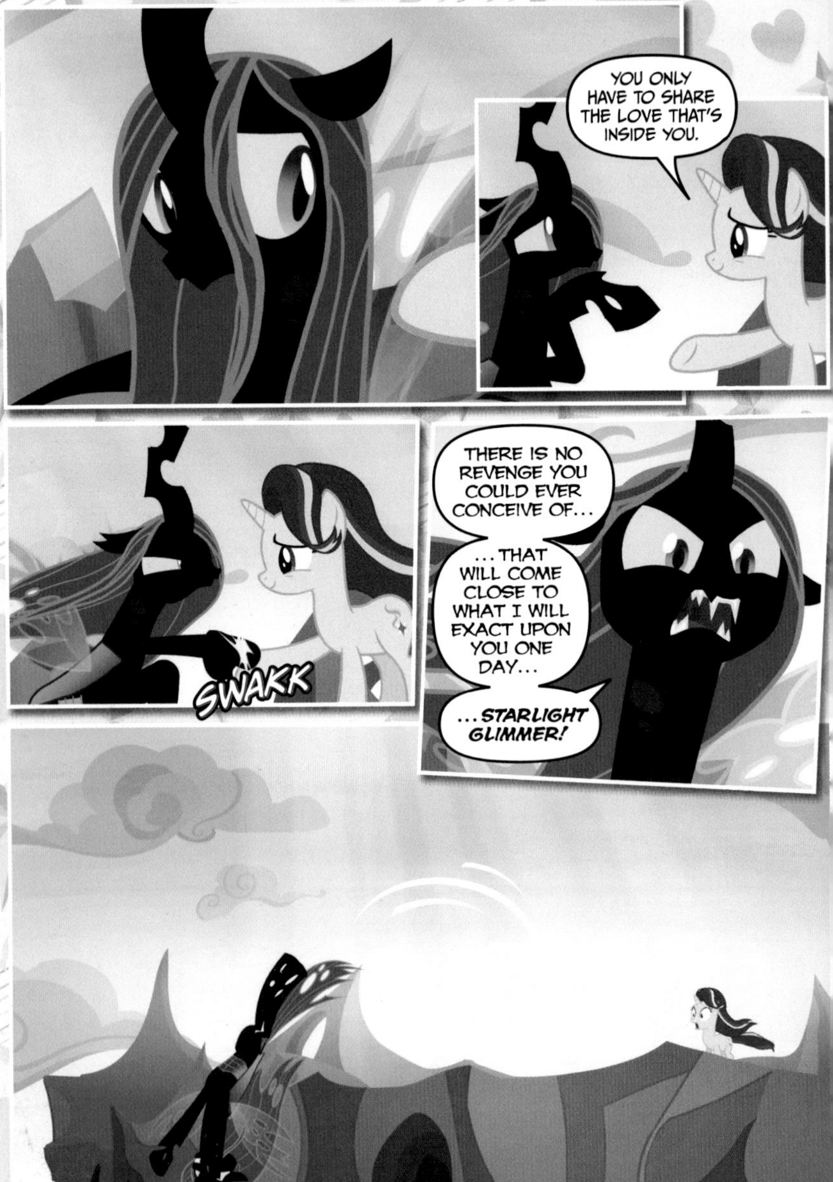
YOU ONLY HAVE TO SHARE THE LOVE THAT'S INSIDE YOU.
SWAKK
THERE IS NO REVENGE YOU COULD EVER CONCEIVE OF...
...THAT WILL COME CLOSE TO WHAT I WILL EXACT UPON YOU ONE DAY...
...STARLIGHT GLIMMER!

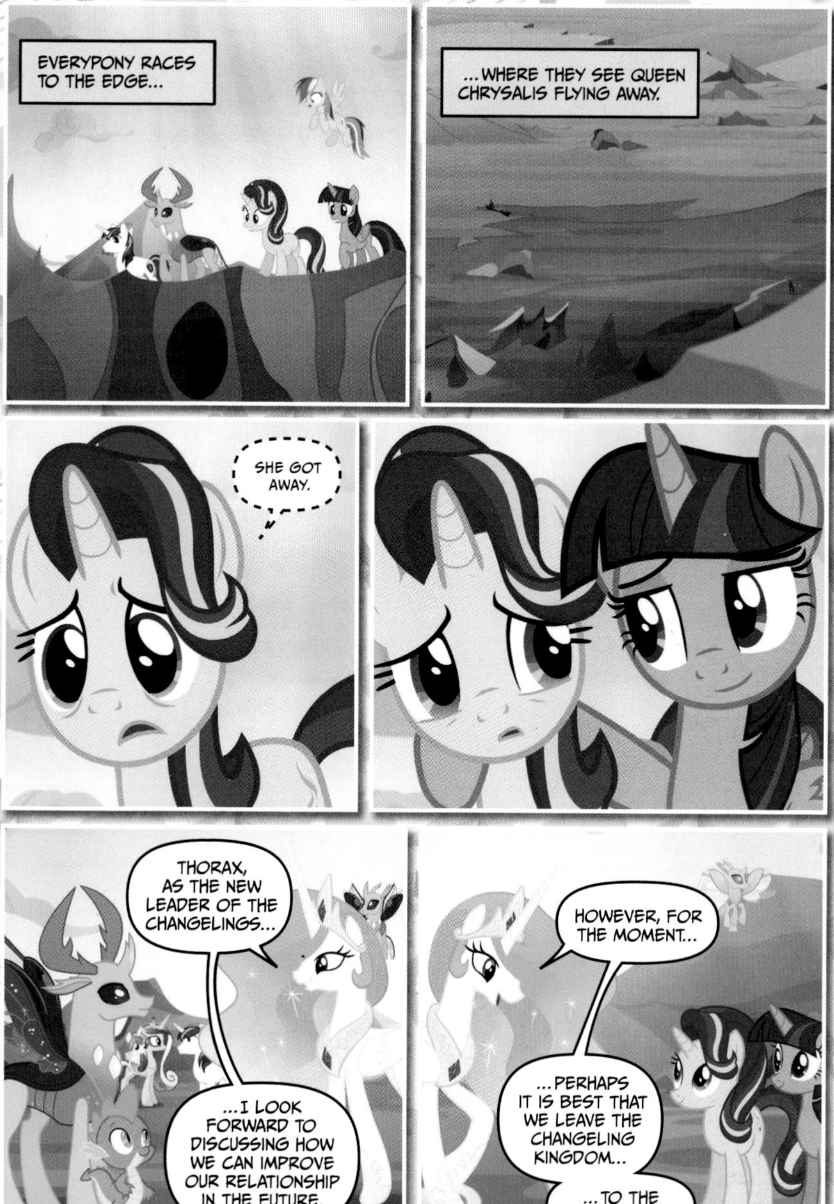
EVERYPONY RACES TO THE EDGE...
...WHERE THEY SEE QUEEN CHRYSALIS FLYING AWAY.
SHE GOT AWAY.
THORAX, AS THE NEW LEADER OF THE CHANGELINGS...
...I LOOK FORWARD TO DISCUSSING HOW WE CAN IMPROVE OUR RELATIONSHIP IN THE FUTURE.
HOWEVER, FOR THE MOMENT...
...PERHAPS IT IS BEST THAT WE LEAVE THE CHANGELING KINGDOM...
...TO THE CHANGELINGS.

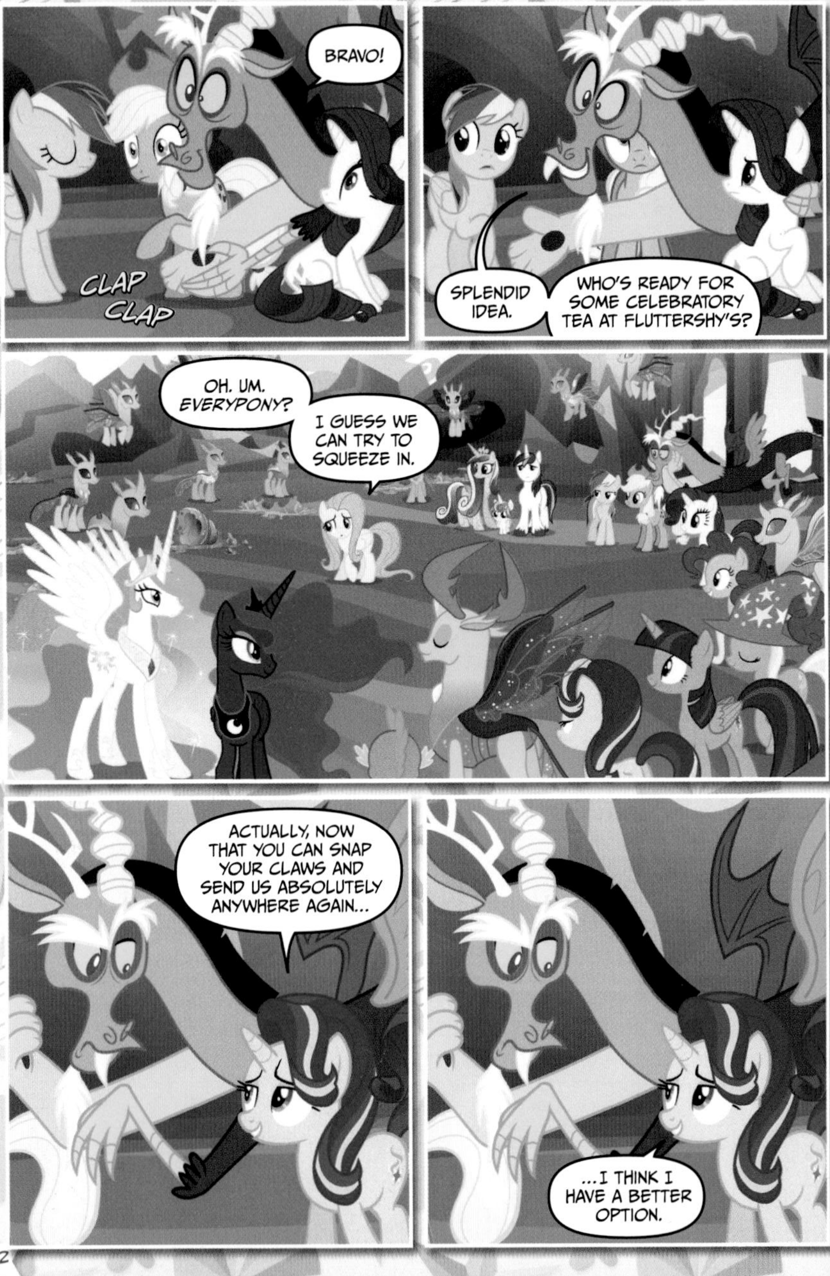
BRAVO!
CLAP CLAP
SPLENDID IDEA.
WHO'S READY FOR SOME CELEBRATORY TEA AT FLUTTERSHY'S?
OH. UM. EVERYPONY?
I GUESS WE CAN TRY TO SQUEEZE IN.
ACTUALLY, NOW THAT YOU CAN SNAP YOUR CLAWS AND SEND US ABSOLUTELY ANYWHERE AGAIN...
...I THINK I HAVE A BETTER OPTION.

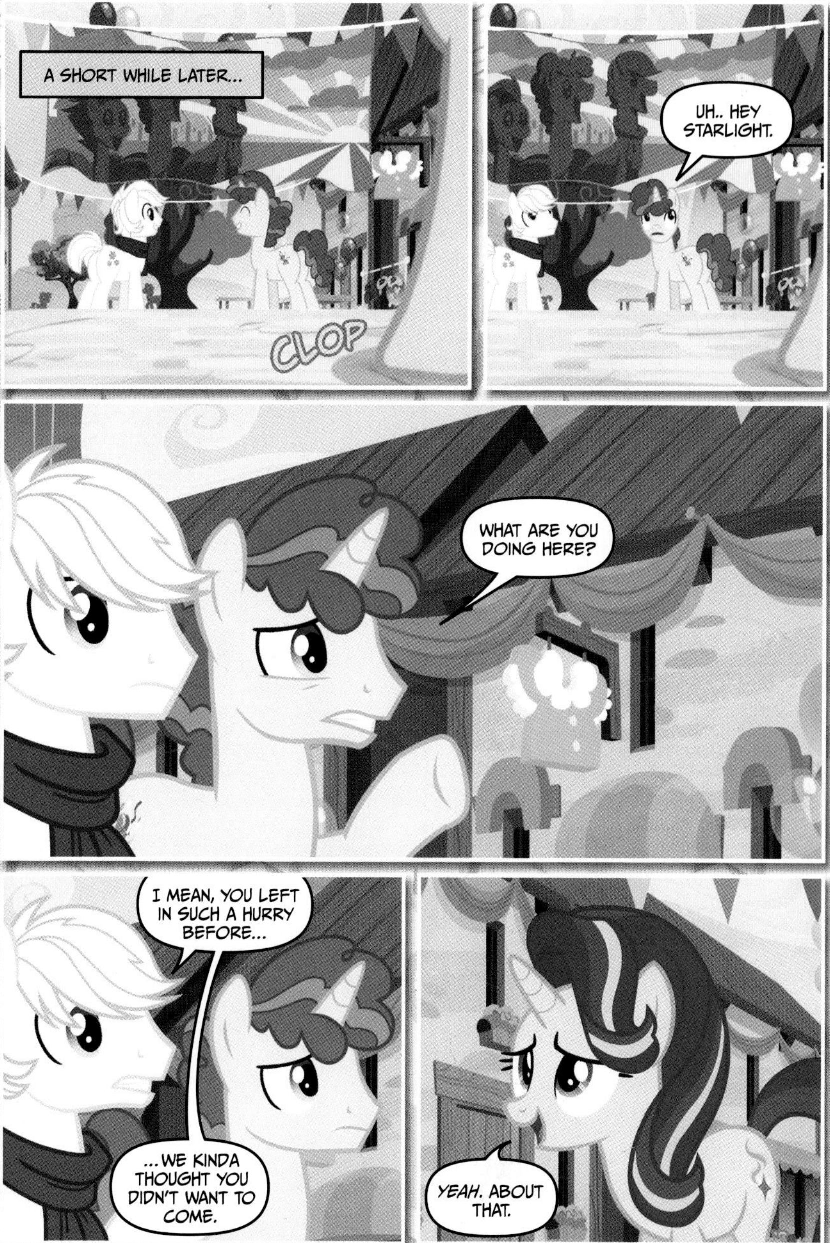
A SHORT WHILE LATER...
CLOP
UH.. HEY STARLIGHT.
WHAT ARE YOU DOING HERE?
I MEAN, YOU LEFT IN SUCH A HURRY BEFORE...
...WE KINDA THOUGHT YOU DIDN'T WANT TO COME.
YEAH. ABOUT THAT.

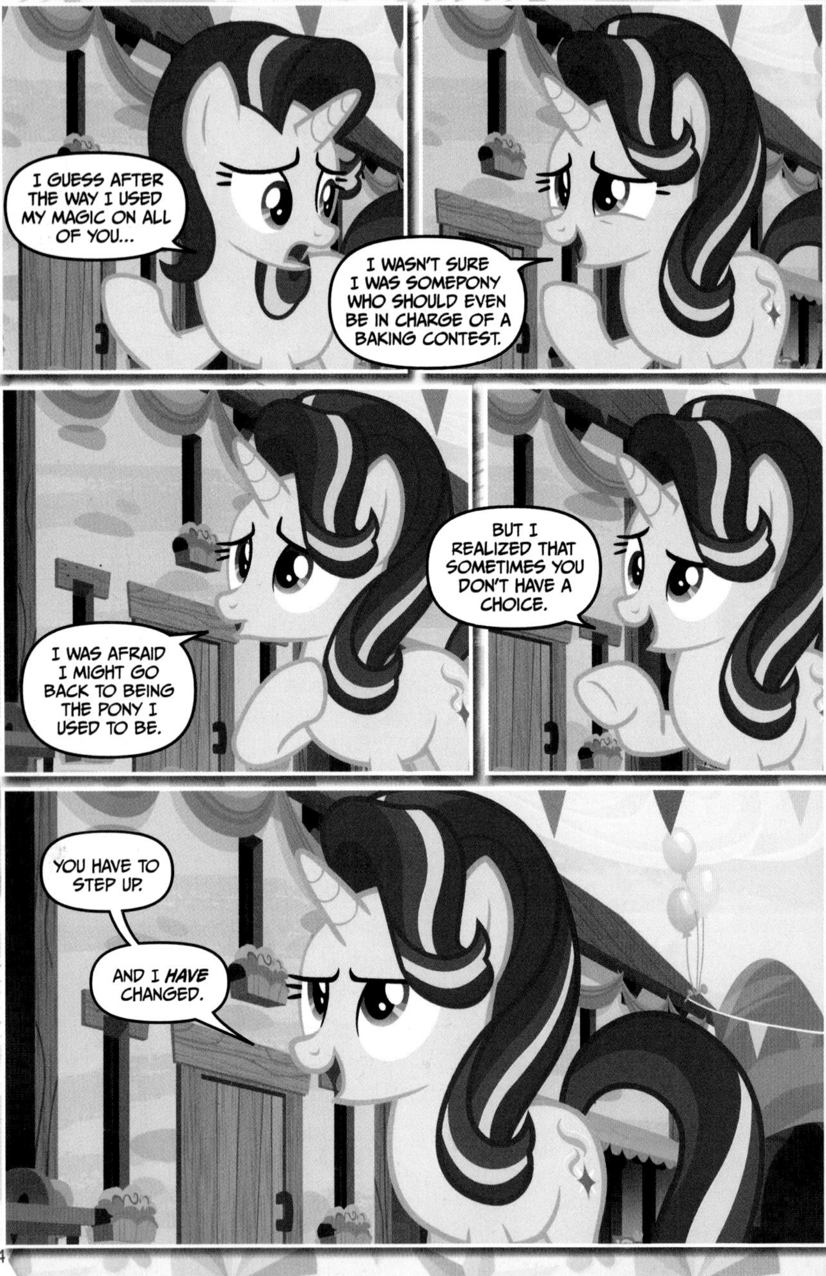
I GUESS AFTER THE WAY I USED MY MAGIC ON ALL OF YOU...
I WASN'T SURE I WAS SOMEPONY WHO SHOULD EVEN BE IN CHARGE OF A BAKING CONTEST.
I WAS AFRAID I MIGHT GO BACK TO BEING THE PONY I USED TO BE.
BUT I REALIZED THAT SOMETIMES YOU DON'T HAVE A CHOICE.
YOU HAVE TO STEP UP.
AND I *HAVE* CHANGED.

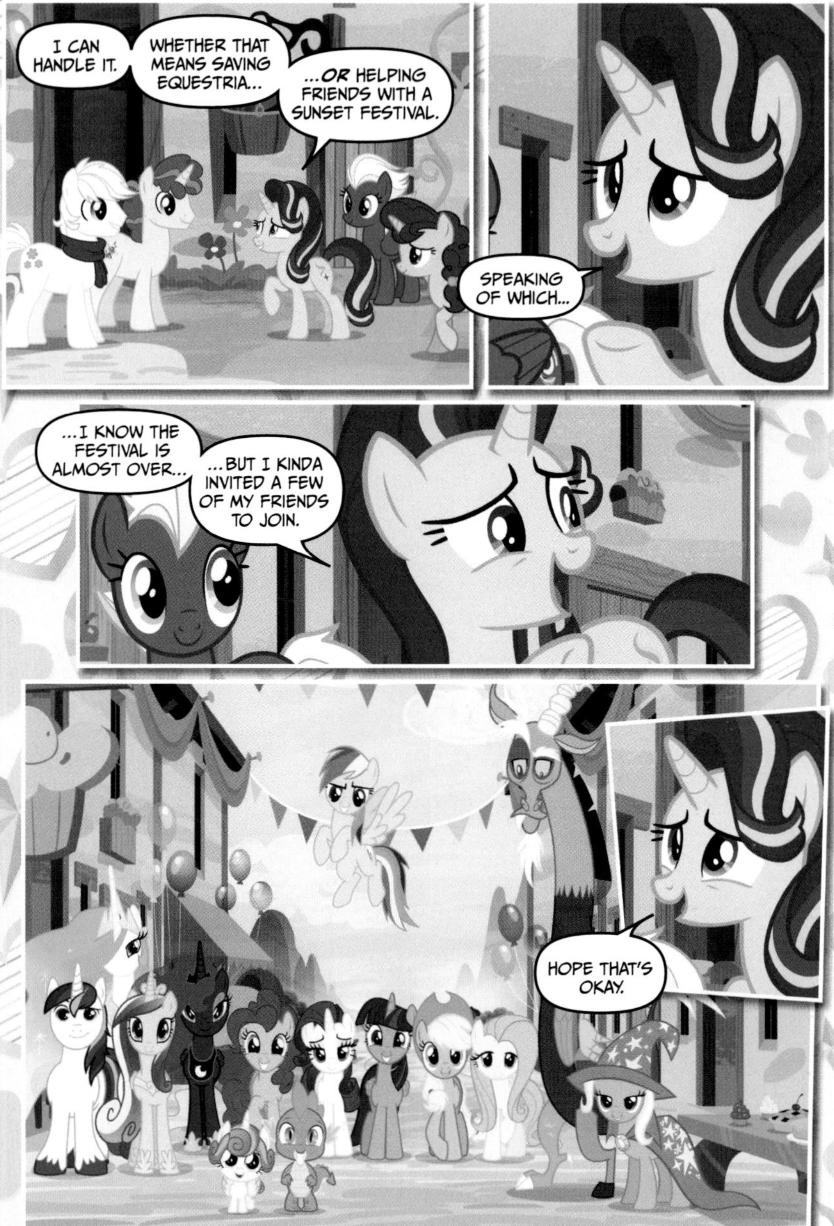
I CAN HANDLE IT.
WHETHER THAT MEANS SAVING EQUESTRIA...
...OR HELPING FRIENDS WITH A SUNSET FESTIVAL.
SPEAKING OF WHICH...
...I KNOW THE FESTIVAL IS ALMOST OVER...
...BUT I KINDA INVITED A FEW OF MY FRIENDS TO JOIN.
HOPE THAT'S OKAY.

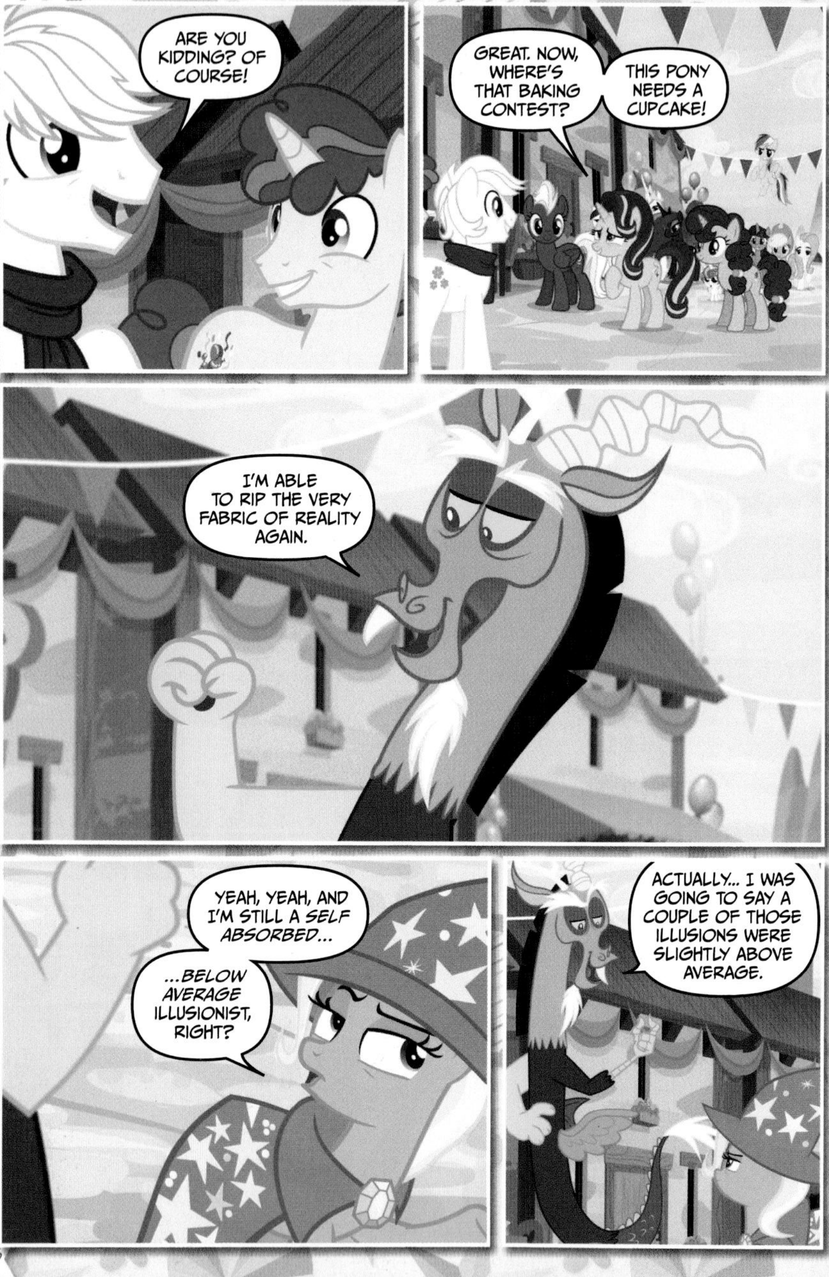
ARE YOU KIDDING? OF COURSE!
GREAT. NOW, WHERE'S THAT BAKING CONTEST?
THIS PONY NEEDS A CUPCAKE!
I'M ABLE TO RIP THE VERY FABRIC OF REALITY AGAIN.
YEAH, YEAH, AND I'M STILL A *SELF ABSORBED...*
...BELOW AVERAGE ILLUSIONIST, RIGHT?
ACTUALLY... I WAS GOING TO SAY A COUPLE OF THOSE ILLUSIONS WERE SLIGHTLY ABOVE AVERAGE.

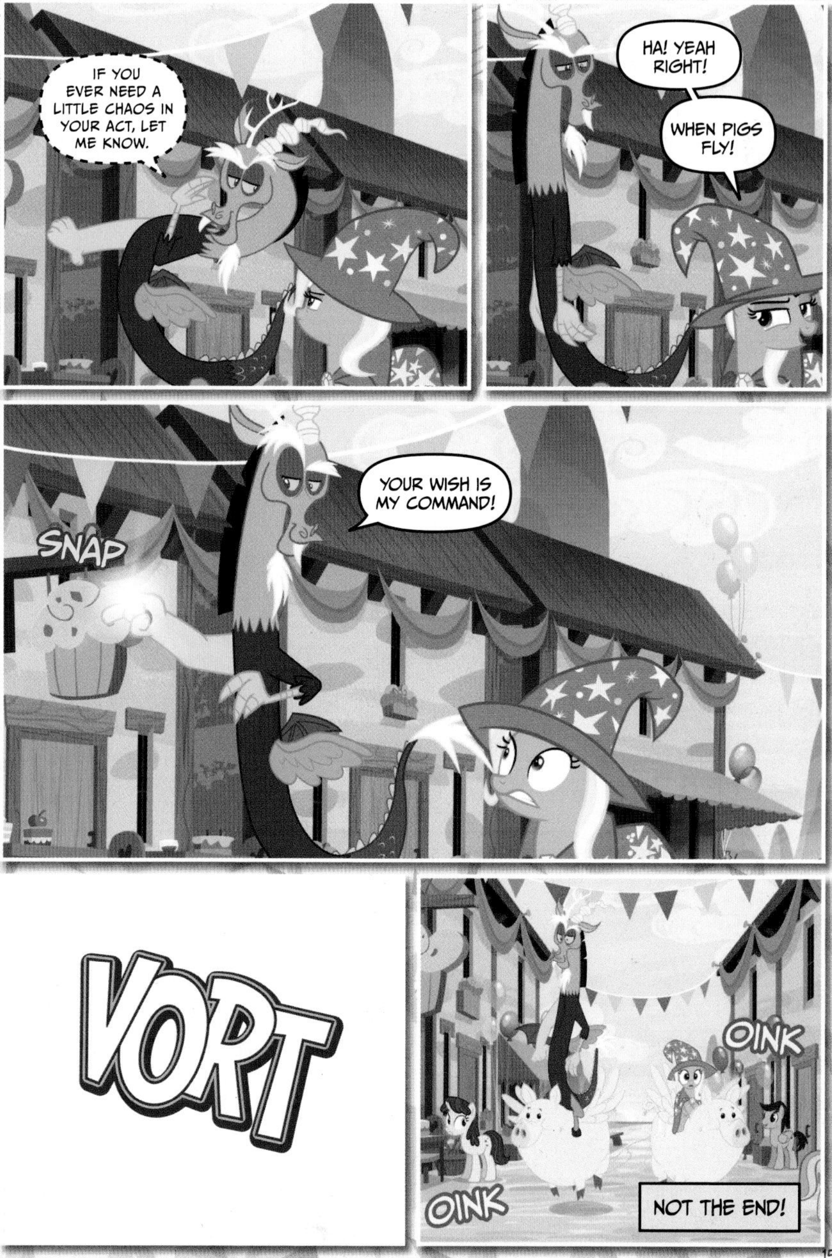

IF YOU EVER NEED A LITTLE CHAOS IN YOUR ACT, LET ME KNOW.
HA! YEAH RIGHT!
WHEN PIGS FLY!
YOUR WISH IS MY COMMAND!
SNAP
VORT
OINK
OINK
NOT THE END!

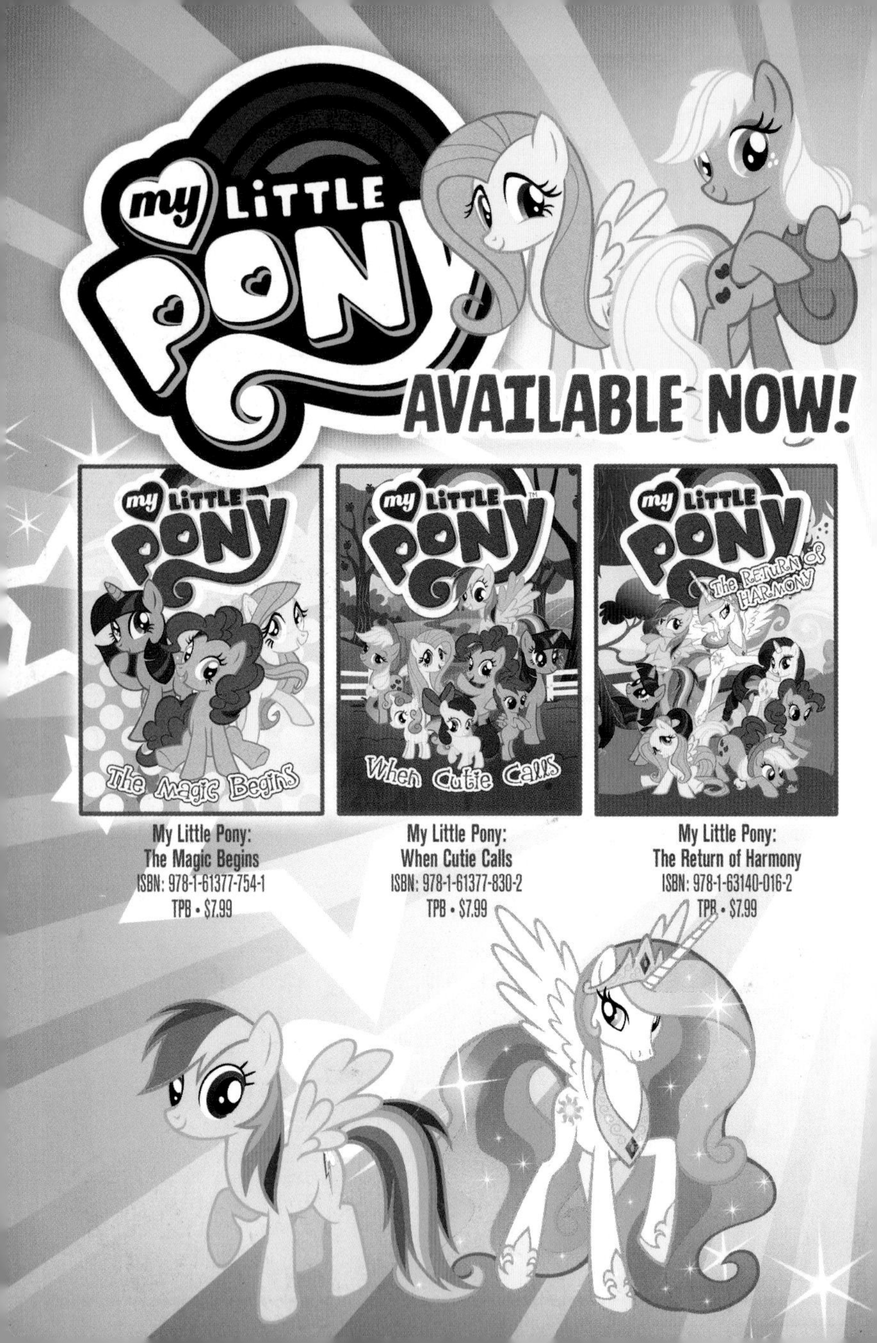
my LITTLE PONY
AVAILABLE NOW!
my LITTLE PONY
The Magic Begins
my LITTLE PONY
When Cutie Calls
my LITTLE PONY
The Return of Harmony
My Little Pony:
The Magic Begins
ISBN: 978-1-61377-754-1
TPB • $7.99
My Little Pony:
When Cutie Calls
ISBN: 978-1-61377-830-2
TPB • $7.99
My Little Pony:
The Return of Harmony
ISBN: 978-1-63140-016-2
TPB • $7.99

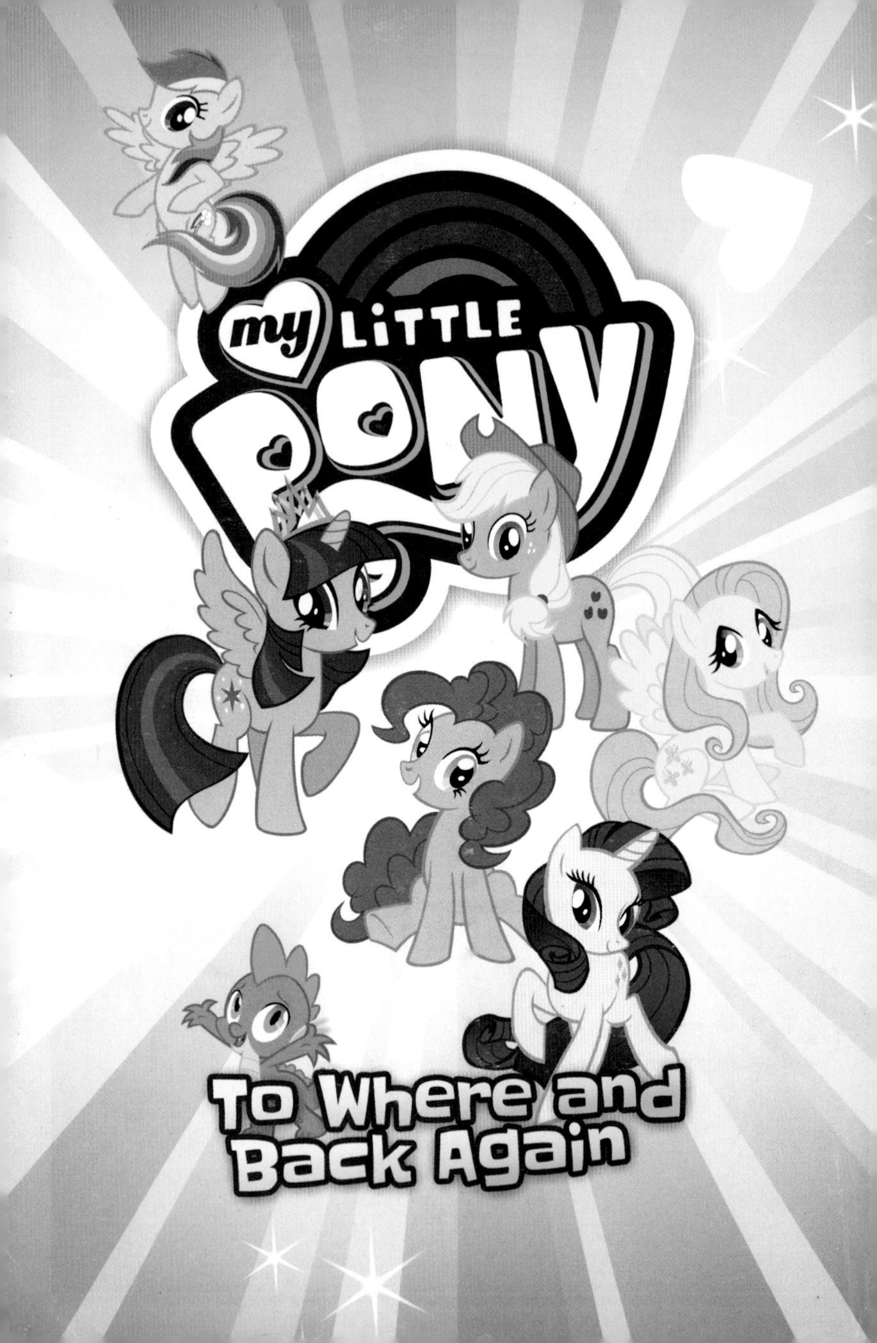
my LITTLE PONY
To Where and Back Again